# FURY IN HISPANIA

## The Celts Return

## A "Wolf the Quarrelsome" Novel

Thomas J. Howley

Lanyard Press
Leesburg Virginia

Other Books by Thomas J. Howley

**Wolf of Clontarf**
***The Irish, the Vikings and the Foreigners of the World***

Thomas J. Howley's books are available at Amazon.com and other purveyors of fine books.

Fury in Hispania

This is a work of fiction. All concepts, characters and events portrayed in this book are used fictitiously and any resemblance to real people or events is purely coincidental.



Lanyard Press
Leesburg, Virginia 20176

ISBN: 979-8-9931250-9-1

Printed in the United States of America.

# Acknowledgments

Two particular people were especially helpful to me in writing this book. I have always been knowledgeable about Ireland, its history, culture and traditions. However, for me, the history of medieval Spain was *terra incognita.* Darío Fernández-Morera, Associate Professor Emeritus, Northwestern University, was an early inspiration and source of subject matter awareness. His outstanding non-fiction book, "The Myth of the Andalusian Paradise," was one of the academic resources I found invaluable in researching "Fury in Hispania." Scott W. O'Connell, USA LTC MI (Ret.) and former Counterintelligence Special Agent, is a prolific author of superb American Revolutionary War espionage novels. And of importance here, he is one of my "old Army buddies." Scott was of immense help in my navigating a new way through the publication of this book. He was also instrumental in assuring I wasn't writing it in the manner of a military field manual, which I am sometimes wont to do. Thanks to both of you guys.

For

Conor Michael Howley

# Fury in Hispania

## *Return of the Celts*

*** A Wolf the Quarrelsome Novel ***

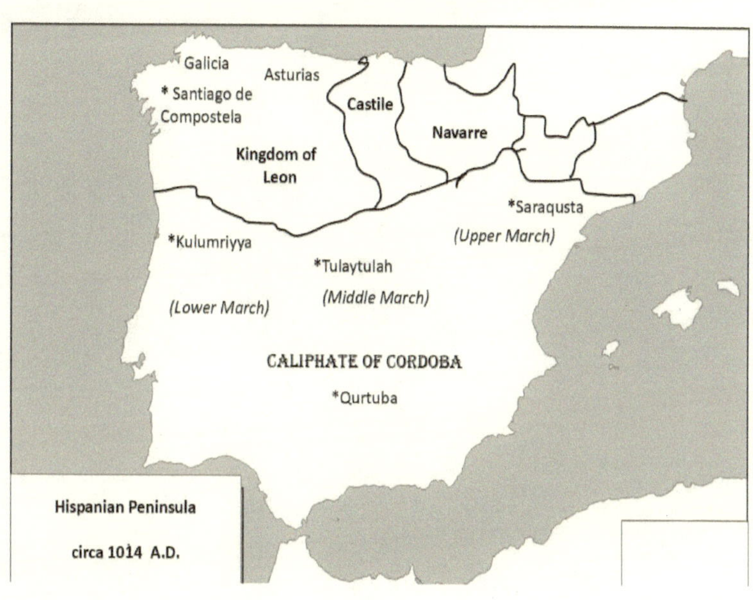
Galicia
Asturias
* Santiago de Compostela
Castile
Navarre
Kingdom of Leon
*Saraqusta
(Upper March)
*Kulumriyya
*Tulaytulah
(Middle March)
(Lower March)
CALIPHATE OF CORDOBA
*Qurtuba
Hispanian Peninsula
circa 1014 A.D.

# Chapter 1

**Off the Coast of Gasconia, France**
**Late April 1014 A.D.**

On a bright, golden sunlit and nearly windless morning under a cerulean cloudless sky, a large hook-beaked cormorant glided effortlessly, eyes fixed on three sleek *snekkja* longships skimming smoothly through the coastal waters below. One boat was slightly ahead, the other two abreast behind it. All three bore the unmistakable form of those feared dragon predators that had unleashed slaughter and terror across the north and west of Europe.

Yet there was something different about this small squadron of swift wooden craft. Two were adorned with the gracefully carved heads of a sleek swan and a regal stag. These figures, thrusting proudly up from the prows of the sturdily built *Snekkjas*, were crafted in the Celtic style harkening back to the time of the ancients. Their artists' work was meant to convey simple beauty, not to intimidate sea spirits nor frighten victims. If the elegant swan and stag seemed out of place upon these fierce Viking ships of war, none among their crews cared a rat's ass. Both boats were mainly crewed by Christian Celts who appreciated the beauty of God's natural creatures above heathen devilry.

The foremost of the three vessels, however, was bedecked with a snarling wolf's head thrusting high above its bow. Along with this ferocious figure, still more features seemed to indicate the Norse pedigree of the craft. Somewhat more blonde and red-haired oarsmen were sprinkled among the crew than on the other boats. Indeed, these were mainly Manx and Icelandic Northmen, good Christians who had allied with King Brian at Clontarf. They had fought against the Viking invaders who had swarmed from across northern Europe to seize Ireland for themselves and their leaders. Now the bloodied survivors had thrown in their lot with the Celtic crews of the other two boats on a voyage to God only knew where.

Foremost among the rowers, taking his place among the oarsmen, sat the formidable and inspiring leader of this seaborne enterprise. He had refused to take a single bench and rowed alongside one of the oldest warriors of this entire band of newly minted reavers, Cormac Mac Mahon. Still, most of his weapon brothers devoutly believed Wolf could, alone at the oars, easily drive the entire ship through the strongest gale.

At 28 years, *Faolán an Trodach* – Wolf the Quarrelsome, once given the name *Ulf Hreda* by the Dublin Norse, sometimes seemed more like some gargantuan and fantastic apparition of dreams, sagas, or nightmares than a simple mortal man. He was a head higher than the tallest of any of them, as powerfully and heavily built as a raging bull but rangier. Supple and swift as his namesake, he had pummeled enormous Viking bear-like *berserkers* to death with his bare hands over the last several years.

Long dark hair, so deeply chestnut-hued it was almost black, hung unkempt to his shoulders. Deeply green and intelligent eyes, which seemed to radiate spark-like golden flecks when he was in his battle fever, now shone with good humor and contentment. He eschewed the heavy beard favored by many of his crew, preferring, it was said, to have his scarred face displayed before his enemies for the same reason ancient Celts painted themselves with blue woad and worked lime into their spiked hair – to shock and imbue awe into the foe. Thin and faint, silver scars diagonally crossed his broad face from hairline to chin, the result of beatings across his head and shoulders with cutting blackthorn staves in his childhood. This, at the hands of his Viking captors, after a jealous and barren Danish matriarch had murdered his mother. These would never completely disappear and were now joined by more recent battle scars won at Clontarf and already healing. Ironically, the same scars that he unashamedly carried with martial pride also attracted women and girls and won him the admiration and respect of his own warriors.

He had deeply mourned King Brian, his foster-father, yet only after savagely hunting down, smashing and legendarily executing the king's killer.

Now Wolf resolved to carry Brian's example of freedom to other lands. The giant leader also recognized his Gaelic blood and soul yearned for adventure and challenge. If he could help others, even strangers, win freedom from subjugation, he trusted he would make both of his fathers and his mother, now watching him from God's heaven, well pleased.

# Fury in Hispania

After the death of King Brian at the moment of victory at Clontarf, the king's youngest son, Donough, was now King of Munster. All of those who fought under Brian's banner felt the pride of victory and the heart-rending loss of a beloved father figure. A diverse band of hard-fighting and trusted veterans of the climactic battle – Irish, Scots, Picts, Welsh, Icelanders, Manx and even a few exotics from the east of Europe – had pledged to follow the charismatic giant as he moved on. So, Wolf had called for a council of his most trusted friends and advisors and, with the blessings of the new King Donough, they had sailed from Limerick into the expanse of the western sea. Once underway, they had discussed their path and destination in earnest while the three boats were lashed together during periods of calm waters. Many of the Icelanders urged they make for Iceland, provision at some good Christian port there and strike out west toward the unknown to gain riches and glory.

Wolf remembered speaking early on with two of the Icelanders about these supposed riches in the far west while they all pulled together at their oars.

"Now then, tell me more about Iceland and what lies beyond. Our clan bards claim that there will be found *Tír na nÓg*, the island of eternal youth, a place with vast forests, flowery meadows, joy and abundance. Though they also say it can be dangerous for travelers who stumble upon its shores."

The two exchanged knowing glances, happy to be making conversation with this colossal natural warrior who spoke perfect Danish and was, by now, a mysterious legend both feared and loved across Europe.

"Well now," replied the youngest of the two, "Iceland is filled with volcanic rocks, geysers of steam and just enough green to yield a paltry harvest but then…beyond to the west, hmmm." He stopped mid-sentence and looked up whimsically.

His mate picked up. "We've not been there ye' understand but we've swapped tales with some among our kinsmen who claim they made the voyage. The first *Skraelings* they found surely didn't match the tale of eternally young Celts."

The younger man laughed at that. "They were short yet sturdy and covered head to toe in some type of fur with only their little black eyes peeking out. At first, it was thought they were sea creatures since they sat so low to the sea. They looked to be moving, immersed in the waves, yet expertly working their tiny paddles. Only later did our cousins learn they were piloting small, sleek hide-covered boats. They flew off when they first caught sight of the dragon ships from afar. Once ashore on their islands, our brothers searched for them in vain."

His friend continued. "Finally, an old man came down from the hills to them, head uncovered. He reminded some of the *Sami* tribes who live in the far north of our people's old homeland, though much shorter and with black hair and strangely shaped eyes. Since the island looked so barren and the old man not to be understood, they gave him some food and a small child's knife and departed to sail further west."

*I can tell their kinsmen must have been good Christian Northmen, otherwise they would surely have killed the old man and hunted down and slaughtered the rest out of long-time custom*, Wolf mused to himself.

"And later," chimed in the older one, "they came, or so they said, to a land so immense, any further sailing voyage to the west was impossible. And this land was as brilliantly green as Ireland and even more deeply forested than Norway or France. As they hugged the coast, large bands of tall and well-formed men, as fair as we and the Irish and clad in well-made skins adorned with colorful decoration, shadowed them as they made their way south. These strangers brandished bows and spears and bellowed deep and ferociously in obvious defiance. They almost seemed to welcome battle with our now depleted and famished kin."

"By this time," his mate continued, "they'd been underway far longer than any who came before them. Their diet of fish, the occasional careless seabird and water and the salt sores which covered them, as well as the exhaustion and lack of free and robust movement away from the rowing benches, bade them return home before all perished. And so, alas, that's all we know about your *Tír na nÓg*. Mayhap, had they made land and explored…well?" The speaker's voice trailed off as they all pondered his words.

This plan of journeying to strange and unknown lands held immense appeal for all the Celts who shared the Norse yearnings for exploration and discovery. Besides, the Irish lads announced to their Icelandic mates, good Saint Brendan had already traveled there, converted all the heathens to the true faith and then returned home in time for Christmas dinner. The Northmen just shook their heads and laughed at that.

Wolf had been sorely tempted to follow that mysterious and entrancing path and voyage to some entirely new land, notwithstanding his long-held disdain for anything that even reeked of Vikings. However, the valiant and true

Icelanders and Manx who fought alongside him against the invaders at Clontarf had severely challenged his beliefs on that subject. The young leader had come to reluctantly realize his hatred and distrust of all Norse had not always served him well. Such had the crew of stalwarts now straining at oars behind him certainly proven beyond doubt. He, who seemed so knowing and all-powerful to all who had seen him and the results of his actions, knew, in his heart, he had much to learn – about hate and, of late, especially about love.

*But then*, he told himself, *these true men and one dear Norse woman are good Christians and they've volunteered to follow me to hell if I but lead them. They are no longer, if ever they ever were, followers of pagan Odin.*

In accordance with the customs of Irish nobility, Brian had assured that Wolf, after liberation from bondage, had been classically well-educated by the good monks on the Isle of Inisfallen. Now he mastered the Gaelic, Danish and Latin tongues, was knowledgeable in the sciences, numbers, geography and engineering of the day and held a deep love and interest for history and world events. He had been taught that there existed rampant evil and that good, gentle Christians were everywhere under oppression across the known world.

So he decided they would raid and harry heathen lands along the route south, then east, until they finally came to the majestic capital, Constantinople. There, they would present themselves to Basil, Emperor of the Christian Greek Roman Empire, and offer their services in defense of Christendom and free people everywhere. Or so Wolf believed, as did his enthusiastic band of battle-tested heroes.

***

"Well, 'my good boy,' d'ye reckon we'll ever round this thrusting French peninsula and make way our due south once more?' asked the grizzled older Gaelic warrior of his oar mate. He used the term of endearment a noble old woman had told him Wolf's mother called him to conceal his true name from the Vikings during the time of their captivity – 'my good boy.'

Wolf laughed. "We hugged the coast of Ireland and Wales not long years now gone, striking that rat's lair of *Fingwalle* in the Danelaw on these same boats. And we were simple Celts with not a Viking among us. And that ended well for us now, didn't it?"

***

The wolf-prowed boat was first to make its way past the narrow tip of the promontory. As the lead pilot gestured with hand signals for the other pilots and helmsmen to turn once more, a keen-eyed, raven-haired young woman standing high at the bow was the first to see the unexpected. She peered intently, assessing what lay before her green Irish eyes, before grasping the pilot's shoulder and directing his gaze to what moved on the waters not overly distant before them.

There, on this almost entirely windless day, sailing southbound with only the torpid and gentle currents to carry them, were three ships like nothing she, nor any of the Celts, had ever witnessed. Unlike the Norse craft, these were high, crescent-shaped and wider with black triangular lateen sails, now drooping flaccidly in the absence of any breeze to fill them. No oars were apparent, yet the decks were manned by stygian swathed figures who themselves appeared as alien as their strange craft.

The experienced Norse pilot turned to Wolf, his voice calm but filled with earnest and knowing intensity.

"Captain, we've come upon Moorish dhows. They'll soon spy us."

With eager concern, he continued, "Those black sails give evidence they're slavers. Two of them will be teeming with fighting men, most likely Berbers, with Arabic officers. The dhow in the center will be carrying their cargo, no doubt Christian slaves. It will contain a few crewmen, guards, merchants and the miserable souls in their holds."

Even before Wolf could reply, the wise Icelander had already flashed more urgent hand signals to double the speed of all three ships – the same deep, slow and powerful strokes through the water but now wasting no time on the upstroke.

Soon, the Moors detected their pursuers. A fair-haired young boy and a limping woman were dragged onto the deck of the black-topped central ship. Wolf watched as two dark figures behind them raised enormous scimitars, which caught the light of the full sun with an arcing flash. Spraying a shower of red, two heads flew off the slight bodies and into the green-blue sea, a warning to the Norse ships to stay away.

Now, not just Wolf but all the fiery veterans of Clontarf, men and women, were overcome with immediate and seething rage at the spectacle. All had the same vengeful and lethal urge as their captain raised his wolf-pummeled sword toward the monsters and shouted in a voice that thundered across the otherwise quiescent seascape.

"For God and King Brian. Let us crush these bloody little heathens."

Fury in Hispania

Nearly a hundred voices rose in a resounding bellow that seemed almost to rip and tear the very ocean. “**Abooo, Abooo, Abooo.**”

***

Each of the Snekkjas had selected a targeted dhow in accordance with the guidance of the wolf boat's wise pilot. This Icelander, called Keli, was a nephew of the beloved and renowned high chieftain, Ospak of Man, who had heard the voice of the White Christ and joined his people with good King Brian at Clontarf. Ospak had fallen in battle on that bloody shore with many of his family. Yet his kin still loved him, their Celtic weapons, brothers and their new faith. Wolf had ironically seen something of himself in the young bearded blonde Icelander and entrusted him with tactical leadership of events arising at sea.

“Captain. We'll be upon them too rapidly for them to kill all the hostages. We can't save every poor captive but we will slaughter the vile heathens and return them to their *shaitan* moon god without their heads. Our task now is to close and crush them with lightning swiftness.”

Wolf the Quarrelsome nodded his formidable lupine head in enthusiastic agreement, raising his left fist then smashing it into his mailed breast with vigor. The plan called for the Wolf and Stag *Snekkjas* to engage the warrior-laden enemy craft while the Swan ship closed with the slave dhow.

By now, the three boats were nearly upon the Moorish ships whose decks were covered with black clad warriors brandishing scimitars and deadly lances while repetitively chanting *Allahu Akbar*. Despite this bravado, the speed with which the Viking ships had aggressively come upon them seemed to have somewhat unnerved the dark foe. The Norse, experienced at ship-to-ship combat, readied grappling hooks along their starboard side, preparing to catch hold and swarm aboard the dhow with celerity and unbridled violence.

The Celtic heavy infantry veterans on the stag boat checked their armor and fighting *scian* long knives for mobility and quick use. They then brought their heavy metal, swagged shields to an upright position and their sturdy, long spears over their right shoulders, ready to thrust up and out. Between and behind them, experienced light infantry brought into play another weapon, casting spears called *darts*. These had been used to great effect by the Irish at Clontarf. Each consisted of an iron-tipped point, sturdy and precisely weighted wooden shaft and a thong of tough sinew, which enabled the weapon to be retrieved after impact. The intended goal was to capture both the enemy's hull and, whenever possible, enemy personnel and drag them to the closest possible combat.

The last of the small allied flotilla's ships, the Swan, had among its crew almost a score of battle-proven, skilled and deadly archers whose deceptively small, recursive bows were immensely powerful; capable of launching well-crafted arrows, which would easily penetrate any Moorish armor. These archers were already pulling the bowstrings to their ruddy cheeks.

Days before, Wolf, Keli and Fergus, Commander of the Irish Spartans, himself almost as immense and formidable as *Faolán an Trodach*, had sat during an early and crimson-hued evening on the bow of the Wolf boat. Faolán had led seaborne raids in these same craft, yet never had even he experienced ship-to-ship combat. The scarred leader was keen to learn from Keli the manner in which the Vikings conducted such seemingly awkward engagements.

The Icelander, who had lived through several such fights, could only relate what he had experienced.

"Captain, I've only been through several such battles. I've met Danes and Saxons on heaving decks, all washed with slick blood. We always treated these forays exactly as they play out on land. I know you may think we live for the sea but we crave firm land under our feet as much as any other man."

Fergus reacted with surprised astonishment as most Irish and indeed, other populations across Europe all believed the Vikings were indeed just some species of sea creature, the frothy waves and piercing winds their natural haven.

"Whenever able, we strove to bring our boats together and bind them to each other. Thus, we created our field of battle to strike with combined force against individual enemy craft. Though I've no knowledge if this tactic would be effective against Moorish adversaries."

"Interesting," replied Wolf. "I believe when we engage a new and strange foe, whose methods we've not yet encountered, we must assure we resort to the most primordial means of combat. First, we must always rely on savage, yet lucidly controlled, ferocity. Tear into them viciously, instilling unrelenting terror. That means there is no substitute for taking the offense at sea, especially with our current small fleet of three."

His two comrades sat listening attentively, enraptured as always when Wolf spoke of battlecraft.

"The longer a seaborne fight ensues, the more chance for unnecessary losses of our friends and possible escape of our enemies. We must end such engagements rapidly to assure we reach land alive to fight and win again."

***

Now the decisive trial was at hand. To complicate the issue, all of the allied Celts and Norse felt an urgency to swiftly rescue the confined prisoners before they could be slaughtered out of rage and spite by the black-clad heathens. All of them knew in their hearts the dreadful certainty. The Moors would give no quarter to shackled captive nor battling foe-man. The time of blood, steel and fire was at hand.

At that moment, almost surreally, an enormous black figure, vaguely familiar but surreally larger than any raven the Celts or Norse had ever seen, flew over the now tightening group of six vessels, rudely displacing the gently soaring seabirds and letting loose a deafening scream as the northerners took solace. For the Celts, this was, of course, Morrigan, the ancient goddess of war who never interferes but promises victory to those who fight valorously. The same apparition appeared to the Vikings as a comforting memory of omens of their own recent pagan past.

Before the allied fleet could close with and assault the black-sailed foe, a whispering flock of sharply pointed death shafts struck with devastation. The score of archers, trained in the Magyar way, rained destruction equally as well on a ship's deck as they ever did astride a galloping Connemara pony. Such was the range and intensity of the volley that all three Moorish ships abruptly lost almost half of their exposed defenders. Those who weren't immediately killed writhed and screamed in agony.

"**Aaayyiiee!**!" bellowed the slavers and hurled curses in their sibilant yet shrill guttural tongue. "**Abooo!**" retorted the allies, including even the Norse, who had learned now to embrace the ancient Celtic battle cry as their own. As more of the slavers rushed to take the place of their fallen comrades, the distance had become too close for the archers to strike effectively. Besides, these same warriors desperately wanted to come to grips with the heathens who had just so recently desecrated a tow-haired lad and lame old woman.

The fearsomely grinning wolf's head of Faolán's *Snekkja* almost gently sidled along the tallest and most formidable Moorish dhow, which now bristled with cursing, fully armed warriors.

“Now”, shouted the dark leader as supple and deceptively strong rawhide tethers, topped by sturdy iron grappling hooks, flew over the gunnels of the enemy’s taller ship.

“Up and at them! Send them all to hell!” With that, he took hold of a tether and leapt with an almost impossibly lofty ascent to land in the middle of the Moorish deck. All alone he was, surrounded by a squadron of demonic foes. Only their eyes were exposed, and these glistened with hate and fury from their dark orbs.

As they cautiously circled the horrific Christian monster of their worst nightmares, Wolf grinned terribly and gleefully.

“Ye’ve the look on you of stunted crows, terrified of some sea eagle come to steal your pickings. Well then ye’ wee heathens, come taste good Irish steel!”

Rushing with uncanny swiftness toward the closest four foemen, Wolf simultaneously swung his ponderous, iron-covered round shield in a wide arc leftward. At the same time, his right hand slashed the deadly long sword through the ribs and torsos of the two Moors there who had been too dumbstruck by the horrific vision before them to assume a proper defense. There were sickening groans to his left and shrieks to his right as the shield edge crushed two skulls and the streaking sword blade eviscerated cloth and flesh to his right.

With four of the enemy dead, Wolf instinctively fell to the deck, rolled to the side and sprang up to face four more of the enemy who had been closing behind him after their initial shock at witnessing their comrades slaughtered so quickly. Just in time, as a long spear flew inches above his head and a razor-sharp scimitar forged of the best Damascus steel sliced down where he had stood just a half second earlier.

But now the Icelanders were leaping onto the dhow like falcons swooping on a school of fish. They spread all over the deck, shields crushing the bodies of their foes while their axes flashed like scythes among the dwindling number of Berber lighter armed fighters. They trusted their keen and swift, incredibly sharp scimitars to make some kind of resistance.

By some weird twist, the six craft were now almost all entangled as if they comprised one teeming platform of sound and fury of shrieking and death. But the outcome was never in doubt. The shock of the unexpected encounter with their enraged opponents was too much for the slavers. They almost threw themselves on the axes, spear tips and slashing swords of the Christians or were smashed by the heavy shields which were wielded as equally offensive weapons.

Above the clamor, Wolf bellowed to Keli with a stentorian roar.

"I'm going to the hostage ship."

The giant leader ran in lengthy and surprisingly agile strides and leapt over and across two decks to alight on the craft upon which the two hostages had been massacred just a few moments earlier.

The huge, red-haired Irish infantryman, Fergus, was hacking at the locked hatch of the cargo hold's entry. This dhow held fewer warriors and those had already succumbed to Fergus' Spartans almost at once in the first sweep aboard.

"I pray we've struck so swiftly, there's been too little time for the poor *créatúrs* below to have been slaughtered," he grunted, finally smashing the entry way and tearing the wood of the hatch off its hinges with a most decidedly unchristian oath.

Wolf sprang to Fergus' side, his muscular frame tensed to crash down into the hold, annihilate any remaining slavers and liberate his fellow Christians.

Before he could leap, a hideous cry of pain and terror arose from the newly opened aperture, immediately followed by the unexpected appearance of a shrieking figure clad entirely in black who sprang into the midst of the half circle of bristling warriors, seemingly oblivious of the deadly threat they posed.

The slaver seemed almost as large as Fergus under the dusky robes of his raiment. Only the space around his eyes was uncovered. Yet to the astonishment of the Christians, *there were no eyes*, only rivulets of blood and viscous fluid where the eyes had been.

Before the onlookers could make any sense of this spectacle, another smaller figure leapt from below. This one screamed with rage, not terror and launched herself onto the slaver's back, one arm wrapped around his throat while the other small white fist pummeled the face and head. This was a woman whose visceral hatred for her Arab captor resonated with Faolán. He instinctively recognized that this poor creature had experienced some similar horror with which he was sadly familiar from his youth.

Another of the Gaels watching felt the same sense of familiarity and empathy for the enraged woman, perhaps even more so, as this Gael was also a woman.

Aoife was the first of the mixed band of Clontarf veterans to have detected the flotilla of slave ships. This was perfectly appropriate as she had been selected years earlier by the Irish leaders to become their Chief of Intelligence and Spy Master in the war against the invading Vikings. Her innate intellect, dedication and love for her people, as well as her ability to see possibilities beyond others' ken, distinguished her most favorably. It also helped that the formidable young woman was a weapon sister and soulmate to their colossal, scarred Battle Captain. As a child, Aoife, too, had endured the same heart-rending barbarity at the hands of marauding monsters as had Wolf and, apparently, this poor woman.

"*Pax*.... Peace, dear woman, you're with friends. We'll take this heathen and deal with him in accordance with your wishes."

Aoife tried to speak these words in a comforting manner, which defied the ongoing events. She used her best Latin, hoping that the rage-filled woman might comprehend that which was the closest thing to a common tongue in the Christian world. A natural polyglot, Aoife spoke Gaelic from birth, Latin from the nuns at Cashel, and, constantly improving Danish, picked up from Wolf and her new Icelandic comrades. Most recently, she was striving to learn Greek from two of her close friends and shipmates.

The woman showed no sign she had listened to or understood Aoife's plea but continued her onslaught as the black-clad figure continued to shriek in pain, trying vainly to throw off the demon on his back.

With a look of concern and sympathy, Aoife dropped her shield and moved closer. The young Gaelic girl tried to comfort and assist the frantic woman. As she gently put her free hand on the woman's back, the distraught captive looked her in the eyes with something approximating recognition and gratitude. Then, almost too swift for the eye to follow, the fist that had been pounding the slaver reached to Aoife's leather belt and snatched the fighting *scian* knife from its scabbard.

She thrust the deadly keen blade up to pierce her enemy's chin, grunting and using all her strength to push through bone and tissue into the screaming wretch's brain. The dark figure collapsed immediately, its attacker on top of the now prostrate mass of blood and robes.

Aoife had seen too much terror in her own young life to quiver before such a horrific stage of events. Now she bent gracefully, softly humming a lilting Irish tune as she stroked the woman's hair.

"*Benigne.*" The woman slid off the corpse and looked up into the loving eyes of the angelic presence peering down at her with radiant compassion. Aoife was about to utter more words of comfort when the woman pulled her down to herself and hugged her tightly amidst tremulous sobs.

Now more captives slowly and timidly arose from the slavers' hold. Mostly women and children yet accompanied by two wizened older men. The newly freed people spoke to each other in a melodious language which sounded to the Gaels like some variation of Latin. The more educated among the Irish could grasp bits and pieces.

"God has saved us. Thanks be unto Jesus."

They looked around them, surprised but not alarmed by the fierce, though strangely familiar and benign countenances of the Gaelic warriors smiling at them in welcome. Then, abruptly, they were taken aback by the appearance of several Norse axe wielders standing alongside their rescuers.

"*Normanni*!" several screamed. "Once again we're delivered into the hands of Satan!"

"No, dear friends. These Northmen are as goodly Christians as are we Irish. None of us will see you harmed. Look about you. Your heathen captors have all been slain. Our only purpose is to bring you to some safe harbor, to restore you however we can to peace."

Aoife, as so often before, was calmly reassuring and endearing and her Latin seemed to be understood by at least some of those listening. The captives slowly relaxed and clasped each other. From the midst of the assembled warriors, a titanic colossus strode to Aoife and gently wrapped his enormous arm around her. His eyes caught hers with unabashed pride and affection.

"And Captain, I request I be allowed to take charge and care for our guests, hear their stories and see to their needs until we can deliver them someplace safe of their choosing."

Aoife knew this favor would be granted as all of her comrades intuitively recognized she was absolutely best suited to set these poor people at ease. And equally important, they knew, she will derive from them the most information and critical intelligence on matters that may be of use in their continuing mission of aiding other oppressed Christians.

"I'm also sure our Greek friends will be of enormous value participating in this task," added Aoife as she looked over with a knowing grin at one among the warriors whose features seemed out of place among the band of Gaels and Norse.

"Helena and I will be most honored to assist you in this noble endeavor, dear Aoife."

Pyrrhus Lakepeno, representative of the Emperor of the Christian Greek Roman Empire, former ambassador to the Magyars, Saxons, Danes and more recently Irish, proclaimed with a courtly bow and almost mischievous smile.

Wolf looked around at those surrounding him with satisfaction and joy.

"So be it. Now let us render aid to our new friends and cleanse the stench of the bloody little heathens from us all." There arose a rousing cheer even from among some of the still reeling former captives.

# Chapter 2

## Tales of Woe

Those of the enemy who were not slain outright under the onslaught of arrows, darts, axes, swords and spears of the Northerners, seeing that all was lost, threw themselves into the ocean. Some, however, dropped their weapons and bared their breasts, offering themselves to be skewered by the all-too-willing Gaels and Icelanders whose shared battle fever was almost palpable atop the bloodied decks of the black-sailed dhows.

While Wolf and the allied leaders organized the disposal of the Moorish bodies, Aoife and Pyrrhus saw that the former captives were provided with food and water. They were assisted in this effort by two other women who were part of the Hiberno-Norse quest. The first was Luta Einarsrdottir, once Viking Princess and lately weapon sister to the Irish "Magyar" cavalry squadron. The robust young woman with shimmering golden hair assumed responsibility for the younger children. Helena Lakepeno, a radiantly beautiful, middle-aged Greek woman with long dark tresses moved among the older woman captives. Cousin to Pyrrhus and his superior in the diplomatic corps of the Greek Roman Empire, she seemed to fit right in with the southern European women she comforted.

Pyrrhus, meanwhile, was drawn to the two older men who had seemed out of place amidst the women and young ones. The Greek ambassador was a master of many languages and soon discovered why they'd been spared in whatever slave raid occurred. One was a fellow diplomat and representative of the Kingdom of Leon in Hispania. The other, whose facial features were immediately recognizable to Pyrrhus, was a Jewish native of Hispania. It took only a few words of Greek, which this man spoke surprisingly well, to learn he was a trained physician and scholar of the physical sciences. While Pyrrhus was older than most of his shipmates, he was nevertheless a sturdy middle-aged specimen of his race whose sharp intellect only enhanced his proven fighting abilities. These two were decades older and he guessed they were in their late sixties.

Several of Wolf's warriors, wounded by arrows or the blades of scimitars, were being attended to by their comrades. Pyrrhus asked the physician, whose name was Schlomo ben Adret, if he would be willing to assist the wounded men. He, in turn, smiled and asked Pyrrhus to lead the way as the two went off together to tend to the casualties.

The two dhows that had carried the Berber fighting men were already in flames and drifting away from the other craft. Wolf had ordered them to be fired after anything of value aboard was salvaged to be later distributed among the now freed captives. The captives would remain on the third dhow and Pyrrhus assured Wolf that the diplomat and the scientist would easily instruct some of Keli's men in operating and navigating the slave ship until they reached some safe port. At this, the Icelanders seemed offended, averring they could master any sailing ship from any origin at any time, no matter how strange it might appear to the Gaels. Pyrrhus could only shake his head at that.

As the Greek and Schlomo were moving among the wounded men and the Jewish physician was working with needles and thread produced from his own meager belongings, Pyrrhus noted that the older Hispanian diplomat had almost physically attached himself at Wolf's side as soon as he was able. Both appeared to be in animated yet amiable conversation. This reminded Pyrrhus of his own extended talks with Wolf aboard one of these same Snekkjas not many years earlier, after Wolf had rescued the formidable Greek ambassador from Danish captivity at a place called Fingwalle.

When he had first seen him, Felix Santos Serra, immediately recognized his savior. The gigantic apparition stood over the prostrate form of the hideous demon and the poor mother who had taken her revenge on the cruel *Son of Hagar*. This woman could not be restrained. The slave master had been the one who had ordered her young son, along with a sad, lame woman, to the deck to be murdered as a warning to the approaching ships. When the battle began and the slaver took refuge in the hold with the terrified captives, she saw her chance.

As soon as her son was out of her sight, she sliced the bindings about her wrists using the sharp edge of a broken piece of pottery and waited for her chance. The slave master sat quaking below amidst the others when there was a loud crash on the hatch leading to the deck. As the monster looked up fearfully at the sundered planking, she exploded out of her crouch, leapt onto his back and drove her long, sharp fingernails deep into his two eye sockets, ripping out any tissue and sinew her strong probing fingers met. He screamed like a woman rushing to escape, with her scrambling behind him. Then she desperately took hold of Aoife's *scian* and avenged her little boy.

Felix had witnessed it all and after Wolf had issued initial orders to his lieutenants, he approached his titanic rescuer.

"My name is Felix Santos Serra of Leon. I told them all that you would come but few believed me," he spoke almost reverently, looking up into the green eyes of the largest man he had ever seen. "I know you will understand my Latin as must all of God's Messengers."

"*Salvus Domine Felix,*" Wolf replied in greeting, "but I'm not sure I'm worthy of being included among God's messengers."

"But of course you are *Angelus,* all of God's angels are indeed His Messengers. For was I not named after Saint Felix of Nola? And was not that dear priest rescued from captivity and torture at the hands of cruel Roman heathens? I knew you would come for me just as the first mighty angel came to free my namesake."

Now, Wolf the Quarrelsome loved history, especially military history and he understood the irony that religious history had a strong martial vein running through it. Yet he knew, he himself was anything but an angel and found some humor in that notion. He also instinctively liked this older gentleman who seemed so earnest.

Felix continued, "I am an ambassador of my King, Alfonso of Leon, captured in a French village by the heathen pirates as I was returning from my diplomatic mission there. The local men were working out in the fields when they came seemingly out of nowhere. Only women, children and I were there to be taken and, after setting aflame the poor tiny settlement, they drove us quickly and cruelly to a nearby cove where small boats were waiting for us."

Wolf nodded in sympathy and melancholy recognition. *Different heathens, same horrific tactics*, he told himself. Vikings had been raiding helpless small settlements, monasteries, and convents across northern Europe for hundreds of years. He liked to think Clontarf may have been the beginning of the end of that terror. That and the fact that the Northmen now seemed to be converting in vast numbers to the true faith as had the Gaels half a millennium earlier. And there was no better example than the valiant Icelanders who were now a trusted part of his small band of warriors.

Wolf gazed down kindly at the older but still vigorous man who stood almost nobly, his posture erect and eyes clear.

"I'm called *Faolán an Trodach.* by my people, Wolf the Quarrelsome, a name given me by the heathen Vikings of Dublin – it is *Ulf Hreda,* in their tongue."

"Well, I suppose Lucifer would find the Archangel Michael somewhat 'Quarrelsome' from his own demonic perspective," Felix quickly replied in answer with a bit of twinkling mischief in his deep brown eyes.

*This one should get along well with Pyrrhus*, Wolf mused to himself; *they both share a wry and humorous way with words*. And he couldn't help but grin now as he let out a muted laugh. Mornak the Pictish warrior, who was somewhere on one of the other craft, had that same inclination to make Wolf laugh at the most inappropriate of times.

"I'm quite certain King Alfonso will be immensely grateful to you and your warriors for your gallantry today in the face of our mutual enemy, these idolatrous followers of a moon god. Our kingdom has been afflicted by their kind since long before I was born. And our young regent's family has personally suffered at their hands not so long ago. Alfonso, despite his young age, is organizing us as a people and as an army, while he simultaneously tries to enlist allies among the other small Christian northern kingdoms of our homeland, Castile, Navarre and others."

"Why then haven't you joined together with your Christian neighbors long before now?" asked Wolf. Though he'd been taught by the monks at Inisfallen about the geography and general history of the other Christian nations, he'd never had much interest in politics but rather an intense desire to understand and master military matters.

"It dismays me to tell you, Leon, Castile and Navarre have often bickered among themselves to our eternal shame and the Caliph's great delight," replied Felix with a sad shake of his silver-haired head.

"No need to feel any singular shame in that friend Felix. On my little island, we've far too many 'kings' and 'kingdoms' often squabbling among themselves, not to mention clan kinships, which can be troublesome to the safety and happiness of our nation and its people. The Vikings often took advantage of that until we finally attained some bit of unity under good King Brian and only then could we throw them into the sea."

Now both men nodded in agreement and Felix clasped the giant's huge arm in a knowing fellowship.

***

Once the wounded were tended and former captives made as comfortable as possible, the three dragon ships and one black-sailed dhow continued their southward voyage. While Aoife, Luta and Helena remained conversing with and reassuring the two score women and children, Pyrrhus and Schlomo seemed delighted in each other's company and it seemed Felix could not be parted from his "guardian angel's" side.

That evening, the small flotilla anchored off a small uninhabited island and let off a small party to search for water to replenish their supply. They soon returned with full leather water bags and even a few baskets of shellfish, which were most welcome. As the newly freed were bedded down with new hope and welcome relief for the first night in some time and most of the warriors took their usual sleeping places on the dragon ships, a small council of leaders sat in a circle on the wide deck of the dhow.

This resolute and trusted band, who had sat in similar circumstances even before the climactic and decisive events at Clontarf, for some strange reason, now included two other newly met members. Schlomo and Felix were welcomed based on the certitude of Wolf and Pyrrhus that they would be of value. And given the two wise older men's recent condition of iniquitous bondage, none believed they were agents of some foul pagan evil. Luta and Helena, still enamored by being among the women and especially the children, chose to stay in their company and continue to soothe their new charges. Aoife, however, Wolf's experienced Chief of Intelligence and Espionage, rightly took her place among the rough circle of Wolf's chosen battle chiefs. Fergus, Captain of Irish Spartans and Cael O'Cadhla, Commander of the former Irish Magyar Squadron, both of whom began service to King Brian Boru as teens, sat together as usual.

While Fergus was a heavily built stereotype of an infantryman, Cael was of middling height yet sinewy and supple stature, well adapted to be the experienced and supremely successful cavalryman as he had shown at Clontarf. Mornak Cennelath also took his place. Back home in Scotland, Mornak's adopted younger brother Partha, was once referred to by Vikings and Scots alike as the "demon of the heather."

Years earlier, Viking marauders had raided his small Pictish settlement on a rocky Scottish outcropping, slaughtering most of the men and carrying off the women and children, including Partha's mother. The small boy had lived alone for months amidst the Scottish Highlands, raiding Norse and Celtic homes and farmlands to steal food to survive. Upon his capture, all were astonished to find the demon was merely a frightened youngster who desperately missed his people.

Thinking of his younger brother, now back in Scotland with Mornak's own parents, Mornak seemed to have a heightened sympathy for the newly freed captives. Now the Pict was at home among his comrades and his warm personality and mischievous good humor tended to make him everyone's best friend.

Of course, Cormac, nephew of the slain High King Brian and father figure to many of the younger warriors, was among this small group. Even as Felix believed Wolf was his guardian angel by delivering him from the slavers, Cormac had likewise rescued Wolf from horrific captivity in Dublin on the first day of the new millennium after the battle of Gleann Mama.

Considering their giant leader's explosive sentiments towards all Norse as recently as six months earlier, it seemed almost beyond belief. This meager band of Wolf's trusted chiefs now included a Northman. Keli, who'd proved his mettle in blood and fury at Clontarf. Keli now sat among the small ring of men and one woman gathered around their revered leader.

"So then ye' pack of wolves. Now that we've added this bit of unforeseen ruckus to our quest, what now?"

Wolf asked, his shining green eyes surveying these men and women who had endured so much, good and bad, with him.

All his veteran comrades hid slight grins, knowing if he referred to them as "wolves," he meant that as a genuine compliment especially as he had never before referred to them in that term. Strange, considering the cruel Dublin Vikings of his youth had conferred that name on him as a reluctantly respectful, albeit derisive, slur.

"I reckon we've at last met a wee bit of his final trust and confidence," whispered Mornak Cennelath to the deeply crimson-haired Fergus O'Roghan, who sat to the Pict's right. For Mornak well remembered Wolf's repeated combat lessons and his outbursts when the warriors around him had failed to heed his guidance during actual battles with the Viking foe. "With what we've all gone through together, I don't think the captain has any doubts about us now, if he ever had," replied Fergus.

"You say that because you've never borne the brunt of his 'counseling' after a fight. He so often seems to want me at his side so that I was almost always the first to be 'corrected' for any lack of martial perfection after even a small engagement. Even my sparkling humor and wit couldn't always save me from his scolding." The Pict's eyes twinkled and Fergus could not hold back a grin.

Wolf's men called him by different appellations – "Captain," "Chief," "Commander," or simply by his name, "Faolán." The tall leader personally disdained any titles for himself and seemed quite content with what the Vikings had called him in Dublin years earlier – Wolf the Quarrelsome. Even his own dear Icelanders still called him - *Ulf Hreda.*

Cormac opined first. "It seems to me we have only two choices. One, we could take the women and children back to what remains of their homes. But, with the burning and pillage, it's unlikely there is much for them to return to. Their menfolk have undoubtedly gone south to look for them, or perhaps just moved on to find new lives. Or we could drop them off at the first Christian settlement and hope the people there will take them in. Yet, as we've seen, times are difficult and those additional mouths to feed would strain most of the small settlements we've encountered thus far. Neither alternative is attractive, I'm afraid."

Mornak injected a happier note upon hearing Cormac's dismal comments. "Yet the fact that they're all alive and free is a blessing. No doubt the women may have endured outrages but they and their children seem to be of good, strong stock and all of them appear robust and resilient to me."

The Pict's always optimistic words were likely based on the experience of his adopted brother, who had survived such hardship and was now a sturdy young man and comfort to Mornak's aging mother and father. There was that and the fact that the raven-haired Pict always seemed to project a cheerful outlook even at the most dismal of times.

Fergus's huge elbow gently nudged Mornak's shoulder at that. "Leave it to you to pull good sparkling mead out of spoiled vinegar."

The Pict looked up at his friend with a feigned expression of injury. "Now then, do ye' not prefer sweet, honeyed mead to sour vinegar after all?"

It was at that moment that Felix unexpectedly addressed Wolf. "I know that after being a prisoner, I remain an outsider and guest but may I have permission to speak my opinion, Captain?"

Wolf turned to the Hispanian diplomat with a kind and gentle expression, which belied his formidable stature and silver scarred countenance. "Friend Felix, you are indeed a highly honored guest and your welcome presence here among us at this small council gives proof you are also a trusted ally. You do not need to ask, please speak freely."

Now, all of these conversations among the diverse participants occurred in multiple languages. Pyrrhus and Schlomo were happy to speak in Greek to each other. Mornak and the Gaels spoke Irish among themselves. All were busy teaching Keli and his Icelanders that same Gaelic tongue, while Wolf and Pyrrhus were masters of Danish and both could translate as needed. Yet the lingua franca of the paltry few educated in Europe was, of course, ecclesiastic Latin. King Brian had seen to it that Wolf and Aoife had been classically tutored by the good monks and nuns at Innisfallen and Cashel and both were comfortable and conversant in that old yet still prevalent language.

Felix began his peroration in that common tongue. "We will soon be off the coast of the Leonese Empire… All of the kings of Leon have loved to flatter themselves by referring to their kingdoms as empires," the last bit added with a self-deprecating smile. He continued, "Whether he's a King or Emperor, young Alfonso has already shown himself a noble regent and a brilliant organizer. Given what Leon has endured over the last three decades through the misfeasance of his father Bermudo and at the hands of the late tyrant and infidel Almanzor, he had no other choice."

Aoife used the speaker's brief pause to translate to the others as Wolf beamed at her, his deep green eyes filled with pride and endearment.

"I am sure, Captain, that our youthful king, who is wise beyond his years, will welcome your comrades and these newly liberated Christians with gratitude and the warmest of friendship. You could use the time to replenish and rest before striking out again on your voyage. Or perhaps and I'll confess my fondest wish, we might convince you to stay among us, to join our people as brothers and sisters and warriors of Christ."

Felix paused momentarily as Aoife translated once again. "As for these poor women and children, you have my word, our king will welcome them as well. He can arrange, if they wish, to have them transported back to their former homes or send word to Gascony through his emissaries and clergy of their safety and refuge in Leon in hopes their menfolk might come and be reunited with them."

While Aoife was converting these Latin words to Irish, Pyrrhus translated them into Danish for Keli. As a diplomat himself, Pyrrhus was impressed by his counterpart and, catching Felix's eye, nodded in humble respect. At the same time, Wolf looked around at his small circle of friends and weapon brothers, trying to determine their reactions to this offer. He read their faces, trusting their judgement of character. All these battle-scarred and hardened veterans seemed pleased and gratified with the sincerity and dignity of the older Hispanian man.

Now Wolf turned to speak directly to Aoife. "Well then, *a stór*, as our Chief of Intelligence, your assessments have always proven wise and prescient. What say you now?"

The young Irish giant and the even younger and much smaller Aoife no longer even attempted to hide their feelings for each other. Even if they tried, it would not only be in vain but also a source of amusement to their comrades. For long before Wolf and Aoife could deign to admit it themselves, all around them could see the pleasure and delight the two took in each other's company. The two former orphans and victims of their family's massacre at the hands of the Vikings always seemed melded in both thought and sentiment.

"Captain, it has ever been the strongest intention of our quest to aid our fellow Christians who may be beleaguered by invading enemies, no matter where they are or how hopeless their lot. This appears to be the case in Hispania and now at the hands of the Moors, who seem a hideous and diabolical foe. I believe if we spend time in Leon we may also have an opportunity to acquire essential elements of information that may be of great assistance to us however we move ahead on our journey."

With a huge grin and, as always, deeply impressed by his beloved's elegant choice of words, he knew his and Cormac's choice of Aoife as their chief for determining all matters about their enemies was divinely inspired. Now, with steeled confidence and total conviction, Wolf addressed his friends.

"So then, it is decided, at the morrow we make for the Kingdom of Leon and King Alfonso." At that, all in the assembled ring joined in an exuberant and joyous cheer which carried into the warm and humid salty mist of the nighttime sky and likely awakened some of the finally relaxed sleepers below them.

# Chapter 3

**King Alfonso**
***Imperator Totius Hispaniae***

Alfonso was born to King Bermudo "the Gouty" and his second wife, Elvira Garcia of Castile, in 994 A.D. His father, Bermudo, died in 999 when Alfonso was but five years old. Too young to rule, Queen Elvira and Galician Count Menendo Gonzalez acted as his co-regents. Upon the count's death in 1008, Alfonso became King of Leon and ruled on his own.

Now, in May of 1014, at the age of twenty, the black haired and tawny-skinned monarch sat upon a crimson and golden-draped throne on a slightly elevated stone platform within the enormous great room of his royal castle and personal domicile. Alfonso's appearance and countenance seemed, at first sight, surprisingly impressive and measured for one so young. Seated, slightly lower and on each side of him were his court cleric and his senior military advisor. The cleric was a slender man in a black robe with silver hair. The military commander and standard bearer of the king was a barrel-chested and mail-clad veteran warrior named Sancho. As oftentimes before, Alfonso looked out upon the scores of members of his royal court who took their accustomed places around the walls of the huge hall. On this occasion, however, a group of obvious newcomers also stood before him. Their garb and features indicated a foreign and slightly exotic origin.

One trusted and familiar figure emerged from their midst and respectfully came forward to bow and beg he be allowed to address his king. All recognized Felix Santos Serra, one of Alfonso's hand-picked advisors. Before he could speak more, Alfonso, whose eyes were now wide and filled with teary pleasure, replied.

"Ambassador Felix, my dearest friend, we had thought you were lost to us. Now, I see that our scouts, who brought word of your return, were happily accurate. You, dear Sir, are once more among us where you belong. And now you bring welcome guests whose arrival we most happily welcome. I look upon robust Christian warriors from the North and even one Northman who we're assured is as devout to the good Savior Christ as ourselves."

Then, looking directly into the eyes of the three women among the visitors, he added. "And three beautiful ladies, all with proud and strong countenances, each different and extraordinary in appearance." Alfonso then bowed slightly and respectfully, his expression earnest and pleased, as Aoife, Luta and Helena all gazed up at the remarkably humble and sincere eyes of the impossibly young king.

Earlier, in a discussion with Felix and the others, Wolf had decided that during their first audience, Felix would first present Cormac among the small group of allied leaders. Cormac was the only one among them who had any claim to a "noble" birthright. His father and uncle had both been kings in Ireland. The humorous irony, however, was that almost every Irishman and woman was certain there was a king or queen in his or her background somewhere. For that reason, none held any great reverence or deference for "nobility." Cormac was older than the others however, presenting a more seasoned aspect than the younger men in the group.

Felix stood erect and observed his king's notice of the visiting women. He decided to use the opportunity to change plans and introduce them first. "Sire, I present Helena Lakepeno, who is foremost among the ambassadors of the Christian Greek Roman Empire."

Helena, dressed in an elegantly flowing green robe, which had somehow survived the voyage relatively unscathed, bowed respectfully, her waist-length dark hair almost shimmering in the torchlight.

"And these two young women are Luta Einarsdottir and Aoife of Cashel. Both are pious Christians and have been of great aid and comfort, tending to the sad captives who were so recently held in bondage by the vile infidels." Luta and Aoife, standing together, also bowed respectfully, though perhaps not so elegantly as had Helena. They were, of course, in their twenties, while the Greek was a sophisticated and handsome woman of middling age.

The snow blonde Luta and the deep chestnut brunette Aoife presented a pleasing contrast as they both gazed up with similar radiant and youthful smiles. Each wore a simple flaxen-colored linen dress which fell to her ankles, all they'd been able to take with them for whatever 'special occasions' they might encounter.

Just at that moment, another figure stood up from her elaborate seat at the very front and to the right of the great hall. Hers was the only position in the chamber with a platform at the same height as the king's. Queen Mother Elvira Garcia of Castile was dressed in an exquisite scarlet gown which covered her stately figure from her regal head to below her feet. The king's mother appeared to be about the same age as Helena and both cast a cultivated and imposing aura. In fact, many of the Gaels, looking upon the two formidable women, observed that the two could easily have been sisters.

"You, dear ladies, are most welcome among us. Your presence cheers my heart at a time when it is especially gratifying. Please do let me know if I can do anything to make your stay with us more pleasant." Elvira looked to her son affectionately and once again took her seat.

The ambiance in the room almost immediately seemed to transform from a formal meeting with new arrivals from distant lands to a warm reunion among long-lost friends. The king and Felix were visibly beaming. That was, of course, the desired effect of Elvira's heartfelt and moving words.

Felix continued, "And this, my King, is Cormac MacMahon, the son of King Mahon of Munster and nephew of the late High King Brian Boru of the Irish Empire, formally deemed *Imperator Scotorum* by our Holy Church." Felix knew from a conversation with Pyrrhus that the monks of the Monastery in Armagh, Ireland, had bestowed that rank on King Brian and he was most pleased to diplomatically make use of the somewhat embellished title in his introduction.

Cormac was a rugged and grizzled warrior approaching his fifth decade. His long, brown locks were streaked with silver and, like all the other visiting warriors, he was garbed in a simple *léine*, a linen tunic that fell to his knees. However, perhaps because of his lineage, he chose to wear a deeply blue-hued *léine* as opposed to the more muted dun or wheaten tunics of his comrades. Folded over several times and draped over his right shoulder to be secured beneath the wide leather belt on his left hip was his woolen *brat*, a hoodless and sleeveless cloak normally an outer garment in cooler weather but easily carried and worn in this manner in warmer times. Most of these cloaks were woolen but some of the Irish preferred a *brat* of cow or deer hide.

Alfonso almost immediately felt a certain kinship with the older Irish son of a king who stood before him proudly. This is what Felix had expected, and the king didn't disappoint him.

"You, Prince Cormac, are indeed most welcome. God be praised, we have lately received word of the magnificent accomplishments of you, your comrades here and the other Irish in the desperate battle against the hordes of heathen invaders who threatened your land."

Then the king continued in a more somber note, "The same traveling clergy have also brought us news of the tragic martyrdom of the brave High King Brian at the hands of the murderous Vikings. Please know you have the sympathies of me and all our people at your loss."

In the same Latin tongue, Cormac replied in his usual tenor-toned voice. "You have our sincere thanks for your welcome and your condolences, King Alfonso. We mourn our great king and hope to someday bring aid to other Christians suffering the depredations of foreign heathen invaders. For, in our moment of need, we were aided by others, including our Scots and Welsh cousins and not least good Christian Northmen, many from Iceland, including one who is with us this moment."

At that, Keli stepped forward, took his place next to Cormac and bowed slightly. Alfonso reckoned he appeared not much different than the other Gaels around him, though there was a type of runic patterning on his tunic and his long blonde hair was braided differently than that of the others. Alfonso's people had also suffered the raids of Viking dragon ships and occasionally still experienced these attacks. But the king was wise enough to understand that the threat was diminishing as the Northmen increasingly turned to the Christian God. And Alfonso knew well, he had a far greater threat to face from the immense occupying presence of other heathen invaders who held most of the Hispanian Peninsula.

Aoife and Helena had been translating the Latin conversation in hushed voices for the benefit of Keli and the other Gaels of the lead band. Now, Felix continued by introducing all together, Fergus, Cael and finally, Mornak the Pict.

Though he was a classically educated Hispanian nobleman, Alfonso had never even heard of, much less been in the presence of, a Pict. He noted there was something alien and, yet at the same time, eerily familiar with Mornak's countenance. With darker skin and hair than his comrades, the Pict almost seemed a primordial relic of ancient times on the continent of Europe.

But then, Mornak bowed with a theatrical flourish, sweeping his hands low and gracefully up from the floor and stood upright again in a grand finale, his sky-blue eyes twinkling mischievously and with a contagious, toothy grin. The king and the other Hispanian members of the court looked on with joyous amusement and could not help but smile with pleasure and applaud their delightful visitor. Fergus and Cael just rolled their eyes.

"I see a noble and powerful group of warriors. All of us are most pleased to have you in our company." The king said this with utmost sincerity as he highly appreciated blooded veteran fighters who fought for their Christian faith and native country.

"And you, Fergus, must be the indomitable war chieftain whose great fame has found its way to us here in Hispania?"

The King's assumption was made in all honesty, as Fergus was tall and immensely powerful in stature. And his red hair no doubt confirmed all the images the Hispanian held about the wild inhabitants of what the Romans had called Hibernia. Fergus looked anxiously at Cormac to explain the reality to the king. Because, as the *Snekkjas* and captured dhow docked at a small but important harbor town which afforded the Leonese access to the seas north of their kingdom, Wolf had first met a ten-year-old French boy named Albin.

***

Since the moment they had been liberated and Albin set his incredulous brown eyes on the enormous leader of the men who had saved them, the boy had been mesmerized. Albin's prior weeks had been a series of horrors for the child. His father had been one of the far too few of their settlement's men who had been selected to look after them while the others worked in the fields. He had been swarmed by a rush of six Moorish men carrying spears and slaughtered within seconds of hearing the alarm being cried out.

Albin watched as his father crushed one attacker's skull with his simple wooden cudgel before being impaled by the long stabbing spikes of five thrusting spears. Albin wanted to run to his father but instead dashed off to find his mother, who was already being harried by a particularly large, black-garbed raider. All he could see were the evil black eyes of the monster as its head was entirely covered in black wrappings.

But Albin knew his mother was no weak and screaming matron to be carried off like a mewling lamb. As the Moor viciously clutched her upper arm with one hand, the other upraised and poised to bash her senseless, his mother deftly extracted a sharp-bladed utensil from her skirts. It was a simple tool normally used to core apples. Now she used it to suddenly and without warning, cut the creature's throat and then drove it in again to skewer where she thought its heart must be.

As the raider fell to the ground, drowning in his own blood, Albin screamed as his mother was immediately surrounded by the same men who had killed his father. Now they used their short swords and hacked the woman to a grisly death, enraged by what she'd done to their leader. The boy howled and rushed to throw himself on his parents' murderers but was struck in the head and everything went black. Albin woke up much later in captivity with the other women and children on the slavers' dhow.

Aoife, wise as always, thought it fit to introduce Albin to their huge leader personally. She had heard his story from the others as translated by Felix during the voyage. They had endeavored to talk with the boy himself but he seemed unable to speak except for one phrase, which Felix thought meant something like "Avenging giant."

When their craft arrived at the small port settlement north of the fortified town of Oviedo, Aoife and Pyrrhus brought Albin to meet Wolf. Upon hearing the boy's tale of woe as described in the words of his dear one and the Greek diplomat, the towering leader bent to gently put one huge hand on the youth's narrow shoulder. The two pairs of eyes, brown and green, locked almost as if they exchanged meaning without words. Then, Wolf spoke softly in his own tongue, his voice deep and sincere.

"Hear me, young Albin. You have suffered irrecoverable loss and hideous pain over the last few weeks. Yet here you stand before me, proud and erect. You are not alone in such pain and you are not without friends now. Trust me in this. You will conquer your sorrow and fears and you will grow up to be strong and intelligent. I see this in your eyes and your valiant bearing."

Pyrrhus did his best to translate these words into what he hoped the boy would comprehend. When he was finished, Albin nodded with understanding, then, seeming infinitely more mature than his young years, he reached out his right hand to grasp that of the giant in apparent acknowledgment and gratitude. The two then embraced like warrior comrades. From that moment until they arrived at the kingdom's capital city, also called Leon, the two were almost inseparable, to Aoife's occasional displeasure. It didn't matter that they spoke no mutually intelligible language. To all appearances, the immense Gaelic champion and the small French boy could get their basic meanings across even when each spoke in his own tongue.

As soon as they came into Leon, even before being presented to the king, Wolf and Felix set about finding a worthy haven for Albin. Felix knew a family of minor nobility who had three young daughters and they said they would be delighted to adopt the orphan boy. Wolf also wanted to assure Albin's education and Felix again knew of a prestigious abbey in Leon, which had students from good families from across Europe. That same abbey agreed to accept and educate young Albin.

Wolf had insisted on touring the place to determine if it met his approval, pleased to acknowledge that it finally met his standards. For that reason, the Irish leader, never one to be overly impressed with Kings and Queens, with the notable exception of King Brian, was a wee bit late for that first important meeting with Alfonso.

***

As Fergus looked anxiously to Cormac to somehow answer the king's confusion about the "indomitable Irish war chieftain," the thick oaken entrance doors to the great hall unexpectedly swung open. There was a tramp of heavy boots as four fully armored Hispanian knights escorted an impossibly massive and almost barbaric figure to stand before Alfonso. There was a collective intake of breath from the assorted onlookers at the appearance of this newcomer who seemed to be a biblical Goliath facing King David. Yet Alfonso was not in the least alarmed. He smiled with good cheer and welcome at the formidable apparition whose eyes were level with his, notwithstanding the elevated platform and high throne upon which Alfonso sat.

"I now see those romantic tales of druidic rituals summoning up some ancient pagan Celtic War god to smite the Vikings were not to be believed."

I must confess," nodding to the priest beside him, "forgive me Father.... I'm almost disappointed. Yet in all truth, you, Sir Knight, exceed the descriptions about you in those early reports."

Wolf had been called many names but never "Sir Knight." Despite his classic education at Inisfallen and a particular love of history and military subjects, he had never heard the term "Knight" until Felix tried to explain it to him. Apparently, it meant something different than a simple cavalryman, heavy infantry warrior, or even an individual clan champion. Knight seemed to connote a combination of devout piety, intense military training and upraised nobility. Wolf immediately related to the concepts of intense military training, piety (though they were all sincere Christians, he knew he and most of his weapon brothers might not exactly be considered exceedingly monk-like in their reverence). But he'd never considered "nobility," upraised or not, to be a positive discriminator for a mighty warrior. Nevertheless, he understood the respect with which the king used the term.

"I beg your forgiveness for my slight delay, exalted King. I was delayed at one of your most excellent abbeys by the good monks who didn't seem to want to let me leave. I am called in our language *Faolán an Trodach* – Wolf the Quarrelsome. It's a name bestowed on me by the Vikings of Dublin when I was an orphaned captive youth there. *Ulf Hreda* they called me. I hated those bloody little heathens but I came to rather like that name and find it as suitable as any other. I hope it doesn't offend you or any in your court."

The titan briefly turned his huge head around to survey the people in the hall with a sincere and contagious smile. They all nodded and it seemed their initial shock had turned to pleasure at hearing their most uncommon visitor's words rendered in such eloquent Latin. He turned quickly back to the king and continued.

"I do hope the men and women of our small contingent have also met your approval. By now, I trust them all with my life and can attest without reservation to their trustworthiness and honor…. despite the appearance of some of them."

Even his Irish eyes were smiling as he added that last and most of his men had to struggle to keep from chuckling as Aoife and Pyrrhus again softly translated. But many in the court were not quite so solemn and there were more than a few subdued laughs among them, including from their own king.

The formal conversations went on for not overly long and it was ultimately agreed that the visitors be welcomed and given accommodations to stay as long as required to recover from their voyage and battle. Comfortable barracks were provided for all the fighting men and a large stone residence was reserved for visiting dignitaries, including the leaders and women. Alfonso had already taken steps to assure their three *Snekkjas* were secure back at the small port. The slavers' dhow was given to their Hispanian host to do as he saw fit. It seemed that there might now be an opportunity to rest and prepare for what was to come next.

# Chapter 4

**The Assassin - Qatil Al Sulafia**

As he sat in a place of honor in the Caliph's palace within the walls of the city of Cordoba, the capital of what was still known as the Caliphate of Cordoba, Bogumir Dalibor exuded an aura of potent controlled ferocity. Of course, he was no longer known by those old and now detested words. His Islamic brothers had bestowed upon him a new and welcome name. They found it fit to honor him as Qatil Al Sulafia, loosely meaning the Slavic Assassin.

***

The man now known as the Assassin was finally in a place and at a station he deemed worthy of his honor and skills. But it had not always been this way. As a young boy from the town of Ragusa on the Adriatic, Bogumir's father, whom he had never seen, was slain while in military service to the Emperor of the Greek Roman Empire. Ragusa, first established by the Romans, was long contested among Slavs, Greeks and Latins. His mother was a Slav but she told him his father had originated from distant lands to the east. He was an only child and his mother was often absent on business that he never learned about. They lived in a small hut just outside the town. There was not much to live on and he was forced to steal to survive almost as soon as he could walk. After he was caught and beaten by a shepherd while trying to steal a lamb, Bogumir learned to stalk with stealth and silence by observing wolves, martens and other predators. He noted their methods of blending in with their surroundings, then striking with lightning speed and savagery.

As he grew into his teens, he saw less of his mother. Surprisingly, this fact did not seem to overly dismay either mother or son. Though nominally a Christian, Bogumir wasn't sure he was ever baptized, nor did he ever attend any formal church ceremonies. What he did know about being a Christian, he didn't like. There just seemed to be too much emphasis on the things he loved but was forbidden to do. He was especially disgusted with the concepts of "turning the other cheek," or "loving one's enemies." As he grew older, simple thievery was no longer enough and he learned to take pleasure and profit in violence and cruelty.

With his blond curly hair, blue eyes and deceptive appearance of penniless innocence, it was easy for him to fall in with itinerant merchants on the roads outside Ragusa. If they were foolish enough to travel alone, it was almost too easy for him to strike with lethality and make off with their money and goods. If there were two or even three of them, Bogumir could still slit their throats so swiftly that the last one's eyes would still be filled with surprise and shock before the first bled out.

It was the same with girls and women. He had no patience with the nuances of wooing, courtship, or working his way into their good graces. He chose to take what he wanted. This worked with a small percentage of them but most resisted vigorously and had to be forced to submit to his cravings. The same furtive techniques he had learned in becoming first a thief and later a murderer - deception, awareness of his surroundings and savage ferocity – served him well until one girl escaped in a moment of inexcusable inattentiveness on his part. She had been too quickly gagged and bound.

As he was about to unleash his inner demons on her, he thought he heard someone approaching. He drew his dagger and crawled out from the small alcove among the thick conifers into which he had dragged his prey. There was nothing to see. But to be safe, he dashed quickly to a promontory from which he could observe the beach below. Out on the waters, some fishermen in a small boat were busy hauling in their catch and bellowing with pleasure at their bounty. Shaking his head, he returned to find the girl gone and the bindings flung to the ground. He knew immediately Ragusa would never be safe for him again.

***

With so many ships from so many nations plying the waters of the Adriatic, it was not difficult for Bogumir to come to a verbal agreement with a Greek captain of a merchant ship and become a deckhand. The ship was bound for the port City of Antiocheia, close by the contested frontier border with bellicose Arab Muslims. It was a large, three-masted craft powered by sails and multiple banks of oars; not much different from similar merchant ships that had been trading throughout the Mediterranean for centuries. The young Slavic man knew nothing of sailing but at 20 years of age, he was robust, tall and lean with rangy muscles across his shoulders and arms. There would be plenty of maritime tasks for which he would be well-suited.

Always a loner, Bogumir had never had a friend during his short and troubled existence. So, it was unusual for him to somehow develop a type of rapport with a shipmate called Jalel. Trade has always seemed to endure, despite wars and strife among nations and populations. It was not unusual to find men from diverse lands, tribes and religions serving as crew members aboard the same ship. This Greek merchant ship was humorously named the "Sea Cow."

So, one morning, as they labored next to each other on the oars, Jalel, a short, dark-haired Syrian Muslim with decent Greek, spoke his first words to the fugitive Slav. "So then, mate, what good fortune brings you to join us on this pleasant and joy-filled cruise across two seas?"

Bogumir, who was so relieved to be safely away from Ragusa and anyone who could possibly recognize him, replied with an uncharacteristic grin, "I was just hoping to get some sun, salty air and exercise as a break from the tedious life of soft luxury back at the palace."

The Syrian laughed unabashedly, taking an instant liking to his new blonde shipmate. Over the coming days, the two of them engaged in long conversations about their lives and hopes. Almost everything Bogumir said was a lie, while Jalel spoke honestly from his heart.

"Why are you always so cheerful Jalel, even as our blisters bleed and our asses chafe?" The Slav was genuinely interested and listened intently as the Syrian answered him. "I'm content because we're still young and I know Allah, the All Merciful, will see to my welfare in the darkest of times. And that He will reward me here on earth and in Paradise."

"And what rewards will Allah shower on you before you get to Paradise?" Bogumir tried not to let his sarcasm sound too obvious.

"With the wages I receive from this, my second trading voyage, I will return to my home tribe in Syria and be able to procure the first two of the four wives I ultimately intend to own. They will take care of my dwelling and property while I'm away on my next and hopefully even more profitable journey." Jalel smiled then in happy anticipation.

"When I have acquired the two women I have already chosen as first wives, I will train them well. After that, I will join the expeditionary forces of the Umayyad clans to gain slaves and booty taken from barbarian *kafirs.* With these new riches, I shall take two more wives, build a new palace and then fill it with beautiful slaves to serve me at all times. And, much later, I shall die and go to Paradise where Allah will be pleased with me for obeying his law, and thereafter I will be rewarded with even more of all that is sweet and luscious."

Bogumir listened to these words, unsure if Jalel might not be merely taunting him. He was not much interested in taking a wife himself, thinking of how miserable his mother's life had been. But he was captivated by the idea of reaping booty and slaves through stealing and pillaging. And all of it sanctioned by a powerful religion. It seemed the antithesis of what he knew of Christianity, where everything he now craved seemed to be forever forbidden to him.

"Does your faith truly allow you four wives? Are you also able to plunder and kill your enemies, take their possessions and make slaves of their people without sin?" Bogumir asked almost hesitantly, fervently wanting to believe it was true.

"Yes, we are told we must do battle with the unbelievers and that Paradise is under the swords of Jihad. But first, we must allow them to accept and submit to Islam or pay the *dhimmis'* tax of *Jizya.* If they resist, we must slay them wherever we find them or be slain fighting against them and thus taken into Paradise."

Now Bogumir felt truly lightning-struck—almost as if the girl escaping his clutches and his hasty flight away from Ragusa was somehow ordained. Everything Jalel, who was otherwise jocular and amiable, had just said to him seemed too good to be true. He had found his true path.

"Jalel, please tell me. What must I do to become a Muslim like you, to fight for Islam, to please Allah? I am ready to do anything to ensure my conversion, to do what is necessary. Please."

Jalel's customary pleasant smile once more appeared on his beaming face. "I have already determined you're no longer a Christian and perhaps you never truly were one. And you should have no worries about any "conversion" for no one "converts" to Islam. They revert to the true faith which Allah has given to all of us. You could do it right now by simply reciting the *Shahada* – the

Declaration of Faith. But I would still advise you to do so in a more formal setting surrounded by your brothers and holy ones."

So, it was decided that after docking at Antiocheia and receiving their pay, Bogumir would accompany his new friend back to Jalel's home tribal lands in Syria. Although a hot/cold war existed between the claims of the Christian empire and the Arab territories, it was a relatively simple matter to cross back and forth without impeding trade, which benefited both sides. Once home, Jalel would bring Bogumir to the Umayyad Emir, where the Slav would be received and formally recite the *Shahada* to be accepted into the true faith.

***

Several weeks later, Bogumir, who was now called Al Sulafia, felt truly at home for the first time in his life. The Emir, who was an energetic and formidable man in his forties, had been impressed by the Slav's apparent earnestness and willingness to serve Allah. Jalel explained how his friend had appealed to him to join the Muslims. He also recounted Bogumir's maritime skills, acquired aboard the Sea Cow and how he appeared stronger and more diligent in his duties than most of his fellow shipmates.

When Jalel returned to his home to claim his wives and prepare for yet another voyage, which was to commence in the near future, Sulafia stayed with the Emir, residing with the guard force that always accompanied their leader.

During this time, the young man experienced his twenty-first birthday and began to grasp the Arabic language so quickly that it seemed astonishing to the guards. He explained to them it was because of his burning desire to speak in the tongue of the Prophet. They also used this time to teach him the ways of the sword and lance, as well as the rudiments of horsemanship. Through all of this, he was an avid student.

When he was brought before the Emir again, the conversation turned to practical matters and the future.

"I have been told you have excelled at every endeavor during your short time among us Sulafia. You already understand the basics of our language and are becoming proficient in the ways of weapons and horses. And that you are improving rapidly in all aspects. Tell me, did you have other skills learned on your own before you fortuitously came to us?" The Emir sounded quite pleased and Sulafia wanted to impress him but knew he must choose his words wisely. They spoke in Greek, which the Emir understood quite well.

"My Emir, I regret to say I've had little formal education back in the land of the infidel, but I am able to converse in Greek and the Slavic tongue of my mother. I also was forced to learn to be swift, stealthy, and very forceful when needed to survive in that vile place where all seemed hostile to me. I can blend in with the background to elude capture and beating. I can silently enter locked structures and abodes to hide from evil-doers. And, at times, I have successfully battled against assailants who threatened me."

The Emir was not only a veteran warrior but also a wise and perceptive man. He knew immediately what he was dealing with in the form of the young Slav standing before him. Sulafia had undoubtedly been an indigent child who had learned to become an expert thief. He also knew that most Christian children, just like their Muslim counterparts, often grew up in difficult circumstances.

But few would actually believe they were in a "vile place" where everyone was hostile to them. And the older man also interpreted the words about "successful battles against threatening assailants" as clearly meaning that those "assailants" had been killed, whether or not any "battle" had truly taken place. There was some almost palpable driving force or energy in this one, which seemed to manifest even as he stood respectfully before his Emir. This could be a gift and, properly honed, the Emir could have a useful tool to employ against his enemies.

"Well done, Sulafia. Based on your blessed admittance into the true faith of the believers and your most excellent progress in learning the ways of the warrior, I have confidence you may advance to greater heights in service to Allah. The skills you just described, though gained only under great adversity in the *Dar al-Harb* - the "Abode of War," will also be of great value in the *Dar al-Islam* – the "Abode of Islam."

The young man contemplated the Emir's words as the older man continued to speak.

"I have a task in mind for you. If you succeed, it will not only further prove your dedication and be to your honor but give you valuable experience for what may lie ahead of us." The Emir caught the glint of eager anticipation in the Slav's blue eyes and went on. "We have learned that the commander of the frontier garrison of the Roman Army along our border has been secretly meeting with the noble wife of the provincial *Exarch* at a secluded spot not far from our own outposts. I have no idea what the two are doing but I'm sure the

Roman governor would not approve of his wife's dalliances with his subordinate officer."

Now Sulafia was listening with rapt attention. Would it be possible that he would be sent on some mission to gain fame and perhaps more? He immediately assented. "My Emir, I have no wish but to of complete service to you and our people."

With those words, the boy named Bogumir no longer existed. The man called Sulafia had replaced him to take part in a new world where he was free to be himself and satisfy his long-forbidden desires. The plan called for Sulafia, whose appearance and accent were typical of the various peoples of the Greek Roman Empire, to lead a band of eight *saqaliba*. The *saqaliba* were freed slaves who had been kidnapped on raids from areas in eastern and southern Europe. Among them were Slavs, Germans, Greeks and Latins, as well as former Christians and former pagans. They were generally considered to be useful savages by the Arabs. Sulafia differed, though, in that he had never been a slave.

The Emir knew that the garrison commander had taken only his personal guard of four cavalrymen with him when the officer and the governor's wife met at the small estate, which was always vacated before their arrival. The only others there would be the family of servants who maintained the estate. They lived in a small house nearby. Wearing uniforms of the Roman cavalry and carrying standards of the Imperial army, the strike force would casually ride up and quickly slaughter the guards. Then Sulafia would enter the abode with another and execute the commander in front of his lover.

The Emir considered this Roman commander to be an intelligent and formidable enemy who had won every one of the occasional battles along the border when his Muslim raiding parties had been intercepted. It was a most welcome development when his spies reported on this uncharacteristic lapse in security on the part of the officer. Now, this would cause confusion and strife among the Christians and the Muslims would not be considered the perpetrators. Perfect *Taqiyya*—deception. Sulafia would now have his chance.

***

The small residence was situated on a patch of green amid surroundings characterized by scrub brush and sparsely vegetated terrain. The small estate did claim its own tiny spring, which provided the gift of water, even if not in great quantity. It sat a bit lower than the area around it, though there were no great hills to be seen anywhere in the vicinity. From a tiny promontory mounted by a scraggly bush, Sulafia crawled up to peer down at his target.

He could see the primary residence, which was essentially three rooms of masonry construction and a small cabin where the family of servants resided. The servants must have been in their dwelling since Sulafia was sure the commander wouldn't want them underfoot while he was "visiting" the Exarch's wife. The four guards stood a short distance away from the residence. One man on each of the cardinal sides so that each could always maintain eye contact with at least two of the others. Now the young Muslim convert developed his first formal plan of execution and explained it to his comrades.

The leader of the commander's guards was the first to see three Imperial cavalrymen trotting toward the estate. One of the men raised his hand and called in greeting.

"God's greetings! We've come to bring word to the commander. The exarch is coming here soon as his visitor from Constantinople has cancelled his trip."

When the party reached the guard, they all dismounted. "One of you come with me. I don't doubt the disturbance will dismay our leader but he'll appreciate the warning."

Sulafia walked to the guard's side and the two made their way briskly to the estate's entrance, where the guard knocked on the wooden door and alerted his superior inside, his voice forceful.

"Commander. Imperial messengers have come. It is urgent! May we have a word?" Sulafia heard annoyed cursing inside and the sound of heavy footsteps tramping toward the entrance. That was his signal.

With a dagger in his left hand, he deftly slashed the guard's carotid artery and he fell to the ground, gurgling. The door opened to reveal the disheveled commander, barefoot and clad only in a quite wrinkled tunic. Sulafia ran him through with his sword before the leader's eyes could even register the crumpled form of his personal guard splayed on the doorstep. He heard the thundering of hoofbeats as he stepped inside.

The eight mounted *saqaliba,* disguised as Imperial troops, made quick work of the other three completely surprised guards, breaking into groups to surround and impale them from horseback with their lances. Then they rejoined to trot to meet Sulafia.

"Is it done? Is he dead?" asked one of their new leader. "He and the guard are both dead, as is the ugly hag who was the wife of the Exarch," Sulafia boasted. "But we are not yet finished." The *saqaliba* were taken aback. There had been no discussion of killing the governor's wife.

Sulafia mounted his horse and the others accompanied him to the servants' quarters. They had known to stay out of sight in their cabin the entire time when the commander made his occasional visits here, so they were completely unaware of what had just transpired. Telling them to wait outside, Sulafia drew his sword. Strode to the flimsy door and kicked it violently, storming inside.

Then, for a few brief moments that seemed like hours, the horsemen heard terrified screaming and the moans of agony. An abrupt and eerie silence followed this before Sulafia appeared once more in the door, clutching a horrified teenager by the lad's long curly black hair. He was dragged before the mounted men, where the Slav screamed at him in Greek, "Thus, the wages of all who threaten our holy Emperor!" Then Sulafia brutally punched the boy in the face, sending him to the ground, where he lay unconscious.

As their leader walked toward his horse and began to mount, one of the *saqaliba* strode into the cabin. Moments later, Sulafia was already trotting his steed back toward their own lands as the man came out of the cabin ashen-faced.

"There's blood everywhere. A man, a woman and a very young girl. All butchered and mangled," he tremblingly informed his comrades. "Why then did he leave the boy alive?" asked one. Another answered. "He wants to let it be known that soldiers of the Christian Emperor killed everyone, even the commander and the Exarch's wife."

***

Later, Sulafia stood before the Emir to render his report. "Praise be to Allah, we accomplished our task and the enemy commander is slain. We left one *kafir* alive to tell the tale but all others I killed."

The Emir immediately discerned two particular facts from the brief report. His orders were to slay the commander. He gave no instructions about killing others. And the Slav had said 'I killed,' not 'We killed.' He needed clarification.

"Did you then actually slay the governor's wife as well? And what others did you kill? I sent others to assist you. Did they play any part?" The Emir saw neither doubt nor hesitation in his eyes as Sulafia replied.

"My Emir, the men you sent with me nobly proved their worth. They quickly vanquished the four Christian guards who had accompanied their commander. I, myself, killed the others, the commander, the woman and the family of servants. However, I left one alive to allow the tale to be told. Now, all will believe Christian soldiers kill anyone who displeases their emperor with no regard for whether they are his own soldiers, his own Exarch's wife, or a simple family of servants. This will sow confusion and doubt into our foe. *Taqiyya* is our sacred ally in war. I most humbly desire that my actions meet with your approval."

The Emir listened intently to the words of the man before him. The logic was unassailable. This successful raid confirmed his initial impression of the gift that had fallen into his lap, a gift he planned to use to great effect in the future.

"You have done magnificently, my valiant soldier of Allah. From this point on, you are no longer simply Sulafia. You are to be honored with the title: *Qatil Al Sulafia* – The Assassin. In the coming days, we sail to the Caliphate of Cordoba in Al Andalus to be amongst our brethren in a new land of plenty. You will be among my most trusted and valuable leaders there."

The newly designated Assassin bowed his head in respect and gratitude, pleased to once again have the opportunity to prove his skills.

# Chapter 5

## Reconnaissance in Force

A few days after their initial audience with King Alfonso, Wolf again called a council meeting of his leaders. This took place in the main room of the stone residence provided by the king. On this occasion, it was formed of the original members of the expedition, as Schlomo and Felix were otherwise engaged. In truth, Wolf was pleased. He was concerned that the two older men, though trustworthy and wise, might inhibit candid comment among the Gaels and their Greek and Icelandic comrades.

"Well, it seems we are, for now, in a position to fulfill that mission to which we are pledged, to aid those who are oppressed and threatened by invaders," he began. Then he gazed toward Aoife.

"Now, to determine how best to accomplish that. We must gather the information needed to develop our own assessment of the situation. Thereafter, we'll design our courses of action to bring to the king. You've all mingled with our hosts over the last few days, I've no doubt you have ideas of your own that I'm keen to hear."

At this point, Aoife, Luta and Helena all looked to each other, nodding in unspoken agreement. They had spent their time thus far speaking to the local women, from servant girls to matrons and noble ladies, including the Queen Mother Elvira herself. Their efforts were not in vain.

Aoife took the lead, speaking with confidence and conviction. "Captain, despite the hospitality afforded us by our hosts, it seems matters here are not much different than those in Ireland before King Brian brought us together. Even faced with the threat of foreign invaders, strife persists among the various small Christian lands and their leaders, not to mention courtly intrigue. Alfonso, like Brian years ago, is still trying to overcome those challenges. So, whatever we decide, we must proceed with caution."

Now Aoife looked in turn to Cormac, Cael, Fergus, Keli and Pyrrhus. "We've had some discussions among ourselves. So as not to be surprised in a strange country with an altogether different enemy, I'm convinced we must make a reconnaissance in force before we can develop a plan of action."

Unsurprised by his Chief of Intelligence's candid comments, Wolf smiled at her. "I had no doubt, Aoife, that you were well ahead of me in determining a way ahead. And what, pray tell, do you suggest we do first?"

Aoife looked to Cael, signaling him to proceed as they had discussed earlier. "Aoife has learned from Alfonso's spy chief that the Caliphate, despite its recent troubles, has imported yet another band of Berber horsemen from the north of Africa. These riders have established themselves just below Leon's southern marches. They've been raiding across the border, pillaging homesteads and attempting to find the best possible axes of advance for a larger force to penetrate deeper into the kingdom."

As Cael continued, all the assembled veterans listened with rapt attention to the talk of a new and aggressive enemy movement. "The Leonese intend to send a force of about 100 heavily armed and armored heavy cavalry to track down and destroy the raiders. They call these men 'knights' and believe they will easily crush the Berbers, who are said to have twice their numbers."

Aoife now spoke up. "They may indeed be able to outfight the Berber cavalry, who are unarmored and only carry light spears and long knives but with their heavy armor and huge lances, the Hispanians won't be able to find and fix such a mobile force."

"And that's why we feel the knights should be accompanied by our two score of good Irish Magyars," a beaming Cael added. "We may not have our much-missed Connemara ponies but our friends have offered to loan us use of trained horses from their own stock. And we each have our trusted and well-blooded Magyar bows."

Cael had spent a full morning with the cadre of organized Hispanian archers and had come away impressed by the men and their weapons. However, they were meant to move and shoot on foot and lacked the speed, mobility and shock power of a company of trained mounted archers.

"We'll be able to ride quicker and quieter in advance of the knights to scout out the presence of the Berbers, especially with the aid of one of the local Leonese militia who knows the terrain and is a very good horseman…
even if he is even a bit older than our own Cormac."

As the eldest of the group, Cormac was used to being teased about his age and laughed along with the others at Cael's hobbling attempt at humor. Still, he had to reply, "I'm just concerned you and your young Magyar louts might fall off the huge steeds provided by the Hispanian. Do they know ye've only ridden stunted dwarf ponies until now?"

The laughing grew more spirited and Aoife chimed in over the din. "And, to keep them out of trouble, they'll be accompanied by an experienced Viking-slayer and spymaster who can ride better than any of those boys."

The mood in the room was buoyant but Wolf knew he had to bring the band back to some semblance of order, even if he was laughing as much as the others. "Very well, even I know the knights plan to move out in the next several days. What else have you all come up with?"

Aoife went on, her voice more subdued and serious again. "As you know, we continue to gain valuable information from the local women. Helena has been particularly welcomed among the wives of the Counts, Earls, and other titles the local nobility may bestow upon themselves. At the same time, Luta is especially popular among the common women and girls. No doubt because of her golden hair. And she has become friends with a learned, kindly nun who serves as her translator. Almost incredibly, this nun even speaks Danish, having been a captive of the Vikings as a young girl."

Luta and Cael looked at each other with disappointment but resignation. For months, they had spent every free moment in each other's company and grown increasingly closer. Yet both knew they had important roles to fill.

"Likewise, Cormac has been especially respected and honored by the King and senior members of his court. Along with Pyrrhus, we feel the two of them will be able to grasp early warning of any threats to ourselves or perhaps to the king himself." Aoife paused and then added, "We know Cormac would prefer to keep our Magyar 'savages' out of trouble himself but he's agreed to sacrifice by staying in the company of the king and the king's mother in this case."

Again, the room was filled with laughter and grins and Aoife concluded her speech. "We knew better than to ever come up with a task for you, Captain. For one thing, everyone is well aware you don't respond well to others' designs for you. And you, no doubt, have your own plan for causing pain to this new slew of 'bloody little heathens'. We also know Keli would not wish to be too far from his dear wee *Snekkjas* and that Fergus and Mornak are happiest fighting on their own two feet on God's good green earth while at your side."

Wolf looked genuinely surprised, "You seem to be able to read my mind *mo chailín deas*. I have indeed been pondering a means to wreak some bit of havoc and confusion among the Moors. And it does, coincidentally, involve our three dragon ships, along with Keli, Mornak, and Fergus. Your insight never fails to amaze me."

Now it was Mornak's turn. "Mayhaps you merely spoke aloud in your sleep, Captain. Our dear Aoife couldn't help but divine your clever plan if that be the case." The entire assembly erupted in good-natured hilarity at their Pictish friend's jibe. Though she blushed just a bit, even Aoife couldn't hide her own slight grin.

***

Cael and his twenty Irish Magyars spent the next two days with their borrowed mounts training in their accustomed way with their recursive bows and slender lances. The Hispanian steeds seemed like enormous and ponderous draft horses compared to the tough and hardy little Connemara ponies they'd ridden in Ireland. Yet, what these huge horses lacked in speed and agility, they made up for in strength and height. It didn't take long for the small cavalry contingent to adapt and regain their former deadly accuracy on the gallop and from long range. The troop was only one-tenth of the size of their 200-strong squadron at Clontarf but they knew they could nevertheless prove decisive.

The Moors, like the Vikings and Irish, never employed organized mounted archers in battle, especially not equipped with finely constructed recurved bows in the manner of the steppe riders of the East. Their cavalry, while swift and effective, consisted generally of lightly armed horsemen equipped with javelins and slashing swords. While in the saddle, they had no stand-off strike capability to equal the maximum effective range of the Magyar's deadly arrows.

At a communal evening meal, the Magyars had an opportunity to spend time with the Leonese knights who were to be their comrades. These warriors with their head-to-foot chain mail, sometimes overlayed with plate armor, massive kite shields, heavy lances and broadswords, reminded the Irish of the Jomsvikings that some of them had faced at Clontarf.

Cael and Aoife also spent time with the promised local scout. His hair was long and silver and he appeared to be in his early sixties. Yet still, he displayed a formidable countenance and walked with a confident swagger. He had been a *Campeador*, a Champion of the nobleman he served, in his younger days. Now he was content to tend his farmstead in the south and play with his grandchildren. The new threat of raiding Berbers had spurred him once again to volunteer his services to the court in Leon. His long years of warfare against the Moors, coupled with his thorough knowledge of every extent of terrain along the vulnerable border lands, made him a most valuable asset for the Magyars and knights.

Even though he was of common birth, as were all of the Irish Magyars, he had spent enough time at various Hispanian courts to speak serviceable Latin. Thus, the scout, whose name was Rodrigo and Aoife were mutually intelligible and she found herself once again translating for Cael and the others. He was quite amiable to the Irish, explaining to them that since he was Galician, they were his cousins. Rodrigo was also completely fascinated by the Magyars' equipment and tactics and the Irish were proud to bring him into their fold.

***

"From what the locals tell me, the raiders send out small parties to harass and when possible, slaughter unguarded travelers on our roads just north of the Caliphate's border."

Rodrigo motioned to the two young men who had accompanied the Magyar troop to this particular place adjacent to the road. "And these two fine and adventurous lads have discovered that a band of twelve vile heathens are camping in a copse of pinewoods just opposite us, south of the road."

It was several days later. The Magyar troop and the hundred-man squadron of knights had been patrolling along the threatened areas, stopping at local towns and isolated settlements to comfort the people and gain information. The knights had remained in a nearby town while the smaller band of Irish probed on both sides of the border to detect signs of their enemy.

While gathered on the slope of a small hill and assuring potential watchers could not see them in the tree line, Aoife translated Rodrigo's words to Cael and the others. Then they went to ground to peer through the grass down to the road below and trees not far beyond. The low hill featured a spur around which the narrow road ran and then continued straight westward. Fortuitously, this was one of the few spots where the Magyars could be hidden out of sight of any in the forest to the south of them.

It didn't take long before Aoife's eyes lit up and she showed the others a mysterious but mischievous smile. "I have a plan which I know the captain will relate to well and would approve wholeheartedly."

Not long after, two black clad figures, prone on the ground at the base of a thick tree with lush green branches spreading to the pine needle-covered ground, spied a curious site slowly moving along the dusty road. A little wagon made its way creakingly along, just beneath a small hill. They were heading westward. A hunched old man with long grey hair appeared to be sitting on the bench holding the reins with unsteady, ancient hands. Meanwhile, a little girl with ivory skin and shoulder length dark hair was holding onto the harness strap, walking alongside the draft horse, singing a lilting song in some strange and alien Christian language.

The two watchers looked at each other with low chuckles. "Not much to be gained here, I'll wager," said one. "We've been here all day and nothing till now. Besides, I like the way that child sings. She could bring us some bit of cheer in this otherwise cheerless land of the infidels. I'll go back and alert the rest to come up and then watch for treachery when the two of us go to collect our booty."

When the ten others of their band walked their mounts up to the edge of the woods and waited, the two watchmen mounted and spurred their swift horses in a dash across the swath of open ground to the wagon, screaming oaths which sounded like war cries to the old man and girl. In the short time it took to reach their quarry, the whooping ceased abruptly when the two raiders noted, to their shock, that the old man and young girl were now smiling just when they should've felt their doom approaching.

At that moment, on closer inspection, the man with silver hair no longer appeared so ancient as he bent to retrieve and make ready a deadly Christian broadsword which had been at his feet. And the little girl, who they now saw was a healthy young woman with strong shoulders and confident posture, slid a deadly looking dagger from a hidden sheath at her side. She assumed a fighting position, ready to leap to either side in a flash.

As the two were focused on the suddenly dangerous old man and girl, they never even saw that a figure emerged crouching from beneath a woolen blanket in the bed of the wagon. Before they could react to the movement, Cael drew and released his first arrow, which struck the closest in the base of his throat. At this close range, its tip pierced through the fabric of the black tunic, the windpipe and severed the spinal brain stem to emerge again on the other side. His second arrow caught the other rider in the shoulder as intended. This one immediately fell from the saddle, howling in agony on the ground as Aoife started toward him, holding her *scian* Gaelic fighting knife at her side.

With an urgent but furtive warning, Cael urged her to stop and drop to her knees. "Scream like a deathly frightened girl! Make a pathetic spectacle of yourself quickly and hide your knife. And tell Rodrigo to drop and hide his sword once more." For Cael had observed at that moment that a line of ten riders had broken from the trees and were galloping towards them with furious intent. They'd been just a bit too distant to observe the specifics but they discerned that two of their own were on the ground, unmoving. Now, as they rushed forward, they could clearly see a terrified girl on her knees and the old man huddled over and shaking in apparent shock.

But suddenly, to their utter consternation and dread, they observed two groups of riders emerging around either side of the hill and across the road, flying toward their flanks at tremendous speed. Inconceivable to the Moors, these two columns of ten men each were knocking and drawing strange little bows as they thundered closer. In scant moments, it was over; all the Moors lay dead on the ground, most feathered by two or more arrows. The two lines of Magyars drew close and rode among the dead, looking for signs of life. There were none. "Seems our training was simply too drilled and instinctive. Let's hope Cael left at least one of his alive," said one of the riders in their own good Irish tongue.

"You performed most admirably, young lady," said Cael with humorous glee to Aoife, "though I was alarmed for a moment that you were about to slit the throat of the one I so deftly wounded." The aforementioned Moor was still on the ground, moaning with Cael's arrow protruding from both sides of his shoulder.

The Spy Chief, though chafing slightly at having to play the role of a whimpering little girl, nevertheless was ready with her own reply.

"It's simply one part of the tradecraft of my business, just another warrior skill beyond the capability of you and your crew of rambling bucks. Now let's see to Abdul here."

As planned earlier, Rodrigo took over the interrogation. While the other Gaels were retrieving weapons and anything else of value from the corpses to later give to the local people, the two young boys joined them, both carrying shovels. They immediately commenced digging a trench in a field at the side of the road. Rodrigo kicked the groaning man onto his stomach and tied his hands behind his back, heedless of his cries. He then looped another rope around his neck and dragged him over to watch the boys. Soon, the hole was quickly completed. It was the length and width of a man and waist level deep.

One of the boys retrieved a sack from the bed of the wagon and brought it to Rodrigo while the other dragged the body of the dead one over to the freshly dug grave. A bloody and intact hide with the still attached head of a huge porcine boar was then wrapped around the Moor's corpse. The two boys then kicked it into the grave. Immediately, the wounded man howled with a shriek of such intensity that was far beyond the pain of anything he had so far endured. He was blabbering in some guttural language, which only Rodrigo among them understood.

The boys were covering the grave with the pig-covered dead raider, its sole occupant. "Now then, my lad, you and I will have a nice little talk," Rodrigo addressed the still screeching man in Latin, which seemed to make the whole situation even worse for the Moor.

***

In the early evening, Rodrigo gave the others the results of his "interrogation." By now, the main body of knights had joined them. The boys had returned back to their settlement with the wagon full of weapons and whatever else might be of value to their neighbors. The Irish had been baffled by the whole affair with the pigskin burial since no one had seen fit to give the other Moors anything like a decent Christian burial.

The former *Campeador* had to explain to them. "You have to understand. Many things are considered 'unclean' to the Muslims: wine, beer, dogs and *kafirs* such as you, unbelievers who don't worship the one Allah. But the one thing that is considered the most horrific to them is any kind of pig."

At that point, Cael felt a need to interject, "That just seems so demonic and alien, Rodrigo. Everything you just mentioned is held dear to me and all of us, especially beer and our good and faithful hounds. And we all love a delicious feast of pork when we can get it." His comrades chimed in with unanimous agreement before Rodrigo could continue.

"So, when the wounded man saw his comrade wrapped in pigskin and dropped into an unmarked grave, he nearly lost his mind in fear and horror.

There is little that can be considered more eternally degrading and damning to the soul of a Muslim than such an atrocity."

The others shook their heads and Rodrigo finished his tale. "Faced with such a fate himself, I promised him he would avoid it by giving me the information we wanted. Where was the main body of the newly arrived Berbers and how many were there? On pain of his soul, he explained their precise location, an area I know well and not too far from us right now. He knows if he has lied what awaits him. And I promised him freedom when we return so I believe we can trust him."

Then, with a wry smile, Rodrigo added, "He also complained to me about you, Aoife. He thought it was most profane that one with such a celestial voice of an angel could, in truth, be so deceitful and evil. I explained to him it was my understanding that all Irish girls are that way."

***

The Berbers had established their base near the remains of an old Visigoth town, which had been constructed on the foundations of an even earlier Roman encampment. There were still existing stone walls that served to provide some shelter for the three hundred Moorish warriors garrisoned there.

Based on the prisoner's information, Aoife, Cael and Rodrigo had ridden out to conduct a covert night reconnaissance to assure they were not being led into a trap. Though the older Leonese man was confident the prisoner's story was the truth, the Irish man and woman could not fathom why being wrapped in hide and suitably buried should terrify anyone with fears of eternal damnation. And Aoife knew at least two sources should vet all intelligence attained. So now they found themselves in the dark up in the branches of a tall tree, looking down upon the Moorish strongpoint and assessing the enemy's composition. Rodrigo was on lookout below as the warming sun was starting to rise.

"The prisoner's tale rings true as far as I can tell," whispered Cael to Aoife, who sat on a neighboring branch, one arm clasping the tree's sturdy trunk. "And it seems he was truthful as well about their plans to move north, maybe even today. Some of them are stirring even at this early hour, packing bedrolls and provisions into sacks. Based on the number of horses, they should number about two hundred and fifty by my count. Any others must be with the small bands prowling the border."

"Which means we haven't wasted our time in this stealthy endeavor. And that we must now depart in haste to return to the others," answered Aoife, already climbing down as dexterously as any red Irish squirrel. The two collected Rodrigo and the trio set off as furtively as possible, given their tall Hispanian mounts. Once they were far enough from the enemy, they broke into a flying gallop.

Having been told that the tribe would be moving in strength northward into Leonese territory, Rodrigo had determined that their most likely first target would be a small Leonese settlement that had been only partially fortified. The inhabitants were mostly families of shepherds with a tiny garrison of Hispanian light cavalry.

Just south of the little town, a rather wide and deep river ran east to west. An ancient but still functioning Roman arched bridge provided a dependable crossing point as most horses would shy at the steep banks and swift current. Examining this terrain feature earlier had enabled the Leonese commander, Aoife and Cael to take the required steps to prepare their battlespace.

***

The long column of Moorish riders, astride their magnificent Arabian horses, moved with sleek and graceful swiftness. Their fluttering green banners, adorned with golden Arabic characters, rose above them. Their scouts had not yet returned with a report on their objective but their leader was unconcerned. With all the internal troubles and turmoil the Caliphate had been experiencing during the last eighteen months, the last thing the Christians must expect is any major incursion northward. His action here, however, would only be the beginning. Soon, *Insha'Allah,* the wrath of the believers would descend upon the last pitiful remnants of the infidels in their small, cold and mountainous northern lands. Al-Andalus would encompass the entire peninsula right up to the border with the Franks. And those *kafirs* would be the next to fall.

He could see the forward riders had already crossed the bridge that they expected to find here. The scouts were moving leisurely but with eyes keen as they knew the little settlement lay not too distant over a small rise ahead of them. There was a swampy wetland on one flank and a wide verdant field on the other as more of the Berbers crossed in columns of four abreast.

Soon, three massed columns of fifty each were across when the forward scout halted abruptly, calling out a warning and pointing northward. Their leader could now observe an ever-increasing troop of Hispanian knights deploying in line formation on the crest of the rise. Overcoming his initial shock, he was surprised though when the huge enemy army he had feared he would witness turned out to be fewer than half the number of his own force.

He called out to the men now, his commanding voice unshaken and confident. "Steady, my brave brothers! If there were more, they would have been upon us by now. Deploy in line for battle, echelon right to envelop them. Avoid the swamp. Prepare now to engage and destroy the miserable *kafirs.*"

The two lines of Cavalry began to canter toward each other, the Moors easily avoiding the wetlands on their left and moving to extend their right flank beyond their enemy's left.

Without warning, Berber riders streaming to the right suddenly seemed to disappear amidst the screams of horses and men. The Moors ran into each other on that side as the foremost came to a complete stop. They could now see the wide and deep trenches which had been hidden under grass-covered nets. Some unfortunate men and horses lay there, pierced by carved wooden stakes dug into the ground.

From above, the Hispanian war cry erupted. ***Santiago y cierra, España!*** Saint James and Attack! For Hispania! As their horses stretched into a full gallop, the massive lances of the Leonese knights lowered almost in unison into a fearsome horizontal killing edge of steel pointed death. The two lines met in a thunderous impact, the heavier armored knights piercing deeply into the ranks of the Berber horsemen.

The Hispanian lances and flashing broadswords hewed into the massed ranks of the Moors, who were hemmed in by the swamp on one flank and staked trenches on the other. Still, the long, sleek Moorish javelins hurled by skilled riders and assisted by the barreling charge of their speeding horses sometimes pierced armor, unhorsing several of the knights. And the Moors' superior numbers were beginning to tell as more of their tribesmen crossed the bridge and joined the tumultuous battle. The knights were starting to give ground and their forward line was on the verge of being sundered when the battle suddenly turned.

More than two score fresh Leonese cavalrymen stormed over the bridge, attacking the Moors from behind. Following the knights came another score of bizarrely garbed riders, already launching arrows over the Hispanians and into the rear ranks of the Moorish lines. The Berber leader turned to discern the nature of this new threat. He gazed upon the newly arrived knights, who were harrying his force from behind. He was even more astonished to see twenty additional mounted archers arrayed in a stationary semi-circle, sitting to horse and leisurely loosing carefully aimed arrows. He had never seen their like.

Their headgear was made of black otter fur over boiled and molded leather caps. They were further adorned with fitted leather jerkins over linen tunics. Most outlandish were their multi-colored leggings. He watched as his entire force was being encircled and crushed by the weight of the armored knights and the additional horror of a rain of deadly arrows falling into their midst. That was his last view before two arrows pierced his thighs and he tumbled to the ground.

It was over quicker than the Christian warriors had expected. Despite their losses, their plan had gone off almost flawlessly. As Rodrigo and the two Irish leaders were confirming the prisoner's story, the main force was busy earlier digging the pits then carefully camouflaging them to create a canalized killing field. Separately, twenty-five knights and the Magyar troop had crossed the bridge to find a concealed spot in the hilly wooded surroundings where they could watch the expected battle develop. Then they were to dash forward and take the enemy from the rear at exactly the right moment.

However, Cael and the others had arrived too late for Cael to lead his Magyars, as they were already deployed and hidden. So, he and Rodrigo had fallen in behind the main body of knights, prepared to plug any gaps as needed. Aoife, meanwhile, positioned herself atop the rise to take note of any unseen developments and give warning if required.

Now, as the Hispanians respectfully buried their own slain comrades, Rodrigo prepared to conduct another "interrogation" of the few Moors who had survived the encounter. Fortuitously, the Berber leader was one of them. The former *Campeador* would start his questioning with this one after the initial "funeral drama."

# Chapter 6

## Gone A-Viking

During long conversations with Wolf and some of his leaders, including Fergus and Keli, Felix elaborated on Hispania's experiences with the Vikings. These discussions were both pleasant and compelling for the Irish Captain, who had a passion for all history, most especially its military ramifications.

"Vikings, some from Norway and some from Sweden, have been raiding our peninsula for hundreds of years, going back to the 800s. They are still an occasional menace even today, though the threat is diminishing as their leaders are increasingly turning to the true faith," explained the Leonese diplomat. "In fact, as recently as 968, a savage named Gunrod led a fleet of 100 dragon ships and sacked our most sacred city, Santiago de Compostela."

Keli nodded, adding, "We were told these same tales for years back in Iceland. And they even raided further south to pillage among the Moors I believe. Is that not right Felix?"

"Yes indeed. The Caliphate despises the Vikings even more than they hate us, considering them godless pagans," Felix answered with a smile. "For they call the Northmen *Majus,* which means Pagans and we Christians and the Jews are considered 'People of the Book' which gives us a slight step up from the other wretched *Kafirs* in the eyes of the Muslims."

Wolf listened intently, always seeking some novel tactic to exploit an enemy.

"You say the Viking sack of the holy site occurred in 968? That's ironic, Felix. In that same year, my foster father King Brian and his brother Mahon, Cormac's father, defeated the Vikings in battle at a place called Sulcoit and sacked their port City of Limerick back in Ireland."

The captain looked then to Keli and asked, "Do you think we could train a crew of Leonese fighting men to join us in manning our three *Snekkjas* to 'go a-Viking' along the coast of the Caliphate? We Gaels can pass as Vikings as we've proved in the past and I suspect some of Alfonso's warriors might enjoy making a bit of mischief on their sworn enemies."

A grinning Keli replied.

"I do think so, Wolf, even with our twenty Magyar horsemen conducting a land reconnaissance, I'm supremely confident that, with the aid of a few of our stalwart hosts, we will be quite capable of launching a three-ship Viking raiding squadron to pillage along the Moorish shore lands."

*Keli seems most exceedingly elated at the prospect*, thought Wolf to himself amused. *Even if he is a good and gentle Christian, the Icelander is, after all, still a Viking.*

"I agree, weapon-brother. And, if done right, we may convince the Moors they have another threat to face besides Alfonso's knights, his foot soldiers and archers."

Wolf then looked to Mornak, who had also warmed to the idea. "I only wish we had a thousand wild and screaming Picts to join us. Just the mere sight of an army of your ferocious kinsmen would chill the bones of the most fearsome Berber."

Mornak, grinning, replied instantly. "I share your passion for that, Captain. The whole world knows very well that all savages, heathens and demons tremble in the presence of manly perfection and beauty."

Good-natured, exuberant laughter always seemed to follow Mornak's majestically rendered pronouncements on matters under discussion and this instance proved no exception.

***

Several days later, the three *Snekkjas* were once more underway, with the Irish Magyar crew members now replaced by twenty Hispanian warriors, all selected for their martial prowess and knowledge of the coastline along the lands now held by the Caliphate. By some good fortune, several of them had earlier been sailors as well. In any case, after King Alfonso's blessing, each was enthusiastic about playing the role of a Viking and proud to be among the Gaels and Icelanders to strike back and confuse the foreign invaders.

The target they had selected was a Moorish outpost located on a small peninsula, a bit north of the major trading port of *Al Isbunah.* It was a strategic location, the furthest point west in continental Europe and had been a stopping point for maritime traders dating back to the time of the Phoenicians. One of the Leonese volunteers had visited it several years back during his time as a maritime trader himself and was familiar with the terrain. He provided the key intelligence to enable the three sleek dragon ships to slip quietly into a small, sheltered cove there. It was very early one morning, before the sun could burn off the nighttime fog, when they beached their nimble craft.

"In my time here, the Moors maintained only a small garrison to serve as a coastal watch. But this spit of land is uncommonly lovely and there are also several small palaces for the use of the Syrian nobility of the Umayyad dynasty to enjoy at their leisure," explained the former trader who was now garbed in the style of a Viking.

The allied band of Christians had earlier scraped together whatever odds and ends they could find to try to clothe the Hispanians in something to make the Leonese appear as like Viking marauders as possible. The tailors in Leon had claimed with pride that they could fashion a quilted gambeson far more expertly than any Viking seamstress. When they were finished, Keli commented with some amusement. "You couldn't fool a toddler back home in Iceland. The children would probably believe you were all some kind of trolls."

Trying to hold back his own laughter, Wolf spoke to reassure their Hispanian allies. "In Ireland, we never recognized the Vikings by their appearance alone. Foremost was the foul smell of them. I suggest you smear yourself with fish guts before we strike, then howl like demons and grunt in roars. Those are the marks of a true Viking." Keli just shook his head but he could not help laughing with all the others.

The hundred or so "Vikings," clutching their huge round shields and carrying axes and swords, sauntered up a grassy slope from the inland side of the peninsula. At the summit, they came upon a tall, narrow, round tower, surrounded by several smaller stone structures that served as quarters for the Moorish guards of the garrison. The towers and quarters were partially constructed of stone but all were braced with timber along their sides and roofs. It was still the wee hours of the morning and there was no need for talking. They had all received their orders from Wolf earlier, given in a manner that left no room for misinterpretation.

Splitting into three groups, they ran silently into the encampment. Adorned with his Viking berserker lupine-styled helmet, Wolf led the smallest group into and up the steps of the tower. This helmet, which the Irishman had torn from the head of its original owner, was constructed on the model of a snarling wolf's head. On the leader's heels came Mornak, his almost luminescent blue eyes flashing. The six Moors on the observation port at the top were quickly overwhelmed before they could offer any semblance of resistance.

By now, there were furious shouts from the surprised guards below as they were set upon by a horde of savages who had seemed to come out of nowhere. The guards, all professional Syrian Arab infantrymen, were outnumbered more than two to one. Not expecting any attack from land, few of them were armed and prepared for battle. Though they put up a short and lively defense, the outcome was pre-ordained. Mere moments passed before all were slain.

The raiding force regrouped and moved off to the leeward side of the peninsula, where the two palaces, close by each other, were to be found. As they looked down upon the shoreside estates, they were pleasantly surprised to observe a ceremony occurring in the lush and well-manicured green expanse that separated the two Moorish villas.

"It seems we've stumbled upon a wedding among two or more Umayyad families, unless it's a funeral but I see neither corpse nor grave," conjectured Keli in subdued voice to Wolf as they and the others lay prone on the ground. "Whatever the case, they are well guarded by a force of men-at-arms who nearly equal our number."

Though surprise was on their side now, Wolf knew when they broke cover, they would immediately be observed, giving their enemy time to react. Whether they would fight or flee, he could not guess.

"Captain, considering the ground we must cover to close with them, I recommend we assume the *Svinfylking* with the 'Spartans' and Icelanders in the fore, followed close behind by the remainder employing darts and slings. That is the swiftest course and it will have the greatest shock of impact."

Keli and Wolf spoke now in Danish, which Wolf had mastered as a young captive back in Dublin. The *Svinfylking* or boar snout was a wedge formation used in place of a lined shield wall when speed and penetration were of the essence. The Gaels and Icelanders were both well trained in it and their Leonese friends brought their own javelins, which were essentially the same weapon as what the Irish called darts.

The entire group crawled back to a position where they could not be observed and quickly assumed their wedge attack formation. Wolf at the very point with Keli, Mornak and Fergus just behind him, the others building on that model. Even before they landed on the peninsula, Wolf had made his rules of engagement incandescently clear.

All adult males and those who wielded a weapon against them were to be slain. All efforts were to be undertaken to spare women, children, slaves and the elderly. All structures and property must be burned. The only words spoken were in the tongue of the Vikings. Incomprehensible and hideous war cries were the exception. Those exempted from harm would live to tell the tale of the ferocity and brutality of this latest 'Viking' attack.

With a sudden bone-chilling howl, the sweeping wedge of armored muscle, steel and heavy round wooden shields cascaded down the slope toward the suddenly aghast wedding revelers. The armed Moorish guards, completely taken aback, attempted to set up a hasty defensive circle around them. This only served to dilute their strength and depth when the unstoppable wedge crashed into and through them. Once in their midst with half the defenders already down from blades, axes, or projectiles, the attackers deployed into a widening wall of shields. Their armed opponents futilely threw themselves against this inexorable killing machine, welcoming a martyr's death.

It took even less time than at the watch tower before all the guards were slain. Now the attackers broke into smaller groups to chase the screaming women and very few children out of the two residences, pausing only to slaughter any adult male who still lived. Both palaces and every standing structure around them were put to the torch. Anything of value that was small enough to be easily transported was carried off.

Other raiders stood over the wailing women who clutched their children in dread. The Viking replicants tried their utmost to appear menacing and sanguinary but this was difficult. The Gaels, Icelanders and Leonese were all good Christians whose faith told them to protect the small and the weak. It was only with the utmost difficulty that they refrained from comforting the pathetic figures. Then, as quickly as they appeared, the raiders were gone.

***

The three dragon boats deliberately set sail southward to appear to continue raiding along the Caliphate's coastline. When Keli was sure they were out of sight of the survivors or any other onlookers, they changed course westward and then looped back north, heading once again for Leon. Their booty consisted of gold-worked headbands, pendants, brooches and shawl pins, along with some silver plaques and diadems. Though of some value, this would not usually be enough plunder to justify a Viking raid, especially when no slaves were taken.

The real intent of the Christians' strike, however, was to attempt to convince the Caliphate that the three dragon ships were simply the vanguard of a far larger Norse attack on the major trading hub of *Al Isbunah* to the south. If the Vikings could take and hold that city, they could then stifle the Caliphate's maritime commerce and threaten the interior. The hope was that the Moors would have to draw their attention away from the Christian kingdoms of the north to deal with a possible separate crippling threat from the seaborne pagans.

During the return voyage, Wolf looked forward to sharing the results of their seaborne deception operation with Aoife. He also yearned to learn any information gained from the riders' Reconnaissance in Force. But even he had to admit to himself the real reason his thoughts revolved around Aoife. He missed her terribly; missed her counsel and her company. He increasingly realized how much she had come to mean to him. With that in mind, he pulled even harder on the oar.

# Chapter 7

**Fracturing the Caliphate 1014 A.D.**

A compartmented group of allied Christian leaders and one distinguished Jewish man sat around a circularly designed table in the anteroom, which led into the now vacated great hall of King Alfonso's royal castle in the citadel of Leon. Elite guards stood outside both entrances to the small chamber.

Next to Alfonso sat his military commander, Sancho and his senior diplomat, Felix. Cormac, Wolf and Aoife comprised the Irish contingent. Pyrrhus and Schlomo were the only others in attendance. The purpose of the gathering was to review the information gained during the recent military actions and for the visiting allies to gain the Leonese perspective on the situation they all faced.

"My knights and the Leonese 'Vikings' have been full of only praise for the valiant actions of our northern guests and I look forward with alacrity to your own account," began the king, again speaking in Latin as the common tongue. The others had already agreed that Aoife would be the primary conveyor of the intelligence they had discovered.

"We also wish to convey our own respect for the courage and skill of our Leonese comrades as we conducted our joint endeavor," replied Aoife. "Good King, I'll be brief and to the point on what we reckon to be the key indicators of enemy intent." Alfonso nodded, pleased with the directness and sincerity of the young and incredibly impressive Irish woman who addressed him.

"As you are no doubt even more aware than us, we believe the Caliphate is in total chaos. There are numerous quarreling factions and shifting alliances among them. This strife is compounded by the nature of the enemy peoples' populations: Arabs, Berbers, so-called Andalusians, *Saqaliba and black African slave warriors have little love for each other,* even if they profess to all share the same faith. This is not to even mention the competing noble families among the ruling Arab ruling classes, long-time dominated by the *Umayyads*.

She paused briefly to gauge the reaction of her audience. As expected, she detected no surprise but was reassured to note the apparent approval for the wisdom of her words.

She continued, "However, notwithstanding their quarrels or their occasional use of Christian mercenaries, the Moors continue to view the northern Christian kingdoms as their main obstacle. From the thorough 'interrogations' the noble *Campeador* Rodrigo conducted with the captive Berbers, we now believe the Caliphate is planning a true invasion, not just a raid, into Leon."

The three Hispanians listened intently. Now Alfonso spoke once again. "You have truly earned my highest regard Aoife. Of course, we are aware of the tribulations the Caliphate is enduring. You have only been among us a mere few days it seems, yet still you have most accurately confirmed our own judgement. The possible invasion, though, is new information and bears our due consideration."

Aoife, almost instinctively, put one small white hand on Wolf's massive shoulder as he proudly sat next to her. "That was one purpose for the 'Viking' attack on that strategically positioned Moorish watchtower – to hopefully disrupt the enemy's possible offensive plans."

"It may not have been much and, indeed, might not even draw the enemy further south to cover his flanks there but it will undoubtedly give him something to think about," Wolf commented with a grin.

The King and his leaders smiled in return. Alfonso, looked to the one non-Christian at the table with great confidence. "You may have wondered why I requested Schlomo join us here today. We believe it is prudent for you to hear a learned and trusted firsthand account of our foe, which will put things in greater context before we decide on the next steps to take. Schlomo, please continue."

As his listeners would soon learn, Schlomo, indeed had an interesting story to tell.

"You know I'm a physician, a scholar of the physical sciences and a Jew. What King Alfonso and his advisors know and you do not, is that for many years I was a senior member of the court of the Caliphate of Cordoba."

Schlomo noted the surprised expressions of the visitors sitting around him, with the one conspicuous exception of Pyrrhus. The Greek exhibited the countenance of a wise man who has just had an uncertain notion confirmed.

"My family has lived in the city of Cordoba for generations. Of course, we were mere *dhimmis*; allowed to retain our beliefs as long as we paid the *jizya* tax and accepted our inferior status among the Muslims. But we were never slaves. And *dhimmis*, both Christian and Jewish, can attain respect and even lofty positions of trust in the Caliphate if they are able to offer particular skills and services. It was in the summer of 981 A.D., as a highly capable scientist and healer of some eminence, that I was first appointed as the court physician in Cordoba during the reign of Almanzor."

Both Wolf and Aoife immediately noted the looks of disgust on the Leonese hosts' faces at the mention of that Arabic-sounding name. Meanwhile, Schlomo almost assumed the role of teacher to his students as he related the relevant history that led to the present situation in Hispania.

The Islamic storm first erupted in Hispania in the eighth century. The Romano-Visigoth culture there was advanced but far from united, perhaps gone soft, said some. Led by Mideast Arabs, a multi-ethnic invasion of peoples from the Maghreb, many rather recent converts to Islam, seemed destined to pour right into the heart of Europe before, in 732, they were thrown on their heels on the blood-soaked fields of Tours in France in by Charles Martel.

Always subordinate to some Islamic entity back in the Mideast, the Syrians of the *Umayyad* dynasty decided to declare their own Caliphate in Hispania and thus was born the Caliphate of Cordoba in 929. Many of the lands on the peninsula were now, at least in theory, under a single ruler. Still, internal squabbles continued among noble families and the various tribes and ethnic groups. There were also incessant battles against the small and equally disunited Christian kingdoms of Northern Hispania. This all seemed to be on the verge of ending with the coming of Almanzor.

Muhammad ibn Abi 'Amir came from a family of minor Muslim nobility in Hispania. In 976, he became vizier, or advisor, to the reigning Umayyad caliphs. Capable and ambitious, Abi 'Amir soon exploited his advisory position and seized control as the military leader of all Muslim armies in Spain. He won a great military battle against rebel Muslim forces at Torrevicente and became Al-Mansur Bi-llah or more commonly Almanzor – "Victorious by God." He was now the uncontested leader of all Muslims in the peninsula, even as he kept the actual young *Ummayad* Caliph comfortably imprisoned in a 'golden cage' for the rest of his life.

Almanzor was an exceptional soldier and innovative leader who turned the main Muslim forces into a more formidable foe by organizing them along functional roles as opposed to solely deploying in their own tribal formations. However, there were some exceptions to this for garrison duty, minor raids and reconnaissance, for instance. But when he massed his armies for major battles, they were an exceptionally imposing enemy indeed.

To even more powerfully assert his dominance and power, Almanzor decided to present himself as the Defender of Islam and take *jihad* to the Christian kingdoms. The Muslims had always carried out seasonal military expeditions called *aceifas*. Still, Almanzor gave them the holy designation of *jihad* even though only a Caliph could legitimately call for such an edict. These religious *aceifas* unified his forces and fortified them in their faith.

In 997, when King Alfonso's father, King Bermudo, refused to pay Almanzor his customary tribute. The Moorish tyrant decided to pillage Christianity's third holiest site after Jerusalem and Rome – Santiago de Compostela, which contained the tomb of Saint James the Apostle. Compostela was deep in the heart of Leon's Galician region and a beacon of devotion and reverence for Christians everywhere. In this manner, Almanzor intended to humiliate and mock the Christians, little realizing the ultimate effect.

Pillaging and destroying homes and monasteries along the way, when the huge invading force of Muslims and mercenaries finally reached their goal, they found it deserted. The citizens had all fled in fear of the despised Moorish vizier. In a rage, Almanzor ordered the entire city razed to the ground. The ancient Romanesque church was put to flames and its priceless bells were removed to be converted to lamps to adorn Cordoba's Great Mosque, a further desecration.

"Still, the Moors never succeeded in discovering the saint's tomb nor desecrating his remains," exclaimed King Alfonso with proud emphasis.

"You are quite correct, my King," replied Schlomo. "For, as you know, I was at the vizier's side as we sat in our saddles watching his soldiers search everywhere in and under the church. I looked on as the majestic bells were removed to be carried on the backs of slaves. Only a lone, elderly monk stood vigil as flames consumed the ancient church. And Almanzor, despite his rage at failing to find the apostle's holy tomb, did not even see fit to have the old clergyman put to the sword. I attribute that not to mercy but rather his desire to deny the sad, broken man a martyr's death. With a final sneer, he turned his mount about and led us back to Cordoba."

In the summer of the first year of the new millennium, 1000 A.D., Almanzor again led an army of 20,000 north. As always, he depended highly on his Berber troops, especially their light cavalry and foot soldiers. This time, he marched against the Christian kingdom of Castile. On this occasion, however, he was met by an almost equally large Christian force at a place called Cervera.

The battle there was hard fought and the vizier's command was on the verge of collapse at several points. But it was the Christians who withdrew from the field, giving Almanzor a bloody and costly Pyrrhic victory. For several more years, he continued the pattern of mounting expeditions against the tiny Christian kingdoms. Upon returning from once more raiding Castile, he became very ill and died outside a small village in 1002.

Here, Schlomo interjected his own impressions before continuing with his narrative.

"I'd been treating him for chronic diarrhea for years. He was always a sickly man who additionally suffered from gout and other wretched ailments, notwithstanding all my efforts. As I observed over time how brutally he treated his foes, the atrocities he committed against unarmed civilians and his disdain and abuse of the many slave women in his harems, I felt God was punishing him on earth even before he would be punished for all eternity. This was one reason for my later actions."

Almanzor was succeeded by his first son, who continued his father's cruel ways. This son did not have the father's luck, however and died in great pain in 1008. Some have even said he may have been poisoned. He was succeeded in turn by his brother, who was derisively called *Sanchuelo.* This newest vizier soon made the critical error of wanting to declare himself Caliph, which neither his father nor brother had ever dared. This extremely dangerous and controversial act turned the vast majority of Cordoba against him.

The Arab and Andalusian aristocracy, as well as the rest of the common people, began to develop a genuine hatred for the latest member of Almanzor's family. Even more perilous for Sanchuelo was the increasing lack of support from the members of the Umayyad dynasty. Complicating his precarious position was his obvious preference for the Berbers in his armies, even greater than his father's had been. *Saqaliba and* especially Berbers, had long been treated with disdain by Cordobans, even though they had consistently proved their worth on the battlefield and were equally devout Muslims.

In 1009, while Sanchuelo was pillaging in Leon, *Umayyad* family members usurped the Caliphate throne from the long cloistered Hisham II and raised one of their own as the new Caliph. With Berber support, this is the man who, incredibly, still rules, however precariously, in Cordoba, Sulayman al-Musta'in. By the time Sanchuelo returned, most of his army had deserted him and he was executed by the latest rulers there. His body was stripped, mutilated and crucified, then hung on the city gates of Cordoba.

As the furious tides of civil war shifted in the Caliphate, Sulayman, whom the native Cordobans had driven out, returned with an army of vengeful Berbers to sack the city in the Spring of 1013. Thousands of Cordobans were massacred and the blood-crazed Berbers pillaged the capital city. Thus, Sulayman rules yet with an unsteady crown and the Caliphate hangs by a fine thread.

All of the visitors listened to Schlomo's narration with captivated attention, especially Wolf. Yet, it was Pyrrhus who commented first. "You said it was rumored that Almanzor's first son was poisoned. Were you still the court physician at that point? And, if so, could you not determine the cause of his death?"

"I examined him in some detail. But despite all my skills could find no obvious or classic sign of poisoning. He was quickly laid to rest shortly afterwards." Schlomo's eyes presented a sly aspect as he directed his answer to the Greek diplomat.

Wolf couldn't help noticing that the two learned older men, who had by now become good friends, looked at each other as if they were silently acknowledging an intricate tale which only the two would ever understand. And both wore barely discernible smiles.

Wolf, who had always avoided any involvement in courtly matters when his foster-father was High King in Ireland, could only muse, *I thought the court dramas back at Cashel were simply distracting but they apparently were children's games compared to whatever intricate and serpentine intrigues must take place in Constantinople and Cordoba.*

"You mentioned your 'later actions.' I think we might be capable of deducing them but could you tell us the rest of your tale?"

Wolf asked, knowing that Schlomo must have come over to the side of Leon at some point.

"Despite my comfortable position and the fact that my family remains in Cordoba, I could no longer abide the horrors I witnessed among the Moors. The Christians aren't perfect either and neither are we Jews but we recognize that we sin and try to do better. Almanzor and his henchmen seemed to take delight in cruelty and dominance.

So, in 1009, during all this contentious struggling for power among the various competing elements, I decided to leave Cordoba and offer my services to a Northern Christian king. Sulayman had just been declared the latest Caliph and Sanchuelo, who was away fighting in Leon, still didn't realize his days were numbered."

"And you came at a most propitious time, Schlomo my friend," added King Alfonso, "as I was just beginning my reign after the regency of my mother and the Count during my youth. You've taught me many things but the most important was the intelligence you provided on the fragile state of the Caliphate, which gave all of us hope."

"Thank you Sire and you and your family have made me welcome and likewise given me hope for the future," Schlomo replied, then turned to the others to answer a question that hadn't yet been asked. "Felix and I had both been dispatched by King Alfonso in February of this year to represent Leon in Rome, where Pope Benedict crowned King Heinrich of Germany as *Romanarum Imperator,* Holy Roman Emperor.

Earlier in the year, King Heinrich had restored the Papacy to Benedict, as an antipope had earlier usurped the Chair of Peter. We were returning from that trip when we were captured by brigands on the road who sold us to those foul Moorish slavers, from whom you rescued us. Obviously too ancient to be of any service as slaves to the Moors, we came to recognize they intended to ransom us back to King Alfonso if he would meet their price. Unfortunately for them, you ruined their grandiose plans."

After a gracious nod of acknowledgement, Cormac spoke up for the first time. "Well, Schlomo, you've enlightened us immensely. After your travels and experiences, I'm afraid we must seem almost backward provincials from some distant and isolated hinterland to you and the king. I've also learned that our Holy Mother Church does indeed love to proclaim '*Imperators*' all over.

My uncle King Brian, you King Alfonso and now this German fellow, Heinrich. All '*Imperators.*' I find it all most interesting."

"Prince Cormac," insisted Schlomo, "all of us have the utmost admiration for you and all of your companions, both as our liberators and now our proven courageous comrades in arms."

King Alfonso now took the opportunity to assert vigorously, "I agree. As I mentioned before, the news of your magnificent victory over the Viking invaders at Clontarf has inspired all of Christian Europe, including our people here in Hispania. You have not only been the liberators of Schlomo, Felix and the poor captives but the Irish people may well have been the saviors of all of us. We shudder to imagine what may have been our fate had you not prevailed. Would we, the Germans, the French and the Italians have been destroyed piecemeal by Viking pagans from the North and Islamic invaders from the South? No, dear friends, you Irish have truly earned your place among the Christian peoples.

But there's still another reason I requested Schlomo join us today. As you may have been told or perhaps seen for yourselves, thousands of dhimmi refugees, both Christians and Jews, have been pouring over our borders for months since the frenzied turmoil in the Caliphate has progressed and seemingly worsened. And now a young Jewish man who had been keeper and healer of horses in the Caliph's stables has appeared among us. And he has brought exceedingly good tidings to Schlomo."

The Jewish physician picked up the story.

"My wife died years ago but she left me a kind and intelligent son. I sent him to the best seats of learning to be educated in medicine. I also trained him myself in the skills I had learned. He excelled and was favored by the elite of Cordoba. I dare say he became even more respected than I was. And naturally, he took my place as the court physician upon my departure."

The father's pride was obvious in the tone of his words. "I tried to convince him to accompany me on my flight but he would not hear of it. He felt he owed the Moors gratitude for holding him in such great esteem and it would be ungracious for him to simply leave. All of my pleas were in vain. Now this keeper of horses brings word that his friend, my son, has relented and desires now to come to us. However, after my unexpected departure, he is now surrounded by guards at all times as the Moors fully understand the otherwise unattainable service he offers them. Yet he is scheduled to make a call soon to an ailing Arab nobleman who resides near their northern border. And we're told his retinue will contain only a score of cavalry."

"And that," proclaimed King Alfonso, "is what we should now discuss."

# Chapter 8

**In the Caliphate**

North of Kulumriyya. The discussion with the King of Leon led to a decision that Schlomo's son must be snatched from the custody of the Moors. They all agreed the younger physician was able to provide new and detailed intelligence information of great benefit. They also recognized that this mission should entail a small force, great stealth and a swift and decisive impact upon initial engagement.

The next morning, Wolf, Cael, Fergus and Aoife came up with the rudiments of a plan. Wolf also invited the former sailor, Diego, who had taken part in the 'Viking raid,' and had great knowledge of the local countryside, where they would intercept the armed column escorting the physician.

"There is only one road that leads along the way north from Kulumriyya to the residence of the *Umayyad* official. That ailing nobleman will have hundreds of hardened fighters around him as they constitute not only his guard force but are also expected to protect that part of the Caliphate's border," explained the Hispanian warrior, proud that he'd been asked to contribute to yet another expedition with these strange but formidable northern allies.

Wolf now expounded on what they had already discussed.

"If the escort consists of twenty Moorish heavy cavalry, we should not exceed twelve in total number. And we should strike in such a manner that negates their mounted advantage and maximizes our own. I believe four 'Magyars' and eight 'Spartans' will do quite nicely. Of course, we also humbly request the pleasure of your company, Diego. You played the part of a Viking most admirably of late. Now you shall be a Magyar."

Diego was not sure what a Magyar was but he was now fully imbued with pugnacious ardor and welcomed any role his new friends felt fit to offer him.

The enormous Irish Captain continued, "We must select the most propitious ground for our battle space. Diego, are you aware of any places on the road where deployment of cavalry in line would be difficult, or better yet, where the riders would be confined to just the road surface itself? We must engage them where they're unable to maneuver as they are accustomed, when they will come upon a force of heavy infantry such as they've never before encountered and where they will be showered with deadly arrows at the same time." Wolf then smiled at Diego and asked another question, "Have you, by chance, had any experience as an archer as well as a foot soldier and sailor?"

***

They had taken only the wolf-prowed *snekkja* on the voyage, once more sailing south along the coast. The sleek ship contained a full complement of thirty-five, including four Magyars, who brought extra arrows since they would not be mounted for this battle. Diego had indeed spent some time in his past as an occasional archer and he became quickly impressed with the small but immensely powerful recursive bow provided by his comrades. In addition, there were eight massively built and heavily armored 'Spartans.' This time, they brought long and stout thrusting spears with deadly, wedge-shaped steel points. The rest of the small crew was made up of Wolf, Keli and Icelanders.

The plan had called for them to sail a short distance up a river which led into the interior from the sea. Diego knew this route would bring them close to the place he had chosen to intercept the physician's column. After Wolf and the twelve selected were offloaded, the *snekkja* would immediately return to the coast so as not to be blockaded by the Caliphate's naval forces. Not far up the coast north of the river, Diego had earlier suggested a small hidden cove in which they could beach, then easily conceal their shallow-hulled craft. Upon completion of the rescue, the assault team would make their way back to that cove on horses, which they intended to steal from the enemy.

When they reached the designated spot, Wolf, Fergus and Cael could see immediately that Diego could not have selected better terrain for their planned scenario. The road itself was quite narrow, flanked on one side by a not overly wide but rapidly flowing stream with white rimmed rapids. On the other flank was a steep rise leading to the crest of a hill covered with hedges and shrubbery. Both the river and road alongside it were sinuous with sharp and unexpected bends and turns. This spot led to one such place where the road almost seemed to twist back on itself. It was here they would await their quarry.

***

One splendidly armored Moorish rider, astride a magnificent Arabian stallion, rode a bit ahead of the column. The clamor of the rushing waters of the adjacent stream masked the sound of hoof beats, creaking saddle leather and the clinking mail armor of the twenty heavy cavalry who followed him. He found the landscape verdant and pleasing but the road itself was almost confining, allowing no more than two horsemen to ride abreast. And the constant twists and angles of both the road and river required him to move slowly and deliberately. As he made his way around a strikingly tight bend, he almost blundered into a gargantuan figure standing in the middle of the road. Except for an instant's disbelief, he had no time to react before a flashing spike-covered ball of steel crushed his skull.

Wolf swiftly pulled the corpse out of the saddle and slapped the horse on the rump, sending it running ahead. Then he dragged the body into the brush on the slope and rushed back to his original position further down along the bend.

When the first section of the column, about twelve riding two abreast, rounded the bend, they thought their point rider must have gone further ahead. However, a strange obstacle appeared to be in their way, a short distance in front of them. As their eyes focused, they could see a novel spectacle. Eight huge, armored figures, with enormous round wooden shields swagged in steel chain, stood in formation four abreast and two deep before them.

They were all adorned in heavy metal helmets that covered their entire faces and more disturbingly, each wielded a long, deadly-looking spear. All wore the same deep scarlet cloaks which flowed over the thick armor that encased them. One of those in front and center was even more massive than the others and this one had a fiery red beard, which was visible even through the partial obscuration of his helmet.

The Moorish leader found this startling but he was an experienced fighter who had fought in the Middle East and Africa. Now he found himself in Hispania. The officer knew infantry would always break when it encountered charging heavy cavalry. He turned confidently to tell his men to prepare to drive these eight *kafirs* into the ground or the river. He didn't care which. But, when he turned back, he noted that the eight had marched much closer to him, not at all what he expected. Now, he was forced to order a charge even though there was insufficient distance for his mounted formation to build momentum to attain the desired shock effect.

With a cry, he led the charge and all the others followed him, dropping their lances to horizontal. But none had time or space to even reach the speed of a trot before they impacted the front line of infantry who had gone down to their knees with spears braced upwards and shields interlocked. The line of four behind them covered both lines with their shields upraised and long spears held overhand to thrust into their enemy.

The initial contact, even without the dominating speed of a full gallop, resulted in a thunderously loud crash as heavy horse flesh and leveled lances impacted against a steadfast and seemingly unmovable wall of sturdy shields, lethal thrusting spears and massively muscled armored men. A raucous cacophony of cursing grunts and the agonized screams of both men and horses immediately followed.

"Remember, avoid injuring the horses!" called out the red-bearded giant who centered the line.

His words, bellowed in Irish Gaelic, sounded bizarre and alien to the Arab riders who could hear them. Regrettably, some of the beautiful animals were already on the ground, injured or dying. The melee turned into a tangled debacle for the Moors as some in the rear crashed into or spilled over their foremost comrades. The situation deteriorated even further for the cavalrymen when, suddenly, well-aimed, bodkin-tipped arrows found their targets, piercing their finely crafted Damascus mail armor with deadly effect.

In the rear around the sharp bend, the physician was accompanied by two Moors riding ahead and two behind as he was mounted on his own white mare. Just as this small group could hear the alarming sounds of pitched battle even over the sounds of the rushing waters, Schlomo's son was startled to witness the two riders ahead of him fall to the ground with arrows embedded deep in their throats. He turned in confusion to the two behind him just in time to see these two go down in the same manner.

He then heard a call on his left and slightly above him. *Shalom!* Diego dashed down swiftly from behind the bushes that had concealed him as another archer stood up not far from the first.

"We've come to collect you to bring you to your father, Schlomo, in Leon. Please help us recover the Moorish horses." Diego knew his Arabic was inadequate but hoped the young man could understand his intention, especially when preceded by the only word he knew in Hebrew.

Apparently, his hopes had been answered, as the still-mounted man replied in Arabic. "I understand and will do as you say. And thank you." Diego still grasped enough of the foreign tongue to comprehend at least the words "understand" and "thank you." As he ran to collect two of the now riderless horses, the other man took hold of the reins of the two remaining mounts.

By the time the physician and the two archers rode round the bend, most of the fighting was over. A closing circle of spearmen now surrounded the four remaining cavalrymen. The few who had tried to escape to the rear were met by Wolf and more archers who quickly dispatched them. The four Moors continued resisting with swords since they had already launched their lances at the others in a desperate attempt to create a route of escape. Finally, these four as well were skewered on the wedge-shaped blades of the Spartans' spears.

"Enough," shouted Wolf in a deep, stentorian command. "We must mount and move out without delay. Fergus, losses?"

"Two of our Spartans went down with injuries to their shield arms from the death throes of dying horses. Though with God's grace, both will recover and can still ride. And if Cael can confirm, I believe we have recovered enough of these superb horses that we can ride to rejoin our mates at the coast." Fergus made this announcement with obvious pride in his men and heartfelt relief that none had been killed or maimed.

Cael's report followed. "Captain, Schlomo's son is safely in hand and his escort eliminated. Even if there were so few of us, I'll admit it's much easier and quicker to let loose deadly volleys while crouching on firm ground. As you well know, we're more accustomed to knocking and loosing from the saddle of a galloping horse. And, if I may be so bold, I humbly request that you allow Diego to be invited into the ranks of our 'Magyars'. He performed magnificently as part of this minuscule but ferocious squad of archers." Cael proclaimed this with the same pride and relief as his long-time comrade, Fergus. The two enjoyed a good-natured rivalry at times but were always the best of friends.

"Right, we've no time to bury our dead foemen. And for all I know, if we did, that might be insulting and offensive to them anyway. Cael and Diego to the fore! Everyone else, pick a steed, mount up and move out."

***

The ride to the coast was not overly protracted nor difficult except for the two injured 'Spartans.' But neither complained and their new attendant physician was even able to fashion makeshift but quite effective slings for both. He was as thankful for his rescue as they were appreciative of his efforts in bringing them some comfort.

Once they reached their waiting comrades, they wasted no time getting underway and sailing northbound. Diego was in for even more praise when Keli told them all of how close they'd all come to disaster.

"The cove that Diego selected for us to await in concealment for your return could not have been more perfect. Less than several hours after we arrived and tucked ourselves away, we spied a fleet of twelve Moorish fighting ships brimming with warriors, plying the coast, obviously having been informed of our presence earlier on the river. They were scanning diligently both to sea and along the shoreline. From our places of hiding in the woods, we could observe just how close they were to us. I believe that had I thrown a well-aimed stone, I could have easily knocked one overboard. Yet they neither discovered us nor our well camouflaged craft."

Keli was beaming now and added, "Captain, we counted more than five hundred fighting men aboard that dark-sailed fleet. Had they come upon us, that may have been too much even for my crew of sixteen Vikings to defeat handily."

Keli and Wolf had been conversing in Danish. When the leader translated the account of their narrow escape into Irish, they all decided to drag Diego from his seat at an oar and place him on a wooden bench in the bow with a woolen blanket to use as a cushion. Fergus then broke out a good-sized cask of the fine Hispanian wine from beneath his own rowing bench and presented it to the Hispanian sailor/soldier/archer with a deep bow, giving thanks, *Míle Buíochas!* A thousand thanks!

The return journey was uneventful but for one ironic encounter. The *snekkja* had deliberately taken a route home further out to sea and away from the seacoast. Nevertheless, as they rowed north under sail, one of their crew, from his comfortable perch of honor - Diego of course – pointed eastward. All eyes turned to where his finger was extended. Southward bound, almost hugging the coastline, they could make out a total of six Moorish ships apparently limping back to their home port of Kulumriyya.

Keli immediately informed Wolf, "Captain, even at this distance, I'm quite sure that's the same fleet of Moorish craft we observed looking for us earlier but something must have happened as they're only half their former strength."

At first, Wolf could only respond with a grin. "Perhaps, they happened to encounter a waiting flotilla of Leonese naval vessels. Aoife suggested that Alfonso be prepared to engage a search party of Moorish warships not long after we set out. I believe he may have taken her advice. Clever girl she is." By this point, Wolf was accustomed to Aoife's tactical insight into the likely intentions of whatever enemy they faced.

Though they were certainly well out of any hearing range of the Moors by this time, most of the crew were excitedly moved to stand up, wave their arms and shout most enjoyable and irreverent curses at the enemy ships that had earlier missed a chance to make a mockery of their happily successful rescue mission. The young physician could only shake his head and wonder what he had gotten himself into. But then he too stood up and joined in the celebration with the rest of his new friends.

# Chapter 9

## Fangs of the Viper

The Caliph's palace in Cordoba was constructed of simple brick yet overlaid with highly polished wood, which braced elaborate and beautiful tiles, creating an imposing appearance from the outside. Within, it was even more elegant. Highly ornamented, arabesque decorations proliferated on the surfaces of corridors and the several lofty halls. All of these were further embellished by being connected through perfectly designed horseshoe arches lined with the same elaborate and stately adornments.

There were no portrayals of holy personages, glorious warriors, beautiful women, or exotic animals. Instead, resplendent and stylized, multi-colored motifs of flowers and other vegetation, along with geometric patterns in symmetric arrays, predominated. Religious texts, crafted with magnificent calligraphy, were also sporadically displayed.

The Assassin lounged in a red-cushioned bench in one of these elegant halls. Across from him, in comfortable repose, Sulayman and Qatil's own Emir from back in Syria discussed matters of import. As he often did, he once again reminisced about how he was so fortunate to come to this exalted point in his young life.

When, along with his Emir and a thousand Syrian warriors, he departed Syria, he knew nothing about this place the Muslims called Al-Andalus. The huge fleet that carried them not only transported the fighting men but also horses, weapons and other provisions. There were also several noble members of the Umayyad clan, along with their wives and slaves. Along the way, as they transited the Mediterranean, they passed numerous islands and long coastlines.

"All of these lands you see once belonged to the infidels. We conquered them all and brought them to the richness of Allah," explained his Emir.

In addition to being a powerful warrior and leader, the older man was wise with great knowledge of the world around them. Qatil, otherwise cynical about most things, took his mentor's words to heart and counted himself blessed to be so trusted by this great figure. He knew he would obey without question whatever command the Emir gave him. And he would do so with the utmost alacrity. So, he had no hesitations about sailing to this strange and alien peninsula far to the west.

"We will be sailing into a place and time of great turmoil, Qatil," the Emir candidly told his young and valued assistant. "The great *Umayyad* Caliphate is under siege from foes from within and without. Since the magnificent Almanzor died some years back, the *Umayyads* have struggled to keep order amidst the squabbling and diverse Muslims who have always been so faithful and reliable.

The most powerful faction presently is made up of Berbers. They are awesomely effective warriors and faithful servants of Allah. Yet, in many ways, they are not far removed from their recent past as pagan, cultureless savages. Magnificent light horsemen, they often seem invincible in battle and were always prized by Almanzor himself. They are the key to the survival of the Caliphate."

The Emir gazed out to the horizon before continuing. "But very recently, the Berbers, under the command of yet a new Caliph, Sulayman al-Musta'in, stormed Cordoba and put many of the nobility and common people to the sword. Sulayman is my cousin and that is the reason we make this voyage. We shall be among the ascendant class there and strive to bring unity to the faithful by assuring Sulayman's uncontested rule. And, Qatil, I know my cousin very well. He will be very appreciative of your extraordinary skills."

Sulayman did indeed have use for Qatil and the Assassin received his first assignment during a personal audience with this latest leader of the Caliphate. Sulayman was a tall and slender dark-eyed man with an almost feminine face, notwithstanding his perfectly trimmed and well-oiled black beard. The Assassin prided himself on his ability to remain calm even in the most stressful situations. Sulayman, in contrast, seemed incessantly tense and consumed even in the familiar setting of his own chambers and amidst his closest confidantes.

Pacing the room while Qatil stood respectfully, the Caliph began.

"Almanzor himself saw fit to keep this befuddled Hisham as a puppet. He has been treated as an unwitting tool for years to be used if needed by those seeking power. Even I have ensconced him in luxury, though he has not the freedom to move beyond the walls of his palace. But he has always been a

Caliph in name only. My Berbers, however, have ever considered me their true leader and their true Caliph." Sulayman's pride and confidence in 'his' Berbers was evident.

"Now I have grown weary of this charade. You, Qatil, will put an end to this game in a such a manner that we will place the blame on the loathsome *saqaliba*."

Qatil could not help but note the sardonic irony. He himself was a Slav as were most of the *saqaliba* slave warriors, though he himself had never been a slave. Some part of him felt pride that Sulayman spoke to him as a trusted equal. No doubt the bonds of family trust between his Emir and this Caliph removed any doubt of his own reliability.

Over sweet tea and out of earshot of others, the two developed the simple plan to deal with the hapless Hisham II.

***

Several days later, a lone figure, astride a piebald steed, arrived at the gate of the opulent compound within which Hisham spent almost all his time. The visitor also held the reins of a separate saddled horse, which trailed behind him. The rider was tall and leanly muscled. He wore a conical steel helmet with a nose guard and chain mail skirting down to his shoulders. A red and white patterned tunic fell to his knees and a long lance, adorned with the black and white banner of the Caliphate, was slung over one shoulder. A round wooden shield, painted with geometrically designed blue and red circles, hung strapped to his saddle. Around his waist he wore an intimidating straight sword, secure in its leather scabbard.

*"As-salamu alaykum!"* the rider called out to the lone guard who stood there.

The guard returned the universally respected religious greeting. He could not make out much of the rider's face except for a glimpse of square-cut blond hair which fell almost to equally blond eyebrows and piercing blue eyes. He immediately determined the visitor was some type of *saqaliba* military officer. From his physical appearance, arms, clothing and accented Arabic, there was no room for doubt. Such were common in Cordoba and many nobles employed them as bodyguards.

"I have been sent to escort our guest to an audience with the Caliph Sulayman. Here is a written authorization." He handed down a scroll to the guard, rolled and bound with an official looking red wax seal.

This was unusual but not unheard of. On a few other occasions over the past months, the guard had greeted other visitors whom Sulayman had sent to summon Hisham. The Caliph frequently wanted to assure himself that all was well with his caged bird. This guard, whose literacy was not perfect, quickly opened the seal without detailed examination and scanned the scribbled lines there. Then he turned, returned the scroll to the rider and opened the wooden gate standing to one side.

"My thanks and we shall not be long," said Qatil pleasantly, casually guiding his horses into the enclosure.

When the Assassin reached the arched and lavishly ornamented entrance, he dismounted. The attentive slave at the door immediately ushered him inside, pointing to the splendidly crafted entrance to Hisham's chambers. Qatil had left his lance and sword outside, lashed to his mount's saddle. He smiled graciously at the few attendants and knocked gently on the red-hued and highly polished wooden portal of the inner chamber.

A sallow-skinned young servant woman, clad in some shimmering diaphanous fabric which did little to hide her lithe figure, opened the door. She startled somewhat at the tall and imposing figure who stood there, then bowed and motioned with her arm into the interior. Hisham was sitting on a luxuriously padded bench, poised over a finely carved slab of very thin and light alabaster wood, totally immersed in painting a sublimely colored and non-existent variety of flower.

"My apologies *Sayid*," said Qatil just loud enough to engage the attention of the artist. "My Master requests you join him to discuss some pressing matters in which he believes you can be of great assistance in preserving our *ummah*, (community of believers) here."

The painter looked up from his work of art to gaze upon an unexpected caller, obviously a foreigner, who nonetheless bowed respectfully. Qatil's talent for feigning innocence and affability had always served him well and this case was no different.

"Is it Sulayman again? He knows I'm excelling as never before in creating the most inspirational and holy art for our people. This is what separates us from the *kafirs* and blasphemers. While they dabble in creating profane and abominable images of the worst kind, we portray the wonders of Allah's perfection."

"Yes but Sulayman prizes your devotion and inspiration and begs you to advise him as he faces threats from the infidels and, worse yet, the heretical serpents among us."

Hisham looked up yet again at the visitor whose accent seemed almost blasphemous to his ears, having been educated in classic Arabic since the time of his birth. The young warrior before him was spawned obviously in some distant and barbaric land yet he seemed earnest and well-mannered. And he stood respectfully with head bowed.

"Very good, Sulayman handles well the tedious tasks of the banality of rule, while he allows me to pursue the work of celestial homage to assure Allah preserves us in these difficult times. I suppose I should not be averse to giving him my guidance on occasion. It is early still and I will accompany you into the city. My sacred art will remain unmolested in the company of my beloved servants here." Hisham placed his brushes aside, stood up, smiled pleasantly at Qatil and moved to the door.

Hisham's cloistered residence was just outside the walls of Cordoba in a wooded setting well-patrolled by Sulayman's personal guards. These had been given orders to stand off for a given time on that day by the Caliph himself. So Qatil and Hisham, astride two fine mounts, rode quietly out of the residence grounds, passing the gate guard with a casual wave. As they made their way along, Hisham regarded a small digging implement lashed to his companion's saddle. He had little to no experience with cavalrymen and considered this just another practical tool of the warrior's trade.

After a short distance, Qatil took note of a stand of tall conifers off the trail. Clumped together, the spruce trees gave the appearance of green pyramids. The Assassin had spent time amidst them earlier in the day. He looked all around them and determined they were quite alone. The two were riding side by side and now was the time.

The tall rider quickly grabbed Hisham by the scruff of the neck and violently pulled him off the horse. As the older man was struggling to recover and bring himself to his hands and knees, Qatil nimbly dismounted, strode over and viciously kicked him in the side of the head with his booted foot. Then he led both of their horses to be tied off securely to a tree branch and retrieved his small shovel from its sheath.

Looking around once more and satisfied they were still alone and unobserved, he dragged the senseless Hisham into the midst of the pines to a prepared place under the spreading boughs. The deep trench he prepared earlier was unmolested and ready. It had been difficult digging as he had to cut through thick roots in addition to removing the densely packed earth. That mound of dirt was piled now to one side of the long, narrow pit.

He heard a soft moan followed by a whimper. Qatil removed his sword from its scabbard and dropped to his knees beside the prone figure. Within the canopy of the trees, there was not enough room for him to stand and slash down with the long weapon. But he could just clear enough space while kneeling. There followed an exhalation of breath and a swishing sound as the blade cut the air, then a sickening crunch and a shower of frothy blood.

The Assassin kicked the body into the grave and shoveled dirt on top of it. He also placed a few heavy stones he'd collected earlier to deter scavenging animals. When finished, he brushed pine needles in place over the disturbed earth until the enclosed area looked exactly as he had first found it. Then he went out to retrieve both horses, again assuring there were no tracks visible leading into the clump of spruce trees. On the pleasant ride back to the Caliph's palace, he was quite content. It had all gone off even easier than he had expected.

***

That task had achieved the expected result. Since Hisham had been out of any position of visibility for so long, his absence did not cause any great discomfit. The few who even realized he was missing blamed his disappearance on some rogue *saqaliba* warrior. This impression was reinforced when Sulayman ordered the execution of Hisham's gate guard for dereliction in protecting his master. Arabs and Berbers alike looked down on the *saqaliba, so such a crime did not adversely impact* the two most important of the Moorish factions. At least for the moment, Hisham was quickly forgotten.

"Now it seems, we have new and unexpected threats from beyond our borders," exclaimed Sulayman to Qatil and Qatil's Emir.

Not long after Hisham's 'disappearance,' all three were once again engaged in serious discussions. This time, however, there was a fourth member.

"This holy man is a learned and respected *Allamah* whose expertise is in dealing with the most hideous of evils afflicting good Muslims." The Caliph gestured to a middle-aged man clad entirely in black with a silver beard and dark, penetrating eyes in a pale face. "He has been made privy to disturbing intelligence we have gleaned from our own spies and from official couriers from other lands of the *Ummah.*

Over a month ago, an enormous battle took place on a small island nation in the distant northwest sea. It seems that the pagan Viking *Majus* attempted a major invasion and were annihilated by the Christian natives of that land at a place called Clontarf. Since then, ominous events have occurred around the periphery of our own Caliphate."

Always appearing to be disquieted by affairs around him, Qatil noted the tense Caliph seemed even more anxious than usual now. The Assassin suspected he should soon be expecting yet another task to eliminate some new problem.

"There are superstitious tidings in the wake of that distant Clontarf battle. Christian and Viking sources both make mention of some colossal and apparently invincible warrior among the Christian armies that fought there. He supposedly defeated a monstrous Viking titan in battle and later tracked him down and strangled him after first cutting out his intestines."

Qatil and his Emir looked at each other with puzzled expressions. What did some far-off battle between obscure Christians and pestilent Vikings have to do with them and what was the peculiar-looking holy man's role?

The *Allamah* picked up the narrative. "He is described as being taller and stronger than any two normal men, face strewn with faint silver scars, with the ears of a wolf. Though that may simply be some outlandish disguise as favored by the Vikings. He is most assuredly no *Majus,* howeve *and* is said to despise heathens and all who are not Christian.

That island nation is called Hibernia by the Romans. Its people call themselves Christians but the Romish hierarchy believes they to continue to adhere to many of the tenets of their former pagan faith. The Greeks named these people Keltoi and were terrified by the supposed supernatural powers of their wizards, whom they called druids. These druids were said to raise up preternatural and ancient gods and demons to aid the Keltoi in their times of need."

The imposing holy man looked directly into the faces of Qatil and the Emir. "That is merely malevolent pagan necromancy for I know what this demon truly is and how to destroy him!"

"What has any of this to do with us or our people here? Should we not be pleased the *kafirs* are making war on each other?" asked Qatil, even more perplexed now after hearing these tales of devilry.

Sulayman took over the discussion once again.

"There is more. Quite recently we sent our court physician to attend to an ill *Umayyad* nobleman who manages affairs close to our northern border. He was accompanied by a troop of twenty heavily armed, veteran Arab cavalrymen. But for one man, all were slaughtered and the physician taken off."

The Caliph paused and clenched one fist. "One of our horsemen, grievously wounded, crawled off to the banks of a nearby river where he was discovered barely alive by a passing courier. He told a harrowing tale. The column encountered a small force of heavy infantry at a bend in the narrow trail. These men appeared to be terrifying specters from some long-dead era. They were heavily armored with enormous shields and employed long, deadly thrusting spears from the impenetrable wall of a tight phalanx. All were clad in flowing red robes and their lances wreaked havoc among our men and horses. While riders were falling to the ground and skewered, arrows rained with deadly accuracy among them, easily piercing their armor and turning the road into a killing field."

Sulayman stopped once more to smash his fist into his palm, clearly infuriated. "And then, claimed the dying man, a terrifying colossus leapt from a height into the midst of the struggling cavalry. He stood even taller than the few remaining men who were still mounted and began to set about a carnage of destruction with an enormous sword and a slashing axe. The monster roared in a guttural and savage tongue unlike anything the stricken man had ever heard. He said its head was covered with a strange, black, lacquered helmet and its ears were like those of a wolf. The sword appeared far too immense to be wielded by a single man and the handle was capped with a steel stylized wolf as its pommel. Finally, the poor soldier coughed once more and died as the courier cradled his bloodied head."

"We call that creature a *ghul,* a demon of pure evil summoned by some pagan conjurer; in this case no doubt a druid," declared the *Allamah*. "If such a blasphemous creature now serves the Christians and if it has, in turn, summoned lesser demons as its minions into the world, as may be the case with these red-garbed spearmen, we must destroy it all costs. And that can only be accomplished by chanting the *Ezan* call to prayer in its presence while wearing white gloves. Then it must be smashed in the head with a blessed sword and finally immolated in searing flames."

"That, Qatil, will be the task I now entrust to you," declared Sulayman, his eyes brimming with total confidence as he smiled at the young but already proven, deadly assassin. "And a most recent and fortuitous event has provided us with a means of inserting you directly into the court of the King of Leon where you will be most cordially welcomed."

***

So, the plan was laid. Sulayman told the others how he had recently come into the possession of a most splendid prisoner. And the prisoner's belongings were even more useful. Moorish pirates had come upon an inexcusably unaccompanied sailing ship just south of the now Muslim dominated island of Sicily. When they boarded, the Christian captain told them they were simply emissaries and no threat to them. They had been sent by the Emperor of the Greek Roman Christian Empire, Basil II Porphyrogenitus, to profess peace to all peoples who lived around the Middle Sea. He had recently made peace and a treaty had been proclaimed between the Empire and the Muslim Fatimid Caliph in the East. Having said that, the ship captain's head flew off his shoulders and into the calm seas of the Romans' 'Mare Nostrum' before he even finished speaking.

"There is only one Caliphate. Caliph Sulayman rules the true believers of the one, true Caliphate of Cordoba," bellowed the leader of the pirates as he wiped the blood from his scimitar. Kill them all."

The boarders rushed among the crewmen with flashing swords. Many of the Christian sailors leapt overboard. But so far from shore, few had any chance of surviving. More marauders surged below deck and there were hideous screams. The three women who tried to hide were defiled hideously, then dragged above with jubilant shouts from the Moors. They were bleeding and sobbing but still managed to look into each other's eyes. Nodding somberly and then making the sign of the cross, they sprang up defiantly. and threw themselves over the sides of the ship. The pirate leader swore furiously over losing such potentially valuable slaves but then one of his men emerged from below, clutching a slight young man clad from head to toe in a brown robe. He also wore a beaded necklace with a wooden cross hanging from his chest.

"He was praying with his hands upraised. We couldn't bring ourselves to slay him. Beneath his robed knees, we found this locked wooden box." A young pirate held up an exquisitely polished small chest with an ornately crafted seal.

Taking it in hand, the captain beamed with elation. "This is the seal of the Greek Emperor. The contents are no doubt of value beyond anything in this pitiful cargo. Well done, brothers!" At that, another head was hacked from its praying owner's shoulders and tossed into the sea by a laughing Moorish crewman.

"Leave this precious parcel untouched. We'll take it to Sulayman. He is wise and generous and will reward us greatly." The ship from Constantinople was put to the torch and the dhow continued its voyage westward under full sail.

# Chapter 10

**Sacred Mission**

A monastically garbed traveler made his way slowly along the same road that led south from the same small port town that had been taken by the veterans of Clontarf weeks earlier. He sat astride a spotted brown and white mule. More intelligent and with greater endurance than horses, these oldest of all man-made hybrids had been ably serving men for thousands of years. The rider was dressed in a long beige and yellow robe which fell to his ankles. He wore a monk's round, flat-topped Greek *skufia* on his head. It was embroidered with bronze and tan crosses on its sides and top. Tufts of flaxen hair, where not covered by the hat, fell to the base of his shoulders. The rider was accompanied by other differently robed clergy members mounted on both mules and ponies.

A day earlier, after sharing his story with a resident Greek trader in that port town, the merchant took him to a local Benedictine monastery, where the monks were delighted to welcome a fellow clergyman, even if he was of the Eastern Orthodox branch of Christianity. Over cups of red wine from the monastery's own vineyards, soft oaten bread and cheese, they heard the tale of this exotic visitor. Since the Orthodox monk spoke only Greek, his merchant companion translated.

"I was among a contingent of distinguished emissaries dispatched by the Greek Roman Emperor Basil II to the peoples of the Middle Sea, with our ultimate destination being the Kingdom of Leon. One morning as we were not far off the coast of Barcelona, our captain spied a sleek Moorish corsair bounding with all haste to intercept us. He knew we could not outrun her and had no illusions of what our fate would be when they came aboard."

The Benedictines listened with apt attention and great sympathy as he continued.

"Perhaps because I was the only clergyman, or because I was the youngest and most fit, the ship's captain decided to give me a small sealed wooden chest with our Emperor's seal. Then I was aided by other crewmen in being lowered overboard and sat alone in a small boat with two oars. This was on the side of our ship opposite the rapidly approaching Moors, so I pulled as hard as I could to try to make it to shore, where I was told the people were Christian. I believe God strengthened my arms as I was able to reach land just in time. I ran into the heavily variegated tree line I found there and dropped to the ground, peering back towards our ship. It had just begun to burn and I could see no one aboard. The corsair was now sailing south towards the lands of the Caliphate."

The assembled Benedictines all made the sign of the cross in the manner of the Latins – left to right to middle – when the monk paused. One put his hand on the speaker's shoulder as a gesture of comfort and reassurance.

"Somehow, with the help of good and simple Christians, even though we were most often unable to speak the same language, I made my way through the County of Barcelona to the north of the Kingdom of Navarre. There, a motley but kindly crew of fishermen, some of whom were Greeks, took me aboard and later deposited me in that small port town, from whence I have just come."

The monastery's Abbot, who had been listening engrossed to this harrowing tale, asked the question they were all most curious about. "And what is your mission now, dear Brother?"

"The senior emissary among my ill-fated fellow travelers confided in me in private almost at the exact moment that our ship departed Constantinople. He told me I was specifically and specially chosen by the emperor himself, who wanted a young, strong and robust monk who had only recently been inducted into the ranks of the monastic clergy. I was to accompany this diplomat to the court of King Alfonso of Leon. There we were to present the king with a precious offering in hopes it could be conveyed to the sacred site of Santiago de Compostela where it should find its proper home."

"Is that what that small chest you've been holding so protectively contains? What is in it?" Even the Abbot could not maintain a stoic countenance when regaled with such an entrancing narration.

"Not even the noble envoy claimed to know exactly what is enclosed therein. He told me it contains a scribed message from Basil in both Latin and Greek. And a small object of immeasurable value." The Orthodox monk gazed upon the faces of his audience, wondering if his earnestly delivered rendition would be challenged.

These gentle clergymen were not accustomed to any type of malevolence in their halls and were filled with wonder, not suspicion, at the words of their now most welcome visitor. By their genuine and congenial smiles, he knew he was among friends.

"Then we shall do everything in our power to see you are safely and comfortably escorted to King Alfonso," pronounced the Abbot.

***

Even before they reached the outskirts of the fortified city of Leon, riders had delivered tidings of a most recently celebrated visitor to Alfonso's court. Any news of an imperial message from the Eastern Christian emperor was welcome. Especially when the tiny Christian kingdoms in the north of Hispania were holding on so tenuously. Word had leaked out as soon as the messengers left the field where the local herdsmen tended their mounts. Mounted knights and common people alike lined the streets after the troop of monks had been led past the gates.

"I do hope the king and his people are not conducting this grandiose welcome just for my humble and pathetic presence," said the Greek monk to the abbot riding at his side. "Please tell me, they're simply cherishing a visit by a venerated Benedictine Abbot."

"I'm sorry to confess we seem not to have concealed news of your arrival more than we should have. My apologies…and I will have a stern discussion with those herdsmen when I return to the abbey. I do believe, brother, these people are celebrating your entrance into their walled and venerated city."

The younger man waved shyly and smiled at the cheering throngs on either side of the broad avenue that led to the King's palatial court. The crowd knew well that Almanzor's horrific sacking of Santiago de Compostela not many years earlier had enraged all of Christendom. From across Europe, distant Christian kings, princes and even chieftains of still half-wild Christian tribes had reacted with fury that some demonic heathen fiend would dare to defile the tomb of the apostle. All knew the flames had been ignited and no matter how much time it took, they would take back these Christian lands from the invaders.

The monk was then ushered into the great hall of King Alfonso. He was surprised to find Leon's ruler was several years younger than himself. The king was surrounded by his court dignitaries as usual, so as to further impress his eastern visitor, Alfonso had also invited several northern visitors, including

Cormac, Wolf and Aoife, along with the recently resident Greek Imperial diplomats, Pyrrhus and Helena.

The Orthodox clergyman looked around with gracious and amiable eyes at all the members of the stately members of the court. When those same eyes eventually fixed on one of the attendees, he froze, his face contorting with a visible start. There stood the most towering and massively statured man he had ever beheld. A head taller than the tallest of the men here, the giant had thick, dark hair, falling in curled locks to his shoulders, so brown it was almost black. His broad, pale face displayed strong, dominating features, including a powerful prognathous jaw. Faint silver, barely discernible scars ran diagonally from his forehead to his chin. His eyes were an almost luminescent green, projecting both intelligence and force. A massive sword was strapped to his back, a hand-and-a-half hilt with an iron wolf's head pommel visible above his colossal shoulders.

Noting, with some amusement, his visitor's obvious amazement at Wolf's presence in his court, Alfonso decided it was time to make introductions. Starting with the Queen Mother, he presented each of his senior advisors by name. Pyrrhus conducted the needed translation.

"And these," said Alfonso, gesturing to the three Irish among them, "are Prince Cormac MacMahon, Aoife, Chief of Intelligence and lastly, *Faolán an Trodach,* named *Ulf Hreda* - Wolf the Quarrelsome - by the savage Vikings. Wolf is an Irish Battle Chieftain and has recently acquired a bit of status as a legend in the wider world. They and their men have been our most welcomed guests for several weeks now."

The king went on as he and his most recent monastic guest exchanged pleasantries, proclaiming the mutual admiration that manifestly existed between Basil and Alfonso. Finally, the monk came to relate the same tale of how he had arrived here and critically, what he had delivered.

After listening to the same compelling and intriguing tale as had earlier been explained to the Abbot, the king decided to conclude the general assembly and invite the visitor to a more intimate council with fewer attendees to take place after a sumptuous midday meal.

Later, in a smaller room around a rectangular table sat six men. Alfonso and his senior military and spiritual advisor, along with Pyrrhus, Cormac and the monk, all gazing with interest at the small wooden chest on the table.

The king took the initiative himself. Drawing an ornate but practical blade from its sheath on his belt, he sliced through the crimson leather sealed covering, then he twisted the blade's point in the crevasse just enough to spring the box open. Inside was a fine parchment with two entries printed in exquisite calligraphy. One ecclesiastical Latin, the other Greek. The parchment was wrapped around a slender, stick-like object, wrapped in purple-dyed linen.

Alfonso carefully unwrapped the artifact and gingerly laid it on the linen. It was white as ivory, articulated in a quite familiar design. It also appeared to be rather ancient as well as incredibly delicate and fragile.

"That is most certainly some person's finger bone," announced the king as the others all nodded in instant agreement.

"What kind of precious gift is that for the emperor to be delivering to our king?" exclaimed the grizzled old warrior Sancho. Always wary of any implied threat, the military advisor was instantly suspicious.

Alfonso smiled and, resting one royal hand on his friend's shoulder, said, "Steady my old warhorse. Let us first read the accompanying scripts and give Basil the benefit of the doubt for now." The spiritual advisor grinned knowingly, already sure what the writings would reveal. As usual, he was certain his King's first instincts would be proven correct.

*My Dearest Brother King Alfonso*

*Greetings from your most fraternal friend and ally. As a gesture of my respect and admiration, please accept this holy relic. It has been preserved in our patriarchal cathedral, The Church of Holy Wisdom, here in Constantinople for 500 years. Our clergymen claim it is the finger of the most Blessed Saint James the Apostle.*

*Whether or not that is true, I feel it is the best for all if the dear old saint's parts are all together in his final resting place. So, I now pass it on to you in hopes you may find fit to unite his finger with the rest of him in Santiago de Compostela.*

*My fondest wishes for your continued health and prosperity.*

*Basileios Porphyrogennetos*

The same message was written in both Latin and Greek by the same hand. There were no other writings nor objects of any kind within the chest. King Alfonso turned to Pyrrhus, his expression one of questioning. Unexpectedly, the Greek diplomat first broke into a wide grin, then couldn't help but laugh merrily.

"Well, most respected King Alfonso, I cannot say for sure if this is or is not the Emperor's handwriting, nor if the relic is genuine but I must admit the style and prose of the message ring absolutely true to the Basil I know so well: laconic, to the point, without flourish and, as always with our Basil, a bit of dry humor even if it might seem bordering on blasphemy."

Pyrrhus looked briefly toward the King's spiritual advisor, hoping he had not angered him.

"Please know our Emperor is a devout Christian but his sparks of amusing wit at times confound the listener. He never means harm nor offense but I don't believe he will ever change."

He was relieved when the King and the others began to laugh as well. Only the visiting monk silently looked on, seemingly perplexed by this display. Cormac especially found the jocularity to be a pleasant surprise, which made him think back fondly to the good humor his own father and his uncle King Brian had often relied on in trying times. It appeared this Emperor Basil would have gotten along just splendidly with either of them.

Cormac now felt it appropriate to add his own perspective.

"You should know King Alfonso that Emperor Basil also sent King Brian a small gift of valuable coins before our great battle with the Vikings at Clontarf. We put it to good use in equipping our warriors as best we could. Somehow, the Emperor knew the final battle was approaching. But I don't remember Pyrrhus translating any accompanying missive at that time, if indeed there was one."

"That's because you Irish are without any sense of humor or fun at all and you would never have understood it," instantly countered the affable Greek diplomat who had spent so much time among the Irish that he was almost one of them.

The laughter grew more boisterous now, with the exception of the Greek monk whose confusion was obvious. And so, it was decided. In one week hence, there would be a royal procession, led by King Alfonso, to the hallowed City of Santiago de Compostela where the beloved apostle would have his errant finger returned to him. And thus could he take his place in heaven proudly and completely intact. Though all good Christians knew well the saint was already most graciously ensconced there among his brother apostles and all true believers in their Lord and God.

***

That evening, Cormac and Pyrrhus relayed the account of the monk, his mission and the contents of the precious gift box to Wolf and his leaders. They spoke among themselves at some length. Aoife, especially, asked probing questions of her two friends who had attended. She was most interested in the tale the monk had told of how he had found his way to Leon. Cael, Mornak and Fergus seemed to be pleasantly impressed by Basil's apparent goodwill and his unexpectedly amusing wit. At the same time, Keli used the occasion to comment with feigned bewilderment.

"You Irish are so often strange and apparently *fae*-touched. Our hosts here in Hispania are equally eccentric. So why should I be surprised that some distant Greek Emperor seems fit to send some weirdly worded message to accompany his outlandish gift? I'm just a simple and devout Christian Northman."

The amiably gathered leaders of this crusading adventure all grinned gleefully at their 'savage Viking' friend and comrade. And then, Aoife wisely concluded the discussion with an emphatic admonition. "We must pay careful attention to what might happen next and in particular to this curious new monastic 'harbinger of solace' from Constantinople."

***

Two days later, Wolf and Aoife decided to take advantage of King Alfonso's offer for them to escape for a night to enjoy the bucolic yet comfortable chalet that his father had built for the Queen Mother long ago. He told them that his mother had recently taken a greater interest in the court's affairs than usual. And he winked when he told them, she seemed especially pleased to converse in mellifluous Latin with their noble comrade, Cormac. Aoife's eyes rose just a bit at that but, as always, she kept her counsel.

It was a small and simple yet elegant two-story stone structure resting in a delightful pastoral setting just outside the walls of Leon. Unoccupied except when Elvira was present, the King assured them that they, if they so wished, could be alone for a few precious hours. He offered to provide a force of burly guardsmen, which they graciously declined. There were two austere yet comfortable bedrooms above and a small kitchen and sitting room below. The Irish couple had also declined the offer of servants, as they said they just wanted to be with each other for one brief and shimmering interlude.

The two bowed and thanked the young king with the utmost sincerity. Then, hand in hand, they departed his chambers, waving happily to onlookers and to the clerics gathered outside the multi-chambered rectory of the king's spiritual advisor, including one who peered with curiosity from the several windows above.

***

Qatil made his way openly and unconcerned along the streets of the city of Leon. He was something of a celebrity among the common people, though all were much too deferential to even speak to a most welcome guest of the king. Especially when he was clad in his monastic robes and walking while praying piously in his exotic Greek tongue. As the afternoon progressed and the sun began to descend, he approached one of the smaller city gates, attended by a single guardsman.

The Assassin knew the man would not understand his Greek words but he tried asking anyway.

"May I just take a little walk outside? Just to see the trees and flowering shrubbery?" He raised one palm and, with two fingers of his other hand, made a sign of walking in circles.

The guard, a young and newly recruited soldier, recognized the exalted visitor and was honored to be spoken to by such a dignitary. He knew, of course, what the hand gestures meant. The poor monk simply wanted to see something beyond the gates. With a flourish, he opened the gate and bowed slightly. Qatil bowed as well and passed, raising his hand and gracefully making a small cross in the air toward the dazzled youth, who immediately knelt and crossed himself.

Once outside, Qatil laughed out loud, telling himself how naïve and stupid these Christians were. And how it was no wonder the faithful had crushed them, taken their land and enslaved them hundreds of years before. *Taqiya* - Deception has always served Islam well and the Assassin had become a skilled master of it. Now, as darkness was setting, he threw off his despised Christian robes to reveal a tight-fitting black wrap of purest Giza cotton. He then withdrew a black hood that covered his head except for his eyes. After questioning other monks and young women of Alfonso's court he knew his destination was not far. And, to Allah's praise, there would be a hidden package awaiting him before he reached it.

The tree was exactly where he was told to expect it. Unlike the pines beneath which he so carefully buried the pathetic Hisham, this was a huge oak. Thick branches spread out above him, just close enough for him to reach up, clasp and climb. Not far above, he found it, a fissure in the wide trunk. He reached in to withdraw the most magnificent sword he had ever beheld. It was the 'blessed sword." Made from the finest metal in the world, finely honed Damascus steel and featuring an exquisitely designed ivory hilt covered with sharkskin, it was richly engraved with sacred writings. There was also a small sack containing white cotton gloves. With a dismissing snort, he threw that back into the tree hole. He had what he needed and wanted. And it exceeded his expectations in all aspects.

As soon as he had initially arrived at Alfonso's court and looked about him to survey those who were there, he had found what he was looking for. The worst nightmare of his most awful dreams stood among them. He was truly a staggering and fearsome colossus. But he was no *guwl*! This was neither a druidic demon nor a hellish angel. This was a man. And any man could be killed. He'd learned that when he was but a child.

Now it was well after dark, and Qatil hastened to the place he was told he would find the enormous warrior, hopefully enraptured in the embrace of that pretty dark-haired, green-eyed waif with whom he seemed so enamored. *Christians don't know the purpose of women,* he told himself, *they should be ever demure and obedient to the men around them. And never should they intrude themselves into affairs of men as had this one.*

It was close to midnight under a crescent moon when he first came upon the dwelling. A simple wooden door was at the center of the ground floor with two small windows below and two larger ones on the second floor. Peering from the trees, he could see it was rather surprisingly small and rustic to serve as a retreat for a queen.

There was just a faint trace of light emitting from one of the windows on the second floor. Most likely from a lighted taper, he thought. All of the windows were open to let in the cool night air. During the day, they would normally be covered with sheets of horn. Staying as much in the shadows of the trees as possible, he crept to peer through a window into the ground floor. He neither heard nor saw anyone inside. Over the years, his sense of hearing and smell had been honed by the necessity of survival. And now he could hear a soft and lilting feminine voice, almost a murmur, coming from above. The Assassin smiled.

Earlier, he had furtively conducted a perimeter search around the dwelling, assuring himself there were no guards in the surrounding woods. He also found no signs of horses or sheds. The two must have been dropped off here by comrades to be collected on the morrow.

The magnificent sword was strapped to his back and he had a pilfered meat-cutting knife in a sheath girded at his waist. The lower windows were too small for him to crawl through, so he carefully tested the door. As he suspected, it was a simple latch which he easily and almost silently opened by employing the knife's blade to lift and release it from the outside. He assumed the Queen Mother would normally be surrounded by guards when she visited, so the little cottage need not be some impregnable fortress.

He padded inside, his nose and ears assessing his surroundings. He noted the strong but familiar and homey scent of the grease and soot of the cooking fire with its mixed aromas of meats, vegetables and various herbs. There was just enough moonlight penetrating through the open door that he could make out some features. The kitchen and the sitting room were open to each other and a narrow staircase at the rear led to the upper floor. The sparse furnishings consisted of a long, well-cushioned lounging bench, several wooden chairs, a table and a shelf for preparing simple dishes. A few empty shelves lined just one wall but there were no closets or storage chests. Confident he was alone, Qatil cautiously ascended the stairs. Hopefully, the two above were, by now, either happily asleep or completely enraptured in each other's company, oblivious to anything else.

The narrow hall, which separated the two rooms on the second floor, was lit by the taper he had spied from outside. The one-bedroom door was open and he quickly determined it was unoccupied after he first took the effort to check under the large bed. Now was the time.

Qatil put his ear to the door of the other sleeping chamber and heard only what he reckoned was the contented and soft breathing of its two occupants. He silently drew the sword from its leather scabbard across his back and slowly opened the door with his other hand, sliding without a sound into the room.

The light from the hall now allowed him to see the short dark tresses of the girl on the bed. Her arm was draped over the enormous form beside her. A sheer white sheet covered both.

He raised the blessed sword over his head and prepared to strike savagely and explosively. And then his blood froze!

Aoife slowly turned to look at the black-clad intruder and, incredibly, smiled at him as she pulled back the sheet, revealing that she was clad in a fine chain mail tunic which fell to her knees and that her sleeping partner was a massive brown bear… or rather, a bear skin stuffed to appear as its original size. The bear's head was well preserved and its evil crystal eyes glared terrifyingly at the Assassin. The most horrifying feature was the creature's muzzle, filled with impossibly large, yellow, glistening incisors.

For a mortifying moment, the deadly assassin screamed like a woman, as four candles simultaneously lit up the room, almost in a single blinding flash. Next to each stood a fully armed northern warrior: Cormac with his broadsword, Cael with a drawn bow, Fergus with a thick, thrusting spear and Keli with his Viking sword in hand.

Qatil turned back the way he had come in to find a leering and fiercely savage figure standing in the door, brandishing a nimble Dalcassian axe. Wearing just a leather breechcloth, Mornak the Pict was smeared head to toe in cooking grease and covered all over with ashy soot. Only his bright blue eyes and grinning white teeth gave him a vague human appearance.

By now, Aoife had drawn her *scian* fighting knife, which she had employed in the past to dispatch even bigger heathen monsters than this quivering figure standing among them. She moved to stand beside red-haired Fergus and then crouched like an alpha she-wolf, ready to pounce at any instant.

The Assassin tried to gather his wits, recognizing his situation was dire. There was one barely possible chance of escape and there could be no delay. Without grace or careful aiming, he flung his sword at the most immediate threat, the archer with the drawn recursive bow. Despite the lack of skill in the execution, the sword would have skewered Cael if he had not leapt to the side at once. As it was, he jostled against Cormac, almost knocking them both over and that was the chance Qatil needed.

The Assassin dove out of the window, hoping he could survive the fall if he dropped and rolled on impact. He had outlived similar escapes in his past. The impact was jarring but he first tensed, then quickly relaxed his muscles.

He was just moving into a crouch, prepared to dash for the dark shelter of the thick woodlands, when something enormously powerful lifted his whole body higher. He felt one immense hand clutching his throat, the other wrapped around his knee. The force seemed inhuman. He heard a thundering roar, then felt himself flying at impossible velocity through the air, directly toward the structure's solid stone wall.

There was a sickening crunch as he experienced another impact, this one horrifically worse than what he had just gone through. Every muscle in his body was on fire, every bone felt shattered. He groaned in agony, reaching for his knife but his hands and arms would not obey his brain. He looked up from the ground to find that same monster of his dreams, his intended victim, peering down at him with curiosity. One huge hand reached down and Qatil winced but the intent was only to tear the black hood off him; even that caused a new wave of red torment in his head and shoulders.

"Are you unharmed, my love? He has a knife in his belt," called Aoife from the upper window with tender concern.

"It's grand altogether, I am, darlin' girl," replied Wolf, "and ye' look like an angel in the moonlight upon that window frame."

Their eyes locked and Aoife could wait no more. She lifted one foot to the window's sill and, without a word, leapt out. Wolf spread his two huge arms and caught her easily, dropping to his knees to soften her landing. She ran her hands through his thick, unruly hair, smothering kisses all over his face. Even with her attired in a chain mail tunic, he felt he was embracing the world's most dazzling and delicate creation.

Again, without warning, the impassioned young woman sprang from his grasp and dashed to stand over the brute who lay moaning and prostrate on the ground. This malignant, diseased creature had meant to kill her beloved. She began raining vicious kicks with her booted foot on his back and legs while execrating the beast with decidedly indelicate curses.

"Ye' vomitous spawn of maggots and worms. Sure, it's to hell ye're on your way and I aim to hasten the trip," she began to draw the deadly *scian* from its sheath before Wolf caught her and gently pulled her away.

"Now then, lass, that's no way to treat a man of the cloth. And you, above all, should know we must drag all the intelligence from him we can." Then it was his turn to rain kisses all over her flushed face.

When he came up for air, Aoife replied, "Sure and he's no more 'man of the cloth' than I am. It's from hell he's come and back to hell he'll be going. But you're right about intelligence, Captain. Please excuse my lamentable rage."

The two blissfully embraced once again as they ignored the bleeding and groaning fiend at their feet.

***

It was Aoife who was most suspicious of the monk's story from the beginning. As soon as this visitor arrived, she sensed some malevolent strategy. After conferring with Pyrrhus, however, she felt the tale of the saint's fingerbone and the emperor's missive might indeed be genuine. Ultimately, the Irish presented their concerns to Alfonso. Together, they decided to surveil this 'monk' discreetly and their doubts grew stronger. Aoife was especially concerned when she learned from Alfonso's sources that the monk seemed to continually be seeking information almost exclusively on one subject: "this Wolf, this exotic and freakish Irish warrior". Finally, they contrived a plan to lure the monk out of hiding and see what might transpire.

***

So, the morning after the incident at the Queen Mother's retreat, a small group of the Irish leaders delivered the now broken monk/assassin to Alfonso. When he was informed of the details of the episode, the king's first reaction was similar to Aoife's. He was enraged but knew he must compose himself. Schlomo and his son were summoned to examine the moribund man who was now muttering almost incoherently in Arabic.

"He has multiple broken bones, arm, shoulder, three ribs and likely his neck as well. That alone would be enough to kill him but he also has internal damage and it seems blood is leaking into his lungs even now. What happened to him? There is no sign of any injury from the blade or the arrow?"

The son asked the question but Schlomo merely nodded in response. "I think I know and I'll tell you later."

In gentle voices, they asked him questions about his mission, since both spoke fluent Arabic. Amazingly, given his grave condition, he was able to respond to most of their questions despite occasionally coughing and spitting up blood.

After a few moments, Schomo translated. "He thinks he's speaking to Caliph Sulayman and someone he calls his Emir. He was sent undercover as a monk to deliver the emperor's gift to King Alfonso. The relic and royal letter are genuine. And they saw no use simply destroying them."

"But he no doubt had an ulterior and evil objective as well. Is it right I am then, Schlomo?" interjected Aoife.

"You are quite correct, of course, dear Aoife. The gifts were merely a means of entry. He had been sent specifically to exorcise and kill what they suspect is a *guwl*, what we call a demon. They'd been told stories of some diabolical creature from the far north who had slaughtered thousands of Vikings. They thought an Irish druid summoned it and is now sent to assail the true believers of the Caliphate."

All eyes turned to Wolf. "You have apparently made quite a name for yourself, Faolán an Trodach, my friend," said the king, who mangled the pronunciation of the Irish name. Turning to the others, Alfonso continued. "And what did he tell you then, Schlomo?"

The Jewish physician reiterated that the dying man thought he was speaking to his two masters. He told them that he was ashamed to admit he had failed in his mission. And that the "demon" is real, is something like a colossal and fierce monster bear and cannot be killed. But Shlomo made it clear the man was quite delirious and may not have known what he was saying.

"That will work to our advantage if the Moors continue to believe some outlandish and preternatural monstrosity has been sent to punish them. Our good King Brian always urged that we cloak the existence of our Irish 'Magyars' and 'Spartans' in mystery to confound the Viking foe. And the Norse, all on their own, amplified their stories of this 'colossal and fierce monster wolf' now standing among us," said Cormac, smiling toward the tall Irish warrior.

"If Sulayman and this 'Emir' had been present to witness Aoife leaping from an upper-floor window in the misty moonlight to so ferociously thrash their most dreadful executioner, they would be much more alarmed that she may be coming to destroy them and not some damned *guwl*," Wolf countered.

Aoife's lily-white cheeks turned pink. "As I already explained, it was but a wee lapse which I heartily regret."

At that moment, the dying man convulsed in a fit of coughing, spitting more blood and rasping out a few desperate words before his entire body stiffened and his eyes rolled up in his head. Then Bogumir, later named Qatil al-Sulafia, was no more.

"Those few final words were neither Arabic nor Greek," exclaimed the King. "Do you have any idea what he was saying?"

"I'm not absolutely sure. In years past, I did pick up a few words of their grunting Slavic tongue from the *saqaliba* slave warriors of the Caliphate. I'm fairly certain he was calling for his mother at the end."

Despite Schlomo's lachrymose declaration, none of those assembled felt the slightest pangs of pity for the hell-bound, merciless murderer.

***

Not two days later, a small, sealed chest was delivered to the Caliph at his residence in Cordoba. It had made its way to him through a most curious and circuitous route. A traveling merchant, plying his goods in the north, had been accosted in the road by five Leonese knights who seemed to appear out of nowhere. Even though merchants were by mutual consent left unmolested by both Christians and Muslims, the trader was certain he was about to be slain, or, at the very least, relieved of his wares. But it did not turn out that way.

Producing an ornately lacquered wooden box, the heavily armored knights explained to him that their King Alfonso had decided to convey a message and an offering to the Caliph. They also told him Sulayman would likely become enraged if it were to be opened before delivery. Most surprisingly, the knights paid him with a small sack of silver coins for his trouble. Then, to his astonishment, they took the time, with good cheer, to purchase a number of his goods, which included fine silks, oils and spices from the East.

Sulayman prudently ordered the Emir first to inspect the chest to assure it was not some infernal trap to cause harm to its recipient, by which he meant himself. But the inspector immediately returned from his task, having not even opened the box.

"My Caliph, this is the exact same chest we received some time ago, the one from the Emperor in Constantinople. How could it be coming back to us now? And why?" The Emir was both confused and alarmed.

"I know not and my patience wears thin. Just make haste, open it and bring me whatever may be inside," ordered the Caliph once more in frustration.

Moments later, the Emir returned, clutching a snugly tied leather sack in one hand and a rolled parchment in the other. "From the waxed seal, it seems indeed to be a letter from King Alfonso, the satchel may hold some gift of tribute or a peace offering from the infidel King. I've not yet read the message, awaiting your permission, my Caliph."

Sulayman nodded and the Emir bowed gracefully and then deftly sliced through the seal with his omnipresent dagger. He unrolled the parchment, surprised to find the words were so few. "It's in Arabic, Sulayman and perfectly scribed, though it includes some foreign phrases in infidel gibberish," announced the speaker. He then read it as literally as it was written.

*To the Ruler of the so-called Caliphate of Cordoba, whomever that might now be.*

*Greetings. Herewith we return to you your recent kind bequest with our gratitude. We are pleased to accept the sacred relic of the most holy apostle and will assure it will be kept in sanctuary with him in heaven. We are equally joyous to also accept the superbly resplendent Damascus steel sword you have conveyed and will without fail put it to best use in the near future after we remove the heathenish etchings which currently defile it. You may keep the rest of your property which accompanies this dispatch.*

*Alfonso*

*Imperator Totius Hispaniaie*

*Beware the* ***CÚ SÍDHE****!*

"What is in the damned bag, you idiot? Bellowed the Caliph, who was both furious and burning with aching curiosity now. "Let us see what gift or insult this insolent boy King sends us. And then we judge what to do next."

The Emir, who suspected with dread what they might find, cut open the satchel's bindings. He then turned it over to rest on a wooden stool beside him. A decapitated and desiccated head, dull blue eyes staring upwards vacantly. It somehow landed upright. Qatil's now ashen hair, formerly bright and flaxen, left no doubt. It was their prized assassin.

Sulayman gasped and stepped backward as if he'd been struck. "Damn them all to hell! And what is this thing of which we must beware?"

The Emir, who not only didn't understand the words' meaning but could never come close to pronouncing them with any accuracy, simply shrugged.

# Chapter 11

## New Arrivals and The Cluniacs

With all of the dramatic events they had sparked, by now it seemed Wolf and his band had been in Hispania for many months instead of just a few short weeks. Then came word of another flotilla of northern sailing ships arriving at the same small port town in Leon. Consisting of ten craft of various sorts, the motley squadron included Viking types: *moras, Snekkjas, knarrs,and drakkars,* along with a Frankish *cog.* Just under four hundred men disembarked, almost all of them Irish with a few Scots and Welshmen among the crews. All were combat veterans of the Battle of Clontarf. The Frankish ship, however, contained quite different visitors. They were black-robed monks from the Benedictine Abbey of Cluny, founded in 910 A.D. by William I, Duke of Aquitaine in France. The churchmen were from different nations and peoples from across Christian Europe.

There were two primary modes for the dissemination of information across Europe – widely traveling traders and clergymen. Both types of messengers had brought tidings back to Ireland, sometimes confused or exaggerated, of the achievements of Wolf and the others in Hispania. These hardened fighters chafed once again under feuding Irish leaders at home, who seemed to be shifting back to the priorities of clan and province, rather than the tentative unity King Brian had established in Ireland.

Because the foreign Vikings had been defeated or driven away and the likelihood of their return was minimal after hundreds of years, local chieftains and petty kings began to focus once again on their own interests. The newly arrived warriors reminisced proudly about their hard-fought victories, achieved almost miraculously under the leadership and inspiration of their Battle Captain, Wolf the Quarrelsome.

After conferring with the king and members of his court, Wolf and his leaders, along with a number of Leonese nobles and knights, rode off to meet and assess these newest visitors. Alfonso, especially, had been pleased to receive news of hundreds more hardened Celtic Christian warriors turning up on his shores. If they were at all as loyal and ferocious as the first contingent, they would be invaluable allies indeed.

From the heights above the port town, Wolf, Cormac and the others looked down at the snug little harbor which now sheltered an additional ten craft of various origins along with the usual fishing boats and merchant ships.

"All those various types of Viking craft in the port bring back dolorous memories of when the Norse invaders first arrived in Dublin just before the battle at Clontarf. I commented at the time that one could walk the expanse of Dublin Bay without ever getting his feet wet," declared Cormac.

"Many others said the same at the time," replied Wolf, "but then there were thousands of savages, bloodthirsty heathens all. And now, we welcome friends and countrymen."

"We'll see just how 'friendly' they are indeed, once we've met and judged them," countered Aoife. Ever wary, as behooves a Chief of Intelligence, she remembered well that some renegade Leinster Irish had taken the side of the Viking invaders at Clontarf.

The great Captain grinned broadly. "Always looking at the bright side of things. That's my darlin' girl."

"And wasn't it I who first distrusted and warned against this 'gentle Greek monk' who turned out to be a murderous viper in our midst? And you, above all, Captain, have seen how merry and cheerful I can be in most instances," retorted Aoife, flashing a victorious smile.

"Ye're right on both counts as always, *a stór*," replied Wolf with unabashed pride and affection.

***

The leader of this seaborne force of Celtic men and eight Celtic women was a robustly built ox of a man named Lorcan. Lorcan had been Fergus's second in command of the Irish 'Spartan' heavy infantry, which had topped out with an end strength of three hundred scarlet-cloaked, thickly armored spearmen back in Ireland. Recruits had been selected for their massive size, strength and stamina. Now sixty of those stolid behemoths, with all of their equipment, had accompanied Lorcan on the voyage. Others of the unit had been lost in battle or simply decided to stay at home and hearth.

The original squadron of Irish 'Magyar' cavalry had numbered two hundred mounted archers when they thundered over the fields and through the hills and forests of Ireland. Now Cael would soon be delighted to be once again joined by forty more of his former comrades. Of course, they couldn't transport their nimble Connemara ponies but all had brought along their powerful recursive bows and a healthy supply of various purposed arrows. Aoife's brother, Eoin, one of the youngest of the group, was especially looking forward to seeing his sister once more.

Many of the others who made the journey had come from the ranks of the *Laochra an Rí* or 'Warriors of the King.' These were made up of former "hostages" sent to King Brian's court. A common practice in Ireland and the British Isles was exchanging young men from allied clans and provinces, as well as friendly foreign territories such as Scotland and Wales. Members of Brian's family also served as hostages in other courts. The practice was meant to solidify alliances and friendships and worked to the advantage of all. Now they aimed to become *Laochra Faolán an Trodach... '* Warriors of Wolf the Quarrelsome.'

A separate and special group among the voyagers was composed of eight young women. They were all experienced scouts and spies who had been hand-picked by Aoife. When, in times past, King Brian had dispatched parties of recruiters to all parts seeking volunteers to join the ranks of the *Laochra* and the special heavy infantry and mounted archer units, Aoife had often accompanied them. In her role as Intelligence Chief, she knew women could frequently gain access to people and places where strange men would be viewed with suspicion. She sought out these women among the common people – field workers, cooks and serving girls. All had two things in common. They were highly intelligent Christians who loved their country and they could ride as well as any of the Magyars. These eight had missed the excitement and thrill of their recent past and longed to serve under their former leader, Aoife, once again. When they learned of an upcoming expedition to Hispania, they joined up with the utmost enthusiasm.

After receiving training by veterans of King Brian's formidable naval group in the handling of the various Viking craft, the voyagers set out from Limerick with the blessing of the surviving members of King Brian's family. The intent was to embark on a type of pilgrimage, to reunite with Wolf and the others and to continue God's holy work.

Though they were all highly skilled, armed and lethal fighters, they viewed this journey as simply "picking up the cross." When and if they returned to Ireland, they would bring the benefit of their experiences and be greatly valued by their clans and countrymen. If they might be equally motivated by the exuberance of youth, the elation imbued by their victory over hordes of Viking invaders and a sense of yearning for adventure beyond their shores, it never occurred to any of them in their religious and patriotic zeal.

When the voyagers made port at the small town, they were delighted to be informed that Wolf and the others had also made their initial entry there just scant weeks back. The townspeople and leaders made them feel welcome, especially when they took note of the clergymen who disembarked from the Frankish *cog*.

The Celts had first encountered the Cluniac monks during a layover in Gascony to replenish food and water. These monks were on a mission of their own. Just as the tiny kingdoms in Hispania were in a state of confused flux, so too was the hierarchy of the Church in Hispania. There was a need for a unified and renewed spiritual vision. And that precisely was the calling of the Benedictine Abbey of Cluny. Free from secular entanglements, the Abbey had first been placed under the protection of Saints Peter and Paul.

Now, Cluniac influence was at its height throughout Europe, with bequests pouring in from England, France, Germania, Italy and Hispania. Ironically, King Alfonso had invited the monastic delegation to come and bless himself and his people with their presence just before Wolf and his three dragon ships fortuitously fell into his lap. For their own safety, it only made good sense for the monks to request joining the flotilla of Irish warriors on their way to the same place. Lorcan and all the rest were only too delighted to welcome the *cog* and its good monks into their midst.

***

The visitors had set up camp in a large clearing outside the town, which the local leaders had recommended. There they awaited the arrival of the delegation from Leon, which they'd been told was on its way.

A young runner rushed into the leather tent, which Lorcan used as a temporary headquarters. The teen's beaming face was flushed red. He was gasping for breath, prodigiously excited and bursting to announce the news.

"Lorcan! Riders coming down the slopes. I recognize Wolf, Cormac, Fergus,
Cael and Aoife among them. Even Mornak the Pict. We've found them at last."

Groups of the warriors of Clontarf began to gather, peering up at the stately procession of riders making their way toward them. It didn't take long.

Dignified pomp and ceremony could no longer be upheld. All proper decorum evaporated. These were Celts after all.

With a deafening roar, the milling horde of hundreds of fierce men and eight equally formidable women surged in a dashing rush up the gentle hill to be reunited with their beloved leaders, who had also been their trusted friends. Almost at the same time, these same 'leaders and friends' leapt from their mounts and sprinted down to become enveloped in the teeming mass of their exuberant countrymen.

'Magyars' surrounded Cael, Lorcan and the 'Spartans' encircled Fergus and larger groups of *Laochra* rushed to meet Wolf, Cormac and Mornak. There were wild Gaelic shouts of welcome as well as 'Thanks be to God' – *Bhuíchas le Dia!* With a bit more dignity, Aoife and her eight young scouts sat in a circle a bit off to the side on the soft grassy slope, catching up and already laughing over shared stories. And then Eoin rushed into their midst. The strapping young 'Magyar' bent to take his 'big sister' into his strong, muscled arms and threw his legs into the air in a dance as the two hugged each other in glee.

Still in the saddle, the Leonese dignitaries looked on with both puzzlement and amusement at the spirited spectacle of all these reunited Celts. Sitting astride his own mount among them, Pyrrhus could only smile.

"I advised you to expect something precisely like this. They're barbarously savage fighters, yet still the most kind, welcoming and gentle of Christians. Even though I'll admit, I sometimes find them not far removed from their untamed, druidic pagan past. Just wait until you see them in the company of good hard drink and the music of their own pipes, flutes, whistles and *bodhrán* drums. I'm sure you'll agree with me."

***

Later that evening, when the ruckus finally settled down, the proper introductions had been made and salutations exchanged, Wolf called for a council of his original leaders and those of the newcomers, which Lorcan thought was appropriate. Fergus' second selected one man from among the 'Magyars' and one from the *Laochra.* Both had impressed him with their innate leadership traits during their voyage. Aoife also invited one of her scouts, a vigorous and sturdy redhaired lass named Saoirse, who had been fearless and invaluable in providing intelligence information from within Viking-occupied Dublin before the Clontarf battle. As always, Pyrrhus took his place among the Celts.

“I do believe we have a respectable force to bring to bear in serious operations against the Moors. Though far fewer than we fought with back in Ireland, we’re now able to provide significant assistance to King Alfonso and his people,” Wolf proclaimed.

“Our new additions are hardened, blooded and motivated fighters and many have the special training and skills which served so well against the bloody little heathen invaders outside Dublin. Fergus and Cael, what are the strengths of your formations when combined with those we already have?” asked the colossal Battle Captain.

“We now have a total of seventy experienced and indomitable Spartan bulls, Captain,’ pronounced Fergus with pride.

“And sixty hard-riding, deadly mounted archers with their own powerful bows along with their own and all the arrows our allies can provide. And though they’re not our own dear wee Connemara ponies, the Leonese steeds are strong and swift,” added Cael, not to be outdone by his fellow captain and long-time friend.”

Wolf turned to his own battle-scarred, long-time friend and personal deliverer from Viking bondage years before on that first day of the new millennium. “And how many *Laochra* and others Prince Cormac?”

“Roughly three hundred and twenty, mostly infantry and all well trained in sword, spear, axe and sling. That’s including Keli and his Icelanders. This latest batch includes a few more rugged Scottish highlanders as well. Good men all,” Cormac replied as he knew many of them personally from past campaigns.

“A total of almost four hundred and fifty vigorous and highly dangerous warriors from the cold distant north, if I reckon correctly. That is indeed a boon to the Hispanians and a nightmare to the Moorish heathens. The time has now come for us to confer with the king and his military advisors to begin to develop a campaign plan to spark the flames that will drive the invaders from this peninsula. It may take time, perhaps many years but we are perfectly positioned to help begin to ignite the inferno which will lead to ultimate reconquest and these lands returning to Christendom,” declared Wolf.

“Now then, Iceland might be cold and distant but our own dear Scotland and Ireland are cool, green, moist and pleasant,” protested Mornak, “and I quite agree if we can banish the northern heathens from those lands, we can begin to see off the dusky little southern heathens from these sultry shores.”

"My thanks for your most gracious support, Mornak. Another reason you're my favorite Pict," said Wolf, jovially clasping one enormous arm around his close friend's shoulders.

"Captain, as you know I've spent much time with the ministers, noble and diplomats among our Leonese friends. It seems you and your men have become celebrities among the common people and soldiers here. I've no doubt hundreds of them would plead to be inducted into the ranks of our heavy infantry, mounted archers and *Laochra* warriors. We could regain our original strength of three hundred spearmen and two hundred riders."

As always, Pyrrhus spoke with authority as he had been the original inspiration for the foundation of the Irish Spartans. And it was he who had shown Irish craftsmen how to construct their own version of Magyar recursive bows. Pyrrhus had, for several years, been the imperial ambassador from Constantinople among the Magyars in the Duchy of Hungary. Just as he had adapted to and become almost a part of the Irish, he had earlier and likewise developed an intense affinity for the Magyars. He rode and even fought at their sides in defensive raids against their Bulgarian foemen. So, the affable Greek diplomat had been perfectly capable of training an unlikely crew of young Irish volunteers to become as effective mounted archers as his earlier hosts.

"You know how much I've always respected your advice, my old friend. But I fear it could be too great a challenge to integrate the locals into our established squadrons. Language and cultural differences would dilute the cohesion that has grown through shared training and battle. Yet again, you always inspire. If there can be Irish 'Spartans' and 'Magyars,' can we not encourage the formation of similarly trained warriors among the Leonese? We must bring this up with the King."

Pyrrhus nodded in agreement with Wolf, once again recognizing how his young friend seemed to have an innate ability for military art, training and leadership. Wolf the Quarrelsome could have succeeded at becoming some version of the legendary and mythical ancient Irish heroes and demigods in the fashion of *Cú Chulainn*, fighting in monumental individual battles against monstrous enemies.

But the Irish giant was not some frenzied berserker. He had been educated by the good monks at the Abbey of Innisfallen. One history teacher had inculcated him there in the necessity of engaging forces of adversaries with discipline, organization and order. Wolf had imbued that same spirit in the fighting men who served under him, always inveighing against fevered battle lust and individual duels long associated with the Celts. So, it made good sense to maintain the unit integrity of the experienced Celtic special units. And Pyrrhus was equally pleased that Wolf found it wise to broach the idea of developing the same type of warrior groupings among the Hispanians to King Alfonso.

Though the native warriors here were of somewhat smaller stature than the Irish and Vikings, they generally dwarfed their Moorish foes, heavy armored formations of Leonese spearmen, along with cohesive squadrons of nimble mounted archers, would prove a distinct advantage on the battlefield.

"And as you know well, Captain, we must endeavor to gain even deeper insight into the intent of our enemy, his strengths, weaknesses and his most critical vulnerabilities. We must rely on trusted human sources, building on the networks King Alfonso already has in place. And he has recently been gifted with a most welcome and intriguing volunteer in that capacity. I'll discuss this further with you later."

There were some knowing smiles among the others who knew well how much Aoife and Wolf appreciated their private time together, which they strove to snatch whenever the opportunity presented itself.

Aoife continued. "Cael and I have been discussing another means of gaining essential information. We propose to combine the swiftness and mobility of the Magyars and the experience of the scouts and spies who have just joined us. We recommend six teams of two, a man and a woman, who will probe deep into the Caliphate's various provinces, conducting long-range reconnaissance. They will be attired in the Moorish fashion and be mounted on those wonderful Arabian stallions so recently captured by Alfonso's knights. 'Tis a shallow cover to be sure but they will primarily rely on stealth and speed to avoid detection and of course, the man will carry his trusted bow and deadly arrows for use if needed. Each team will be given ample provisions and be prepared to live off the land for the duration of their patrols, which will be limited in time."

Aoife continued. "And each of these grandly motivated women can ride as well as any Magyar. True, they can't launch an arrow from the saddle but woe to the enemy who comes too close. Each lass has her own fighting *scian* and five deadly throwing knives. I've no doubt they will be as dangerous to the Moors as they've been to the Vikings," added Saoirse with spirited conviction.

With a flourish, the crimson-haired young woman drew aside her *brat* to reveal the long-bladed dagger and five sleek darts snugly sheathed on her leather belt.

"We can only hope none of these finely honed killers mistake one of Cael's poor innocent young lads for some evil foe in some deep woodlands in the dark of night," jibed Mornak, reliable as ever.

Not being as well acquainted with the speaker as the others, Saoirse glared at the grinning Pict. But when Aoife and the others all laughed at the same time, she relented and the traces of a smile began to appear at the corners of her rosy lips.

As the meeting broke up and the leaders moved off to sleep or take an evening drink, one of the newcomers stayed back, gesturing as if to speak alone with Wolf. This was Brother Cillian, a Benedictine monk from Cluny. He was dressed in a full monastic black habit with a red sash and a simple, beautifully carved and polished wooden cross on a sinew binding visible on his breast. He wore his long, raven-black hair combed back and held in place by a narrow, reddish leather headband. His eyes were so light brown they almost seemed bronze in color. The dark raiment and hair contrasted with the paleness of his face. His countenance seemed to radiate conviviality combined with intelligence as he stepped toward the Irish leader who towered over him.

"*Dia duit a chara.*" "God be with you, my friend."

"*Dia is Muire leat.*" "And God and Mary with you," replied Wolf, almost by habit, smiling at the black-robed man. "You seem to speak my language with some facility."

"I should hope so. I was born in Connaught and schooled at the Abbey of Clonmacnoise before reporting for duty at Cluny," replied the amiable monk. "There are not many of us wild Irish there but I do believe our presence conveys a wee bit of dignity and grace to our foreign brothers who labor in God's service at that holy sanctuary."

Cillian's broad grin beamed radiantly as he recognized that he had surprised the legendary Battle Captain.

"I should've known you might be one of us. I do believe if I were to travel across the great oceans to the most alien and distant of lands and nations, I'd find an Irish clergyman already among the strangers there. And it's glad I am that you represent us with such elegance and modesty." Wolf was now grinning.

Though Cillian was shorter than the towering Irish leader, he was still of formidable stature with broad chest and shoulders and narrow hips. In fact, he reminded Wolf somewhat of Mornak. If the monk had blue eyes and let his dark hair grow wild, the two could pass as brothers. And the canny Wolf began to suspect another similarity, this one of temperament. The two also seemed to share a sense of mischievous humor and, surprising given the monk's calling, a certain charming irreverence.

"Just as the tiny Christian nations of Hispania - Leon, Castile, Navarre and Barcelona - are in disarray, so too are their Church leaders," Cillian said with some frustration. "Instead of focusing on the souls of their flock, many of the bishops seem to ally with this or that nobleman's political cause."

"We experienced the same in Ireland and King Brian used it to his advantage in uniting the country under his High Kingship. He visited the central seat of the Church in Armagh at the Abbey there and presented a sizeable gift. Not perfect but it gained at least the tacit support of the Northern Kingdoms. Even if most of them didn't join us at Clontarf, we were still victorious over the Viking invaders with the allies who did choose to fight at our sides."

Wolf had always been antagonistic to political intrigue of any kind. And he was also a devout Christian who agreed the church's fight should be to save souls, not to push the aims of secular leaders.

"So, I assume you, the Cluniacs are here to reinforce the people's spiritual will just as we Celts hope to invigorate and ignite their combative resolve?"

The monk gazed into the faintly silver-scarred face of the Irish leader with newfound appreciation. "Precisely, Captain. Each of my brother monks brings certain knowledge and skills. As do I. I've spent my last years at Cluny studying everything in the church's collected texts about the Muslims and especially that belief as practiced here in Hispania. I've even mastered the Arabic tongue to read their scripts in their original. As a matter of course, I've also become knowledgeable about the history and geography of the peninsula, though this is my first time actually setting foot on its soil."

Wolf's interest piqued as he could immediately perceive another distinct asset so fortuitously presented to him along with the addition of hundreds of experienced Celtic warriors.

"So, we've an understanding of what each is about. Can I ask if ye'd be willing to put your particular knowledge and skills to the aid of our quest as well as your own? Our Leonese hosts have been hospitable and exceedingly helpful but I'd be lying if I didn't admit how pleased I'd be to hear such useful intelligence in my own language. Even if you were schooled at Clonmacnoise and not the good Abbey of Innisfallen, where I spent two youthful years.

Wolf sometimes pondered whether he hadn't spent too much time with his Pictish friend, some of that sardonic banter rubbing off on him. But one glance at the amused expression on the face of this very unusual 'Mornak-like' monk assured him he had nothing to fear.

With a countenance of feigned indignation, Cillian replied without hesitation. "Captain, 'tis true I'm a monk of Cluny and committed to carrying out that sacred calling. But I'm also an Irishman and am dismayed ye'd even consider I'd not apply my humble efforts to the service of my own people, especially when they overlap so well with that of my brother monks, foreigners all."

Cillian's eyes were sparkling as he continued. "My answer is, of course, yes and I should have thought you would've known that on general principle. But then, you were schooled at Innisfallen and not the much finer Abbey of Clonmacnoise."

# Chapter 12

**The Reports of Aoife and Brother Cillian**

Later that same night, Wolf and Aoife were finally by themselves. They had politely turned down the kind offer of a rich merchant of the port to spend the night in his small but comfortable seaside watch tower. Both had wanted to remain alone and together but still close to their friends. And since the failed attempt by the assassin on the leader's life, Aoife had insisted he be under the protection of a Life Guard squad she had personally chosen from among the *Laochra.* Despite his vociferous protests, she had insisted, reminding him that even the 'mighty and legendary' Champion of the Irish must at times sleep like a mere mortal.

It was a warm and beautiful evening with a gentle breeze wafting ashore from the frothy foam of the small cresting ocean waves. They decided against staying within the confines of the leather tent set aside for them. Instead, after informing the guards where they would spend the night, Aoife took her beloved's large, calloused hand in her own smaller one and led him to the top of a diminutive hill which was bedecked with a verdant stand of tall fir trees. They had brought with them only a small flagon of wine, one loaf of warm brown bread and their woolen cloaks, wrapped under their arms.

He parted the soft, needle-covered limbs of one of the largest trees and led Aoife to the base of the fir where they could spread out their good cloaks of finest Irish wool and recline. There were stray traces of moonlight that shone through the piney roof in places and the aroma of the sea air mixed with the arboreal musk of their shelter was almost intoxicating. Aoife leapt upon her beloved giant with a joy-filled squeal.

Later, as they shared the moist and delicious bread and exchanged draughts of wine, each taking small sips, Aoife told Wolf what she had learned of Alfonso's recent visitor. And how proud she was that the young king had sought her own advice on how best to proceed.

"Her name is *Zaynab bint Hasan*. Her tale is one of woe, in some ways even worse than what many of us experienced at the hands of the Vikings. She is from the city of Tulaytulah, one of the largest in the north of the Caliphate. Called Toledo by the Hispanians, this city and its inhabitants have in the past vied with Cordoba to be the seat of power there. Zaynab was born to one of the most noble families of Syrian heritage. Her father was particularly influential and one of the region's provincial leaders. He died several years ago, leaving her mother, his two daughters and one other."

Wolf tilted his head questionably to one side, wondering where the story of this Moorish Princess was going. Still, he knew his own 'Princess' was not one to engage in idle banter or gossip. Aoife's compassion was evident even as she relayed the events.

"The other was her older step-brother, her father's son by another of his wives who had been put aside in divorce. Then this other wife disappeared without a word being spoken by anyone else. But the brother remained to make her and her sister's lives miserable and it only got worse with the death of her father. Still, this family was from distinguished old and noble Syrian stock and the brother was able to assure a man was present to maintain their wealth and holdings."

At that point, Wolf stopped to ask Aoife a poignant question.

"Do you mean the mother may have lost their property and family rights if there were no man there after her husband's death? Such an atrocity would never happen in any Celtic land. I don't believe even the heathen Vikings would do such a thing to their own women. Brother Cillian has studied these people in detail back at Cluny. I must have him help me understand them further."

"Yes, according to Zaynab, a man, any man, must always be the master of the family among the Moors, even if her mother was a learned and formidable figure in her own right. And it gets much worse."

Aoife stroked his faintly silver-scarred and chiseled cheek and, in her lilting angelic voice, whispered in his ear.

"Do you realize, my love, how blessed we are to be Irish, to be Christian and to have each other?"

She pressed a soft kiss on his lips, then continued. "At first, even after the death of her father, it was not so bad. Her cruel older brother lived for battle, often away taking part in cavalry strikes and what the Moors call *aceifas,* campaigns against the Christian lands intended to despoil religious sites, take slaves and steal cattle. Their strategy is to cause chaos and insecurity and prevent any semblance of organized and ordinary life for Christians outside of their castles and fortified cities. In essence, to prevent them from uniting and moving south to regain their own lands. These raids are always of short duration but frequent and wide ranging."

"That sounds familiar. The Vikings did the same to the English Saxons and the French, demanding tribute or Danegeld, which they received year after year. Some of the Christian lords here in Hispania continue to pay yearly tribute to the Moors. An abomination, I'm proud to say, we Irish never sank to in our affairs with the Norse, even in the worst of times," said Wolf defiantly.

Aoife nodded, continuing. "As an established and noble family, Zaynab was served by a retinue of slaves and even received a rudiment of education from some learned Jewish and Christian *Dhimmis*. As long as these wise teachers remained subservient and paid the *Jizya* submission tax, even the best of Moorish families tolerated their presence. One of these teachers was a young Christian youth who had an affinity for languages, numbers and the study of nature. This man, Alvaro, became Zaynab's and her sister's primary tutor. Alvaro was two years older than Zaynab, who, at nineteen, is two years older than her sister. Both girls were very fond of Alvaro, especially Zaynab, who endeavored to spend all her free time learning from him. He taught her how to calculate; to add, subtract, divide and multiply and how to speak, at least in simple terms, in his own Hispanic language. He also spent much time with her walking in the fields, forests and through mountain passes. He told her the names of the trees, flowers and animals and how they interacted with each other and with the people who lived in the region. And that was what led directly to heartbreaking tragedy."

Aoife sighed sadly before continuing, "As Zaynab and Alvaro were returning to her stately home from just such a pleasant walk, a servant rushed out toward them. He was panting in fear and informed them that her brother had just recently returned from a raid and that he was on a rampage after speaking to Zaynab's mother. From the open windows, they could hear his ugly, screeching voice. He was barely coherent, yet they could make out enraged fragments – "off alone with an unclean *kafir!* Dishonored me and my family! You allowed it, encouraged it!"

There was a terrible, rending scream from her mother, followed by horrible gurgling, then silence. Alvaro grabbed the daughter's hand and quickly sped her away from the house. Zaynab was in a state of shock as the two ran through woodland trails for what seemed like hours to his family's simple farmhouse."

Wolf listened to this story and could feel his own rage building. "You mean the warrior murdered his own step-mother because the girl was with her tutor?"

"Yes, it's called an 'honor killing' where a man can murder any woman in his family who he feels has brought shame on the home. But even there, it is extreme to object so drastically to a *dhimmi* teacher whom the family has entrusted to teach their student. Nevertheless, their faith and their laws permit such atrocities. As soon as they reached the farm and told Alvaro's father, the older man immediately put Zaynab on one of the family's ponies, telling her to ride for her life to the north, to his brother in the City of Leon. He added that he and Alvaro would find her younger sister and then the two would join her there. But it didn't work out that way."

Aoife's emerald eyes were shimmering with tears as she went on.

"Alvaro had also taught Zaynab to ride, so she sobbingly followed the roads north, critically avoiding any stranger she came upon and not stopping until she arrived in Christian-held lands. She came upon a group of Alfonso's knights who appreciated her attempts to speak their language and took pity on her when she told her story. They took her to Alvaro's uncle. He is a well-off merchant who had emigrated from the Caliphate during the time of Almanzor, while his brother decided to remain. Not long after, word came that Alvaro had been hunted down and slaughtered by the demonically evil brother while he was trying to worship at Holy Mass furtively. His disguise had failed or some other dhimmi had betrayed him."

"And the younger sister?" asked Wolf with genuine concern. Even though he didn't personally know any of those involved in this tragic saga, he always felt great empathy, given his own family tragedies when he was but a young boy.

"Alvaro's father has spirited her away to some sanctuary where she is well-cared for but lives in constant fear. The father's spirit is crushed as Alvaro was his only child and he now considers Zaynab and her sister to be his own daughters to be protected always. It is an appalling and heart-rending story in every way. But, having met and spoken with her *a stór*, I strangely believe Zaynab may have a bit of our Irish blood coursing through her veins."

"And what makes you say that, *a chuisle mo chroí?*" aksed Wolf tenderly.

"It has been only a brief time but now, despite the loss of her mother and beloved tutor, she is intent upon returning to rescue her sister and take revenge on the hideous murderer. And that is why King Alfonso thought I may have a notion of a way to help this girl and bring confusion and dread on our enemy at the same time. Zaynab is a sophisticated and elegant Arabic Princess and can move easily among them. The Berbers, the *Saqaliba and* the various *dhimmis* all defer to such a personage from force of habit. Our aim is to fracture the Caliphate, to encourage distrust and disunity among them and to gain further intelligence. We should be able to devise a plan to do that and to assist Zaynab in her most Celt-like endeavor."

"That we should, dear girl," responded Wolf, smiling with the familiar assumption that his Intelligence Chief had already designed a shrewd and effective plan of operations which merely awaited staffing with the others and the blessing of King Alfonso before moving forward.

***

Brother Cillian and Wolf the Quarrelsome, sat on a giant felled tree, perched on a cliff which rose majestically up from the green-tinted coastal waters. Wolf always found the subtle differences in the colors of the same ocean interesting. In Ireland, it seemed the waves were always a cold slate grey, with occasional slashes of the deepest blue. He knew this was an idle fascination but considered it harmless. With all the horrors and cruelty extant in their world, the Irish always took time to take pleasure in the wonder of God's nature, its seas, its forests, its hills and meadows and the spectacular creatures which shared that glory with them – horses, hounds, sheep, cattle, fowl, fish and more.

"The founder of 'Malikism' was Imam Malik Ibn Anas, who lived hundreds of years ago. The Maliki school is one of several schools of Islamic jurisprudence but it has been deemed the only official religious and legal source of law in the Caliphate."

Cillian spoke as if he were giving a lecture to monastic students, yet Wolf's interest was unfeigned. He had loved history since his days at Inisfallen and, when it gave him insight into the ways of an adversary, he paid the utmost attention.

"Abd al-Rahman III, first Caliph of Cordoba, perfected a system whereby he devised an inquisitorial system of surveillance using Maliki clerics. These clerics kept the Caliph informed of what was going on throughout his realm.

The practice continues today but there are more challenges for Sulayman. The Arabs are the upper classes of Cordoban society but the North African Berbers and the *Saqaliba* who are mostly descendants of Christian slaves, are ironically beginning to question not only the religious devotion but the political motives of the Arabic *Ummayads.* And by now the two non-Arab groups make up the largest segment of the Moorish fighting forces, as the bulk of local elite have become comfortable and increasingly demilitarized."

"That certainly seems to provide an opportunity for us to exploit," Wolf interjected.

"But as you have no doubt also noted, these Hispanians are also not as united as they should be, even though most are of Romano-Visigoth stock, excluding the Galicians. I must talk more of them at another time, a subject you will find of great interest. You no doubt already know of our own ancient pagan tales of the Book of Invasions. Mayhap you will find some truth in those old stories, long thought myth."

Cillian grinned, for he, like all Irish men and women, counted himself a gifted *scéalaí* — a Gaelic storyteller and historian.

"I look forward to that, Brother. However, as for the current lack of unity among our fellow Christians here, nothing brings people together more than a shared victory. Even small victories begin to cement adherence to a just and holy cause. We Celts just might be the kindling spark that ignites the flame of liberation for all of Hispania."

# Chapter 13

**Direct Action**

An intentionally small and limited council sat in King Alfonso's personal chambers on plush, velvet-cushioned chairs that had been arranged in a circle. Its members included the king, his military advisor Sancho, Wolf, Cormac and Aoife. The assembly aimed to finalize a plan to assist Zaynab in rescuing her younger sister and to take vengeance on her mother's murderer. Additionally, the city of Toledo and its surroundings were of strategic importance. If the centrality of Cordoba and thus the Caliphate itself, was to be threatened, Toledo and its Moorish inhabitants might actually find that to their advantage. Sulayman's connections with the nobility of the region were not close. Even the Arabs there, not to mention the other groups, realized the current Caliph was no Hisham and certainly no Almanzor.

And at the moment, Sulayman, however weakened, was the one link holding the disparate provinces of the Caliphate together. If he could be discredited in some way in the eyes of the Moors of Toledo, that would, of course, benefit the cause of the Christian kingdoms. Aoife and Wolf had discussed this and forged a concept of operations for discussion with the king whose cooperation and support would be essential. Zaynab was also critical and the Irish couple was relieved to see she was not acting out of irrational rage and fury but that the young Arabic girl displayed a calm, cool and calculated resolve to accomplish her goals. Zaynab was also highly intelligent and, interestingly, beginning to express an interest in the Christian faith of her current hosts.

Zaynab's bona fides had been verified through three separate human intelligence networks: first through her slain tutor's uncle, with whose family she was now staying, secondly through Alfonso's established source networks among the Christian dhimmis and finally by Schlomo's own contacts among the Jews of Toledo. All corroborated precisely the facts of her sad story.

The plan was exceedingly risky but dangers would be mitigated by acting swiftly and stealthily. Zaynab would travel to Toledo on established roads in a fine carriage, worthy of an Arabic princess. She would be accompanied on the coach by three slavish servants – a handmaiden, her porter and a driver. Her escort would consist of six regal Arabic heavy cavalrymen, well-armed and resplendently garbed. Her cover rationale would be that she was a niece of Caliph Sulayman on a tour of the realm. They would take pains at all costs to avoid any prolonged contact or conversation with travelers along the road. Maintaining a haughty and impatient demeanor, typical of ruling family members, would serve them well in that purpose.

They had determined that her stepbrother was currently back from raiding and had taken over the family villa, where he was served by his own slaves and a small harem. He had sold off the former servants as he did not consider them trustworthy after recent events. Their group would proceed directly to Zaynab's family home but arrive during late-night hours. She and her entourage would present themselves to the household, Zaynab's entire face and body covered in the manner of a pious Islamic woman. Whereupon she would unceremoniously and violently take her revenge, her escort was more than sufficient to deter any resistance. Then, she would explain to the servants that the brother had displeased his Caliph by his cowardice in battle. And that Sulayman judged his execution would be even more dishonorable when carried out by a woman. That, of course, was untrue and the brother was a notorious and savage fighter on raids. But the word would get out in time. Finally, they would arrange to have the younger sister collected from her place of refuge and delivered to their keeping for the journey back to Leon.

Alfonso listened intently to the outline of the plan as explained by Wolf and Aoife. He decided he should provide a cadre of his knights and all the mounts, as well as an elaborate carriage captured from the Moors.

"I admire the simplicity and audacity of your plan, my friends and it most certainly has my approval. Among my knights is a sizeable contingent of 'Mozarabs' – Christians who were raised and lived among the Moors in the Caliphate. Some even fought in the Moorish armies. Many fled to ours and the other Christian kingdoms after the death of Almanzor. They have proven themselves and their devotion while fighting alongside us and are superb warriors. I offer you a selection of these to join whatever force you deploy and we also have ample stocks of Moorish arms and armor, along with a splendid and regal Arabic carriage."

Aoife was first to respond. "God's blessings to you, King Alfonso. You have already identified much of what support we had meant to request from you. We have selected from our own ranks, along with Zaynab, what we believe is a dynamic group to play their parts. We would also like to request that the *Campeador* Rodrigo accompany us as well. He has impressed us all. And, despite his years, is a capable and intelligent warrior who speaks the Moorish tongue."

Alfonso looked to Sancho, who nodded while smiling his own approval. He raised one fist in the air, his pure golden bracelet catching a ray of light from the torches and radiating a radiant golden beam.

Then the king proclaimed, "So be it. Confusion to our enemies!"

***

Shortly afterward and very early in the morning, just as the sun was rising, a squad of six galloping Irish Magyars recrossed the border into Leon, where an unlikely party was awaiting them in a wooded clearing. The Magyars, each wearing their usual boiled and molded leather caps covered with otter fur, multi-colored leggings and fitted leather jerkins over wheaten wool tunics, encountered a formidable group of six fully armored Moorish cavalry. They were formed around a splendid, colorfully painted carriage that carried two women in its cabin. One of these was clad in lush silken robes with exquisite gold and jeweled bindings. The other's raiment of robes was of contrastingly drab grey wool bound with rope. Both women were fully veiled.

Two men sat above them on the upper steering platform. One, with his hands on the reins, was older with silver hair peeking out from his crimson turban. A short slashing scimitar was belted at his waist. The other, much younger, was an odd character with wild black hair, which appeared to be spiked with some type of lime. He was clothed in a patched-together tunic of indistinct origin. Both he and the one woman inside were obviously servants of some type.

"The road south and its surroundings are clear for some distance. No foemen, no eyes peering from the woods and only a few simple dwellings of commoners along the way as far as we rode. You won't be detected crossing, though you'll certainly come upon others further south," announced Cael in a halting yet basically understandable version of the tongue of Hispania. Most of the Gaelic leaders had been assiduously attempting to learn enough of the language of their hosts to make themselves understood. Not all Gaels or

Hispanians spoke Latin. To Cael's surprise, he found their language mellifluous and far more charming and sweet than the guttural Danish grunts of the Vikings. Even the two Magyars, now appearing as heavy Moorish cavalry, attached to Alfonso's four Mozarab knights, were able to get the basic meaning of their leader's words.

"Right then, we're off," said Rodrigo, snapping the reins as the four horses pulled on their harnesses.

Four cavalrymen led the convoy with the other two trailing the carriage. Inside the cabin, Zaynab and her 'handmaiden' Saoirse were conversing in a combination of hand signals, simple words in that same Hispanian tongue and occasional flurries of soft laughs. Zaynab, especially, needed this after the tragedies recently inflicted on her by fate. She thought it most fortuitous that her new friend, with her ivory skin, shining emerald eyes and fiery red hair, was fully covered and veiled. Now, only her shining eyes might be a source of attention to the Moors. And Zaynab, like most Arabs, had a natural ability to pick up new languages. This trait was reinforced further by her innate intelligence and curiosity. The two young women, one a veteran of bloody combat and the other soon to be, got along in grand fashion, notwithstanding differences in language and background.

Several hours later, the convoy came to what appeared a military checkpoint along the main road. A group of twelve Berber riders was lounging around a small structure, their horses staked to a railing.

"*As-Salumu Alaykum, Sadiq* – Greetings Friend. And what is your destination?' asked the apparent leader of the guards.

"We are escorting the niece of Caliph Sulayman on her tour of our lands. She wishes to observe for herself the beauty and kindness of all the Caliph's people," replied the foremost of the Arabic riders with an air of obvious authority in his tone.

"Very well, we are both honored and flattered by her visit. Please accept my apologies, though, as my orders are to search, however briefly, any wagons or carriages passing by."

"Just be quick about it and do your best not to disturb her." Then the rider grinned furtively. "She can be a bit of a bitch at times."

The Berber appreciated the jest and smiled back at him, then walked quietly toward the carriage to address the driver. "Greetings to you as well. And what may I ask is this strange apparition beside you, pointing to the other man on the platform?"

"He is the servant of the Princess and a type of savage barbarian from some obscure land. She has a fascination for strange things and he certainly qualifies. Still, though, he's a pleasant enough fellow. Say hello to our Berber friend, slave."

Mornak looked down, cocked his head to one side and let his eyes roll wildly. He took several deep sighing breaths and addressed the curious Berber guard in a staccato and bizarre tone.

"Hello, you ghastly vision from hell, all dressed in pitch black with just your little ebony eyes peering out. And aren't you a grand and magnificent rat-tailed maggot?"

Mornak spoke in the native Pictish tongue of his youth. Then he broke into a mad grin and laughed with enthusiasm.

The Berber recoiled, notwithstanding the apparent good humor of the speaker. "Those are the most horrible sounds I have ever heard uttered. Is he wrong in the head? You can't possibly understand that drivel, can you driver?"

"Not a word and he speaks no civilized language at all. But by now, I've become used to it. And he always seems cheerful and helpful, even if he is peculiar to us."

The guard then moved to the curtained window of the carriage. "On orders of the Caliphate of Cordoba, I must briefly examine the interior. Excuse the interruption."

He gently parted the curtain to peer inside and was immediately presented with an outraged shriek from the interior.

"How dare you! You Berber savage! I am the Caliph's niece, as I'm sure our escort informed you."

Zaynab's angry words were delivered in impeccable and cultured Arabic in the most imperious tone. She glared at the poor guard as if he were slime, then closed the curtain dismissively.

Stepping back, the Berber could only say "Move on," and send them on their way. From the top of the carriage, Mornak waved cordially to him with a good-natured smile.

As the column turned off the main road and onto the worn riding path which led to the home in which she was raised, Zaynab's eyes moistened. She looked out on the apple and pear orchards where she and her younger sister had played together and partaken of the sweet fruit until they made themselves sick. Thinking of her sister and any possible threat to her welfare once again strengthened her courage for the dangerous enterprise she had undertaken. She thanked God for providing her with these valiant allies who would be at her side through the worst. Only a month before, she would have found their kind alien and grotesque. Now, they were prepared to fight at her side and possibly die with her.

"As we will be arriving soon, please refresh us once more on what we might expect on arrival, dear Zaynab," requested Rodrigo. "Feel free to describe it in Arabic and I, in turn, will attempt to translate it for the benefit of Saoirse and Mornak."

"When we reach the gate leading into our home, I expect a servant will be present. This far into the Caliphate, there is no need for armed guards. I will explain yet again that I am the niece of Caliph Sulayman, come to express his deep gratitude and praise for the bold warrior and officer who has been reported as the most valiant of the fighters in our raids against the *Kafirs*.

We'll be allowed through and the guard will enter the villa to announce our arrival. By custom, no proper Muslim woman must ever be unaccompanied outside her home by a single man. I will assure you, Rodrigo and Mornak, my 'servant,' are both at my side along with my most trusted handmaiden. The armed riders will be told to wait outside until the business is concluded. Just past the entry foyer, there is a main room where the audience will take place. We traditionally kept four servants, two men and two women and the killer has most likely maintained that arrangement. You will do the initial talking, Rodrigo. The monster won't recognize me by sight through the robes and veil but if I dare open my mouth to speak too soon, our ruse will be ruined. Still, you need not worry about any elaborate speech. In my hand, I will have a sealed parchment, a 'commendation' from the Caliph. I will move to present it to him, then draw out the dagger it conceals and thrust it into the heart of my mother's murderer. Afterwards, we will take our leave."

Zaynab watched as Rodrigo translated her words into basic Hispanian for the Gaelic woman and the Pict. She felt confident they both comprehended enough when Saoirse put one arm around her shoulder and Mornak nodded with a gentle smile and gave her a confident wink.

Rodrigo then took the time to pass the same information to the cavalrymen escorting them, reminding them once more not to harm any servants or Moorish civilians unless they were first attacked.

It began just as Zaynab had expected. A servant was walking around the grounds and came to the gate when he heard the heavy hoofbeats, which announced their arrival. After listening to Rodrigo's explanation for their visit, the servant bowed gently toward the carriage and led them into the courtyard. He requested that they please wait for the barest moment while he informed the Master. In no time, he returned to them.

"My Master welcomes you and bids you enter. The armed and mounted warriors, however, must wait without. They are free to water and feed their mounts from our stock if they wish. And bread, fruits and fresh water are being brought out to them even as we speak." At that, the door opened and two serving women came out with wicker baskets filled with the viands just mentioned.

*So far so good*, Rodrigo thought to himself, *just as the wise young lady predicted.* The gate guard opened the door for them and Rodrigo entered first, followed by Zaynab, Saoirse and finally Mornak. Passing through the entry hall, they entered the main room, which Zaynab knew so well, with its warmly illuminating torches and colorful tapestries.

But then, as the time-honored and universal soldiers' maxim stipulates: "*No military plan, however well-wrought, survives first contact.*"

Zaynab's brutal stepbrother lounged on a plush, cushioned chair and around him sat four well-formed and fiercely countenanced Moorish warriors. One, who swayed somewhat in his seat, appeared to be a teen. The others were strapping men in their twenties. None wore armor but were all comfortably garbed in loose-fitting garments, though each was belted with his own slashing scimitar and deadly dagger, as was their host. They were a diverse group, a Berber, a *saqalib* and two Arabs. All were veterans and comrades of the *aceifa* raids against Christian lands.

The killer got to his feet, a bit awkwardly it seemed and gave a slight bow with an apparent smirk. But then, he had been told the messenger was a woman. That meant there was no need for sycophantic obeisance.

"Welcome to my home. My comrades and I salute you and bid good health to our Caliph."

All the new arrivals immediately noticed something odd among the Moorish fighting men. The host's words were a bit slurred and his eyes were not fully focused. It seems the group had been quite recently engaged in a bit of *haram* – forbidden revelry. In fact, though none was present, a scented bouquet of good wine wafted through the room. They had expected to find only Zaynab's step-brother and a few servants. The initial surprise of coming upon not one but five armed and dangerous enemies may have been staggering to any other band. But this deceptive group of visitors included a Hispanian *Campeador* of multiple decades, an accomplished Pictish veteran of the Battle of Clontarf and many other brutal clashes, a formidable Gaelic woman spy who had dispatched more than one savage Viking warrior on a dark night in the streets of Dublin and a highly motivated and steadfast Arab girl out to avenge her mother's murder.

Rodrigo began his peroration. "Caliph Sulayman ibn al-Hakam sends his compliments. Tales of your valiant deeds in battle against the Caliphate's enemies have pleased him immensely."

The lounging warriors beheld the assembled visitors with interest. A grey-haired old man with the air of a seasoned warhorse about him was the speaker. He spoke with an accent and was likely a former slave or mercenary of some type. A fully veiled and plainly robed woman who stood with head bowed and eyes to the floor was, of course, a servant. Beside her was an outlandish-looking younger fellow whose clothes were mismatched both in color and fabric, brightly-colored with patches and swathes of both leather and wool. He had an odd bronze-hued visage capped by harshly barbed black hair and his azure eyes appeared to be strangely peering in opposite directions as he surveyed the room. This one was either a servant or someone's pet curiosity. Finally, an obvious woman of nobility stood next to the speaker. Her green silken robes were secured with golden braids and two intelligent and quite focused dark eyes flashed above her gossamer, shimmering veil.

"The Caliph has dispatched our small party to accompany his beloved niece, who will convey to you this scribed commendation which proclaims his deepest appreciation," continued the speaker.

While he was still speaking, he noticed the youngest of the warriors' eyes had closed and he was slumping back in his seat into a languid, wine-induced torpor. It was plain to all that the youth must have been unaccustomed to spending an alcohol-drenched evening of hard drinking with comrades.

As the old man continued his speech, the elegantly dressed young woman strode purposefully toward the master of the house, one hand wrapped around a rolled and sealed ivory parchment bound with a red ribbon. She curtsied and extended the parchment toward his outstretched hand. As he eagerly clasped the document and prepared to open and read its contents, the girl withdrew a long, narrow stiletto that had been concealed inside and thrust it viciously into his heart, almost too swiftly for the eye to follow.

Before the monster's corpse even collapsed to the floor, the serving woman pulled two sheer and weighted black throwing darts from sheaths concealed beneath her robes. As the more sober warriors looked on in horrified astonishment, she brought both her supple, sleek arms back behind her head and cast them with precision and force at two men who were just rising to their feet. One struck home directly beneath a bearded chin and into the soft tissue of the throat. The other was off as the warrior slipped, trying to stand and the dart pierced his shoulder.

The wounded man made the mistake of delaying to try to pull out the long shaft embedded in his flesh. Saoirse used that moment to spring on him, her fighting knife already poised and, making up for her first missed throw, she slit his throat from ear to ear.

Another warrior had time to rise and draw his deadly scimitar, wary of the two women. But as he moved toward them, the strange black-haired servant launched himself from the side, flying through the air to fall upon the last victim. With no way to bring his blade to bear as the assailant pinned his sword arm in a strangling hold, the sword fell. Mornak coiled his left forearm inexorably around his enemy's throat, then grasped one side of the foe's jaw and twisted. There was an audible and sickening crack as the man's spinal column broke and his body was released to collapse to the stone floor. Incredibly, the drunken younger boy had slept through it all. Almost comically, he was snoring loudly and Saoirse noticed his youthful face was flushed in a drunken stupor with the barest trace of a smile. She moved to dispatch him but Rodrigo waved her off. The *Campeador* was right, she concluded. There was no need. So, she merely relieved the recumbent Moor of his scimitar and moved to take a position next to Mornak.

Two of the household servants used that moment to dash into the room, saw the carnage and began shrieking horribly. Zaynab raised one hand in a gesture of peace, putting a finger over her lips, bidding silence.

"You have no need to fear. We mean no harm to you. I have indeed been sent by the Caliph but the actual reason was to punish this coward and traitor to the Caliphate. Our spies have informed us this villain always withdrew from battle at the most critical times, leaving others to die in his place."

She picked up the parchment, which only had one word scribed – *Coward!*

"The Caliph hopes that this execution, even more dishonorable because it was carried out by me, a mere woman, will serve as a warning to any others among the nobles of Toledo who might show inklings of cowardice in the face of the enemy."

The visitors, still wary of their surroundings, moved through the foyer to the front door. Zaynab turned just before leaving and left a final message for the servants.

"Take care of that fool of a young boy who even now sleeps off his sins. Perhaps when he awakens, he will have learned not to drink from the fruit of the grape as do the *kafirs*, nor to evermore associate with traitors and inebriates."

When they returned to their waiting escort, they found only two of the riders standing attentive by their mounts and next to the carriage. They had only enough time to water the horses during the short time the delegation was in the villa. The other two had gone to fetch Zaynab's younger sister from her hidden place of refuge. After mounting and once more boarding the carriage, the party moved out along the same route they had taken earlier, this time northward once again.

It wasn't long before the two cavalrymen, one with a diminutive young girl sharing his saddle, joined them along the way. Her wide eyes shone with radiant glee when she was handed over into the welcoming arms of her older sister. The two hugged each other tightly as they cried and laughed together.

Without excessive delay, they continued north until they came to a precipitous height at a narrow point along the road. To their east, a mountain's slope climbed even further upward and just to their west, a deep crevasse descended down to a rushing river. This was the spot they had chosen earlier. The four horses pulling the carriage were unhitched from their harnesses and a new saddle was strapped onto each of them. Mornak and Rodrigo placed kindling wood and straw into the carriage's cabin and struck a few sparks. Each took up a wooden harness trace and, when the flames started to engulf the wagon, they pushed it over the slope to careen and crash down in flames until whatever remained splashed into the river.

Rodrigo, Mornak and Saoirse each mounted a horse and the two sisters sat together on the last of them. Saoirse was pleased to see that Zaynab handled her mount well, even though she had only received rudimentary training in horsemanship. The young Arab woman had overcome every difficult challenge with fearless determination. By now, Aoife and Saoirse both thought of her as a kindred sister.

The road continued downward from there until they once again reached the lowlands and came to a fork. A logical spot for a Moorish checkpoint, the band counted their luck that it was unoccupied now. Now they split into two smaller groups to move more furtively with a smaller footprint and a lesser chance of observation and interception. Rodrigo and one of King Alfonso's Mozarab knights, both familiar with the terrain in the Caliphate's northern lands, led each group. The plan called for staying off the main roads while maintaining the same general course along parallel routes. They rode cautiously but steadily throughout the night and, by noon of the next day, each group had safely crossed the border into the relative safety of the Leonese kingdom.

# Chapter 14

## Affairs of the Court

One week after the return of the rescue mission to Toledo, a familiar small council sat together in a comfortable circle within King Alfonso's chambers. The only new addition was Rodrigo. The purpose was to discuss what had been learned from that mission and from that of the six teams that had conducted the long-range reconnaissance operations deep into the Caliphate. The king, after conferring with his advisor Sancho, had approved that plan as well, though with one proviso. Each of the Irish spy/scout teams must also include one of the King's Mozarab knights who would also be in attired in Moorish garb. This had the strength of including a warrior familiar with the terrain and local languages, critical to such a deep probe. It was hoped the difficulty of the language barrier between the Irish couple and the Hispanian would be overcome by good fellowship and common purpose. Ultimately, the strength of this approach in gaining even deeper intelligence far outweighed any potential disadvantages. Wolf provided the initial summary of the two separate operations.

"As you're no doubt aware, Alfonso."

By now the two were comfortable referring to each other as familiarly as weapon brothers.

"Both the effort in Toledo and the deep penetration of the Caliphate were conducted with no casualties, at least on our side."

The Irish giant grinned and continued in his best monastery-educated Latin.

"Aoife, Sancho and I have spent time with your own Intelligence Chiefs here to gauge the reaction to the execution of the Moorish raider by the Caliph's 'niece' and it has exceeded our expectations."

Sancho nodded to the King and Wolf went on. "Though Zaynab's brother was a murderous villain in our eyes, he was considered a brave and loyal warrior by the better Arabic noble families of Toledo. They considered it the mother of all insults to their honor that some woman from Cordoba decided to judge and assassinate their friend and comrade.

Sulayman had denied having any part in the deed, insisting it must have been the result of a drunken brawl among party goers, which put even more shame on the Toledo aristocracy. And now they consider their Caliph a liar and are concerned for their own safety. Relations between the Moors of Toledo and Cordoba have never been good and, exactly as we planned, now they are even further and perhaps irreparably strained," Sancho added.

Rodrigo took over to give his King his own first-hand account. "I was so impressed with all the members of our unlikely 'strike force', my King. Zaynab, Saoirse and Mornak were spectacular in action. I'd welcome any one of them to be my *Campeador*. In retrospect, it is quite obvious the servants believed every word we said to them was genuine and truthful. And, the boy warrior present witnessed our arrival as well, even if he did pass out drunk before the ending. One wonders if he still has his head."

None in the chamber, however, seemed to feel much sympathy for the miscreant youth.

"Toledo and its outlying districts and peoples are among the most important of the holdings in the Caliphate. If we have contributed to dissension, vexations and chaos there, that counts as a significant first of what we must hope will be many more victories to come," Alfonso pronounced, manifestly pleased.

"And we have also furthered God's work by rescuing an innocent young girl from almost certain death at the hands of a monster and reunited her with her loving sister. Both girls are now safe and well, I hope."

"Both are comfortably and welcomingly ensconced here in the city of Leon amidst the bustling household of the good Christian and kind merchant who is the uncle of Zaynab's former tutor. He and his wife already consider both girls to be the daughters they never had. And the lasses have two young boys, one still a toddler, for brothers now," said Aoife in answer.

"And finally, Zaynab has offered her services if needed in any capacity in the future. I imagine there may come a time when she may be of great value to our cause."

"Agreed, she has earned our appreciation and most certainly our trust," responded the king. "And what of our six teams of riders?"

Wolf again continued the report. "Our intention was at first simply to get 'eyes on' potential targets but your suggestion, dear King, to include a knowledgeable Mozarab warrior with each team gave us greater insight than we otherwise could have attained. It also had the advantage of increasing the potential striking power of each of these probes.

The riders tasked with covering the greatest distance, to the distant south on the outskirts of the city of Granada, capital of the province of the same name, were able to confirm the most striking discovery. The wealthy city and province, strategically located, are in essence completely independent from the Caliphate. Notably, Granada is under the control of a Berber dynasty known as the Zirids. This same dynasty also rules much of the north of Africa, homeland of the Caliphate's reinforcing Berber tribes. The team covertly observed an official delegation from the Caliph arriving at the gates of Granada and being turned away amidst threats of their destruction.

"The situation you've described confirms what some of our sources have told us, though we were unsure whether Granada was still sending tribute to the Caliph. Based on what you just said, that no longer seems to be the case. Excellent!" said Sancho, grinning with pleasure."

Wolf paused and then continued once more. "Our riders who deployed to Toledo were able to return with further confirmation of the effects of our rescue mission. Another advantage we had was the cultural and religious hospitality of the Moors to other 'believers.' We're told this tradition dates to ancient times in the Middle East, where trade was precarious and travelers, of necessity, had to rely on the kindness of strangers. Who knows? In any case, our Mozarabs, holding to their own stories, were able to casually strike up short conversations with locals of all castes and learn things our Irish teams could never have discovered on their own."

"This business of 'hospitality' and 'kindness of strangers' still doesn't make up for the enemy's religiously sanctioned doctrine of deception and lying to Christians – *Taqiyya,"* sneered Sancho, who had been deceived by Moors during treaty and diplomatic meetings on many occasions over his decades of military service to various Christian kings.

Remembering King Brian's dealings with various Viking Chieftains years earlier, Wolf could only nod in agreement before continuing.

"Other teams found the same type of discomfort and disdain for Cordoba in general and Sulayman in specific, throughout the various provinces of the

Caliphate. Though none had grown so bold as Granada in completely rejecting that Caliph's authority, there seems to remain beneath a seething anger. Questions are also raised about the disappearance of Hisham, who many remember fondly.

"Of course, with our Irish Magyar riders, fiery Gaelic woman scouts and gallant Christian Mozarab knights, there were also several opportunities to conduct a few select offensive and forceful acts to further the sentiments of dissolution and disunity within the Caliphate. On two occasions, our teams were able to intercept and annihilate tribute-collecting delegations dispatched to the outlying provinces from Cordoba. These tax collectors were far too comfortable in their surroundings, showing little awareness of their surroundings. And with only four cavalrymen for escorts, our teams were able to strike unawares, quick as lightning. Two of the enemy would be feathered by Magyar arrows before they even knew they had a whirlwind of three slashing and stabbing *kafir* devils in their midst."

Wolf was now fully energized and grinning broadly, always most enthusiastic when lauding acts of valiant combat.

Sancho's earlier sneer was now replaced with a contented and good-humored smile. "And King Alfonso, I'm pleased to report, three of these teams returned with the booty 'liberated' from Sulayman's tax collectors. All of this has been deposited into Leon's treasury, taking its place among the gold and silver already there."

"One team took a quite different approach, however," Aoife added.

"In this case, there were women among the tribute-collecting delegation. Wolf has always commanded that none of us ever harm any innocent woman or child of the enemy. No doubt a lesson from his own childhood." She gazed tenderly at her beloved, intimately familiar with his tragically painful experiences.

'As am I also quite aware of your own sorrowful girlhood, *a stór,*' Wolf said to himself, his eyes fixed with unbridled love on hers.

"A small group of fierce warriors from the province had been sent out to meet the Cordobans," Aoife said.

"Apparently, they wanted to prevent the Caliphate's people from entering their city and spare themselves the shame of ceremoniously greeting them within its walls. After reluctantly handing over the tribute, they turned around to return home. Our team struck them from the woodlands at the side of the road at the next turn. All four of the warriors were slain quickly, their bodies left conspicuously in the middle of the trail. The armed Cordoban tax collectors, with the women among them, were left unharmed. The intent, of course, was to convey the impression of the Caliph's rage at his delegation not being welcomed into the city."

Aoife was pleased that the reconnaissance teams never established a set pattern. Some had gained information from observation and surveillance. Others struck swiftly and decisively. All physical contact with the Moors was fleeting and the actual origin of the strike teams was never in danger of compromise.

"Based on what we've learned from all of this and from the similar reports of our people spread throughout the Caliphate, Sulayman's control is most tenuous and degrading rapidly. It is not just rivalries based simply on geography – the provinces and cities," said Sancho. "The anatomy of the Caliphate itself exacerbates the problem. Berbers, *Saqaliba,* Arabs and *dhimmis* of various sorts all contend to elevate their positions within the realm. This lack of unity and innate cohesion is a decided weakness. If Sulayman is perceived as favoring any one of these groups, the others become resentful." Sancho's words reflected his usual optimism.

"Thus has the situation presented itself in the Caliphate for generations, yet the Moors continue to hold almost the entirety of the lands of our peninsula," countered the King.

"We ourselves are divided into small and cramped kingdoms, though without the particular issues of the Moors. They seem to devise some diabolical means to overcome their weaknesses despite all appearances."

The time seemed ripe for Wolf to speak up once more. "You're well aware of the recent arrival of a band of monks from the Abbey at Cluny. One of these, Brother Cillian, has turned out to be an Irishman, much to my surprise. All those young men are wise and learned beyond their years. Cillian's particular field of study has been the history of the Moors and their faith here in Hispania."

The Irish leader noted expressions of surprise and interest come upon the faces of the King and Sancho.

"I've had the pleasure of experiencing several enlightening and rewarding conversations with this very engaging clergyman. And King Alfonso, Cillian has developed his own assessment of what 'diabolical means', the enemy has employed to maintain dominance.

"First is the combination of reverence, loyalty and deference that the Muslims feel they owe to a divinely chosen leader. The Caliph is both the head of state and the supreme religious leader. All have traditionally viewed the nobility of the Syrian Ummayads as embodying everything that is required. Even the Chancellor Almanzor, the Caliphate's most successful leader on the battlefield and a scourge to Christendom, never dared to proclaim himself Caliph. Instead, he kept the weak and ineffectual Caliph Hisham, a good *Ummayad*, in puppet status.

"Now it appears to us and apparently to many others in the Caliphate that Sulayman has had Hisham eliminated and appointed himself Caliph, a miscalculation on his part. The diverse warriors of the Caliphate need a transcendent and heavenly-inspired leader they can believe in. Sulayman is failing."

The assembly was listening to Wolf's account of the monk's judgement with riveted attention to every word. Those veterans of Clontarf present were also keenly engrossed as well as surprised. Their Battle Captain had not yet shared the details of his talks with Cillian to any of them, not even Aoife.

"Second, one of the reasons for the tyrant, Almanzor's, success was his zealous and repeated calls for *aceifas*, those frequent deep and extensive raids into Christian lands to gain booty – cattle, slaves and anything else of value. And in the instance of his sacking of Santiago de Compostela, out of pure hatred and spite for Christianity. Historically, back to ancient times, both Arabs and the Berbers, the latter increasingly becoming the strongest component of the Moorish warriors, have cultures rooted in raids for foodstuffs, slaves and, in the case of the Arabs, even for water.

"Those frequent raids kept the Moorish armies occupied, constantly tested in combat, battle hardened and confident in their leadership under Almanzor. The captured booty, after being fairly distributed among the worthiest of the warriors, served to increase the wealth and splendor of the Caliphate. But there have been no successful and extensive *aceifas* similar to those of Almanzor of late."

Wolf paused to let Cillian's assessment of past Moorish success sink in among his comrades. Alfonso and Sancho had been nodding in agreement throughout the Irishman's peroration, recognizing all he described, yet never before had they heard these obvious truths put together in such a concise and revealing manner.

"Your monastic countryman, Wolf, seems clever and discerning but he sounds more like a frustrated fighting man than a pious monk," Alfonso exclaimed. "I do hope we can keep him among us for some duration."

"Exactly what I thought as well after speaking to him, King. He reminds me intensely of my favorite tutor of history while I was a student at the monastery of Inisfallen. Perhaps they are related."

Quiet laughter reigned in the room for a bit after the more serious and somber earlier ambience. Thus far, they had spoken of events already undertaken and their impact on the current situation. All realized there was a continued need to devise a dynamic and effective means to further exploit the weaknesses of their foes and, more importantly, to lay the groundwork for the eventual expulsion of their long-time oppressive foreign occupiers.

Cormac, who had listened quietly throughout, now chose to give a recommendation of his own.

"With your indulgence, King Alfonso, having learned much from our council this day, I have some ideas for us to move forward."

"Prince Cormac, your sage advice is always welcome here. Do carry on," answered the King.

"Our efforts thus far have met with success but they have been limited in scope. We should continue them, however, in preparation for some greater and more decisive action soon. I don't mean to imply we can win all in one great stroke but we can most assuredly strike a lethal blow that will eventually lead to the disintegration of the Caliphate. Once the Caliphate is destroyed, we Christians can, over time, defeat whatever splintered Moorish holdouts remain in sequence. It may not happen overnight but if we can ignite the sparks of the Moors' destruction, your people will again regain their country for themselves."

Then it was Aoife's turn. "Sulayman knows he is in a most hazardous position. Our recent diversionary and disruptive enterprises have no doubt hastened his desperation. However, like most of the Arabic nobility, he is intelligent and resilient, having recovered from near disaster in the past. While Faolán has been in discussion with Brother Cillian, King Alfonso, I have spent time myself with your various spy chiefs."

She cast a sly smile in Wolf's direction. "They have inferred the Caliph's strengths and weaknesses from his past actions. They and I agree. Sulayman must emulate Almanzor if he wants to hold the Caliphate together. He has already committed the mistake of doing away with the most recent Hisham, it seems. So, his wisest and safest option now is to prepare for a large-scale *aceifa.* As the grandest, wealthiest and most troublesome of the Christian kingdoms, Leon will be the likely objective. If he can strike here, return with booty and leave some indelible stain upon the kingdom, as did Almanzor at Santiago De Compostela, he will be perceived as being the strong and chosen one. If we can preempt that, his and the Caliphate's time will not be long."

The king had been keenly listening to all his advisors, one hand stroking his chin, the other on the hilt of his sword, his knuckles whitening at various times.

"My friends, you all have my heartfelt gratitude. I am blessed to be surrounded by such comrades and allies as you. I can find no fault in anything any of you has said this day. I believe now we must have two priorities. The first is to increase our efforts in discovering any buildup of the enemy's hosts as he prepares his attack. I don't think this will be a simple raid.

Secondly, we must, in turn, prepare to mass our own armies for a first strike before the enemy can consolidate on his chosen target. This must be accomplished while concealing our own intentions and capitalizing on surprise to conduct a swift and decisive assault. We have talked enough for now. In the coming days, let us begin to plan our counterstrike for Hispania's eventual liberation."

***

After a sumptuous meal at the king's generous table, the visitors decided to enjoy a pleasant walk back to their various places of lodging on such a fine early evening in the mild Spring weather. There was a cool but comfortable breeze filtered by surrounding woodlands and the mood was cheerful despite their earlier discussions of more somber matters.

Wolf, Aoife and Cormac walked abreast along the well-packed path, others others strung out behind them engaged in genial conversations of their own. At a certain point, Aoife gazed up questioningly at Wolf, who nodded gently toward her. Then he fell back to join Rodrigo and the others.

"Prince Cormac, may I speak alone with you for a wee bit?" asked Aoife, her voice soft and lilting yet with a serious tone of concern.

“Since when do you start ‘Prince Cormacing’ me, dear Aoife?’ he answered jovially, since the two had always been as close as endeared uncle and niece.

“Cormac, you know well how I’ve always loved you as Wolf’s savior and felt of you as family to myself. From the earliest days, no other has ever come to you asking for advice and guidance as much as I have.”

The expression on her sweet face was imbued with unfeigned affection and respect.

“Now then, lass, nothing you can say could ever diminish the warmth in my heart for you. Spit it out.”

Aoife then pointed to a crossing just ahead of them, where another well-maintained path meandered slightly eastward. “Let us go by this road, it doesn’t take us far out of our way.” They both had become quite familiar with the paths, trails and roads around the King’s residence in the time since they had arrived in Leon.

As they walked along the route indicated, Aoife began.

“You do know another of my dear friends and trusted advisors is the Lady Helena. She is so wise, experienced and kind. And, in my case, she has the added advantage of being a woman.” Aoife smiled at him with certain knowledge he would not be offended by the jest. “I’m sure you agree with my opinion of our Greek lady friend, Cormac?”

“Most assuredly, Aoife and as you certainly know, Helena and I have also become quite close over the months, especially during the trying times leading up to and immediately after our battle at Clontarf and loss of our great King there.”

“I am quite aware of that, Cormac and thus the reason I wished to speak with you.” She stopped to look him in the eye before continuing. “Helena and Pyrrhus have never been forced to take on any of the hardships they have endured at our sides. Both have gone through all this adversity willingly, thanks to their friendship with us and our cause. At this point, I consider them as Irish as we are. You and Helena were ever at each other’s sides when not actively engaged in battle with our enemies or preparing for further battles. However, since your arrival here in Leon, you seem not to have so much time for her.”

A certain sternness hardened Aoife’s emerald green eyes as she continued to gaze up at the older man.

"Well, we've all been occupied with forays, planning, intelligence gathering and diplomacy in the time we've been here, Aoife. Don't you agree?" said Cormac by way of explanation.

"Aye and your 'diplomacy' with the Queen Mother Elvira has most definitely occupied much of your time here Cormac, or don't you agree?"

"Now then, Queen Elvira is a figure of the utmost respect to all here in Leon and she remains their beloved Queen Mother. Is it not natural that I should cultivate a warm friendship with her to gain her trust and learn from her? 'Tis to the benefit of us all. You must surely understand." Cormac replied in chosen words that he thought provided a virtuous and altogether innocent explanation.

"And have the two of ye been merely that, Cormac, naught but friends and allies?" Aoife's arms were now folded across her breast, her fingers tapping along the sleeves of her white cotton blouse as she stood facing him directly.

"Aoife, I know you think of me as a mellow and seasoned elder but I'm not as aged and time-worn as your young eyes might seem to view me. Can you not believe women of a certain age, yes, perhaps somewhat older, may find me attractive and take comfort in my company?"

"Enough, dear Cormac." Aoife would not be stopped. "Everything I say is spoken out of my respect and fondness for you, for the welfare of our people on our quest here and, yes, out of my friendship for Helena. You've not even taken the time to realize how you have hurt her and I feel you may be making a bit of a fool of yourself with these antics with the Queen. The women of Alfonso's court speak of it with open amusement. They say you are Elvira's latest shiny toy but she now may have eyes on a newer bauble."

Cormac's face reflected his embarrassment and surprise as Aoife continued without pause. "A newer visiting delegation has arrived in recent days to present to the king's court."

At that, Cormac interrupted her. "Yes, I've heard; two or three quite effeminate looking blusterers from some distant little land in the far northeast of Europe. They're supposed to be nobles seeking the king's support in a dispute among royals there. They offer nothing of use to the king and have naught to do with us or Alfonso's truly pressing concerns."

Aoife raised a hand to stop him. "Well, I'm all woman, Cormac and I find the countenance of Duke Vladislaus of Moravia anything but effeminate. He is quite handsome and elegant. And I note ye've not called on the Queen Mother since their arrival, nor has she requested your company even once."

"You can't be saying Elvira is wasting any of her time with that supercilious dandy? And I have most certainly never intended to hurt dear Helena. You've given me much to ponder, Aoife." Cormac wasn't sure how he felt but none of it was good.

"You must do more than ponder, dear friend. You must be shown. Only then can you take the proper steps to make it all up to Helena and regain your proper course. That's why I chose this path. You know what is on the side of the road not much further ahead, do you not?"

Cormac nodded his head. "Aye, the Queen Mother maintains another of her small villas there, this one to be close to the King."

"Indeed. And, since it's not quite dark, we're to pay a short visit to say 'Good Evening.' If we're told the Queen is otherwise engaged, perhaps you'll take the hint."

Aoife also felt slightly guilty for putting her good friend through all of this but consoled herself knowing it was for his own good.

Presently, the two companions came upon the quaint but distinguished-looking structure, which was surrounded by a low rock wall with a front gate manned by two burly Leonese guards. Each looked upon Cormac in shocked surprise, instantly recognizing both him and Aoife.

"God's greetings, Miguel and Ferdinand. Might we bid a short 'Good Evening' to the Queen Mother on our return walk home to our comrades?" requested Cormac with pleasant familiarity. Of course, the two stout soldiers knew him well. They bore him the same admiration and respect all natural warriors feel toward each other. He felt the same way toward them and they'd all become friends by now.

"Prince Cormac. I hesitate to say but you're not at all expected. I...ummm...I'm not sure if the Queen is disposed to receive visitors now. I'll be delighted to tell her you stopped by." Miguel was noticeably unnerved, flushed and completely uncomfortable. Then he added in a low voice, "Cormac, it is my fondest wish to fight at your side, or at least, in the same battle as you against our common enemies. I appeal to you now as a friend and hopeful weapon brother, not to pursue this visit at this time." His eyes were pleading and somewhat ashamed.

The other guard had gone to the villa's door upon the pair's arrival and he returned alone now, sadly shaking his head. So, with a cheerful 'Good Night, my friends,' Cormac and Aoife walked back to the road, taking up a brisk pace.

"I'm so sorry, Cormac," was all Aoife could bring herself to say at the moment.

"Not at all, dear Aoife, I'm the one who is sorry. Have a wee look back at the upper window of the villa."

Aoife turned around. Peering down at them from the window with its parted curtain were two faces – the luxuriously dark-haired and luminous visage of the Queen Mother and a pale blue-eyed man with long blonde hair - Vladislaus.

"When we arrive back at your lodgings, Aoife, I'll say good night, then I must hurry immediately off to find Helena. I pray it's not too late." Aoife hugged the dear older man with both arms, her head pressed to his chest, then they both picked up their pace.

# Chapter 15

## Galicians, Milesians and Gaels

For obvious reasons of prudence and secrecy, Wolf kept the results of the king's decisions on his two priorities for confronting the Moors from all but his usual trusted leaders. But now, another had been accepted into this close-knit group. The colossal, still young, Battle Captain considered the erudite and amiable Cluniac a most valuable asset for both him and King Alfonso. Besides, after all, wasn't he a man of God, a learned scholar and an Irishman? That alone assured he passed muster, thought Wolf, a bit humorously. And now, the two of them sat together around a small fire in the early evening, leaning against fallen timber logs and drinking locally brewed beer. Though most of the Hispanians preferred wine, some, especially Asturians and Galicians, loved their ale.

"Shortly after our arrival, Brother Cillian, one of the Galicians among our allies referred to we Irish fondly as his 'cousins' and with some degree of familial certainty. We are most assuredly the same people as the Scots and also somewhat similar to the Welsh, through perhaps a slightly more distant kinship. But I never heard of these Galicians until we set foot on these shores. Perhaps, you know of what he spoke?" asked Wolf.

"I believe I do," answered the monk. "Before the Romans arrived, much of Hispania was populated by various tribes of Celts. Many of them became Romanized and later came under the rule of the Suevi and other Germanic groups. However, the two northwestern provinces of Asturias and, especially, Galicia not only maintained a continuing Celtic cultural identity but also a fierce sense of independence, successfully expelling Moorish invaders during the most difficult times. Both Asturians and Galicians are ferocious fighters and the terrain did not suit the preferred Moorish styles of combat. Also, both peoples formerly spoke a decidedly Celtic language but sadly it isn't so prevalent any longer as it was in past times."

"That is indeed tragic, Cillian. We and the Scots are easily understandable when we speak with each other. I must admit it's quite a bit more difficult to ken what the Welsh are on about when they speak in their own tongue, a few words perhaps," interjected Wolf.

"Nevertheless, they still hold on to that old culture and consider themselves of a different breed than their fellow Hispanians. If you wander around Galicia, you will find thousands of hill forts; perfect matches to the many in Ireland still there since the time of the Druids. And then, in the fifth and sixth centuries, Celtic Britons fleeing the pagan Saxons arrived in Galicia from Britannia, even as others escaped to Amorica in western France, where they still thrive. These Britons, apparently feeling at home among their own in Galicia, soon lost their own language and melted into the Galician fabric, indistinguishable from their new countrymen.

"The Galicians have their own Celtic style of music, which is said to be similar to our own. They even have their own bagpipes, similar to our own *píob mhór*, great pipes. They call their version the *gaita*. That, I reckon, is what that Galician fellow was meaning when he called our people his cousins."

"That is most interesting. There are some pipers among our Irish and Scots Highlander warriors who have brought along their own instruments. You're giving me the kernel of an idea to meld the Galicians even further to the cause of King Alfonso and all Christian Hispania," said Wolf, whose affinity for history was always palpable.

"In your time at Inisfallen Wolf, were you told anything of a people called the Milesians?" asked Cillian pointedly.

"I have once heard the name before but with some skepticism from my dear teacher of history. He was a monk like yourself. A good and devout man of the cloth but he had no use for using church doctrine to create a false history. He explained a group of clerics from around Ireland were just beginning to develop a grand epic of the origins of our people by imparting elements from the bible onto some of the ancient pagan myths from the time of the druids and claiming they are the truths of our history. My instructor monk would have nothing to do with them."

"Your history teacher was quite correct and he was a wise man indeed," Cillian said. "I'm aware of those efforts and share his skepticism. The old tales, replete with fantastic myths of giants, magical bards, wizards and creatures of all types, are wonderful but not to be taken literally, especially not when overlaid with biblical slants. These clerics' intents may be innocent – to unite the Irish around a common history and give us a sense of purpose but that should never be done by contrivance. That only serves to distort our faith and the true history of our peoples."

Wolf listened to his friend with fervent interest, having heard something similar from his foster father, King Brian, when he was a teen just back from his time at Innisfallen.

Cillian continued. "One of those old tales from the so-called 'Book of Invasions' speaks of the Milesians, a tribe of Celts from the northwest of Hispania, just one of many different groups of tribes who supposedly invaded Ireland in successive waves. These Milesians are claimed by some clerics as the original Gaels. Ironically, parts of that story may indeed hold some aspects of truth when we observe the Galicians of today."

"I'm curious Cillian, did you ever, by chance, have the pleasure of meeting with King Brian yourself? Some of what you say puts me in mind of long discussions I had with him on this and related matters in times past."

"I regret to say I never had an opportunity to meet our former great king, though when I was a boy, I saw him from afar as he was assuming the High Kingship in Armagh. He struck me as much a scholar as a great warrior. You are fortunate indeed, Wolf, to have had such a close and abiding relationship with such a magnificent man," replied the Cluniac monk.

"I count myself blessed that first Cormac rescued me from Viking bondage after the murder of my parents and then I was taken in by High King Brian. He not only saw I was properly educated but also intensely trained in the ways of war by a most skilled master. Though there were days when I felt the training was perhaps too intense and I just wanted to stop and run away from it all. But the grizzled man who taught me the ways of weapons, muscle and grit never allowed me to quit. Only later did I learn he was also a comrade and former trainer of King Brian when he too was but a novice warrior, aiding his brother Mahon in battling the Vikings of Limerick."

Wolf was silent for a moment, then looked to his friend with a conspiratorial twinkle in his gold-flecked eyes. "But the king saw fit to keep some secrets to himself and but a few closest family members, which I'm proud to say included me."

Noting Wolf's visage was one of amusement and mischief, Cillian dared to ask, "And am I lucky enough to be about to hear the details of one of these royal secrets?"

Wolf broke into a huge grin, his broad, prognathous jaw and flashing ivory teeth taking on the aspect of the fierce maw of his namesake for a brief instant. "Now the first thing you must understand, Brother Cillian, is that Brian was a devout and committed Christian whose faith in the divine trinity was absolute. He proved that in everything he fought for throughout his life."

"No man could ever doubt Brian Boru's zeal in defending our faith and any who did so would be cursed to hell," the monk replied.

"And you also know that even though we Irish have become good, pious and civilized Christians by now, there are yet some believers and seers of the old religion who withdraw themselves into remote wooded glades and hidden warrens beneath scattered hills, stealthily watching the affairs of our island, only injecting themselves into our lives on rare occasions."

Cillian answered, "That I know indeed, early on our church tried first to bring them to Christ's light and, when that failed, banish them. But now we're more tolerant of their presence. We've even identified some of their pagan gods and goddesses with our own dear saints, Saint Bridget being the most notable.

"But did you know that King Brian loved our countrymen of the old religion and sought them out for advice in their shrouded dwelling places on many occasions? He was always furtive about doing so lest he create the wrong impression. He never did so with any belief in the pagan gods or rituals but for a more practical purpose. Brian was convinced these people, especially the ones who still call themselves druids, knew things about our land and our people, things that have long been forgotten by us and lost in the mists of time."

"That I did not know," replied the Monk. "But Brian was right to be secretive about such assignations with pagans. Not all my brothers of the cloth are as tolerant as I am. I just find the whole subject fascinating."

Cillian was smiling openly, obviously unoffended upon learning this one of Brian's secrets.

"When you spoke of the Milesians here in Hispania, I recalled one of the related stories told me by the king. As far as the druids were concerned, Brian informed me, we Irish are indeed Celtic but this aspect of our character is confined to our culture and language, not our blood. The vast masses of our Irish and Scottish people and even many of the 'Celts'of Britannia were here long before the coming of the various continental Celtic adventurers. The druids claim we are the *first people.* They don't believe in Noah's great flood but rather that much of northern and western Europe was covered by ice in antiquity. As those great sheets of ice retreated, first from the coastal areas of Hispania and France, then Britannia, Scotland and Ireland, our ancestors, primitive and just advancing from working with only stone to primitive bronze, crawled into the newly open and lovely lands left behind. All of this was well before the times of the Celts and Gauls of Greek and Roman times."

Cillian interjected. "Some of my brother monks and I have suspected as much. We believe the stone circles, standing stones, dolmens and menhirs of Ireland, Scotland, Britannia and Amorica were not raised by Celtic peoples under druidic guidance but by a quite different race of people and far, far earlier," Cillian agreed. "And any claims of tying these ancient ones to some Mideast origin to reinforce some biblical connection defies true scholarship."

"That is exactly what Brian came to believe as well. He acknowledged the later arrival of Celtic travelers to Ireland. The Druids he met with explained the multitude of the first peoples adopted over time to the advanced culture, language and religion of the Celts. Yet the newcomers were never vast in numbers and became absorbed into the fabric of the far greater original inhabitants. Some of these later arriving Celts could have been very much like the Galicians," Wolf explained. "But then, they would have reflected the same pattern. The *first people* in northwest Hispania would have absorbed Celtic migrants from further east and north, just as would occur later in Ireland and Britannia."

If I follow that logic correctly," Cillian interjected, "we and the Galicians could indeed be the same race, Celtic by culture and original peoples by blood."

"And if that is the case, then the myth of the Milesians from Galicia who became the original Gaels of Ireland may have strains of inadvertent truth. I've noted how similar in appearance we are to the Galicians, Asturians and even the few Basque people I've encountered since we've been here. There is a clear difference between them and Germanic Saxons, Scandinavian Vikings and Mediterranean folk, all of whom bear features which seem to reflect some mixture with more exotic strains. All of this is interesting and ironically amusing to contemplate, at least that's what King Brian felt," Wolf concluded.

"Agreed. Yet all men are God's creatures and, independent of origin, will always be welcomed into the arms of Christ's church." Cillian made the sign of the cross and smiled up at his friend sitting across from him, in the light of the small fire.

The two sat in silence for some time, gazing into the flaming embers, just as their ancestors and all men had done for millennia. There was simply something about the flames of a controlled, warming fire that imbued a sense of both comfort and contemplation in men and women sitting contentedly around one. While Wolf pondered their words with both wonderment and practicality as to their mission, Cillian examined his own line of thinking. He truly felt that all were brothers and needed to embrace the gift of the true faith to bring everyone together.

"Now then, *Cú Sidhe,* care to share with your confessor your 'kernel of an idea' from our talks this day?" quipped Cillian whimsically.

*Cú Sidhe* - hound of the Celtic mythical and ancient fairy people, the *Cú Sídhe* – was a monstrous beast of legend, a huge black hunting dog of *Crom Dubh*, the old black twist of the many glooms. The monstrous brute hunted in silence but when it did let out a dreadful howl, many times its victim would perish from that terror alone.

"I'm glad my Viking captors never laid that name upon me. I prefer their *Ulf Hreda* or Wolf the Quarrelsome," replied Wolf humorously.

"After your tales of the Galicians, I've a notion to lead a sizeable band of our warriors along with an impressive but smaller escort of noble Leonese knights to confer with the leaders of our 'cousins' in Galicia. I realize the Galicians are subject to Leon and King Alfonso but as you said, they have always had a commendable attitude of Celtic independence and the King has, in turn, ever treated them kindly. Perhaps we can encourage and motivate them to join even more enthusiastically with us in the coming trials against the Moorish foe.

Wolf continued. "We can also make a grand spectacle of it; an extravagant display as King Brian did during his dramatic circuits across Ireland and the ostentatious visits of the *Laochra* and other elites of his warriors to impress his Viking subjects in Weisfjord and Vadrafjord. Except that we will go not to intimidate our hosts but to cement and strengthen the already good relationships and I suppose, in our case, kinships. We're not able to take our entire contingent while many are engaged in continuing reconnaissance and raids with our Hispanian allies. I believe several hundred will suffice, assuring we include a good number of Spartans and Magyars clothed and armed in their accustomed manner. We should, however, also include with us those musicians and their instruments I mentioned earlier, along with some of our women warriors. I can already envision a resulting magnificent *Feischeoil* of music, dancing and storytelling."

"I should like to witness that myself," agreed Brother Cillian, with a cheerful grin.

***

Not many days later, after conferring with the king and Sancho, who both concurred enthusiastically, an intriguing column moved north from the heartland of Leon to cross into the lands of the Galicians. Thirty splendidly outfitted Leonese knights carrying the banners of Leon were accompanied by a marching group of fifty elite Celtic *Laochra*, kilt-clad Scots highlanders among them, forty Spartan heavy infantry, their red cloaks swirling about them and thirty Magyars. These were now mounted on fine Hispanian steeds and clad in their multi-colored leggings, otter skin caps and loose tunics with bows sheathed and strapped to their shoulders, thin lances crossed over their backs. Another thirty assorted Irish warriors, scouts and their leaders, most of them mounted, made up the rest of the group.

Leading the group were Sancho and a Leonese knight of Galician origin, along with Cormac, Wolf and the rest of their leadership group. As this was a mission of peace and fellowship, the column was not arrayed in battle-ready formation but more in the manner of a parade of celebration. Cael, leading the Magyars, was delighted to have at his side Luta Einarsdottir, her long blonde hair trailing in the gentle breeze.

Riding alongside Wolf and Cormac were Aoife and, to Aoife's welcome approval, Helena Lakepeno. Cormac was even more delighted, wishing his lady were riding in his arms in the same saddle as they had when her Greek ship had first arrived and she was escorted to Cashel, King Brian's court. Four of Aoife's scouts, including Saoirse, along with Pyrrhus, were also on hand. They had decided to leave the Icelanders behind, given the Galicians' recent history with Vikings and were relieved when Keli informed them, he was not the least offended.

He laughed and told Wolf, "They're your 'cousins', not ours. Please enjoy your revelry while we Christian Vikings remain on guard in the field of battle with our Hispanian allies. Besides, many of my fellows have become quite good friends with some of the finest Hispanian ladies here in Leon's capital and these beautiful women would sorely miss their company if they were to be away in Galicia."

In the still mild mid-spring weather, the march had been a comfortable one; the going was a bit slower, though, as they moved only as rapidly as those on foot could maintain. All of the settlements along the way cheered them as their parade had been earlier proclaimed throughout the realm and announced in person by advanced riders. As they trekked through the countryside of Galicia, the Irish could not help but note the similarity between this province and their own homeland. Both were cool, green and moist, brimming with verdant woodlands, lush meadows and rushing rivers.

As they drew closer to the coastline, the tangy scent of ocean breezes became more pronounced. Both Celtic lands contained large and small hills, as well as low mountains and lofty cliffs along many portions of their coastlines. It seemed it wasn't just that Galicia's people were very much like them, so was its landscape and climate. The Irish and Scots felt a pleasant and relaxed ease as they wandered along roads, trails and woodland paths. For those northern Celts, however, the old Roman-era roads seemed most wonderful and well-preserved, a novelty.

Once inside Galicia, the Magyars and Spartans had donned their armor and arms. Luckily, the local temperatures were far cooler and breezier than further south and they had no fear of baking in the hot sun.

Some Galician nobles had joined them along the way, friends and former weapons brothers of Sancho. They regaled each other as they rode along with old stories of glory in battle against the Moors. The common Galicians, who gathered in crowds on the roadsides to watch the spectacle, were delighted to see King Alfonso's Campeador surrounded by their own leaders amidst a squadron of thirty imposing Leonese knights, all carrying on so cheerfully. Word had spread that foreign warriors from the north were also among the newcomers. The people had been told stories of these fierce men, Celts like themselves, who had, in recent times, defeated and thrown into the sea a massive horde of savage pagan Vikings who had attempted to invade and take over their home island of Ireland. Some of the most educated among them also knew that other Vikings had successfully conquered Saxon England in the previous year and now a Viking King ruled there.

When the mounted squadron of strangely garbed mounted archers with their small, peculiar bows rode past them, they were surprised as these cavalrymen were nothing like the heavily armed and armored knights they knew. They waved heartily to the onlookers as they rode by. And behind them came an even more astonishing sight, a marching column of colossal, fully armored behemoths, scarlet robes wrapped around mailed armor, huge round shields strapped to their broad backs, round steel helmets with mail skirts falling to their necklines, allowing only their eyes to peer out, stout and long thrusting spears with triangular blades carried under their thick mailed arms. These marched in silence and the road almost seemed to shake under their booted feet. Finally, behind them came another troop of mixed warriors and women, only a few mounted. These had their weapons strapped and any armor and shields were slung over their shoulders or strapped to their backs. They strode more leisurely, often leaving the road to jovially shake hands and clasp shoulders with some among the exuberant crowds.

At one point, the marchers were celebrated with music as local Galician pipers with their *Gaita* regaled them with stirring Celtic jigs and reels. This, of course, delighted the veterans of Clontarf and even the Spartans had to struggle to resist breaking into dance as they maintained their stolid march.

It had been decided earlier that the formal meeting would take place within one of the largest and most beautifully situated of the ancient hill forts of Galicia. This one had never known Roman modification, so, as the wood and thatched structures which had once served as houses and halls were long gone, there remained only the enormous circular outer wall of packed earth and stone and the equally round, earth-covered foundations of the former smaller dwellings. Still, the site was magnificent enough. The outer mound was as tall as two men and sloped up rather steeply. On the top were the remains of what might have been battlements. Below them, an even steeper slope fell to a bottom which at one point no doubt contained a water-filled moat.

There were several open fields within the spacious interior, which could have almost housed a small city and the smaller stone circles where structures had once stood. In advance, the Galicians had erected a number of cone-shaped, treated cotton pavilions over some of these smaller circles, giving the ancient site an air of festive liveliness once more. The site was surrounded by broad, open fields covered with red and yellow flowers and just beyond them, a river ran north-south. On the opposite side and closer, another river ran east-west. The sun was high and the slight breeze carried a faint hint of salt air, indicating that the coast could not be too far away.

It was early afternoon when the column arrived at the immense old hill fort. There was a large delegation of Galician nobles and intelligentsia awaiting their arrival, as well as food and drink and fodder and water for their horses. Squires took their mounts to a specially constructed corral and the visitors were directed to various pavilions to stow their gear and rest after their journey. There, wooden buckets of water for washing were at their disposal and they were also advised that the nearest riverbank was a short walk and featured bracing, swift-running current if they wanted to bathe more assiduously. Most of the Gaels, including the women, elected to take advantage of the frothy, cool waters of the river.

After stripping down to as few clothes as needed to preserve modesty, these supposedly fearsome and savage warriors frolicked in the rapids. They sang old songs under the few waterfalls they discovered along the riverbank. Somehow, almost intuitively, they knew they were among friends and felt safe in what should have been a strange land. They had also observed the Galicians had posted roving patrols out past the periphery of the hill fort. When they were satisfied that the trail dust which had coated them was washed away, they returned to the pavilions in small groups to enjoy pears and apples that awaited them there. They were advised not to eat too heartily as there was to be a sumptuous feast laid on later in the evening.

Shortly afterwards, the Gaelic leaders, along with Sancho, the Galician Leonese knight, Pyrrhus and Helena, went to a separate pavilion for a meeting with the nobles and military leaders of Galicia. When formal introductions were made, the hosts were amazed and quite impressed that Pyrrhus and Helena, senior members of the diplomatic corps of the Christian Greek Roman Empire with its capital in Constantinople, seemed to be such an integral part of the contingent of Gaels. The talks were straightforward and not of overly long duration. The visitors described the recent assessment of new expected major armed incursions by the Moors into Leon. They added that there were also opportunities to exploit the enemy's growing weaknesses. They reiterated that the threat was to all Christians in the northern kingdoms and conveyed their fervent hope that the Galicians, always among the fiercest of warriors, could continue to be counted on to vigorously defend their common shared faith and homelands.

As it turned out, the Leonese and their Gaelic allies had no need for concern. Notwithstanding their culture of independence, the Galicians assured them they were part and parcel of the Leonese Kingdom and would fervently heed the call to arms when summoned. Then the Galician senior military representative, smiling broadly, announced, “And with our own dear Celtic cousins fighting along with us, it would be difficult, if not impossible, for me to keep any of our young men home when the hour of desperate battle comes upon us.” With that, the formal talks ended, followed by bouts of happy laughter and eager anticipation of the coming feast.

As it was springtime, the days were getting longer and the sun was still not quite set when they sat to eat. Long, rough wooden tables had been set up in one of the expansive interior fields. They were lined with rough-hewn stumps and stools for sitting. Amazingly, there were places for the hundreds of visitors and an equal number of Galician leaders and lucky commoners whose clamors had won them a place at the table. Cook fires scattered throughout the fort had been roasting beef, venison and sides of pork for hours. These were now delivered to the scores of long tables where rustic wooden bowls and simple metal spoons and tongs awaited their users. Other servers brought loaves of dark and lighter bread, cheese blocks and a variety of early spring vegetables and herbs. Finally, tankards of beer and clay pots of country wine arrived along with cups made of local pottery to drink from. The visitors took up seats generally aligned with the groups they had marched in with and selected their implements. At exactly the right moment before anyone had touched a bite or supped a drop, a horn sounded.

In the very center of the diners, a small stand had been erected. On it now stood a black-robed figure. In the Galician dialect, he called out in a long, practiced and strong voice, “In the name of the Father, the Son and Holy Spirit…”

Even the Gaels who couldn’t understand a word followed along to make the sign of the cross as the priest concluded the blessing. He then, with deft crossed fingers, blessed those on all sides around him and told them. “Eat heartily and God bless you all!”

After that, amidst a merry chatter of praise for the food and drink, the entire assembly tucked in. There were toasts and cheers in multiple languages. None of the Hispanian nobles present and certainly not Pyrrhus or Helena, accustomed as they were to fine cutlery and exquisite dining, could take anything but the greatest pleasure in eating outside, in a field within the interior of this ancient monument. All sat in the company of the greatest of friends, comrades and fellow Christians, regardless of origin. Among the most pleased, joyfully sitting together, were Cormac and Helena, Wolf and Aoife, Cael and Luta and, to everyone's surprise, Fergus and Saoirse. Someone, somewhere, was playing a melody on a type of stringed instrument but not much could be heard over the cheery clamor of the diners as they told old stories and ate as if they were, for some reason, famished. Still, no one became too boisterous just yet. All knew there was more to come as this evening of delight continued.

When the meals were finished and the crockery collected, the men of the assembly, visitors and locals were directed to pick up the long tables and the stools and move them into two lines facing about three hundred paces across from each other on the field. With all the strong men present, it didn't take long and the guides directed them where to go. In the very center of the field, a sizeable fire pit had been dug earlier. It was filled with thick logs cut from elm trees and laced with dried kindling.

While the tables and stools were being repositioned on both sides, others were erecting an array of staked man-high torches into the ground around the outer periphery of the field. These were constructed of resinous wood and covered with multiple layers of fabrics soaked in beeswax. Just as some planner decided the sun had indeed set to his satisfaction, a horn blared out again. The fire pit and the torches were simultaneously ignited and a golden radiance immediately blossomed over the venue. It was a gloriously clear night with a brilliant three-quarters moon and the stars shining brightly. The ambience seemed almost to turn magical as groups of festively garbed musicians gathered together in a crescent, perpendicular to the lines of tables and chairs, all carrying instruments of various types.

There were Scots and Irish with their great bagpipes and Galicians with *gaita,* stringed instruments of various types and flutes and whistles. *Bodhrán* and other drums for percussion were also readied for use. Six Galicians stepped forward with the first gaita players and drummers among them and from the other side of the field, twelve more rushed to join them comprising six women and six men. The women were dressed in black skirts, topped by sheer white blouses with elegantly embroidered yellow vests, the men in black pants and loose, flowing white shirts. When the musicians and dancers were in the correct places, the blaring horn sounded yet again, a drum crashed and the music began with the dancers springing to frenetic action.

All eyes were upon them as their audience looked on with glee. Flashing happy grins to the onlookers, the six couples kicked their feet, swiveled their hips and raised their arms over their shoulders in unison as they moved in circles to the music. As the melody came to an end, the dancers bowed to great applause and cheers from those at the tables. Then, even more musicians joined the first groups. Irish, Scots and still more Galicians took places in the now much larger crescent and began to play the wildest jigs and reels that came to them. It seemed incredible but the Galicians were easily able to immediately adapt to the northern Celtic tunes and add the unique sounds of their own instruments to the bagpipes and drums of the others. It was almost as if there were some ancient, racial shared memory as the players all played off of each other seamlessly, regardless of the origin of any particular Celtic theme.

"We've waited long enough," shouted Cael. Taking Luta's ivory hand in his own, he dashed to the center of the field just as the next piece began. The two, still holding hands, began swirling around to the delirious resonance of pipes, flutes and drums.

"Once, in Scotland, you had to drag me to dance with you," Wolf whispered in Aoife's sweet, soft ear. "Now, it's my turn." Taking her in both arms, he sprang from the chair and ran in long strides to join Cael and Luta.

With more grace, Cormac gently bent to kiss Helena's hand, then, looking up to her expectantly, asked, "Dear Lady, will you grace me with this dance?" Trying vainly not to laugh, Helena responded, "Yes, Kind Sir, I believe I shall." The two erupted into laughter and walked with feigned elegance toward their dancing friends.

Watching this all, Saoirse felt the heat of Fergus' gaze, so she turned coyly toward him. "Are we just going to sit and watch?"

Fergus reached for her hand and the two, being younger and wilder, dashed enthusiastically to the center. Both had fiery red hair, which hung in long locks to well below their shoulders, now flowing freely behind them as they sprinted. Comically, with the ambient light of the fires reflecting glowingly off their scarlet tresses, they almost appeared to be two more torches rushing over the field.

Scores more revelers joined them now. Some of the bravest Irish and Scottish warriors tread shyly towards the few groups of Galician women sitting together, smiling and requested that the ladies join them in dancing.

Although the languages were mutually unintelligible, the Celtic women knew exactly what was intended. Each stood gracefully, reached out her hand and was escorted by her partner to join the others.

Seabirds of various types flew and cawed overhead, somehow attracted by the firelight, the strange and beguiling sounds and the view of the hypnotically dancing figures below them. Off in the surrounding woodlands, wolves howled, apparently in some affinity for the celebration of life they heard. Perhaps, it was something just like this that had brought their distant ancestors to the campfires of primitive peoples thousands of years ago.

The music seemed to grow louder as the dancers reeled over the packed earth of the field. Those still sitting at the tables pounded their hands onto the wooden surface in accompaniment with the beating drums. Flagons of wine and beer were being delivered nonstop to even further increase the merriment. The wail of the pipes, the lilting of the flutes, the rhythm of the various stringed instruments, melded together to lift the hearts and move the hands and feet of all present. It was easy to imagine that this same hill fort may have been filled with a very similar sound and scene millennia ago. The communion of the Celts, met and unmet, seemed to assure it would last forever as the glorious and delightful night continued.

# Chapter 16

## Scourges of God

The journey to Galicia had exceeded even the most optimistic expectations of the Leonese and Gaels. Galician leaders were keen to greatly increase the number of their levies who would support King Alfonso against the possible renewed onslaught of the Moors. They could clearly perceive that the threat would affect Galicia as severely as the rest of Leon and the other Christian kingdoms. With Santiago de Compostela having been sacked twice in the last half century by two different foreign enemies, first the Vikings and then the Moors, the Galicians knew, despite their fearsome strength and independent streak, that they could never be immune. Even, Ireland, a smallish island in the distant northwest, had almost been conquered by invading heathens from afar.

It was the Irish contingent among the visitors that particularly sparked the enthusiasm and admiration of the Galicians, especially their young men of fighting age. Hundreds pleaded to accompany the Irish back to Leon and begged to be accepted into the ranks of the Gaels. Of course, the Leonese would not be averse to adding more recruits to the Christian cause. The Irish leaders, however, were wary of absorbing new fighters into their warrior groups. The normal challenges of training and integrating were complicated even further by the lack of a mutual language. Still, in times past, the *Laochra* had experience in successfully absorbing foreign-speaking Welsh and Breton young men, so there was precedent.

Cael had the greatest reservations. “Yes,” he complained, “any eager young volunteer can quickly learn to become a sword swinger or spear thruster, all the while standing on his own two feet. It takes great skill and dexterity as well as precision timing to become a mounted archer in the ranks of the Magyars.”

It would have been easy for Fergus, Cormac, or even Wolf to take umbrage at what might have been perceived as a slight to the Spartans and Laochra but each of them had to admit to himself that there was a grain of truth in Cael’s words. The actual Magyars in Hungary had been living in the saddle and sleeping with their recursive bows since birth. It required becoming acclimated to an entirely distinct style of riding and fighting when learning these skills as an adult. Yet it was Pyrrhus who spoke up for the Galicians in this instance.

"Now then, Cael, you were a capable horseman when you first came to our Irish Magyar camp but you had barely ever seen a bow and arrow before that time. Did you not look about you as we rode through Galicia? Horses and riders abound. I'm sure there are at least a few experienced riders among the young men here whose fervor to join you would make their training less arduous."

"And, dear Cael, was it not yourself who took me out of the kitchens at that same camp and became my 'personal trainer' in the ways of the Connemara pony and recursive bow? I'd never done either before. Was I such a burden to you? And am I not now as adept as any of the lads in these skills?" asked Luta, with an affectionate though, decidedly mischievous, smile.

Feeling abashed, Cael replied, "My apologies, friends and leaders, my pride in my hard-riding Magyars was clumsily spoken at the cost of unintended derision upon the rest of my weapon brothers."

Unsurprisingly, it was Mornak the Pict who brought this awkward conversation to its quick conclusion. "Apology accepted, Cael. Now, how many are we going to take and how many new friends and comrades am I about to meet?"

Ultimately, with the assistance of various experienced military leaders among the Galicians, the recruits were selected. As the Hispanians, in general, were slightly smaller in stature than the Gaels or Vikings, there were not as many massively built young men to fit the requirements of the Spartans. Luckily, however, the Galicians were, in turn, somewhat larger than the rest of the Leonese and twenty new and eager and powerful brutes happily joined their ranks.

The militia levies of the Galicians numbered in the thousands. From their ranks, with the permission of their own leaders, eighty were accepted to become part of the elite *Laochra* as well as the combined armed forces of Gaelic infantry. Among them were included mounted infantry who could deploy rapidly and fight on foot. For the Magyars, ten new mounted archers were welcomed. Although Galicia was primarily an agricultural and fishing region, there were still families of hunters who used bows, along with other hunting implements. Each of these ten was an able horseman as well as being proficient with their own long bows. It would not happen overnight but by necessity, it must be accomplished expeditiously and these young men were to become welcome additions to the ranks of the Gaels.

Since, for most of the neophytes, Latin was as foreign a language as any other and for matters of urgency and simplicity, it was decided to teach them to converse in Irish Gaelic. They would learn it alongside the intense and regimented martial training they were about to endure. The Irish, like all native speakers regardless of language, considered their own tongue to be so natural as to be ridiculously simple to learn. Pyrrhus, now a master of Gaelic himself, chuckled when the others told him that.

"I speak multiple languages, including the most exotic: Arabic, Hungarian, Latin, Danish and others. None are so arduous, convoluted and demanding as your own," he told them.

"You're quite right Pyrrhus," replied Brother Cillian, laughing. "But our speech is beautiful to hear; lilting and lyrical, you must most assuredly agree."

The leaders of the various warrior groups left to welcome the newcomers personally and then introduce them to the representatives of the bands that had made the trip to Galicia. The young men had already bid farewell to their friends and family and cheerfully took their places among their new comrades for the return trip to Leon.

***

Upon their return, they were told the King and his counselors were in the main chamber of the court discussing a matter of great concern. The Leonese had established a series of minimally fortified outposts just inside their southern border. These were generally built on the remnants of old Roman fortifications. They were reminiscent of ancient Galician hill forts in some respects: an outer wall of raised earth with stone material interspersed and the ruins of structures within. The differences were that Roman forts were rectangular in shape, as opposed to circular and they were laid out geometrically, with straight roads and even boulevards. The structures had been designed for different purposes: barracks, headquarters building, stables, dining facilities, baths and storage areas.

All were now long gone and the Leonese had built over them. These outposts served as billets for Leonese scouts and administrators and traveling squadrons of knights, as well as assuring a place of refuge for the local farmers and animal herdsmen in the event of Moorish raids. Perhaps the most important of their functions was to provide early warning of any major movements of the Moors along the borders. The King considered these outposts and especially the courageous and far-ranging scouts stationed there, to be his eyes and ears.

Now word had come that one of these outposts had been besieged and sacked. Except for a boy and a girl, sibling twins who had escaped during the worst of the destruction, all within had been put to the sword. The pre-teen boy and girl had been hastily brought to the capital to safety and to tell the story. At the time of the attack, about half of the scouts had been deployed, out in various nearby provinces of the Caliphate and no traveling knights were in garrison there. The attackers were not in immense numbers but, for the first time, they came well-prepared and equipped for their mission. Their siege equipment, never used along the borderlands and copied from that employed by the Christian Greek Roman Empire made quick kindling of the wooden palisades the Hispanians had erected over the old outer wall of the outpost. Flaming arrows from the curved bows of the attackers set some of the interior structures aflame. Through the breeches poured infantry in quilted armor, turbaned helmets and heart-shaped shields adorned with four or more horsetails.

The young ones had crawled through the smoke to a tiny back gate from which they ran hunched over into the nearby wood line. Ironically, the attackers had struck so quickly that none of the local population had time to rush in for sanctuary to the outpost. The escapees watched in horror from behind the cover of thick brush as the Moors finished their grisly work. They then attached the siege equipment once more to the wheeled platforms and their teams of six horses stashed whatever plunder they found onto another wagon, mounted their own steeds and galloped off once more back to the Caliphate. At that point, the two small refugees sped to the home of a local farmer who promptly loaded them and his own family onto a cart and made for the Leonese capital.

The members of the court had already been informed of the trip's success in Galicia by riders who brought the message in advance. So, when Sancho and the Irish leaders joined the others in the main chamber, the King's congratulations were sincere but terse.

"But now, it seems, Sulayman is trying to blind me, to take away my eyes for some nefarious purpose which he no doubt is darkly conjuring as we speak.

We have discussed this in some detail, even before this latest outrage and have agreed he is planning some new horror against us."

Alfonso bade the newcomers take seats and continued. "Our recent diversions may be causing him to speed up his plans, even if he is unsure whether we, the other Christian Kingdoms or, indeed, some new and strange foe is working against him."

Wolf took the opportunity to respond to the King's assessment of the situation.

"That makes perfect sense, King Alfonso. I suggest we provide him additional 'diversions.' This time these tactics should be even more dynamic, offensive, harmful and alien in nature to compound his troubles and delay any grand *aceifa,* giving us more time to prepare a 'grand' response to his planned great raid."

***

On the return trip to Leon, Wolf, Cormac, Pyrrhus and Cael discussed their near-term options for meeting the threat. They all knew they would need at least some time to integrate the nearly three hundred Galicians into their own bands. Yet the enemy would not calmly extend that grace period to them. They had already struck the foe from the sea in the guise of Viking marauders, engaged and largely eliminated a newly arrived tribe of Berbers who had sought to impress their Caliph and conducted small-scale, direct action special operations in rescuing Schlomo's son and Zaynab's sister. They had also returned the Caliph's assassin to him. Or at least part of him.

Pyrrhus brought up his time as a diplomat among his much-admired Magyars. "Before they were finally defeated by Saxon King Otto in 955 in southern Germania, they had been threatening to push all the way to the French coast and had encroached deep into Italy. What I neglected to tell you is that the pagan Magyars also struck into the Caliphate as recently as 942, causing panic and fear among the Moors.

In a sweeping raid, they invaded *Thaghr al-Aqṣa.* This is the 'furthest March,' the northwestern frontier province of the Caliphate. As they pillaged further south, devastating towns and cities, they began to run out of provisions and were unable to procure local forage, so they retired from the field. Yet the damage to the Caliphate was done and the Christians of the time were vigorously inspired once more to fight for their own freedom."

"Your good friends, the Magyars, seem almost to have been as far-reaching and rapacious as the Vikings in times past, Pyrrhus. 'Tis glad I am they never took to the seas or we may have experienced even more troubles at home," Cormac commented. "Ah, well, thanks be to God, those of the Duchy of Hungary are all good and decent Christians now."

"I regret I hadn't told you that about the Magyars before now," exclaimed Pyrrhus. "I wonder. Does it give any of my dear friends any notions of how we might make use of those savage Magyars of old?"

"Well, you wise old Greek wizard, it does indeed. And have no care that you haven't told us until now. Better late than never and the timing is exceedingly auspicious," Wolf replied, quite pleased.

The three Irishmen were all thinking the same thoughts and nodding when Cormac laughed and announced, "Tis true, we Irish may have thick skulls but that's only to protect our bright and brilliant brains."

***

Wolf continued with his recommendation to the king, given the Moors' latest atrocity and how they might quickly respond. "We discussed this idea of a new 'diversion' on our return trip from Galicia after Pyrrhus informed us that Magyars had bedeviled the Moors but a half century ago. They are still remembered with fear and loathing. And, as you know, Alfonso, we have 'Magyars' of our own, though perhaps too few to invest the entire Caliphate."

Wolf had an intense, though slightly mirthful, expression on his face as he looked first to the king, then to Cael.

"They even had four genuine Magyars among them during the Clontarf battle. These had been the escorts and guards for Lady Helena when she visited us as an emissary and gift bearer on behalf of Emperor Basil. And, being good Christians, though still quite savage Magyars, they begged to fight at our sides against the Vikings. We couldn't turn them down."

Wolf kept the other reason for Helena's visit – to scold her cousin Pyrrhus for his protracted absence – to himself.

"With Pyrrhus' assistance and the example of their four actual Magyar weapon brothers, our lads were quite convincing when in the saddle, attired in the style of the steppe riders and using almost identical weapons and tactics. The slew many times their numbers in Vikings. Of course, there were two hundred of them then and our own dear ferocious Irish hounds aided them. God bless them all," said Wolf with a smile.

Cael now chimed in. “With the addition of more of our comrades on those ships from Ireland, we now number sixty riders. Ten young but experienced horsemen and archers from Galicia have also asked to join our ranks. These, though, must be trained in our ways before they are committed to battle. We have tasked ten of our own to personally tutor the Galicians, which brings our total to fifty. I can employ this small but exceptionally agile and deadly squadron to strike any targets of our choice throughout the Caliphate.”

Alfonso and Sancho both took on pensive expressions before traces of smiles began to curl almost simultaneously at the corners of their thin lips.

“What we would request, King, is that no more than six of your valiant knights who would also be disguised as Magyars accompany us. They should hopefully be familiar with the terrain and perhaps have knowledge of the local languages and dialects. We have used this model of combined operations since our arrival and it has been invaluable to our mutual efforts,” added Wolf.

The king’s response was most positive. “In the brief time you’ve been among us, you’ve never failed in any of our joint endeavors, my friends. This too seems a novel and, I must confess, quite devious concept. I very much like it. If Sulayman is now worried about Vikings and Spartans as well as you mysterious Celtic ‘savages’ from the cold northern seas, then the introduction of a new threat of returning Magyar ravishers back to harry the Caliphate once more must surely impede any precipitous plans he has for a major *aceifa*.”

“And to make the impact even more agonizing to our enemies, I recommend these new Magyar barbarians strike across that same northern province as they did a half century past,” added the King’s *Campeador*, Sancho.

“Felix, how are our current relations with Castile and Navarre in your opinion? And do you have trusted contacts still there?’

Luckily, the king’s ambassador at large and friend to the Irish was also on hand for the council.

Felix addressed the old warrior with a note of respect and appreciation.

“I do believe I grasp your intent, Sancho. If our tiny group of Magyars can do most of their traveling across friendly lands and then strike southwards across the borders there, they will be more secure. It so happens that we currently enjoy quite collegial relations with our fellow Christians. If I can convince my contacts of the need for secrecy and that they themselves will not be held accountable for these raids, this all may work out splendidly.”

***

Felix had alerted his contacts and given them the basics of the plan. They, in turn, assured that only the uppermost among the nobles of Castile and Navarre were given any details. The nobles found no objections to acting against the Christians' common enemies and were actively supportive. So, trusting there would be no compromise of their true intent, fifty-six riders, all attired in the same drab garments of simple workmen, set out eastward.

They crossed the border into the south of Castile, where they were met by an escort of four Castilian knights garbed in red and gold tunics. The cover story for those they met in Christian lands was that they were a party of skilled mining engineers dispatched to conduct complicated drilling and extraction operations in the Pyrenees mountains. They crossed over towering mountains of Castile of such heights as none of the Irish had ever witnessed. Here and there, they passed other travelers as all struggled and, in some parts, were forced to walk their horses. Behind them came a baggage train of three wagons which carried the supposed tools of their trade and other sundry objects.

Upon reaching the border of the Kingdom of Navarre and with the mountains behind them, they were met by a new escort group of Navarrese knights. The land here was lower and more level as they continued east and rode downward towards the confluence of several rivers. The plan called for them to cross the border south into the Caliphate from Navarre's easternmost marches.

After crossing, they would no longer be 'mining engineers' but rather ravenous Magyars storming once again into those lands they had pillaged in the past. When they reached the pre-selected assembly area along their point of entry but still hidden from view from the other side, they were met by more Navarrese who had brought provisions of dried fruits and breadstuffs. They would leave the wagons with the men from Navarre and these would drive the carts back to another pre-selected site. Their re-entry point, if everything went well, was to be in Castile and the carts and new escorts would await them there in one week's time.

Now, garbed once again in their familiar Magyar panoplies with recursive bows secure in their sheaths, quivers stuffed with arrows in their quivers and thin lances strapped over their backs. They prepared for seven days of fury in the style of their adopted namesakes.

Cael looked to the oldest man among them and had to comment. “Sure now, Rodrigo, you’ll be the oldest and swarthiest Magyar any of these Moors has ever beheld.”

They had been delighted when their friend and weapon brother Rodrigo begged to join them and was given the approval of King Alfonso to do so. Notwithstanding his age, he had proved himself in battle at their sides, was skilled in multiple languages and had knowledge of the terrain from his younger days as a roving *Campeador* who conducted far-ranging missions in service to his lords. He was even familiar, he said, with *Thaghr al-Aqṣa*, the far northern march of the Caliphate and its capital, *Saraqusta*, or what the Hispanians called Zaragoza.

Rodrigo had been endeavoring to learn Irish Gaelic but found it more difficult than all the other tongues he had mastered. Cael, for his part, had been struggling along with Luta to master Latin with Pyrrhus and Cillian as tutors. He had improved greatly and the two men were mutually intelligible now to their great pleasure.

“This grand plan of yours requires every detail to be carried out without the slightest failure. And you know, Cael, that’s never possible. So just be content, a seasoned and sophisticated warrior of my age is at your side to see you and your young pups don’t make a total shambles of it,” commented Rodrigo as both friends broke out in laughter.

Cael and one of the Leonese knights, now robed and equipped as a Magyar for the first time, rode off swiftly and stealthily to reconnoiter the area around their planned insertion point. The ground was level but varied heavily with bushes, shrubs and small trees covered in broad leaves. This terrain would aid them in concealment but would slow their progress as they penetrated enemy territory. They returned shortly to announce that the way was clear and that a road was not too distant from them.

And so it was that after an absence of sixty years, a mounted raiding party of fifty-six Magyar heathens once again thundered over the lands of the Caliphate following a similar trail as had their fathers before them. Some carried standards of ox tails which flowed in raven swirls from their lances. Long feathers from hawks and other birds of prey adorned their helmets, which were constructed of boiled and molded leather covered with black otter fur. Fitted leather jerkins draped over red and wheaten-hued woolen tunics made up their only armor. They followed Cael’s lead in a column of two abreast until they reached the mentioned road, which turned out to be merely a dirt-packed track. They stopped for the briefest of moments and Cael sent two of them ahead to ride swiftly but warily as their forward scouts.

"Outside of the few cities and settlements, the only traffic on the roads will be small Moorish warrior groups or merchants with armed escorts of several mercenaries. Their main concern here is bandits who might strike from the wooded areas since there has been no major incursion by the Christian kingdoms in some time," explained Rodrigo, not for the first time.

"Right," proclaimed Cael. He turned to the others. "Remember, we must not engage any force that outnumbers us. If we do meet such a Moorish squadron, we will turn and scatter to come together at rally points I will designate as we move on. No harm must come to any non-combatant but all property should be either seized, if small, light and easily carried, or destroyed. All armed foemen will be slain except for those wounded. Those we must keep alive to bear witness to our depredations. We have by now all memorized basic commands, terms of communication and curses in the Hungarian tongue, courtesy of Pyrrhus. We must assume the mantle of the pagan Magyars of old; raiders, pillagers, barbarous destroyers out of the Moors' worst nightmares. We must become as those so designated by past pontiffs - the *Scourges of God*."

"I know I've already given them those orders but there's no harm in repeating them once more," said Cael more quietly to Rodrigo.

The older man merely nodded and replied, "Well said. There is an old commander's adage – 'Tell them what you're going to tell them, tell them and then tell them again.' You're learning, young man. Now we must take steps to assure our entire enterprise here in enemy-held lands is as well done."

***

The first planned objective was a silver mine on the side of one of the few hills in their chosen area of operations, which was essentially a green depression bisected by several large and small rivers. This was certainly not favorable terrain for cavalry operations but it was offset by the fact that the target was relatively soft. They could expect up to forty slaves to conduct the arduous work of silver mining and less than half that number of guards. The guard force would be made up more of simple slave drivers than trained Moorish warriors. Since the silver ore had to be transported and further processed at a separate site, these mines were not usually at risk from robbers.

From a distance, they could see most of the slavers standing at the mouth of the cave or walking around five wagons, which were being loaded by slaves. Few of the guards would enter the cave for any period of time, as the interior was so stifling and dangerous, with a putrid air quality. Except for the few slaves working around the wagons, all the rest were within the tunnels dug deep into the hill. It was remarkably simple to distinguish between guards and slaves. The slavers were well fed, comfortably dressed and armed with short swords or truncheons. Their charges were nearly naked, clothed in only loincloths, emaciated and wearing leg irons. It wouldn't take long.

As soon as Cael thrust his hand forward, fifty Magyars yelping and cursing in their guttural Hungarian tongue galloped at full speed, their horses' hooves thundering over the packed earth that surrounded the hill. The startled guards were easy marks. Their bodies were feathered with multiple arrows before they could understand what was happening. The slaves looked on awestruck as their captors were slaughtered in mere seconds. Upon reaching the cave's entrance, four of the attackers dismounted and dashed inside, careful to communicate only in rudimentary Hungarian single words or in strings of curses. These four were the Leonese knights, garbed as Magyars but they couldn't bear to be separated from their fine Hispanian broadswords.

The two slavers they found cowering just inside were slashed to death in a fury. Scores of slaves laboring within dashed to the entrance to find a scene of red massacre. Yet their fellows above were uninjured and just beginning to cheer. The wagons were already in flames and some of the attackers were gathering the arrows from the corpses of the dead. Then all at once, they remounted and rushed off toward the northeast in a whirlwind, leaving the bewildered but now liberated slaves to find the keys to their chains among the carnage of their former masters.

Six other Magyars who had been posted around the perimeter of the attack site as security joined the main group, which only slowed when they were out of sight of the mine. They then circled around, prepared to ride southeastward, generally toward the city of *Saraqusta* once more. The intent was to prevent any of the slaves who may be captured or turn themselves in from divulging their actual course.

"If all goes as easily as that, we may take the entire Caliphate by ourselves," said one of the younger Irish Magyars in jest and within hearing of Cael.

"Overconfidence is lethal. Those miserable wretches were mere slave drivers, not warriors. Never forget, the Moors have ruled most of Hispania for over 300 years. Their success has come from force of arms and trust in their faith. If our meager band becomes ensnared through some mishap by a group of warriors who outnumber us and are on lands they've held for centuries, we will have no chance," Cael counseled the young lad, though his admonishment held no harshness in its tone.

"We must strike targets of our choosing swiftly and disappear, always assuring we don't compromise our identity. You, Cathal, for instance, if slain in battle and your body discovered by the foe, would make an unlikely Magyar."

He directed this to the original speaker, now chagrined, who could only hang his long red-haired head in silence as a pink blush spread on his pale, beardless and boyish, freckled face. Then, with a hearty laugh, he slapped the young lad on the shoulder, announcing, "No worries, my friend, I once had far more brazenness than you until Pyrrhus and Wolf trained me otherwise. Never lose your aggressive spirit. You'll be just fine."

Not long after, two forward scouts galloped back to report that twelve mounted Moorish warriors were escorting a horse-driven carriage just on the road before them. There was some discussion of the value of engaging the target. Perhaps, they were escorting a tax collector, tribute gatherers, or a mere traveling nobleman.

"No matter," said Cael, "Magyars would make no distinction; they would simply attack and slaughter their armed foes and so shall we."

The Moors heard them before they saw them. Looking behind, they were stunned to observe dozens of bizarrely garbed riders screaming and bearing down on them. The column made a doomed attempt to outrun their attackers but it was too late for most. Arrows, accurately aimed from the bows of the galloping Magyars, took down most of them. Several tried to make a fight of it but as they were jousting with lances at those closest, other archers simply picked them off their saddles. It was no contest and the twelve were slain quickly along with the coach's driver.

When several Magyars dismounted to examine the carriage's interior, they were greeted by a strident and high-pitched scream. *Allahu Akbar!*

An enormous Moor, clad entirely in black, sprang out of the carriage's door, brandishing a deadly and gleaming scimitar. Only his eyes were visible as his head was covered by a turbaned helmet topped by a steel spike and his face was swathed in black fabric. But the Magyars approached the carriage with vigilance and leapt back agilely. Still, the giant's defiant howl was all that saved them as he burst from the door, landing in their midst, wielding his sword in sweeping arcs that sundered the leveled lances of two of the attackers who surrounded him. These two jumped back, defenseless as he advanced toward them. Their two comrades used that instant to impale him from side and back with their own lances. The huge Moor crumpled to the ground with blood erupting from his mouth. Now, more Magyars surrounded the carriage, grunting and growling with hideous Hungarian curses to any still inside.

"This monster is certainly burly enough to be one of our Spartans," exclaimed one whose lance had been shattered.

The other moved to tear off the helmet and face covering from the corpse's head.

"And he is ugly enough to be one of them as well," replied the second man.

To their astonishment, the slain Moor's hair and beard were abundantly thick and tinted reddish orange.

"Some Muslims follow that practice, believing that their faith's founder dyed his hair with henna as well. Yet it is ironically forbidden for any of them to dye their hair black since most of them are raven-haired from birth. Others believe such men want to stand out and think they are more beautiful when so adorned," explained one of the Mozarab Magyars.

The now wary Magyars surrounding the carriage on both sides began to hear subdued whimpering from its interior. With bows knocked, two others violently pulled open the side doors. Screams of terror rang out from the cab when the attackers peered inside. Three young dark-haired Moorish girls, hugging one another in mortal fear, looked back at them with wide, frightened almond eyes.

"Are these poor girls slaves?" asked Cael. "Why were they alone with that brute and escorted by twelve armed warriors? They're mere wee lasses, dressed in Moorish fashion though better attired than most waifs I've yet seen in Hispania.

He was careful enough to speak those words out of earshot of the girls. All knew the youngsters could neither be harmed nor kidnapped, even if they were Moors.

The Mozarab who had spoken before brought his horse close to Cael's. "They are young Arab women, as the Moors would say, 'of good quality' and prized. They were likely sold by their fathers as payment for some debt or taken in a tribal dispute. They were no doubt on their way to be paired up as third or fourth wives with some Moorish prince or princes, or perhaps, to be sold yet again to meet an even worse fate."

"Such a thing is not to be believed," countered Cael in abject disgust. "They are but babes. The oldest can be no more than eleven. Among us, a girl should be over sixteen for marriage and most are older than that indeed."

"Their ways are not ours as you have plainly seen, Cael," replied the Hispanian.

One of the Mozarab Leonese knights, who had been raised in a small settlement just outside of *Saraqusta,* now took the opportunity to explain that there was a grand and opulent villa, owned by one of the region's leading nobles, just off that same road a short distance ahead of them.

"He is a particularly wealthy Arab, quite moderate and well-liked by his neighbors for his kindness and generosity. He and his family entertain many visitors, both rich and poor, Muslim and *dhimmi*. He is a good and decent man and, I believe, incapable of deception. I once met him and thought he would make a pious and righteous Christian, yet he is devout and happy in his own faith," said the knight. "I know he would assure that these innocent girls would never come to harm."

Cael could only shake his Magyar-helmed head.

"Every day I continue to learn there is good and evil among all peoples. We were raised in the rock-solid belief that all Vikings were servants of the devil. Then at Clontarf, many, like Keli, came to us in their multiples of hundreds to fight at our side. Meanwhile, other Irish from Leinster fought against us and the High King. Such must it be among these Moors as well. I know what you're thinking, Sir Knight, though you haven't admitted it. And I quite agree," he replied. "We should somehow deliver these girls to that honorable Arab nobleman. But we must do it in such a manner that doesn't detract from the bloodthirsty and pillaging aspect we wish to convey."

The knight nodded and continued. "You perceive my intent exactly, Captain. I have a notion of a plan that hopefully accomplishes both. The villa is within plain sight of the road. There will be some guards and a gatekeeper keeping an eye on the place's surroundings. We should gallop up altogether with the carriage in our midst, the girls still inside, when we reach a point where we can be easily observed from the villa. We should make a savage display of barbarity by setting the carriage on fire while we curse at the girls inside and cast mocking gestures toward those watching. It will be that time just before dusk when it's neither light nor dark and the flames will be impressive."

Cael stopped him abruptly. "You expect us to incinerate these three poor girls?"

The knight grinned and laughed. "Of course not. As the flames begin to singe the carriage's exterior, we will thunder off back the way we came. These youngsters are terrified but not stupid. When they hear us tearing away, they will throw themselves out of the wagon. But, lest I'm wrong, we should leave one man to lie concealed alongside. If they don't manage to get out in a timely fashion, he will jump inside and drag them to safety. In either case, he will then slink along like a snake out of view of the girls and the villa to return toward us. We'll pick him up and then begin again our long circle around to continue generally toward *Saraqusta*."

"That will work I hope and pray," Cael agreed, as he directed another Magyar to climb up on the carriage's driving bench and take the reins. Then the entire column rode as a mass down the road with the carriage in their center.

It didn't take long before they reached the cut-off that led to the plush estate, which they could easily see. They could even hear sounds coming from within its walls. Most of them directed their steeds to face the structure as they began to whoop and shake their lances threateningly. Others surrounded the carriage, still directing malicious invectives with deep fearsome voices toward the children inside.

The sad truth was that each of them would have given anything to take the girls protectively in his arms and whisper soothing words into their young ears, anything to give them comfort and hope. All felt the same deep shame at what their mission forced them to do at this moment.

As one of the men dismounted on the far side of the carriage and slunk off into a close place of concealment behind a hedge row, others placed dried wood and tinder on top of and underneath the vehicle and, using flints, sparked a low flame. Almost immediately, the Magyars rushed off together back the way they had come.

Cael, of course, elected himself to be the one man to stay behind to assure no actual harm came to the lasses but he needn't have bothered. As his comrade had predicted, while struck with fear, these brave young girls were neither helpless nor stupid. As soon as they heard the sound of hoof beats thundering away and became aware of the scent and sound of the flames and smoke, all three leapt from the carriage and ran some distance to catch their breath in safety.

Relieved to see the girls' escape, Cael ran bent over along the hedge row following his squadron. The shrubbery, oncoming dusk and now fiercely burning and smoking carriage were his allies in covering his withdrawal from observation by the band of ten riders who were cautiously riding out from the villa to examine the scene. They had watched the strange riders disappear in a rush and meant to see for themselves what had truly transpired there.

After a long and rapid sprint, Cael came to the first bend in the road, where he was met by a weapon brother with Cael's mount trailing behind. The two galloped off together to join their comrades, feeling much better now. There had been no injury suffered by the girls, beyond the situation to which they had initially been subjected. And, as far as they could determine, their cover as savage and cruel Magyar pillagers had not been compromised. Upon rejoining the others, the compact horde of fierce riders once again circled back and around to continue their original course on the road to *Saraqusta*, making quite sure they would neither be seen nor heard by those who had been riding to examine the smoking wreckage of the once-elegant carriage.

***

A distinguished-looking, older Arab man led the party as they rode out from the villa. His silver hair spilled down from his black turban to his shoulders and he was elegantly robed in a red and white linen tunic and loose-fitting black cotton pants. His eyes were kind and his concern at what might have occurred was evident. While the group approached the still smoking corpse of the vehicle, he directed his magnificent white horse around it. As he dismounted, what he saw on the opposite side filled him initially with alarm then blessed relief. Three young girls, attired in elegant apparel, fit for their ages, were huddled together on the ground by the hedges, crying and laughing at the same time.

"Have no worries, young ladies, no harm will come to you now. You're safe and I'll see you stay secure and free from any additional evil," he said with a soft voice in refined Arabic. His gentle eyes and elegant grandfatherly appearance removed any doubt they might have had. All three stood up and ran to him as they raced for the protection of his welcoming arms. The others from the villa came upon a familiar sight when they rode up. Their leader was hugging his charges with affection, calmly reassuring them and all of them had tears in their eyes.

***

As the night wore on, the Magyars finally stopped to spend the night atop a tree-crowned hill just far enough from the road to make their discovery difficult for any searchers. They were running low on provisions, having only enough left to take a quick bite of bread and dried fruit and another course of the same viands to break their early morning fast. That was why their next objective was yet another pre-planned target. This was an open-air farmers' market, serving the locals who lived just a bit too distant to make frequent trips into *Saraqusta* to purchase the more ample and exotic goods and foodstuffs available in that city.

They had debated among themselves the morality of striking against simple farmers and merchants. This was certainly no military target. Two factors convinced them their choice was correct. First, true Magyars of yore often stole cattle and crops to sustain themselves on raids. In this case, they were more concerned with making off with their edible booty and eating once again than with hunting down and slaughtering the producers.

Still, farmers or not, the Moors, despite three hundred years of occupation, were still invaders in a country they had stolen, oppressing and displacing the original owners. Thus, they designed their rules of engagement. There would be no killing of unarmed farmers or merchants unless they themselves were attacked. They would achieve shock and terror by slaughtering the score or so of Moorish mercenaries who would be present to prevent robbery or disorderly conduct among the locals. This would likely scatter most of the hundreds of sellers and buyers. They would gather all they needed to replace their own stocks of victuals, then they would smash or burn every bit of property or goods they could not carry. After, they would hasten southeast toward the capital city and later turn abruptly westward, ultimately heading back to their rendezvous point in Castile.

The next day, around noon, one of their forward scouts rode back to report that the market was rather close and it appeared exactly as they expected. It was set on a broad, flat meadow with numerous stalls, tables, bright, multi-colored tents and simple awnings. There were also small throngs of sheep, goats and cattle clustered around the periphery contentedly munching the moist green grass that grew abundantly. The terrain prevented the scouts from approaching too close without being observed. However, they estimated that there were around two hundred sellers and customers and they could only count fifteen armed mercenaries, although they acknowledged that there could be more, hidden in tents or among the crowds.

The Magyar impostors realized that this undertaking would not necessarily be as simple as it seemed. Just over fifty light cavalry archers investing a crowded and obstacle-strewn space would not work to the attackers' strengths, especially when they were trying to avoid killing or injuring most of the people gathered there. Fighting in such a forced, dispersed fashion, they could be dragged from their mounts and swarmed. Even those not carrying visible weapons would likely have knives of some type since such tools were ubiquitous. The solution they chose was to employ flaming arrows to set several large tents ablaze. Then they would come forward as a slow canter, once more cursing and howling ferociously. The hope was that the flames and the fearsome display of strange alien warriors moving towards them would cause most to rush away in terror from the attack. They moved off at once, intending through sheer shock and audacity to instill panic and dread into the hearts of the unsuspecting Moors.

***

The shrill, piercing blare of an animal horn overcame the hubbub of the hundreds of people at the market fair. Voices stilled as they all looked in the direction from whence clamored the ear-piercing bellow. To their initial amazement, their eyes met a seething crescent of outlandishly garbed mounted warriors slowly trotting toward them, roaring rage-filled invective in some hideous tongue that seemed unfit for human utterance. Amazement was quickly replaced with first fear and then panic as scores of fire arrows fell onto the tents, awnings and then the wooden tables covered with goods for sale. Flames began to encompass those targets, followed by wafts of smoke.

The crowd hadn't come here today to be slaughtered by gruesome demons from some unknown macabre hell. Both sellers and buyers fled in all directions, never stopping. Some were carrying little ones or helping older ones. For the farmers and merchants, their wares weren't worth dying for. The attackers moved into the interior as the fabric of the tents was consumed and fell into the interior. The Magyars were now able to more easily distinguish the mercenaries with their belted scimitars and turban helmets. These guards were running away even faster than the others. Still, they could not escape the well-aimed arrows flying toward them. The Magyar recursive bows had incredible power and range and twenty-six mercenaries, almost half the strength of the attackers, were soon lying face-first on the ground, pinioned by one or more arrows.

When the fleeing Moors were far enough away that they wouldn't detect yet another strange language, Cael called out quick orders. "Swiftly gather as much food as you can carry and any other valuables small enough for transport on our still dangerous journey. Then put everything else to the torch in any fashion possible… but do it quickly!"

While some of the warriors retrieved arrows from the bodies of the slain guards, taking care to allow the few wounded to live on to tell the tale. This act of mercy didn't prevent the Magyars from continuing to heap the same garish Hungarian curses on the few moaning survivors. These repeated insults in Hungarian by now came amusingly easy to the young Gaels, who had little notion of what they actually meant. There was plenty of smoked and dried meats and fish, vegetables and fruits and even exotic dates, to be stuffed into the Magyars' saddle bags. They would have been happy to take some of the cattle along with them, too but that would simply slow them down now that they were ready to return to safety in the northern Christian lands. And none among them would even consider killing the livestock out of spite.

Later, as they rode to the northwest, their scouts discovered a Moorish checkpoint set up on the road consisting of a dozen warriors. Four were posted around a simple wooden crossbeam barrier meant to halt the movement of passersby, who would then be questioned. Another eight reclined, taking repose in the grassy meadows along both sides of the road. This obstacle did not present much of a challenge to the onslaught of the massed Magyars. Since they had inevitably failed to retrieve all the arrows employed thus far, they made use of their thin, lethal lances as much as possible in annihilating the enemy. One, however, was sitting alone with his horse alongside at some distance from the others. This Moor was allowed to escape, though he would later tell himself and others how he had daringly eluded and outpaced his hideous pursuers.

The Magyars took no time to tarry. Late in the afternoon, on the next day, as they approached the Caliphate's border areas with Castile, they set out flankers on both sides as well as before and behind them. The enemy's forces would undoubtedly have a larger presence here than in the interior. It didn't take long for their assessment to be confirmed when a young Magyar scout riding ahead of them galloped back to render his report.

Pulling hard on the reins to bring his mount to an abrupt halt, he breathlessly cried, "Large column of the enemy to our front and marching directly toward us. Perhaps three score infantry and a dozen Berbers on horseback. I don't believe they're aware of our presence but will be on us in not too long. We've not much time."

Nodding to Rodrigo and looking to Cael, the scout inquired in Irish Gaelic, "What are your orders, Captain?"

"What think you, Rodrigo?" asked Cael. "They outnumber us but not by much. If we attack and rout them, we will be able to cross the border into safety by late tonight. I know that we've agreed not to engage with any foe who outnumbers us, yet the lads may feel shamed if we decide to run now. Should we deploy to make a fight of it, or should we be satisfied with our successes up till now, withdraw out of sight and let them pass? You've much more hard-fought experience than I with these Moors. I defer to your judgement."

The older *Campeador* took on a pensive countenance, his gaze was cast up and to the right and he appeared to be chewing on the tip of his thumb for a moment. Suddenly, all the bright eyes of the young Irishmen around him grew wide and some of them gasped audibly. The youngest could not help but say aloud what all of them were thinking.

"Finn Mac Cumhaill….the Salmon of Knowledge."

"What is that youngster prattling on about and why are you all looking at me like that, Cael?" asked a perplexed Rodrigo. Then he continued without pause. "I judge it's best to fight, lest we regret our caution and reluctance years from now when we're all old." His comment, though heartfelt, was not without humor, as the speaker could have been a father or even a grandfather to most of his Irish comrades.

"I'll explain later about Finn and the Salmon, Rodrigo, though I'm sure you'll judge us even madder than you do at present," said Cael to the advanced scout. "But right now, we prepare for battle. Ruairi, did you detect a spot ahead where it would be best to await their arrival?"

"Indeed," answered Ruairi. "A long, low hill at the side and following the trace of the road. Unless they post flankers, which I didn't detect before, we can rush down in total surprise from there as they come alongside. But we must move up at once to properly deploy and position the squadron before they arrive." He smiled, pleased with himself for having paid proper attention to the terrain as he scouted.

"Right," said Cael, "and even if they do post a flanker, he'll be feathered with arrows before he can cry a warning. Lead the way!"

The column rode off swiftly yet just below a full gallop, keeping to the side of the road to minimize the chance of raising a dust cloud above them. Not long after, they observed Ruairi moving off to the right. Now they could detect the low but extended rock and shrub-covered hill that paralleled the road. It was close enough to be easily within bowshot range of their primary weapons, yet at sufficient distance that they could gain overpowering momentum when the time came to initiate a full mounted charge. The hill almost seemed perfect for their needs since it obligingly featured a 'military crest' as well. Just below the actual summit on the side facing the road, there was another ridge behind which they could remain concealed. This crest was topped with scrubby brush, providing cover but sparse enough that their horses would easily traverse it, enabling their riders to emerge seemingly from nowhere and descend in a thundering onslaught.

Soon, they came to an ideal initial deployment location. It provided them advantageous positioning to establish a maximum killing zone as they struck from their enemy's flank when he was strung out along the nearby road in marching columns. They set up in an extended line just behind the military crest. Horse holders stood behind the main formation. Each held the reins of six horses. The others crawled forward to lie or sit in the bushy shrubbery where they could peer down onto the road below. They estimated their extended line would generally approximate the length of the column they were expecting shortly.

Cael and Rodrigo established themselves at the center of the line as they waited for the enemy's arrival.

Rodrigo took the opportunity to inquire of Cael about the business of the lads acting strangely while deciding the course of action.

"Now what's all this about the 'Finn and the Salmon' story," asked Rodrigo in a quiet but curiosity-filled voice. "And why were they all staring at me as if I were some sort of troll?"

Cael had almost forgotten the incident and he had to stifle a laugh.

"I'll give you the mercifully short version for obvious reasons. The story originates from myths and legends, dating back to our ancient pagan past. Finn Mac Cumhaill was one of our heroes from antiquity. He was a valiant hunter-warrior and led a fierce and indomitable band of warriors called the *Fianna*. As a boy, he left home to live with a wise old man who lived along a great river and became Finn's tutor. A strange and supernatural fish was rumored to swim the river's waters on occasion. This fish was the 'Salmon of Knowledge.' It was said whoever caught the fish and was first to eat it would gain the power to see into the past and future and become the wisest of men. But he must assure he never looked into the eyes of the fish, or he would go into a deep slumber."

Cael noted an expression of amusement on his older friend's face as he continued.

"One day, there was a stirring in the water. An enormous and radiant pink fish jumped out of the water toward Finn and his tutor. The old man could not help but look at the fish's eyes and promptly fell asleep on the riverbank by the fish. Later, when he roused somewhat, though still exhausted, he told Finn to cook the fish but to avoid its eyes and not to eat any of it."

"And does this 'mercifully short story' have an ending?" asked Rodrigo in jest.

Unperturbed, Cael went on. "As young Finn was cooking the salmon, a drop of cooking oil splashed up and landed on his hand. Without thinking, Finn brought his hand to his face and thrust the tip of his thumb in his mouth to relieve the pain. Later, the tutor noticed a change in Finn. His eyes were luminescent and shone with brilliance and his entire aspect radiated an aspect of greatness to come. When Finn explained what happened, the tutor knew immediately. Just the tiny drop of oil that had been on the fish gave Finn this great power. Not in the least upset, his tutor congratulated him. From that day on, Finn became Ireland's greatest hero of legend and leader of the mighty *Fianna* warriors. And whenever he had to contemplate the correct way to solve some critical issue, he would bite on his thumb to be immediately infused with great and supernatural knowledge. Do you now understand, Rodrigo, why those lads were so suddenly awestruck by you?"

Without a moment's hesitation, Rodrigo grinned prodigiously and responded, "Of course I do. I understand quite well and am very fond of this legend. Please assure you relate this exact same tale and my role in it to King Alfonso and the *Campeador* Sancho upon our return to the court. Perhaps I should assume 'Finn Mac Cumhaill' as my battle name in the future."

Not long after their discussion, a runner dashed up to the two of them and reported the column was in sight and approaching a slow marching pace. It did not appear they had posted flankers. There were six mounted Berbers in advance and six more in the rear. The North Africans were armed with light throwing lances and large, straight swords. The infantry seems to be a mix of Arabs, Berbers and *Saqaliba.*

"Did you notice anything different about the steeds of the cavalry?" Rodrigo asked the runner.

"Yes, they were smaller than others I've seen among the enemy here. And their swords were different too; larger and with straighter lines. To me, they seemed to be formed similarly to those the Vikings used at Clontarf."

"Those swords are called *Takobas.* Those riders are from a particular tribe among the Berbers. They are Tuaregs. Their mounts are smaller than others, almost like large ponies, incredibly agile and hardy. They use those lances like javelins from the saddle or in tandem with the swords when the owners fight using two hands. They are the best horsemen among the Berbers. Indeed, they constitute the Caliphate's most formidable cavalry," explained Rodrigo.

Cael concluded the discussion. "Let us be glad there are a mere twelve of these Tuaregs, then. Now, please return to your post. We will attack as planned on my signal."

They had judged the expected length of the column and their own pre-strike positions accurately. By the time the enemy reached the selected target position, only three of the advanced riders and three of the rearmost riders would be out of the killing zone. These would have to be dealt with by arrows at a somewhat extended range.

The shrill blare of the animal horn blasted once more, maddeningly loud and piercing. When the Moors turned their turbaned heads in the direction of the hideous clamor, they observed what they thought was an enormous flock of long, pointed and thin, dark birds flying on a course to pass just over them.

When the first of their comrades screamed in agony and fell to the ground, the horrible truth made itself clear. They were under attack from multiple unseen archers above them on the hill.

Each of the Magyars was able to let off two well-aimed arrows before they mounted their steeds. Loosing from stationary positions on the ground seemed almost childishly easy as they were accustomed to employing their bows from the backs of speeding mounts galloping across varying and uneven grounds. Over one hundred arrows poured into the ranks of the sixty Moorish infantry with total surprise and deadly accuracy.

As the Magyars thundered over the slight rise, then down the gentle slope of the hill to close with their enemy, they continued to nock, draw and loose from the saddle, spreading even more havoc in the midst of the enemy. By the time they were on target, the battle became a simple matter of mopping up the shattered remnants. Those still standing were impaled from multiple directions by prancing horsemen.

The three lead riders of the column did not hesitate to rush off to escape southward upon seeing the fate of their comrades. Incredibly, the three who were well behind surprisingly decided to conduct a suicide attack against the wild and strange enemy force that was mercilessly dispatching the last few survivors. Two of them were brought down by what were near the last of the unused arrows. But another got close enough to cast his slim yet large-bladed lance, which pierced the breast of one of the Magyars, who crumpled and fell immediately to the ground. Before the attacker could close and engage with his huge sword, he was felled by another arrow.

It was over. The slain Magyar was one of the Hispanian knights. This poor soul was the only casualty of the week's long and dangerous raid into the Caliphate until then. Rodrigo dismounted and cradled the man's head as he knelt beside him. Standing again, he made the sign of the cross over his long-time friend and weapon brother as others came and gathered his body, wrapped it in a shroud and respectfully strapped him over his mount. The gelding whinnied but soon calmed, carrying his former master with dignity. Despite the need to hasten away, they collected as many arrows as they could before they struck out north toward the Castile border.

They fortunately encountered no other Moors and by riding through the night and after ascertaining there were none to observe them, they silently crossed into Castile just before dawn. As the morning sun was rising, casting a golden red glow over the treetops, they arrived at their previously designated assembly area. They were met by a small and trusted band of Castilian knights who were said to be from the family of Alfonso's Queen Mother, Elvira.

These greeted them as comrades, brought along provisions to make them a breakfast of pork, trout, toasted multigrain bread, local butter and oranges from the distant south. The Magyars changed into conventional Hispanian traveling clothes, which were waiting for them in their original wagons. After several hours' sleep, they set out with their Castilian escort toward Leon. One of the wagons contained the body of the slain Leonese knight. Their escorts had procured a wooden coffin for them from a nearby woodworker when they learned of his death.

As they entered Leon once again, they mourned the loss of their one comrade. Yet all knew they had accomplished their mission and had succeeded in their risk-filled mission with a success that exceeded even their initial expectations. They had penetrated deep into an armed and hostile environment, spread alarm, dread and chaos among the populace and slew scores of enemy warriors. Against all odds, they had lost only one of their weapon brothers and apparently done nothing to compromise their cover as a ravishing band of Magyar savages. They could return to the capital and their leaders with their heads held high, proud of their victory.

# Chapter 17

### The Caliph's Quandary

Within the walls of Caliph Sulayman's lavish and opulent palace in the city of Cordoba, all was not well. Seated cross-legged on plush cushions around a low table, gathered the Caliph, the Emir and several diplomatic, religious and military advisors.

"Has Allah abandoned us or are all of you merely cretinous and benighted imbeciles? Or, worse yet, are you plotting against me?"

Sulayman was on another tear of rage, as occurred more frequently of late. His inner circle had borne the brunt of these blistering tirades before and had learned to let the fiery accusations continue before any of them spoke.

"What *Shaitan* has caused Viking *majus* to plunder our coasts and islands again? And now we learn pagan Magyars have once more stormed into our lands in the northern marches. The reports of arrivals of new and strange Christian barbarian warriors, be they Keltoi or Hibernians, into Leon are also evil auguries."

The Caliph then directed his stern gaze at the Emir. "And your 'Master Assassin' sent with great care to eliminate the vaunted champion of these barbarians failed miserably. We have only his bodiless and desiccated head and a mocking note from Leon's boy king to show for our efforts."

The storm raged on. "Our court physician is either kidnapped or allowed to escape to the north. In any case, he is gone and his replacement is far less skilled. Then, as outlandish fables of ancient Greek warriors emerge, our specially equipped siege and destroy detachment has gone missing after sacking but one of those infernal Leonese border dens from whence they launch spies into our lands."

He paused for a moment, took three deep breaths and exhaled, then began to regain some of his composure, his fury extinguished for the moment. "So, my sage counselors, what now? We have attempted to crush Leon's eyes and ears, to send our own tribes of Berber ravagers to harry them and to insert a meticulously selected executioner into their midst. All to no avail."

Sensing the worst of the storm had passed, the Emir took a chance on speaking, "In the past, we have discussed conducting a decisive strike into the Leon's heart, which would discourage forever any further assaults on the Caliphate. We are now in a position where we must rally our people across all the provinces. That in itself presents a challenge, given recent events, as some of our provinces have become restive of late."

"Still, in recent weeks, we have loosed yet another arrow from our quiver into Leon and it may be seeking its targets even as we now sit here," advised one of the military leaders among them. "This one may soon become a holy *shaheed* and eradicate what we perceive as some of our greatest threats."

All present knew of what he spoke and nodded their heads in hope and prayer.

"There is that, thankfully," remarked the diplomatic advisor. "Yet there remains the need to unite and unify our peoples once more. We all have agreed we must strike a blow against our Christian enemies with indomitable force. The question is where, when and in what strength. I suggest that, instead of sending out the periodic tribute-collecting delegations, we send formal diplomatic and religious emissaries, in this instance to inform the various provincial leaders of our general intentions and gain their support. In doing so, they will also announce that the Caliph has decided to forgo the collection of this season's tribute. This will convey to the people the Caliph's munificence and inspire them. When these parties return, we will be in a better position to prepare the hammer strike."

The senior religious representative now spoke up.

"As Caliph, Sulayman, you may take the most serious road of calling for a holy war – *Jihad* - against the unbelievers. Yet you must do so with the utmost caution. Even the great Almanzor did that only in the name of Caliph Hisham. And Hisham is, apparently, no more. You were proclaimed Caliph by the Berbers and they remain your stoutest supporters among our peoples. In any case, declaring a jihad turned out to be Almanzor's greatest success in uniting our peoples in a time of similar strife. All rallied to him and he was perceived as the strongest horse and thus was he called 'the Victorious' by the masses."

The Caliph's demeanor visibly changed as the religious scholar talked about Almanzor and his deeds. His back and shoulders straightened and his voice regained a more confident timbre as he again spoke.

"Much of what you have just voiced is not without its merit and you have my appreciation. I admit I have reservations about not collecting the taxes of tribute that are needed to maintain the apparatus for governing our Caliphate. However, I see the wisdom of projecting an image of empathy and grace in the cause of preserving our unity."

Sulayman then stood up, his hands folded behind his back and began to stride slowly around his circle of seated advisors as he announced his decision.

"Select six contingents of trusted religious men and diplomats. They need only be escorted by enough warriors to see to their personal protection and that number should be limited and non-threatening. Assure they are all aware of what we have discussed here today, especially about the dire need to strike out at our most serious enemy in Leon in defense of our people and our Caliphate. In two days, they should be prepared to travel to the major provinces – to the upper and lower marches, to the coastal areas of the middle sea and importantly to the cities of Saraqusta, Tulaytulah and Kulumriyya."

The Caliph concluded with an ominous assertion. "When they return and I hear the results of my beneficence, I will decide whether to declare *Jihad* against the North. In any case, we must even now prepare to gather warriors to strike the Christians. And, when we have finished successfully punishing Leon, that same army will be used to bring into tow by fire and fury whatever treacherous provinces do not choose to join us. My Berbers will see to that. Let it be done."

***

While the Magyars were away on their wild excursion, causing havoc, mayhem and chaos in the north of the Caliphate, not all their Irish comrades were at rest. On the morning of the riders' departure to Castile and then on to Navarre, word had arrived at Alfonso's court yet again from the southern border. Leonese scouts had furtively observed an odd column moving north along a main road. They counted eighty mounted warriors, though none appeared to be typical cavalry but rather infantry in quilted armor, with heavy slashing scimitars and crescent shields affixed to their horses' saddles. Horse-drawn siege engines accompanied them, mounted on wheeled platforms. Of course, the scout had never seen a siege engine but he described what appeared to be a type of catapult with ropes and wooden beams. Sancho knew at once what that meant. The Moors were moving again on the nearest Leonese border outpost.

Alfonso thought he had time to reinforce the likely objective before the enemy arrived if they moved quickly enough.

As they discussed the plans, Wolf looked at Fergus and nodded. The big red head then began.

“Sancho, with your permission, I have a suggestion which follows the pattern we’ve established of heaping confusion on our enemies. I believe I can deploy fifty of my Spartans to give the besiegers a surprise when they breach the wooden palisades there. Naturally, they would augment those Leonese knights already there,” offered Fergus, proud Captain of the Spartan heavy infantry.

“But Fergus, can your armored titans actually ride horses?” asked Sancho in all seriousness.

The Irish leaders, among them, laughed together at that.

“Perhaps not as well as our little Magyar satyrs but yes, we’re all cross-trained in the basics of horsemanship.” Fergus continued, “If we can arrive quickly enough and conceal ourselves within some structure inside, we can allow the Moors to breach the walls quickly and pour inside. Then we emerge from inside, the defenders fall back around us and we advance on and slay the enemy warriors.”

King Alfonso grinned at the massive crimson haired young man. “You make it sound so simple, Fergus. Are you really so confident this will succeed?”

The Spartan leader did not hesitate. “One can never be assured of unimpeded victory but we have carried out something very like this not long ago against our Viking foes.”

All the Irish smiled in unison, remembering King Brian’s siege of Viking-occupied Dublin before the Clontarf battle and the Spartans’ role in that siege.

“Among our Viking enemies was an enormous force of what were called Jomsvikings. They are a semi-monastic and zealous warrior caste whose first loyalty is to the Norse gods. Their only occupation is warfare and they eagerly do battle with any foe, even other Vikings who are not deemed devout enough. They receive vast amounts of wealth as paid mercenaries from many leaders across Europe and Britannia. We surprised them on a bridge as they tried to move out from the fortified city of Dublin. My Spartans slaughtered them in their hundreds and watched their heavily armored bodies plunge off the bridge into the cold, muddy waters. We were three hundred then and slew twice our number in that single battle. I reckon our fifty will annihilate eighty Moors, especially if we come on them unawares."

"And if you manage to let a few survive, the tales will be told of a band of formidable and ghostly ancient Greek warriors to be counted as enemies of the Caliphate along with Vikings, Magyars and we Christians of the North," added Alfonso, immediately discerning the intent of Fergus' request.

"I will select six of our knights to accompany you, Fergus and I believe we should include a few of our women to go along with them. If the raiders believe a number of local women are also present at the post, they will assume their presence has not been detected," Sancho said.

At that point, Aoife decided to leverage an opportunity. "May I suggest, Saoirse, go along as well? I've noted she has spent much time with Fergus and his Spartans and knows them well by now. She has also proven to be a skilled scout and spy, not to mention her skills with her throwing knives, as we've learned recently in the affair of Zaynab's half-brother."

"Agreed to all. Let us commence as quickly as possible to arrive well before the enemy comes on the scene," concluded the king.

The next night, the Spartans and the others arrived after dark. Several riders had been sent ahead to have those in the garrison send out scouts to assure the outpost was not already under active surveillance. Sweeps around the periphery of the site out to some distance disclosed no furtive observers yet present. So, the Hispanians put out manned observation posts to prevent surprise.

This outpost was similar to the other old Roman fortress ruins but it was also strategically placed on the flat summit of a low hill, offering a commanding view of the surrounding fields and meadows. A small, bubbling stream ran along the northern base of the hillside, providing fresh, cool water. As was the usual case, many of the garrison were now deployed in the Caliphate, acting as Alfonso's early warning screen. However, a few locals who occasionally came by to sell provisions to the scouts were present when the Spartans arrived in the dark under a moonless sky.

As Sancho's knights explained the plan to the post's commander, Fergus was pleased to find there was a large warehouse structure appropriately built on the site of a previous Roman warehouse. It was quite spacious and since it was meant to store barrels and casks of local wines, it was constructed primarily of stone and earth with a slate roof. This kept the wine cooler and fresher for longer. Because it was early in the growing season, the warehouse was essentially empty. The structure would certainly be large enough to house the fifty Spartans, though they would be dismayed to discover it was quite devoid of wine, Fergus was sure.

Also, because the outpost was on an elevated summit, there was no chance of observation from outside. The Spartans would not have to be confined in the building for an extended period, as they had been back in a similar barn-like structure outside the formidable walls of Dublin. They could walk about in the post's interior, hidden by the log palisades, until the time came for them to conceal themselves inside the warehouse.

The Spartans and the knights bedded down in the warehouse after eating from the victuals they had brought with them from Leon. The women, assembled from Alfonso's kitchen staff, shared a much smaller building as sleeping quarters and Saoirse enjoyed their company even though she couldn't understand all of their conversations. She became fond of them mainly because they were cheerful and laughed a lot, notwithstanding the fact they had been brought along primarily as bait and decoys.

The next morning, as the Spartans exercised in the interior spaces of the outpost, the women and some of the men began a series of continual trips to the river to collect water, filling it into clay urns with curved handles. Fergus and some of the post's garrison used the time to make a modification to the warehouse's front entrance doors. At mid-afternoon, a rider came galloping up the incline pathway to the post's main gate which opened to the west. He reported breathlessly that the enemy was approaching at some distance and would arrive from the west around dusk. He had observed them from a tall tree within a heavily wooded area which formed a crescent running from the south to the west around the outpost. The scout was told to return to his post and conceal himself, then withdraw to the outpost after darkness fell.

Around midnight, the vigilant guard returned and announced the siege party had arrived and set up a camp in a wooded glade just inside the tree line to the west of the outpost. Its composition mirrored what the young survivors of the previous attack had described – about eighty heavy Moorish infantry and two siege engines on wheeled platforms drawn by teams of horses. The previous siege had taken place in mid-morning and the guarded assumption was that this surprise attack would occur similarly.

In the early morning, it was decided that several women should once again retrieve water from the stream, keeping a close eye to the west in case they had to dash back to the main gate. Naturally, Saoirse was one of those chosen as she was an actual scout. The formidable red-haired Irish woman was accompanied by one of the kitchen servants, a young but feisty and fearless girl who pleaded to accompany her. The purpose was, once again, to lull the Moors into thinking they had arrived unseen since two bucolic country women were collecting drinking water, seemingly oblivious to the oncoming threat.

Meanwhile, Fergus' Spartans, the Leonese knights and the garrison scouts were preparing the battleground in the interior of the palisaded post. They positioned wagons, wooden storage containers and small sheds in a manner that inevitably canalized the attackers into a somewhat narrower maneuver space directly in front of the large warehouse. The urns of water were placed around those structures that would be preserved from fire arrows.

With its slate roof and water-doused timber walls, the warehouse would be unlikely to catch fire. The knights assured all the fighting men outside of the warehouse would be issued stout wooden, water-drenched shields when the first arrows were loosed into the compound. Alfonso's brave women joined the Spartans under the slate roof and Fergus saw that each of them was issued a short sword to defend themselves if need be. But the Irish titan was confident that he need not worry, as he was certain no harm would befall them. His Spartans would see to that.

As Saoirse and the Hispanian girl were approaching the gate, the guard announced their return, proclaiming, "They're back safe and no sign of the enemy."

However, once Saoirse was inside and the gate was closed, she broke into a run, rushing to report to Fergus and the senior Leonese knight.

"Six archers, crawling like snakes on their bellies from the west through the meadow, clad in grass-draped robes and by now within bow range of us. And I'm sure I heard straining wheels and the *clomp* of booted feet coming from the forest towards us," she declared with confidence.

"Fine lass ye' are!" replied Fergus, feeling immensely proud of her as he tried his best to convey her Gaelic words in an understandable way to the Leonese leader. Grasping the basic gist, the knight cast a stern glance at the gate guard and shook his head.

"Please don't blame him, Sir. I had a good vantage point and I've a wee bit of experience at doing this," said Saoirse with a smile to the Hispanian.

The Spartan and the knight were both fully armored and garbed in the panoplies of their warrior styles, while she was clothed in the manner of a simple country girl.

Fergus didn't even bother trying to translate the girl's words in defense of the guard as the first few fire arrows flamed from the sky into the enclosed spaces. One struck the packed earth while another landed on a shed which was allowed to burn. At the exact moment, three of the women decoys rushed out of the side of the earthen structure and began to dash about the interior, screaming in feigned fear. Having spent time with the Spartans as the armored behemoths prepared for battle, Alfonso's audacious cooking women were smiling between screams, certain of what was to come. Some of the men inside also began to call out in feigned alarm.

The gate guard called down again. "Two catapults deploying and aiming toward the gate. Heavy infantry in line on either side of them. Archers continuing to knock and loose, all flaming arrows."

When a fire arrow narrowly missed his head, he leapt down to join his comrades who were taking positions in a semi-circle around the previously positioned obstacles. Others were dousing some of the interior structures with water from the urns that had been placed around them. All the men were under the cover of water-drenched wooden shields. The women had returned to the shelter of the patiently waiting Spartans inside the slate-roofed warehouse.

The first huge round stone landed in the interior, smashing a feeding trough for horses and other livestock. The animals had been sent to neighboring homesteads earlier. Other stones struck the palisaded walls, breaking holes through them. Yet it was obvious their primary target was the main gate. As the incoming arrows came to a halt, the warriors within braced themselves. Two heavy projectiles struck the gate at almost the same time sundering the wood and leaving a gaping cleft.

With a resounding war cry, which may have been a prayer, the first of the heavily armored warriors burst through the breach and crouched behind their huge heart-shaped shields. Those just behind cleared the debris to widen the gap and let the others pour in five abreast in an onrushing tide of spears and deadly scimitars. These were the cream of the Caliphate's Arabic foot soldiers. They all wore exquisitely designed chain mail tunics down to their knees, over which were leather jerkins studded with metal plates. Steel helmets, overlaid with a type of white turban wrapping, protected their bearded heads. Interestingly, some carried spears with short swords at their sides while others seemed to prefer their razor-sharp curved scimitars.

The Leonese within let fly spears as the Moors spread out and deployed into a line formation four deep and began moving into the interior. Very few of them found a target. When one lucky cast dropped a man, the warrior behind him moved into his place. Like an irresistible juggernaut, the disciplined formation moved deeper into the outpost interior as the few Leonese defenders ran back, disappearing behind a large earthen warehouse.

The formation paused to survey their surroundings. Around them on all sides were burning sheds, wagons and other containers. Yet other objects had proved to be seemingly immune to the fire arrows whose shafts were protruding from them. On closer examination, the sheen of a wet coating was easily observable. They now realized for the first time that they were standing amidst a cleverly designed field of battle meant to minimize their ability to deploy on a wider front.

At that moment, a loud crash assaulted their ears as the wide doors of the warehouse structure were smashed to the ground. A strange and almost preternatural sight greeted them. A solid line of fully armored warriors emerged from the structure. They marched silently, five abreast and ten deep. All wore thick steel helmets, reinforced at the top with crossed iron studs, a nose guard and a mail skirting to cover their necks. Each carried a thick, round wooden shield, swagged with iron chain. Over their shoulders, they effortlessly bore heavy spears with long and deadly triangular blades. All of them were swathed in the same scarlet robes which fell below their knees. The robes covered the well-made chain male jerkins each wore underneath.

Some of the Arabs had previously served in Muslim occupied Sicily, where they had seen paintings and statues of ancient Greek hoplites. But all knew such warriors had not existed for more than a thousand years. What was even more unsettling was the sheer massive stature of these new enemies. These were the largest men, if men they were, that any of the Arabs had ever seen. Even those not immensely tall were built in the fashion of rampant bulls, brawny and robust with rippling muscle. Their biceps, easily visible as they held the deadly stabbing spears on their shoulders, were as thick as the thighs on some of their own men.

The Moorish infantry was deployed within the confined space, five abreast and about fourteen deep, given their few losses to the Leonese spears. This was still a formidable striking force indeed and they outnumbered their strange foes. They were also seasoned warriors, most of them having seen combat on foreign battlefields all around the Middle Sea. They were accustomed to neither defeat nor fear. With a renewed roar, they hurled themselves at the slowly and silently approaching phalanx.

What followed was a cacophony of groans, grunts and curses on the Moorish side and an eerie whir, almost a buzz, from the other side. This was a mechanical slicing sound, as powerful and continuous thrusts of murderous Spartan spears drove in and out of the enemy's armor and flesh. Most of these young Irish men had trained exactly for this scenario, hurling their bodies behind huge shields, first against huge trees and then lines of wagons filled with heavy boulders for hours. Push and drive one’s legs until the obstacle yields or they do; all the while thrusting their lances repeatedly at well-aimed targets on the enemy’s body.

As one Spartan’s strength waned from the constant effort, he would fall back in practiced movement through the ranks to be replaced by the man behind him. The inexorable drive penetrated through the unsuspecting Moors like a scythe. The boots of the Spartans trampled those Arabs who fell wounded and those behind used their spears’ butt spikes to end their fallen foes’ agonies as they moved continuously forward.

The carnage was ghastly and gruesome but mercifully brief in duration. The confined field was now covered with the crushed and bleeding bodies of much of the attacking force. Spartan spears had skewered most, though the force of the iron-swagged thick wooden shields had also crushed many. The Spartans had trained intensely in using the heavy round shields as weapons as much as their spears and fighting *scians.* Close to sixty armored Moors lay dead.

The dozen or so Leonese now moved around the area of battle toward the gate to prevent any withdrawal. But they were too late as a handful of Moorish warriors, who had been at the rear of the formation, took the opportunity to fly out of the outpost shouting to the men at the siege engines.

“It was a trap! Hundreds of alien warriors were waiting for us. They’re built of iron and muscle and cannot be slain. Unhitch the horses. Leave the machines. We must mount and fly before they come out to murder us.”

Those manning the siege engines needed no further prompting. They swiftly unhitched the harnesses from the stays, then removed the bulky harnesses themselves. Few had ridden bareback in the past but whatever demons might emerge from the sundered gate would no doubt prove to be a greater threat.

Altogether, nine Moors managed to mount and gallop off to the east. Three soon fell clumsily from the backs of their mounts and bounced on the ground, rolling several times. One was unable to rise and lay still, his body twisted in an unnatural angle. The other two limped unsteadily following the path of their mounted comrades. These would be allowed to escape if they proved sturdy enough to walk to the border.

Fergus now walked among his warriors, who were exultant even as they strove to catch their breath and stretch their muscles after the frenetic battle. Sweat lathered their arms and the exposed portions of their faces under their helmets but there was little to no blood to be seen. Then Fergus caught sight of one of his warriors crumpled on the ground. The man was unmoving and surrounded by four of his comrades who knelt over him.

"Young Pádraig slew six of the enemy on his own but he tripped over the body of one of them whose scimitar was angled upwards. The slicing blade caught the poor lad under his chin," dolefully explained the young man's best friend.

Like all commanders, Fergus was crestfallen at the loss of any of his men. But Pádraig had been the youngest among them, which somehow seemed to make his death even more poignant. The red-haired giant removed his own helmet and knelt beside his comrades. Then he gently released the strap of the boy's helmet and put it aside, letting loose a mane of flaxen hair. He bent to kiss his fallen warrior on the forehead and made the sign of the cross. Finally, he stood again and continued checking on his Spartans. There were only two additional injuries, both relatively minor. One received a gash on his calf from a luck spear thrust. The other had broken his nose on his own shield when one enormous Moor had fallen into it in his death throes.

Considering the outcome, the mission had been a stirring victory for the Spartans but the loss of Pádraig was bittersweet for these tough and formidable men. Fergus' decision was to spend the next two days at the outpost to assist in repairing damage, dispose of the slain enemy in a mass grave and await any possible move of retaliation. The Leonese knights left immediately after the battle to report to King Alfonso and arrange for a new contingent of Leonese warriors to support the garrison at the outpost. The Irish used the time to bury their comrade, accompanied by the most welcome blessings of a local priest. A local mason had fashioned a small stone Celtic cross and Fergus had Pádraig's good Irish name engraved on the crossbeam.

On the third morning, after their horses had been returned from their shelter among local homesteaders, the Spartans and the now proven courageous and resilient women of the King's kitchen slowly made their way back to the capital city. It was a glorious morning, the sun shining golden with a refreshing breeze from the northwest. Saoirse rode contentedly at Fergus' side. With words of comfort, she spoke to him.

"Can ye' feel it, dear Fergus? This cool and fragrant breeze wafts all the way to us from our own beloved island to cheer us along the way. Do ye' not catch the scent of the Irish sea, the good aroma of dark turf and a lingering aura of sheep, Connemara ponies and our precious hounds? It's sure I am that Pádraig feels it as well as he watches us right now from his place in heaven."

# Chapter 18

**Return of the Count**

While the Magyars and Spartans were deployed in the Caliphate, events and preparations continued inside Leon. The Galician recruits for each of the special Irish battle groups were being drilled intensely. Every recruit had an individual tutor and mentor, allowing them to be trained both individually and as a group. The Magyar trainees already had experience in riding and in employing bows and arrows. Now they were being taught the Magyar techniques of doing both at the same time – an entirely different skill set.

The burly Galicians, who would be Spartans, were strong young lads and competent swordsmen. Their trainer mentors had the challenge of teaching them the classic tactics associated with taking their place in line in the phalanx and using spears and shields to overwhelm and crush their opposition. This particularly required building expanded muscle mass in their legs and backs.

No matter how excruciating the training was, their mentors were pleased to see that not a single Galician quit. The trainers also used the time to conduct language instruction; first, simple Gaelic vocabulary and tactical commands, then the rudiments of basic grammar. The instructors were amused to find that trying to learn the Irish tongue was more stressful for their trainees than was the rigorous martial and physical training they endured each day without complaint.

Noting the effectiveness of Aoife as chief of Intelligence for the Clontarf veterans, Sancho appointed his own counterpart. This man was the most experienced and successful of the Leonese scout rangers; his reports, filled with accurate details and his assessments of Moorish intentions, had always been proven prescient. His Latin was flawless and this man, Miguel and Aoife exchanged information and ideas to great effect. The experience and knowledge of Pyrrhus, Schlomo and Felix also benefited both of them. The older men had the advantage of being able to analyze the current situation through the lens of past events. All knew, however, that while the past does not always predict the future, history has ways of repeating itself more often than not.

Meanwhile, Felix led Cormac and Helena on a goodwill tour of the other Christian lands of the North – Castile, Navarre, Barcelona and some of the smaller holdings. In each, they visited first the regents, then the estates of some of the other nobility. For Felix, as senior diplomat from the Kingdom of Leon, this was an opportunity to display the prominence of King Alfonso. Helena represented the Emperor of the Christian Greek Roman Empire in Constantinople.

Prince Cormac was introduced as a member of the royalty of Ireland. This island realm had just won an enormous victory over a horde of invading Vikings and delivered the land from foreign occupation. Cormac may have been a bit embarrassed by the pomp and ceremony but that didn't matter. The seasoned Irish warrior just cherished the opportunity to travel to new lands with the exquisitely alluring, dark-haired Greek woman at his side.

Despite the appearance of a simple diplomatic excursion, these visits were meant to acquaint the Christian allies with the developing threats from their great enemy and to forge personal ties with leaders and military commanders. Though he would not admit it, Felix relished showing off the foreign guests of Leon by riding through the populated cities and towns with Cormac and Helena. Since neither was traveling with anything resembling a national standard, the Leonese were bold enough to fabricate one for them. For the Irish, Leonese seamstresses had designed a banner with a field of brilliant green centered by a golden Celtic cross embroidered with black triskele spirals. For the Empire, they contrived a flowing flag with a royal purple background centered by the Greek chi X and rho *P* Christian cross. Both Helena and Cormac heartily approved of them.

So, the sight of the exotic and resplendent visitors riding through their streets on splendid horses, accompanied by an ambassador of Leon, riding under that kingdom's maroon colored, rampant, golden-crowned lion, stirred the passions of the town folks and filled them with confidence that they would never be alone against the Moorish invaders.

Riding close beside his elegant Greek companion, Cormac leaned toward her to whisper in her ear. "I must admit my lady, I much prefer riding alongside you in the company of admiring throngs than sitting on the hard benches of those damned Viking dragon ships for days on end."

Then, to the cheers of the onlookers, he bent even further to kiss her on the cheek. She beamed brightly at him, then turned to the crowd with a contagious smile and they were both hailed even more boisterously.

***

After a pleasant time on the road and having met with many of the nobles, warriors and common people of their neighbors, Felix was satisfied. They had gained assurances of support whenever needed to counter the evil power that threatened them. Likewise, Felix assured his counterparts and their regents that Alfonso would rush to their aid when summoned.

Back in the capital city of Leon, a miraculous event occurred that thrilled all of Alfonso's court. Late one morning, just before noon, two Leonese border scouts appeared in the courtyard, escorting a scruffy-looking man in a worn and tattered tunic. They declared to the surprised guards that they wanted to bring this man to the king immediately. The guards looked dubious but the scouts told them they had found him limping alone in a meadow as they watched from a nearby hill just across the border with the Caliphate. When he fell to the ground, they rode to him, believing he might be a Christian slave or *dhimmi* in need of assistance.

As they approached closer, he took note of their good Hispanian faces and then announced in a weak voice that he was Count Ramiro of Asturias. Though his tone was pained, his words were conveyed in the most elegant and refined manner of their native tongue. The scouts and the guards all knew the name of Count Ramiro. He had been a grand champion of Leon and a cousin of King Alfonso. Yet they also had been told he had been slain in battle three years earlier.

"He explained he'd been knocked from his horse by the blow of a Moorish war club when his small troop of riders was overrun by an enormous band of Berbers those years past. When he awoke, he was in chains and delivered to an Arabic nobleman who put him in slavery to work in a silver mine. Quite recently, by some great fortune, a huge flood rolled through the site of the mine, chaos ensued and he was able to steal a hammer and chisel, remove his leg irons and escape to the north. This had been several days earlier and we can attest there were indeed monstrously heavy rains to the south," said one of the scouts.

"He insisted on first being reunited with the king before anything else," the scout added.

"After seeing to it that he got a good wash, a full meal and refreshing fruit juice, we acceded to his wishes and brought him directly here after first acquiring simple yet clean raiment for him. We've ridden straight through for the last three days."

"Then, by all means, let us bring him to the king. And welcome home, Count Ramiro!" proclaimed the senior guard.

The king and his court were sitting in the main dining hall inside his residence at long tables when a young guard walked quietly and respectfully over to Alfonso.

"With your leave, my King, there is a visitor who says that he is Count Ramiro of Asturias, who begs the honor of joining you. Shall I tell him to wait until your meal is concluded?"

The king pushed back his chair to stand erect. "This cannot be. My brave and noble cousin was slain in battle against our enemy years ago. He was among the greatest of our knight defenders. How can he be here now?"

Alfonso looked to his mother, Queen Elvira. "He was almost like an older brother to me. I must see him now." Then, turning to the guard, he said, "Advise Ramiro that his king awaits his company with great pleasure and no delay. Bring him to us now."

The score or so at the table, which included Wolf, Aoife, Mornak and Keli, watched with interest as a somewhat unkempt yet still imposing man strode in escorted by two guards. He appeared to be on the cusp of entering his third decade. His hair was long, black and quite unruly, given his recent trials. His dark beard was scruffy and he walked unevenly toward the seat of the king. The dark brown eyes, however, never wavered.

"Is it you, Ramiro? Have you truly come back to us?" exclaimed the king excitedly, uncaring of any perceived lack of decorum.

"It is my King and my cousin. My only hope over these three long years of enslavement was to survive somehow and return to once again serve Leon and Asturias. To manifest to my countrymen that none of us are killed so easily." Ramiro paused and looked about those assembled, his eyes blazing with almost unfathomable solemnity. "And to once again grow strong and defiant in the face of the true and evil enemy."

All the Leonese cheered and many wept at the words of their now returned hero and champion. Alfonso sprang towards him and clasped both arms around the shoulders of his cousin, apparently risen from the dead. Others likewise arose and gathered around Ramiro, gently stroking his arms and back and giving praise to God.

"Have no care of your current raiment and appearance, cousin, sit now with us and partake of good Leonese food and wine," said Alfonso, making a place at his side.

The newcomer sat comfortably beside the king, apparently relishing the sumptuous meat, bread and vegetables. Still, he declined the wine, telling the servants he needed time to once again be in the right condition to quaff such a strong, delicious and sparkling drink without embarrassing himself. Cool water from the springs of Leon was all he needed at the moment, he told them with a gracious smile.

Alfonso and Elvira both took delight in conversing with Ramiro, for he was a particular favorite of the King's father, Bermudo, because of his dedication to soldierly duty and his aristocratic family background. They were somewhat dismayed to inform him his wife had remarried into yet another noble family. But both they and he knew a young noble woman who'd not yet had children was expected to find a new spouse of good breeding upon the death of her husband.

"I bear her no ill will," replied Ramiro, "I would have expected her to do such. Though I'm happily obliged, my dear uncle has kept my land and holdings in good stead and I've a home to which I may return."

"And return you shall, Ramiro but not for long, I must confess. There is much afoot within the Caliphate and none of it bodes well for us or our peoples. Still, we have secrets and plans of our own to secure our kingdom. And new and formidable allies. Of this and more, we will talk after you've spent this first night with us and then go home to recover. But please don't tarry there long, I beg, we will have need of your strong arm and courage in the coming days," said Alfonso, feeling comforted by this unexpected miracle.

"And cousin, we do pray that we will not only defend and protect our own kingdom but spark the flame which will collapse the Caliphate and begin the long but inevitable road that will lead to the expulsion of the foreign invaders from our beloved Hispania."

Ramiro stayed that night in the royal chambers and after having been provided with suitable garments and a powerful horse to carry him, made his way alone to his Asturian homeland. Upon returning to his estate, he bestowed curt greetings and thanks to his uncle and retired to his former quarters. His parents were both dead and he was an only child, so it was an expensive but lonely home that greeted him. Even though he knew well the few remaining servant staff who had been there since his childhood, his interactions with them were minimal.

They did take note when he departed on his second day home to travel to a heavily forested local range of low hills, where he apparently spent the night in prayer. On the third day, Ramiro bid farewell to his uncle, telling him that his king needed him and that the older man should continue to manage the estate, drawing from the family's accrued wealth as needed. With that and now garbed in the raiment and armored panoply of a regal knight, with his hair properly trimmed and beard shaped and oiled, he trotted back to the capital city of Leon.

***

All of Leon's nobles were delighted with the return of Count Ramiro and there was little talk of anything else, especially among the women, while he was in Asturias. The men took his liberation as an augury of victory in battle. Some of them were aware there was a small horde of Christian 'Magyars' causing havoc in the Upper March of the Caliphate, while another group of Christian 'Spartan' ironmen had been deployed to a frontier outpost to serve as a nasty and brutal surprise for Moorish ravishers. At the same time, they knew the king's senior diplomat had been dispatched on a goodwill tour to the other Christian lands of the North and that he was in the company of an Ambassador from Emperor Basil of the Christian Greek Roman Empire and a Prince of the Irish. All of this seemed to bode welcome tidings after years of reversals and disappointments for the Kingdom of Leon.

The Irish warriors continued to train with the Leonese foot soldiers to the point they could seamlessly conduct a series of offensive and defensive tactics, melding the most effective combat techniques of both groups. Linguistic differences presented a lesser challenge than originally suspected, as all fighting men seemed to possess a common language of their own.

When Wolf and Aoife first witnessed the surprise arrival of the returned warrior count, Wolf was as pleased and charmed as all of the Leonese at his unexpected appearance.

"This Ramiro has the look of a powerful fighting man. Considering what he has endured and survived, he must be destined for greatness in battle in the service of his king in the days to come," Wolf remarked later to Aoife. She said nothing in reply, merely nodding with a slight smile.

Wolf continued, "I must admit Alfonso has taken quite an attachment to me of late. I believe he knows the most trying of times is approaching for him and he wants to be totally prepared mentally and physically. He understands we Irish also recently underwent a monumental trial in battle against a steadfast and cruel enemy and that we prevailed. He has respectfully requested that I spend a few days alone training him, just he and I."

"And how, exactly, do you intend to do that?" asked Aoife impishly.

"At Innisfallen, my battle trainer was quite fond of drilling me in and around the shores and icy cold waters of Loch Léin, which, as you know, appropriately means the 'Lake of Learning.' And learn and grow I did in stamina and the various techniques of combat. I shall take the king to the much smaller and warmer lake on his private hunting grounds and try my best to emulate the dear trainer of my youth who was simply called 'Trainer' by everyone," said Wolf, smiling with pleasant memories.

"Alfonso will be made to swim the extent of the lake repeatedly with one of our heavy shields strapped to his back. He will stand on the bench of a small rowing boat and continually slash, thrust and slice at the air until he can do so without losing his balance and falling into the water," Wolf continued mirthfully. "On shore, he will be strapped to a wagon stripped of its wheels and loaded with rocks and he will pull that like a draft horse around the lake until he has worn a new and smooth path there. We will spar with wooden training swords, where he will learn that a deadly aimed thrust is much more effective in ending a fight than a wild slash."

"You seem to be enjoying this too much already and you haven't even started yet. I feel sorry for the poor boy. He is only twenty years old," interjected Aoife humorously.

"I was only fourteen when I began my warrior training," replied Wolf defensively.

But then he paused for an instant and broke into a self-deprecating laugh, realizing that his sweet girl was just playing with him. After all, he thought, hadn't she slain her first Viking when she was but fourteen years old herself?

"You're right as usual, *a stór.* Perhaps I just crave a chance to relive the days of my youth once more. And this Alfonso is a sturdy, brilliant and likeable young Christian man and makes for pleasant company even if he is a nobleman of the highest pedigree," Wolf admitted, grinning. "Besides, even though Cormac, Pyrrhus, Helena, Fergus and Cael are away performing God's work, I trust you, Mornak, Keli and Brother Cillian can look after our people to assure all is well for a few days."

"You're quite right, Captain, even you are not indispensable, though I'd never risk trying to tell that to all those men who would gladly follow you through hell's gates," agreed Aoife, again displaying her customary sly and cunning smile.

***

It was Alfonso's second day of rigorous training under the tutelage of the Irish titan. The first day had been dedicated to physical conditioning. Wolf wanted to assess whether he was dealing with a soft aristocrat or a budding Warrior King. He was reasonably sure the young monarch would allay any concerns he might have. The two were clad in light sleeveless cotton tunics, which fell to their thighs and woolen breeches, which reached just to their knees. Both were barefoot.

Though a full head shorter than Wolf, the King was a strapping figure at twenty years old with wiry muscles and not a trace of fat. He was strong with lightning-quick reflexes and possessed admirable natural balance. He was put through some of the same trials that Wolf had endured himself as a youth, as earlier described to Aoife. The king spent the morning dragging a boulder-filled wooden box that had been the bed of a cart before its wheels were removed. After two lengthy circuits around the entire periphery of the lake, he had indeed left behind a smooth and visible walking path devoid of obstacles.

At noon, he was allowed to stop and collapse onto the soft grass gratefully. While he had been dragging his ponderous burden across the grounds, Wolf had attacked the base of an oak tree with an axe, felling it, then removing the branches and hacking until he had a thick, round log the same height and weight as a grown man. He allowed Alfonso to have a bit of a rest, quaff cool water from a skin and dine on common people's simple brown bread.

"You've succeeded in creating a lovely, flattened walking path which encircles the entire lake, dear King. I think you should now be the first to tread upon it. I will walk beside you to assure no mishaps occur if you'll allow me," said Wolf.

Alfonso stood up once again and began to walk along the path he had so laboriously constructed.

"Not just yet," Wolf exclaimed. He was carrying a huge length of timber in his enormous arms. "Please assist as I position this splinter on your shoulders for the hike we will now begin. As my own dear trainer used to say, 'Better well-earned sweat in training than needless blood lost in battle,' and 'pain and prayer build character.' I do miss him at times."

Then he eased the wooden trunk onto the king's shoulders and was pleased to see only the slightest and briefest buckling of knees before Alfonso began walking at a good pace. That was how they spent the remainder of the afternoon, stopping only when dusk was approaching. Though he breathed heavily, the king never faltered and most of the time they walked in silence.

They slept that night in the royal lake house after a sumptuous meal. Alfonso immediately retired to his bedchamber. Wolf was pleased with his regal charge. He could already discern that Alfonso was indeed a formidable and fit warrior. He was wanting only in reliable endurance and stamina. That was understandable, the Irishman thought. Alfonso had already received exceptional schooling in horsemanship, the use of a sword and probably other weapons as well. Still, he had not been put through the rigors of sustained physical drilling. He knew that he would ultimately advise his student to conduct long sessions of running, swimming and other physical exertions as often as his duties would allow.

The next day's training would consist of water drills to build resilience and strength. They stripped off their cotton tunics for the day's activities. The King could only marvel when he observed the legendary Irish Captain's bare torso. The muscles were massive, solid and rippling but supple and sinewy at the same time. Alfonso could only compare Wolf's astonishing physique to a few still-extant ancient Roman statues of Hercules and other Greek and Roman gods that he had encountered during his travels.

They began in a small wooden boat with Wolf rowing and Alfonso standing on a bench at the tiny craft's bow. When they were some distance from shore, Wolf handed over a large Hispanian broadsword and almost bizarrely instructed him to simulate combat with an invisible demon that was flying unseen all around him. As the swordsman began slashing and thrusting about himself, Wolf pulled viciously on one oar while pushing with the other. There was a cry of surprise as the noble King fell most unceremoniously into the blue-green waters, creating a rippling splash that soaked the smiling but sympathetic oarsman.

When Alfonso broke onto the surface again, still tenaciously clutching the hilt of the big sword in his hand, Wolf called down to him.

"Well done altogether. I dropped the sword the first time my trainer performed that trick on me and I was immediately forced to swim to the lake's bottom to retrieve it. You've truly outdone me in this initial trial of water and balance, Alfonso." Wolf did not choose to inform the King that he was only fourteen when he had gone through that same experience.

They continued with this balance training throughout the morning. At first, they exercised with the little craft floating free, oars stowed. In this position, Alfonso was able to synchronize the movement of his feet and legs, having some restraint over the boat's movement, with the controlled slashes, thrusts and defensive blocks of the heavy steel blade. Next, Wolf again took the oars and directed the boat in circles and turns while the King stood heroically, wielding his sword nonstop at the bow. As midday approached, the Irish Captain was satisfied that his student now realized the significance of balancing his stance and being conscious of the motion of not just his upper body in combat but his feet and legs as well.

"You've done well, Alfonso," stated Wolf with all honesty. "You should practice this periodically and eventually it will come naturally to you. So, now we move back to endurance and confidence building once more but first, we'll pause to allow you some rest and sustenance. Again, not your usual fare but pure and clean cool water and good brown bread baked by the country folk. This time, however, they've gifted us with golden butter to spread upon it."

They sat on the plush, verdant grass along the lake's shore and leisurely took their time resting and eating the simple meal, which Alfonso praised as tasting more delicious than the most lavish foods served at the royal Leonese great feasts. Still, Wolf advised him to eat sparsely, as a heavy stomach would ail him mightily in the afternoon to come.

Presently, they strode again to the small boat. A thick, round oaken shield with a huge iron boss at its center rested on its rowing bench.

"'Tis a loan from Keli and his Icelanders. Those belonging to the Spartans are all in use in training or in battle at the moment," explained Wolf. He heaved the shield onto the King's back as he stood to accept it, then passed the leather strap over his shoulder and Alfonso drew it tight.

"You should now swim across the lake at your own pace with the shield as your companion in the waters. I'll be rowing at your side. I advise you to use the least strenuous means of swimming—on either your side or your back. And remember, speed is not the objective. Staying above the water and not drowning is,' said Wolf with a knowing smile.

The king swam with slow and smooth strokes, alternating between his side and back as Wolf had recommended. The buoyancy of his body and the wood of the shield battled with the iron of the boss and the natural inclination of the lake's waters to envelop him as to which would prevail. Eventually, they reached the opposite bank and Alfonso was allowed to sit and rest but with the shield always strapped to his back.

Wolf surveyed his surroundings. The setting was truly lovely. The small lake was surrounded by a narrow strip of soft grass and flower fields on all sides. These fields were, in turn, encircled by deeper green woodlands consisting mostly of Aleppo Pines and Mountain Elms. And now, he thought wryly, a smooth and well-worn walking trail also encompassed the lake. The Leonese royal family had indeed chosen a charming tract of land for their royal hunting grounds.

As they rose again, Wolf explained that they would conduct a half-circumnavigation of the lake. This would be almost twice as long as the simple crossing of the oval-shaped lake but now Wolf was confident he wouldn't have to dive over to save the King from going under. So, they made off once more, Alfonso biding his strength and taking easy and steady strokes, never far from shore with his escort rowing beside him. Eventually, they returned to their starting point. The king stood only slightly puffing while Wolf relieved him of the heavy and now sodden shield.

The swimmer was allowed another rest period to recover, his body already feeling buoyant and unburdened with the removal of the Viking shield. When he stood, stretched his arms and seemed to have recovered his natural strength, Wolf addressed him again.

"You've impressed me once more, king. You're a durable and resilient distance swimmer even when weighted down. Now, let us test your speed in the water. I'll ask that you repeat your original crossing ending in the same spot on the other side as before. This time, you must power through the lake as swiftly as you're able, using whatever style of swimming suits you. I expect it to take much less time than your last crossing. Please inform me when you're ready."

"I'm ready now, Captain," replied the king, standing erect with his shoulders back, proud of his accomplishments thus far and the encouragement he'd received from the enormous Gaelic warrior.

"Right, this time I'll wait here and watch you. I'm told I have a deep, loud and powerful voice and will call over to inform you of your next task when you complete the crossing."

Alfonso sprinted to the shore and dove into the clear, bracing water. He glided across the surface with only the top of his head and his arms and shoulders visible. With the rapid, long and graceful strokes of his arms and flurry kicks of his legs beneath the surface, he slid through the water almost effortlessly, leaving a subtle wake behind him. His face turning up to take breaths at intervals, he fell easily into a steady rhythm.

*I see he has received excellent instruction in the techniques of distance swimming*, thought Wolf, reminding himself to congratulate Sancho later. *With his youth, strength, intelligence and spirit, the Leonese should consider themselves fortunate to have Alfonso as their king.*'

It took much less time on this second crossing as he was freed from the weight of the shield. Nevertheless, when Alfonso emerged from the water, he was gasping for breath and again collapsed onto the soft grass on his hands and knees, winded but pleased with himself for his swift crossing. As he looked up in the direction of the trees, he thought he recognized the dear and familiar face of the elegantly dressed figure who was approaching him. The King smiled and raised one hand in greeting.

The man was clad in a refined, forest green cotton tunic with leggings of the same color. He was robust in stature and armed with a formidable hand-and-a-half sword belted at his waist in its polished black leather scabbard. He pointedly did not return the king's smile. Instead, his eyes were hard and filled with a zealous passion and cold hate as he deftly drew out  deadly blade. The sun glinted off its sharpened and oiled steel as he lifted it over his head.

*"Allahu Akbar!"* The furious cry, howled in splenetic rage, rang out over the waters of the lake as the man began to run madly toward the still prostrate King.

*"Verte Proditor!"* —Turn Traitor!  An equally enraged cry of command, this time Latin and in a strong feminine voice, replied to the first ferocious call.

The swordsman stopped, looked over his shoulder and began to turn around when the first arrow struck his thigh. The mail armor under his tunic, which reached his knee, blunted much of the effect but still his legs buckled momentarily. The next arrow was better aimed, striking him directly at the base of his throat, penetrating with such force that two-thirds of the arrow's length protruded from the back of his neck. He fell backward, his eyes frozen forever in an aspect of surprise, now staring ironically toward his executioner with his head at an awkward angle as the arrow lifted it slightly from the ground.

The archer and another woman ran toward the body. The second woman was carrying a Celtic leaf-bladed sword at a ready position to strike him again if he moved.

"No need for me to run him through," said Aoife, "he's deader than a bee in a blizzard."

Upon first hearing the cry and seeing the strange man approaching the king from his position on the other side of the lake, Wolf had immediately rushed to the little boat and begun rowing powerfully across. Several of the king's guards who had been further back in the woods also rushed to the shore to find boats to cross on their own.

The king himself had witnessed the short but incredibly violent series of events from close range. He was now fully recovered and strode over to the grisly scene.

"Aoife," he said, "I'm not quite sure what I've just seen. Please help me understand all this." Then shifting his gaze to the other woman who still carried the recurved Magyar bow, he said, "I remember meeting you, Dear Lady but forgive me as I cannot recall your name."

"I am Luta Einarsdottir, King Alfonso. I've been living and traveling with the Magyars for a number of years, though I'm originally from Norway." Though she'd spent most of her time in Ireland in Connemara at the camp of Magyars, Luta was an extraordinarily devout Christian and made it a point while there to learn Latin from the local nuns who often visited and stayed for days.

"Be you from Norway or Egypt, I'm most grateful to God you were here this day, Luta and you as well, Aoife," replied the king, still confused by events but gracious as always.

By now, Wolf had arrived, quickly surveying the scene and the sprawled body of the dead man and, like Alfonso, eagerly awaited hearing the explanation of what had just transpired.

"I felt something was wrong the moment this man arrived at your court, King. His story, like that of the false monk who came before him, did not ring true. Yet when you all recognized and seemed to be pleased at his return, I was not sure myself," Aoife said.

"Though he was besmirched with dirt and dust and poorly clothed, this Ramiro did not have the look of a slave who had been conducting the dismal and brutal work of a slave miner for years. He seemed too well fed and his face and features were clear and healthy in all apparent aspects. Nor did he walk in a stooped manner as I've noticed among many other miners," she added.

"What really stirred my suspicions was when all of us together delivered a prayer of thanksgiving to God for Ramiro's safe escape and return from the hell of slavery under the lash of the Moors. As we were all praying with our heads bowed, I raised my eyes for a moment to glance at him. He was neither bowing nor praying but rather looking around at the rest of us with an expression of disgust on his face. I was afraid he'd see me observing him, so I quickly bowed my head again. Finally, at the very end, when we all made the sign of the cross as one, I looked up again. His arms and hands had never left his side."

Despite the solemnity of the moment, Wolf could not help smiling at his darlin' girl with the utmost respect and admiration for her acute intellect and seemingly ineffable shrewdness.

Aoife continued. "So, I decided at that moment to follow him. I asked Luta to accompany me and Sancho recommended a young member of your Leonese scouts to come with us. We trailed him furtively to his abode in Asturias and lurked on the outskirts of his estate. The second day there he struck out for a nearby forest where he, for some reason, decided to spend the night. Equally strange, he chose to retreat to an old, abandoned cave on the side of a hill which projected up from a clearing in the center of the woods. Just before evening fell, an oily-skinned, black-clad man joined Ramiro, his face bearing a suspicious and evil countenance. They were only together for moments and then the other man galloped off, apparently wanting to get out of the forest before dusk set in."

Luta briefly took over the narration. "We talked among ourselves at some length and decided whoever this apparent conspirator was, he could not have learned much from Ramiro, as the count had not been with us long enough to learn anything of great intelligence value. So, we didn't pursue the dark man but remained watching Ramiro. The next day, the count mounted up and returned to the capital city with us trailing behind him."

Aoife resumed, "Almost as soon as the count was back in the capital city, he inquired as to the location of the king and was told you were engaged in individual training at the royal preserve with the giant wild Irish Captain."

She couldn't hide her faint smile as she nodded toward Wolf before continuing.

"So, Luta and I carried on with our surveillance and the pleasant young scout returned to his duties. Ramiro, no longer wearing the blue and gold raiment of Asturias but now clad in the same dark green apparel you see at your feet, spent the previous day watching you from this side of the lake. He was unaware, however, that we were watching him. We had earlier informed the king's guards, who know both of us well, that we were also guarding our own Captain."

Luta took over once more. "When we saw the count come out of the woods as you were recovering from your sprint across the waters, King, we were not sure of his intentions. But when he lifted that huge sword over his head and howled some barbarous curse at you, I was particularly gratified that I had my Magyar bow with me. Neither Aoife nor I could have reached him in time before he would be upon you. With you defenseless and still huffing and puffing."

Both men, Hispanian and Gael, could not help but be enamored by these two ladies. It was an exceptional example of remarkable irony that these two young women could be so formidable and deadly in the face of their enemies. Yet, at the same time, each exuded a natural and magnetic tenderness and charm.

"I regret I missed the proper target with my first arrow but the second, however late, ended the threat," stated Luta with apparently genuine contrition. "I ask you to please not inform Cael about that errant first arrow. He would never let me forget it."

Notwithstanding the macabre turn of events and the grisly corpse at their feet, Aoife and Wolf broke into an inappropriate but stress-relieving laugh while Luta blushed.

"I'm sure all three of us will swear to protect your secret, dear Luta," said the twenty-year-old Leonese king, wise and charismatic beyond his years.

"It has now become quite clear what happened. Everything Ramiro said was a lie. He may indeed have been knocked from his horse by a war club three years ago but it's quite clear he either immediately or sometime later apostatized. He was known even among the Moors as a valiant warrior and man of noble birth. However, many of us here also knew he was unhappy with his wife and, lacking parents or siblings, he felt no particular ties to his birthright. We tried to assure him he was a much-appreciated soldier of Leon but it always seemed he wanted something more," said Alfonso sadly.

"The capture and display of the Leonese hero, Ramiro, as a proud convert to Islam would have been a great boon, reflecting magnificently to the advantage of the Caliphate. But Sulayman is crafty and devious. I've no doubt that upon Ramiro's conversion, he was soon showered with wealth and provided four young wives to occupy his time and leisure. He no doubt received a new name and may have been sent on special assignments to the restive provinces of the Caliphate. But he was being kept and prepared for a much more important mission."

By now, the king's four guards had joined them on the shore after casting disgusted glances at the corpse on the ground. These were the most loyal of men and held Alfonso's full trust.

"The count must have been tasked to learn as much as he could of our plans, then assassinate me and flee back to the Caliphate. But when he saw me lying unarmed, unprotected and exhausted on the shore after my rapid crossing, he could not resist the chance to kill me. He probably hoped, disguised in his green raiment, that he could do it quickly and would not be personally recognized by Wolf and my guards on the opposite bank. Then he could go back to the capital, once again don his regal Asturian robes and feign the same shock as the rest of the court when they learned of my fate."

"That sounds entirely plausible, Alfonso," said Wolf and the others all nodded in agreement. "Then he could continue to gain intelligence and later select a time of his choosing to return to Cordoba to be feted as a Moorish hero and rejoin his four young wives," concluded the Irish Captain, shaking his great dark-maned head. "And I believe, King, you have already passed your abbreviated training session. I see no need to have you run through the woods in the dark tonight, trying to elude the obstacles I've placed in your way. I don't expect you'd ever be called upon to conduct such a midnight reconnaissance mission during battle, considering your lofty position as Leon's King.

"Thank you, Captain," replied the King. "Perhaps it is indeed better we make our way back to await the return of our various expeditionary contingents.

Then Alfonso stepped demurely to stand before Aoife and Luta and bent to kiss each of them on both cheeks. Though each lady was slightly older than he, except for two of the guards, none of those present had yet to age beyond their twenties.

As both ladies blushed simultaneously, the King proclaimed. "Now, let us go home."

# Chapter 19

## Strategies, Tactics and Prayers

It had been an eventful two weeks for the Leonese and their allies from the North. By now, the Magyars and Spartans had returned from their dangerous but ultimately successful excursions and the diplomatic representatives, whose mission was also fruitful, were back once more at King Alfonso's court. Cormac, Wolf and Sancho agreed it would be sensible to convene another small and limited counsel to assess their recent actions and the likely reaction of the Caliph and his advisors; a kind of after-action summation, as Wolf termed it.

All the key military and intelligence leaders among the visitors were present, including Pyrrhus, Helena and Brother Cillian. Alfonso, Sancho and the royal spiritual advisor were, of course, in attendance along with Felix and a small cadre of senior warrior knights of long experience and great renown, including the venerable *Campeador,* Rodrigo, who had proven himself yet again in combat while in action with the hard-riding Magyars.

The King bade Cael and Rodrigo speak initially as their 'Hungarian' deception mission was the first to launch.

"Rodrigo and I, along with others of our band, have conducted our own evaluation of our recent raid to examine what we did well and what we should improve. The loss of one of our warriors was tragic. Yet still, we both acknowledge we came out of the Caliphate in far better condition than we had any reason to believe prior to undertaking our extended ride. We recognize that most of our targets were rather soft except for our final engagement with that column of infantry. Still, even when we achieved total surprise, those among the enemy who resisted us fought valiantly despite their apparent shock at confronting an enemy long thought vanished," spoke Cael without any trace of braggadocio.

"In short, we feel we were most fortunate. With our limited numbers, we would not have fared well against a committed force of heavy Arab cavalry or a typical squadron of formidable Berber riders. We also often rode over terrain that would have proven at best disadvantageous and at worst disastrous for our own battle tactics. So, even with our new additions, there will be only seventy of us. Unlike the Vikings back in Ireland, our Moorish foes may potentially have enormous formations of organized cavalry and we must struggle against overconfidence," Cael warned, casting his glance around the table where the others sat paying rapt attention.

Rodrigo continued the report with the good news.

"We are, however, confident we achieved the objective of deception we intended in carrying out this raid. The people of *Saraqusta* and the Caliphate's Upper March are now convinced they are under threat of attack from Magyars at any time. Their caliph seemed unable to protect them and the one relatively sizable force of Moorish warriors suffered almost total losses. Now they are wondering where we are and when we will strike next. There are two possibilities. One, *Saraqusta* and the rest of the peoples of the northern provinces will be even more eager to join the Caliph in hopes of protection. Or two, they will feel abandoned and look to their own defense, denying the Caliphate any further support. Cael and I believe their choice will be to serve under their own leaders and defend their own home provinces for now."

"I tend to agree, Rodrigo," proclaimed the king. "And, if you're correct and they have no suspicions that we or the other northern Christian realms were involved in this raid, they will be even less likely to desire to join with the Caliphate in a major strike against us here."

"Are you quite sure, Cael, that you maintained complete security at all times? That you neither spoke any words nor left any trace of anything to be later found that would lead the Moors to believe you were anything but true Magyars?" interjected Aoife.

She spoke in Irish Gaelic but the words were quickly translated by others around the table.

"Yes, dear Aoife, both Rodrigo and I took great pains to assure our covers were maintained throughout," replied Cael, unoffended by her question.

Now, in Latin, Wolf addressed Aoife with unabashed candor so that all could hear. "I would have been surprised if our Chief of Intelligence had not endeavored to make fully certain we've not been compromised. Well done to all."

Fergus spoke next, relating the details of the engagement at the frontier outpost. Translations were again required.

"Since we arrived well before the Moors attempted to besiege the garrison, we enjoyed the advantage of being able to prepare the battlespace, which we were confident would occur within the confined grounds of the post's interior. By positioning obstacles in specific locations, we created a proper killing zone that leveraged our tactical strengths. Still, most of the enemy fought with zealous determination and I'm sure they were all seasoned warriors," remarked the Spartan Captain with honest respect for their foemen.

"I agree with the prior advice given about not becoming overconfident because of our successes in several small-scale encounters. Still, we have shown that we can prevail over larger numbers if we correctly choose the terrain and, if possible, leverage the benefit of surprise against our enemies. The Leonese have been holding out against the Caliphate for hundreds of years and are still unconquered. Your people, King Alfonso, are magnificent fighters and we are honored to fight alongside them. Not just their arms and backs but their souls and spirit are imbued with the strength of our shared faith."

The king cast his glance first among his most welcomed guests. They had thrown themselves into the cause of his and his people's freedom.

"No, Sir Fergus, it is we who are honored to have you, not only among us but joining with us in giving up your blood in battle for our freedom from the foreign invaders who have cursed our lands for so many centuries. Until you arrived, we had no reason to even hope for liberation. Your own victories against an equally evil invasion inspire us, here in Leon and in the other realms of the North. It is God who has sent you to us and it is your presence among us, I'm told by my bishops and clergymen, which has spread his Holy Spirit across our lands," replied Alfonso.

All of those present made the sign of the cross after hearing the king's gracious and pious remarks. Alfonso smiled at his friends and advisors and continued.

"Now then, I ask Felix to advise us how he feels his visit to our northern allies helps or harms us," stated the king with a mischievous smile to his senior diplomat and long-time friend.

"There is no need to be cynical, my King. We all know Leon has experienced occasional difficulties with our Christian cousins over the years. But, as you are no doubt aware, many of our good common people attribute that to aristocratic bickering. Thankfully, you've never been guilty of that and our people know it well, I'm proud to say," answered Felix as he observed the nods of others around the table.

The king beamed a self-effacing smile allowing Felix to continue with his report of the diplomatic tour of Castile and the other Christian realms.

"First, let me say, I am convinced conducting our business with our elegant and stately Greek and Irish allies, Helena, Pyrrhus and Prince Cormac, at our sides reflected most highly on Leon and yourself, my King."

Cormac struggled not to grin too prodigiously. He was still unused to being referred to as 'Prince Cormac' and that no one in Ireland had ever considered him as either 'elegant' or 'stately,' he was quite certain. *No harm, Felix, I'm sure you were speaking of Helena and Pyrrhus*, he thought to himself.

Felix continued, "There was, of course, the usual salutations of Christian solidarity and diplomatic decorum. They all seemed genuinely aware of a renewed threat from the south and pledged that we should all band together to repel the Moors. Importantly, they also seemed to agree the first strike will be directed at Leon."

"If that is true and I dearly hope it is, we may expect to receive considerable support in motivated and faithful warriors to fight alongside us when they are most needed," remarked Sancho with great hope and optimism.

"Alas, I believe that would be the case if we were conferring with only warrior knights during our visit. However, our primary interlocutors were nobles and diplomats, Sancho. What those gentlemen say and promise, while sitting comfortably in good cheer around a sumptuous table and amply provided with good wine does not always translate to solid support when evil is bursting in fury over our border. Still, let not my words overly dismay you. I believe our Christian cousins will indeed come to our aid, though perhaps not in the massive numbers you may envision. Thus, the advice offered earlier by our Magyar and Spartan friends should be closely heeded. Make the most of well-selected terrain, employ surprise as able and commit our warriors wisely where their tactics, skills and relatively smaller numbers will be most decisive."

"Thank you, Sir Felix, foremost Knight Champion of the realm," replied Sancho in good-natured jest while grinning broadly. "At our next council, I must be sure to provide you with my sage diplomatic advice."

Everyone chortled at Sancho's light-hearted jibe. Felix laughed heartier than any of them. The Gaels were pleased to see their friends and allies could resort to humor as a palliative even in dark times. Apparently, it wasn't just an Irish characteristic.

"Very well," said Alfonso. "Earlier, we already concluded that Sulayman must be in the preparatory stages of planning an *aceifa* of some type against us. And that it will be on a larger scale and more significant than the harassing raids we've endured until now. We also concurred that he is becoming increasingly desperate and has no other choice but to adopt a strategic offensive in hopes of once again uniting the peoples of the Caliphate.

Now, based on the two insidious attempts at treacherous assassination in our midst, our most recent incursions into the South and your reports and assessments of what is required for us to proceed, I believe we have two sequential priorities at present. First, we should endeavor, however possible, to acquire more finite detail, something we can act upon, on when and where Sulayman will conduct his offensive. Second and directly related to the first, we must then conduct a detailed analysis of the route and terrain which will comprise his axis of advance."

Wolf and Aoife looked at each other and smiled. Both had already discussed in detail a course of action almost identical to what the young king had just described.

"I'll leave it up to all of you, my most esteemed and respected advisors, to collectively develop a plan to execute each of those activities. I need not remind you, *Tempus fugit.* Time is of the essence." With that, the King brought the present council to a close.

***

The "Ambassadors of Kindness" – the contingents of religious and diplomats, who had set out to announce there would be no collection of taxes this season and to solicit pledges of support for the Caliphate in making war on Leon, had by now returned. They had traveled through the upper, middle and lower marches as well as the coastal regions of the middle sea and the great ocean. As was to be expected, their missions met with mixed results, even though all those visited had been pleased to have been excused for once from paying tribute to the caliph in Cordoba.

The only province of the Caliphate where the Cordobans were outright denied entry was the southeast, most pointedly the newly formed city of Granada, where the Berber Dynasty of Zirids was on the verge of declaring their own independent Muslim Kingdom.

In Saraqusta, the diplomats were tolerated, if not welcomed, probably because of the quite recent raids by apparent Magyars, who all had previously thought were a distant nightmare of the past. In Toledo, which the Hispanians called Tulaytulah, a similar reception was given. Though not overtly hostile, the people there were still suspicious of the caliph himself. The strange affair involving the death of one of their local warrior heroes at the hands of a woman who called herself the "niece of the caliph" was a cause for estrangement among some of the locals. Even though the caliph had vociferously denied any knowledge of the man's killing, many had their doubts. The coastal regions along the Middle Sea maintained a position of non-enthusiastic support. None there professed any disdain for the caliph but neither was there any fiery zeal to join in great numbers in a campaign against the Leonese.

Sulayman's senior diplomat summarized. "So, my Caliph, the areas of our main potential support will be the provinces to our west and, perhaps, directly south. The nobles there acknowledge their allegiance and seem ready to answer your call if needed. The Zirids, while not joining us, will not take any steps against us lest they be accused of siding with the Christians. The other provinces of the East and Northeast may send some token groups of warriors to our aid but not enough to significantly augment our armies."

The caliph's Syrian emir then took the opportunity to add a word of caution.

"Earlier, we discussed the possibility of you declaring a holy *jihad* against Leon, my Caliph. If you proceed, that may prove to be a double-edged sword. You were elected caliph by our Berber warriors. If you call for holy war, all of the provinces must rise to their call of duty or else be considered enemies of Islam. That fear may prompt some of them to declare you illegitimate and so not be obeyed. If that happens, the Caliphate's rupture and disunity will be complete. But if we conduct a large-scale aceifa and win a glorious victory over Leon, even if it is but one great battle, our triumph will be even sweeter."

The room became still and it was obvious the caliph was pondering his emir's words with great intensity.

"And after our defeat of the Leonese foe, the word will spread and these recent troubling incidents concerning alleged Magyars and phantom nieces will be forgotten. You will again be viewed as the strong leader and uniter of all our peoples. Then we can deal with these treacherous Zirids at our own leisure," concluded the emir.

Initially disconsolate at the lack of total success of the diplomatic teams he had dispatched across the Caliphate, the words of his optimistic emir had rejuvenated Sulayman and he stood, now with confidence, to address the group.

"I choose to ignore, for the moment, the less than hearty welcome some of your teams received in several provinces. Granada and the Zirids are an exception, of course. But my esteemed emir is quite correct, we will extinguish that nest of traitors at a later date. Of that I'm quite sure."

Sulayman looked to the others with an expression which seemed to indicate he had already designed a solution to that problem.

"We will follow in the footsteps of the great Almanzor. I've already alerted trusted leaders to prepare an expedition into the enemy heartland. You all remember the mocking letter and grisly 'gift' bestowed on us by the upstart boy king in Leon. We are going to sack Santiago de Compostela once again, this time leaving nothing standing. Once our leaders have presented me with a plan of attack, we will consolidate all the available bands of warriors. The weather grows hotter each day, which works to our advantage as our fierce fighters thrive in the heat while the Christians seem to wilt. Though not all the provinces will join us, I've already set in motion a plan to assure us victory."

All of those in attendance listened raptly, curious as to the caliph's strategy.

"Based on the recommendations of two of my most loyal chieftains, I have invited fierce tribesmen of the Latumna Berber peoples to come up from the west coast of North Africa and join us. These savagely daunting warriors, always hostile to the Zirid Berbers and intensely devout in our shared faith, will increase our numbers by multiple thousands. The Latumna are known for their skills as vaunted horse warriors, yet they still maintain the capability to fight on foot. They are noted for raiding to the south of the great African desert in search of slaves and other booty. With such ferocious believers at our sides, triumph will not elude us."

# Chapter 20

## Sea Eagles and Ferrets

After the council with the king and his advisors and the decision on the two priority efforts to meet the inevitable attack from the South, the leaders of the Clontarf veterans gathered among themselves to discuss how they might optimize their own role. They also invited Brother Cillian whose scholarly knowledge of Hispania's history could be of singular assistance.

Aoife spoke first. "I don't believe there is much we can undertake on our own to attain deeper insight into the mind of Sulayman. Leon's network of established sources in the Caliphate is our best hope in that case. We had our own network in Ireland and Britannia, which proved to be of immense benefit but we had ample time to develop it. That is not the situation we find ourselves in now."

"I agree," remarked Wolf. "Though our Magyars make for outstanding scouts in conducting reconnaissance and surveillance, this task calls for a deeper penetration into the enemy's midst, which is best met through human assets— spies."

The monk from Cluny now took the opportunity to contribute his own thoughts on the matter.

"For hundreds of years, the invaders have shared one single faith, Islam. Now there are different 'schools of teaching' but the differences do not rise to the level of heresy. That has been advantageous for them. However, at the same time, the Moors differ from each other in a variety of ways. They are a combination of Arabs from the Mideast; *Saqaliba* slave soldiers, many of them from Christian lands; Mozarabs or converted descendants of the Romano-Visigoths and significantly .... Berbers."

Cillian looked around among the faces of his audience. He understood they had been in Hispania long enough by now to understand already the basics of what he had just explained but he was trying to make a particular point.

"The Berbers, though falsely considered not far removed from savages by the Arabic nobility, have always been the pillar of the Moors' military successes. But there are Berbers and then there are Berbers. The name they call themselves is *Imazighen and* they are the original inhabitants of North Africa. They have tribal, dialect, dynasty and lifestyle differences among themselves. Almanzor imported Sanhaja Berbers who were part of the Zirid dynasty. Now, some of those same Zirids are established in Granada, where they are getting close to establishing their own kingdom independent of the Caliphate. That is a predicament which must heavily grate on Sulayman."

By now, Cillian could see that he had won the attention of his listeners, who were undoubtedly considering what this might mean and how it might be exploited.

"If our efforts at alienating the loyalty of the provinces in the Upper March and the Middle March have been even partially successful, the caliph must presently be finding himself in the position of having a finite number of forces at his disposal to conduct an *aceifa.* So, what must he now do?"

"March on Granada?" offered Fergus.

"Unlikely," answered the churchman. "I believe he will do what the Moors have always done. Import more Berbers. However, he clearly does not want more Zirid Berbers, who are now supreme across the northern part of Africa. He must find other Berbers who are not Zirids and possibly may be antagonistic toward the Zirids, as they exist in northwest Africa along the coast of the great ocean. They are the Latumna people, formidable fighters and devout believers."

Now, somewhat unexpectedly, it was the Icelander, Keli, who spoke up.

"I do believe I know where you might be heading, dear Brother Cillian. These Latumna must cross the waves to come to the aid of Sulayman. And if we can detect them, it will be the signal that the attack will be forthcoming."

"Quite correct Keli. I'm impressed. You must have received an enlightened classic education on whatever glacier you grew up on back in your arctic homeland," quipped Cillian, grinning jovially at their Viking friend.

"And I also trust you have a suggestion on who and what we send to detect such a crossing? I'm equally impressed they teach such excellent tactical subjects back in your French abbey," retorted Keli.

"I do have a suggestion indeed. Now, Keli, can you, your Icelanders and perhaps some of these upstart Gaels take several of your dragonships and sail to provide us early warning of such a crossing? You must play the part of a Sea Eagle who uses only his eyes and not his talons in this case."

And so, it was settled, after conferring with the king and Sancho, Keli would lead three *snekkja* craft to patrol around the ancient 'Pillars of Hercules' to detect any major movement of Moorish ships from the continent to Hispania. And they must depart without delay.

***

After their king announced his critical information requirements, these were issued to Leon's intelligence gatherers. The Leonese then held their own council. In attendance were selected senior diplomats, led by Felix and a mix of officials involved in scouting and spying activities. Also invited were Schlomo and his son, along with Aoife and Brother Cillian. The purpose was to assess what had been most recently learned concerning potential Moorish intentions, especially the possibility of a near-term large-scale *aceifa.*

Felix, who was as much an analyst as he was a diplomat, took the lead in summarizing what had been learned by Leon's Christian network of sources among the Caliphate's *dhimmis*, chattel slaves and those Mozarabs who had feigned conversion to Islam to avoid paying the jizya tax and thus escape *dhimmi* status. These had been instructed to act as cagey ferrets in prying the deepest secrets from the heart of the Caliphate.

"As we had hoped, our diversionary Magyar raids in the Upper March around *Saraqusta* were effective. Not only are the people there wary of more onslaughts from ghastly mounted archers from the distant East but they are dismayed that the caliph has not yet sent a punitive expedition to find and eliminate the strange marauders. They are unlikely to send any but the token contingent of warriors to strike Leon. If anything, they are more concerned with the Christian realms of Castile and Navarre closest to them," advised Felix confidently.

"The situation is the same in the eastern provinces along the Middle Sea. Many of them engage in piracy, which has proven to be a lucrative enterprise for them. Leon is not a threat that overly disturbs them. Granada is even worse, of course. They are their own masters and likely consider the caliph himself to be more of a danger to them than Christian knights from Leon."

Yet another diplomat, whose main function was dealing with those Christians still abiding in the Caliphate, added the likely reaction of the provinces of the Middle March.

"The outlandish affair associated with the execution of a popular Moorish warrior from the environs of *Tulaytulah*, what we call Toledo, though recent, has risen to almost fabled status among the Moors there. The insult of a local hero being deceived and stabbed to death by a supposed niece of the great Sulayman.... a woman of all things... has instilled great resentment. Despite the caliph's denials of any involvement, few believe him. As in those Moorish provinces further east, I assess that there will be only minimal support, if any, offered to Cordoba in carrying out a renewed *aceifa* against Leon."

The council took some comfort in these tidings, though all knew such reports might be subject to wishful hoping, or worse yet, outright deception from those same sources. Such had occurred all too tragically over the decades. It was evil enough that Christian kings had betrayed their own allies in the past. Though diabolical perfidy was a dangerous possibility, all knew just how much their allies in the south risked in transmitting such information to Leon.

Schlomo, the physician, long considered as much one of their own as their own kin, now offered his own insight.

"We all know my people, those of my own ancient tribe, hold a peculiar position among the Moors. We seem to share a kinship of origin with their Arabic ancestors. Our first languages are not so dissimilar. Many of us seem to resemble cousins to many of them. They consider both us and you, Christians, people of the book. Yet, they seem to have an underlying understanding of us from past eons. Though we are also *dhimmis* among them, they cannot help but recognize something of themselves in us."

He smiled now and continued.

"After all, you are pagan barbarians from the north, or at least they think you are with your Galicians, Basques and Asturians. In any case, our own trusted believers, long-time servants among them, have heard things whispered by our enemies while they, with feigned obsequiousness, seemed to be ignored."

All the ears of those assembled were now eagerly attentive in anticipation. Their Jewish countrymen had always been faithful and of assistance since the time of Almanzor.

"From the courts of Cordoba and the villa of Sulayman's harem, the name of Santiago de Compostela has been murmured repeatedly. It seems the caliph wants nothing more than to become the next Almanzor. Even our people know his rule is becoming unsteady. His Caliphate is splintering. He needs a magnificent and glorious accomplishment to restore both unity and obeisance. And he knows he must strike with overwhelming strength, a strength of numbers which he now lacks. And, as our friends here have already surmised, he won't get it from the outlying provinces of his tenuous Caliphate."

The assembled Leonese were aware that their Jewish friends often seemed to have access to the deepest secrets of the Moors. Schlomo's tales of his peoples' and the Arabs' shared ancient origins rang true.

Schlomo carried on. "If, indeed, Almanzor is the caliph's inspiration, which makes perfect sense as that monster's triumphs over all others are legendary among his people and still well-remembered, Sulayman may choose to closely imitate that Vizier who was named 'the Victorious' by all the Moors. Almanzor looked to Africa as the source of further victories and accomplished that by inviting various groups of Berbers in their thousands to join him in battle against the infidels. Despite his current problems with some of the Berbers of the Caliphate, especially the independent Berber dynasty in Granada, he may recruit new and different Berber peoples from more distant parts of Africa. We all know what ominous and forceful warriors they are and so too does the caliph."

Aoife looked to the king with an unspoken, though clear, request to speak in her soft green eyes. Alfonso, in turn, nodded to his Irish friend and recent benefactor, smiling his welcoming assent.

"Prince Cormac, Wolf and others among the leaders of our small band of Gaels and Icelanders have also discussed among ourselves what form the enemy's next actions might assume. Our assessments align closely with the views expressed here. However, we were unable to agree on a most likely target of Sulayman's offensive.

The reports from Schlomo's people in the nerve centers of our enemies are of great interest, the likely attempt to duplicate the successes of Almanzor and, of most significance, the repeated mention of Compostela. Striking such a treasured and symbolic target would bring fame and adulation to Sulayman, replacing the suspicion and doubt that now seem to prevail among many in the Caliphate. It would replicate Almanzor's boldest accomplishment and demonstrate Leon's weakness. I now believe we have a good indication of both what is coming and where. Your advisors and their own sources have performed superbly, King Alfonso. We salute you."

Brother Cillian swiftly took the opportunity to address those present once again.

"And as many here know, we have dispatched Keli with three *Snekkjas* full of genuine and impostor Vikings, to act as our sea eagles and provide us with first warning of any large sea crossings of Berbers into the Caliphate. Now, though, we must examine the most likely routes and terrain through which Sulayman must pass to try to storm our holy city."

Those present knew well the situation was gravely serious yet there was an almost palpable sense of confidence and resolve which seemed to infuse all within the chamber.

"You are entirely correct, dear Brother Cillian," pronounced the king. "And now we know what and where we must be most vigilant to crush the malevolent shadow which is coming to fall upon us. And perhaps, this time, we can deliver our own surprise shock to shatter our long-time oppressors."

***

The straits between the great ocean and the middle sea, which characterized the Pillars of Hercules, were much broader than some simple river or stream. Yet still, this was the closest to the great continent of Africa that bordered the Iberian Peninsula. Historically, the crossing point between the two continents was the launch site for the first Moorish invasions into Christian lands hundreds of years earlier.

It was mid-morning and Keli had aligned his tiny flotilla of three dragon ships in a line north to south. He took his place on the stag-prowed boat in the center with the swan-topped craft to his south. The northernmost *snekkja* with the fierce wolf carved into its bowsprit was just to the west of the opening of the straits. The other two were further south, in positions where they could detect movement from the northwest of Africa, the homelands of the Latumna Berbers. All three of the northern craft were well offshore with sails covered and furled, holding their positions by use of their oarsmen. Yet each was still at a range where they could detect any ships sailing north. They were also within visual distance of each other and had prearranged communication means, using colored pennants.

This is exactly what they had planned and, to their surprise, the events they had expected commenced in less time than they had anticipated.

"Captain, sails to starboard, scores of Moorish dhows hugging the coast and sailing north!" shouted a lookout from his elevated perch above the prow.

All aboard cast their eyes to the east. Even from the deck, they could observe the triangular-shaped sails of forty or more dhows just offshore, moving steadily in the breeze.

'We've arrived not a moment too soon. I only hope we haven't missed other convoys which may have already made way to Hispania,' Keli said to himself.

As they had planned, now was the time for him to direct his stag boat nearer to the convoy to gain closer detail of the nature of their foes. His men didn't need to wait for orders. The entire crew was pulling at their oars while Keli stood on the bow. The sun was now high enough in the sky that he wasn't staring into its glare. In a brief time, he had seen enough and ordered his crew to come about.

He had observed the dhows were packed with what were certainly hundreds of men that even he could detect from a distance. That meant the full numbers aboard the other dhows might possibly be in the thousands. He had also seen several dhows transporting horses and what seemed to be wooden cargo crates, no doubt filled with gear for the men.

When they had returned to their original position, Keli flashed the pre-arranged signal to the wolf boat to his north. Those aboard would immediately row west into deeper waters and at a sufficient distance, let out their sails well beyond sight of the convoy and strike out northward to warn their comrades. Large numbers of Berbers were on the move to the Caliphate.

Meanwhile, the other two *Snekkjas* shadowed the convoy's route northward, keeping a respectable separation in hopes that even if they were dimly seen, they would be mistaken for small fishing or trading boats, too unthreatening to be of concern.

By the next morning, Keli and the others, still maintaining prudent distance, were confident in being able to confirm that the large convoy had indeed weighed anchor in the southernmost port of the Caliphate and appeared to be disembarking passengers and unloading cargo. Then they noticed a somewhat strange anomaly.

A single dhow, with its rudder apparently damaged and now blown off course, was drifting off to their south, further from shore than the others had been. The Icelandic leader now had to make a weighty decision. He could break contact and return northward, or they could attack and board the dhow in hopes of gaining more finely grained intelligence on this migration of Berbers. He'd been told that his 'sea eagles' should make use of their eyes and not their talons. Still, he also knew from experience that their huge Gaelic Battle Captain always lauded those who took initiative when promising events presented themselves. And, after all, he was a Viking….

"Prepare to close with and assault the Moorish ship. We'll come at them from their port and the 'swan' from their starboard," ordered Keli. The instructions were enthusiastically welcomed by both crews, who now rowed furiously toward the dhow.

"Looks like they're going to make a fight of it, Captain, though it appears this dhow is carrying more cargo than warriors," reported the lookout perched on the bowsprit.

Keli could clearly see the deck of the dhow was now manned by about two dozen Berber spearmen, carrying round shields similar in shape and size to their own but seemingly constructed from the thick hide of some African animal. The Icelanders on Keli's boat held their own wooden shields protectively, while others behind them held grappling hooks and still more readied stout throwing spears. The *Laochra* Gaelic warriors on the other boat, also covered by men carrying their shields upraised, prepared their grappling hooks and the darts which had proven so effective in their only other battle at sea. When they boarded, they would resort to their Dalcassian axes and trusty Celtic swords. The Berbers would be outnumbered more than two to one unless they were concealing other warriors lower in the dhow's hull.

As the two *Snekkjas* came closer, the northerners noted a distinct change come over the faces and demeanors of the Berbers. It appeared they initially believed they were going to be challenged by local ragtag pirates aboard sleek rowing craft with shallow draft hulls. As the Icelanders and Gaels in their now-recognizable Viking dragonships approached, the spearmen realized their opponents must be the savage, sea-faring Northmen of terrible legend. They also now recognized, as their enemies were almost upon them, that they were far fewer in number than the fierce northerners. Nevertheless, they howled defiantly and shook their spears, apparently hoping the northern marauders might hunt elsewhere for more docile prey.

When the two attacking craft came alongside the dhow, grappling hooks fell along both sides, most of which took hold. Even more dangerous and lethal were the spears and darts which fell into the ranks of the Berbers from opposite sides. About a third of the defenders on the dhow fell to these projectiles. To their misfortune, this ship of the Moorish convoy, which had already suffered the bad luck of losing its rudder and straying from the others in the night, contained no archers aboard.

As the screams of the stricken and wounded Berbers grew more frenzied, Northmen and Gaels clambered aboard the dhow behind their shields, their flashing axes and swords cleaving through the fabric, tissue and bone of the surviving defenders. Some of these leapt overboard in desperate and vain hopes of escape but splattered blood, which had already spewed overboard, soon attracted sea predators and triangular-shaped fins quickly surrounded those in the water. More hideous shrieks ensued.

The outcome was preordained. The deck was awash with blood and bodies. The Berbers, surrounded, stood no chance. One Icelander fell to an enemy spear in the breast when his shield slipped too low and a Gael was struck in the shoulder causing him to fall back into his own boat, where his fellows rushed to his aid. No Berber survived. Keli ordered details to toss the bodies overboard while others examined the wooden cargo containers. Most contained mundane items: rope, strands of woven hide, tents, blankets and, ironically, iron-tipped arrows. There were also additional spears and shields.

The searchers abruptly ceased their efforts when they heard a muffled sob issuing from a tight space between two large wooden crates. While several of them pulled the two containers apart, others stood poised with shields and weapons ready as the gap widened. A frightened figure sat with his arms raised protectively over his head. His skin was duskier than any Arab or Berber. His eyes were wide and white with dark pupils staring up at them in confusion.

"This poor soul is a black tribesmen taken in some Berber slave raid from the deep jungles which lie below the great desert. The scars from the iron fetters on his wrists and ankles show he has been in bondage for some time," explained one of the few Hispanians who had taken part in the voyage, again using Latin as a lingua franca.

Weapons were immediately lowered and the fierce warriors regarded the stricken man with sympathy. One of the *Laochra* smiled warmly, bent toward the man and extending his hand to help him stand. Some of the fear and bewilderment seemed to dissipate from his face as the black man took the offered hand and stood among them. When he caught sight of the few dead Berbers still aboard, his jaw clenched and his eyes narrowed. Then he unexpectedly put his hand on the Gael's shoulder and nodded in apparent appreciation for a service rendered.

When the Hispanian regrettably acknowledged he didn't know enough of the Berber dialect to try to speak with the man, Keli told him not to worry.

"I'm quite sure this unfortunate fellow is unable to comprehend good Danish or the 'barbar' of the Gaels but if we take him with us to safety and freedom in Hispania, we'll surely find someone in Leon who may be able to communicate with him. And then perhaps we'll know a bit more than we do now."

The two *Snekkjas* then lowered sails and made full haste back to Leon to report back to their friends, comrades and King Alfonso.

# Chapter 21

## Movement to Contact

Sancho addressed the war council assembled now in the king's great chamber. "In 997, when Almanzor conducted the most infamous of his many *aceifas*, the satanic sack of Santiago de Compostela, he led an enormous army. In those days, he also had command of a formidable fleet at his disposal. The tyrant was further benefitted by demanding and receiving the allegiance of a few Portuguese Christian counts along with their knights and foot soldiers.

"On his march north, he hugged the coast, shadowed by his navy, which carried provisions, supplies and slower-moving, horseless warriors. The going was slow but the Moors had the advantage of the treacherous counts who acted as guides. In any case, their flank was protected by the great ocean and their great fleet."

King Alfonso then continued the narration, which was based on study and analysis by many of those present.

"Seventeen years later, Sulayman enjoys far fewer of those advantages. His own fleet is much smaller and less cohesive than Almanzor's and he can no longer count on the support of our good Christian and formidable allies in the county of Portugal. Even in the best-case scenario from his perspective, he would not try duplicating the route of his predecessor in marching to Compostela."

To the surprise of some of those assembled, the king then nodded to Wolf.

"We and Sancho's senior officers agree he will strike northward from further inland. The terrain may be more mountainous in many places but there are also gaps of plains here and there, easier roads and occasional broad passes. This provides a better opportunity for maneuvering than that which exists right along the coast. We have ridden over the grounds there and have found the most opportune routes for such a northward advance. And we are sure Sulayman and the Moors still know those same grounds from back in the days when Almanzor plundered all around Leon."

The huge Gael looked to the king, who nodded sadly, recalling tales told of some of the past disasters.

Even more astounding to many in the chamber, Wolf's Chief of Intelligence, the young and wise Aoife, now resumed the discussion in her lilting and mellifluous Latin.

"From the reports of your far-reaching scouts, the recent forays of our special warrior bands into the Caliphate and the wide array of sources among the dhimmis, we are all agreed Sulayman will be quite unable to assemble as large and capable an army as did Almanzor," she said, reiterating what had already been considered.

Smiles appeared on many faces at her choice of the expression "special warrior bands," by which she undoubtedly intended to indicate the sorties of 'Spartans,' 'Magyars,' and 'Vikings' into the south.

"And now we have even more recent information from an unexpected source," Aoife continued.

"Keli and his crewmen aboard the three dragonships returned from their seaborne confirmation of Berber reinforcements with a surprising passenger. They discovered a slave hidden within the bowels of a stranded dhow, which they assaulted. When the Berber defenders were slain, they liberated the man and brought him back to Leon.

He is a black tribesman from the enormous, dark and imprenetrable forests of Africa, which lie beneath the great sandy desert. In his confusion and surprise, they were at first unable to communicate intelligibly with him. But this impressive man turned out to be craftier and more capable than his slavish circumstances initially seemed to indicate."

Cormac and Wolf both knew, from long experience, that it wasn't just Irish men who reveled in being a great *scéalaí*—storyteller. Aoife not only excelled at it but took great pleasure in relating such intelligence reports.

"During the return voyage, he became much more comfortable with his new shipmates. By the time they all arrived here in the capital, he had become a new comrade despite the language barrier. To our great fortune, we found out he had learned the Berber dialect to a much greater degree than he ever let on to his captors. Held as a slave for two years, he had ample opportunity to gain that skill. The Berbers consider these tribesmen savages and they spoke freely around him in apparent disbelief that he was capable of mastering their tongue."

Now, all of those present, except the few who knew the details, hung on her every word.

"As you know, King, there are a number of Berber speakers among your retinue. The Latumna dialect he learned, along with the Berber dialects studied by the linguists here, was sufficient to enable a good understanding. While we feared the possibility of tens of thousands of new warriors arriving to aid the caliph, this man assured us there were no more than twenty five hundred. Still a formidable threat but as we know, the Berbers' greatest strength is their ferocity as agile, swift mounted warriors. Their deadly spears come upon their foes before they can react. Whether they hurl them or thrust them into their enemies, they immediately afterward resort to their curved slashing swords, which they wield with savage skill."

Aoife, a sad veteran of her own tragedies, seemed to now remember her comrades knew better than her the terror of Berbers and other Moorish invaders. Bowing her head slightly, she offered amends.

"My apologies, my dear friends, to presume I deigned to tell you something unknown to you. Yet, this man told us what he witnessed. He knew most of those on the dhows had never been on a horse. Perhaps five hundred or even fewer of the Latumna horsemen, who had driven into his homeland to take him and his people boarded the Moorish boats. The rest who boarded, he judged, were simple commoners swayed by their chieftains."

This was indeed good tidings for the Hispanians. While the Berbers' cavalry was indeed daunting, their common foot warriors were often unreliable. Some of them were eager to join in hopes of booty, while others were happier to remain at home among their kin and their holdings.

"And what if this is simply a ruse by yet another Moorish spy?" questioned one of Alfonso's advisors.

Aoife looked to King Alfonso, who was smiling at all of them. He then picked up where Aoife left off.

"This is one of the women who helped raise me when I was very young. She is an important part of who I am today. She is certainly no slave, nor is she a simple servant. I call her Aunt Isabella."

A regally clad, older black woman stepped to the king's side. She was a formidably tall figure with intelligent eyes and a most dignified bearing.

"It turns out Isabella is originally from the same tribe as the former slave. She speaks his language as it was also her first tongue. Long ago, she also shared a similar fate when a Berber raiding party captured her. Isabella has spoken with this man at length. Even though she doesn't know him, she is quite convinced he tells the truth. I understand there is always a chance of deliberate deception by our enemies. But, in this case, I trust Isabella's judgement completely."

With the concern resolved, at least for the moment, Sancho then continued.

"So, it appears we are soon destined to be attacked and Santiago de Compostela and its destruction, yet again, as the primary objective. Like Almanzor before him, Sulayman's campaign will be designed to loot and pillage, not to conquer. Sacking Compostela will seriously elevate his prestige, not only among the Muslims in Hispania but even in North Africa. It would represent a renewed and decisive defeat of Christianity."

Eyes narrowed and jaws clenched among those in the chamber.

"Though, by God's grace, the caliph doesn't have the numbers, the fleet, nor the intelligence of Almanzor. This time, it appears, we have the *intelligence,"* he smiled at them all and his appreciative gaze lingered upon Wolf and Aoife.

"We have already been preparing our own warriors for rapid mobilization, both knights of the realm and foot soldiers. We've additionally advised our Christian allies of our expectations. At the first sign of major movement north from Cordoba, we will send our armies to prepared positions on the likely axis of enemy advance, while simultaneously summoning whatever additional warriors Castile, Navarre and the others might spare. God be with us and God save the king."

***

The caliph had summoned all his most trusted leaders to his palace once more to announce his final decision and give them their orders. By now, most of those present were quite aware of the arrival of new Berber reinforcements as Sulayman had spared no expense in providing them with quarters and provisions in the city of Cordoba. Their leader now sat among them on a plush cushion.

Sulayman stood in their center, his aspect buoyant and assertive.

"We have summoned warriors from throughout the Caliphate. They continue to arrive as we speak. As our advisors expected, we have promises of only paltry numbers from the Upper and Middle Marches and all of them are common foot soldiers with neither cavalry nor heavy armored infantry among them. They are supposedly on the march to join us here in Cordoba. Altogether, they number less than eight hundred."

There were angry grumbles among the Cordobans, even though this news came as no surprise to them.

"The provinces along the coast of the middle sea have delivered us gold and jewels instead of warriors. In truth, this is perhaps a boon in as most of those there have become sea pirates of late. They acquire great wealth through that endeavor and don't feel the need to maintain any armies of substance. After we plunder Compostela, I will use some of the riches gained along with this pirate booty to reward our valiant warriors for their victory in battle."

Grumbles turned to pleased murmurings among those present upon hearing the Caliph's promises of booty to come.

"Our loyal provinces in the Lower March have promised us two thousand experienced fighters, including five hundred heavy and light horsemen. They will meet us on our march northward. Our own Cordoban forces consist of two thousand five hundred, with about one third of them mounted warriors of various types. And, most exquisitely, we are now joined by almost two thousand newly arrived fierce and skilled Latumna warriors from Africa. Please join me in welcoming our new brothers."

All eyes now turned to the African Berber chieftain, followed by salutes and praises to Allah for him and his men. He smiled back to them, accepting their welcome with grace.

"We will cross into Leon with an irresistible formation of nearly seven thousand indomitable warriors of the faithful, including almost two thousand swift and deadly mounted horsemen, many of them skilled Berber squadrons, along with our own armored cavalry. We will not take the route of the great Almanzor along the coast but rather proceed from further inland, where it is more sparsely populated and trading roads, plains and mountain passes abound over which we may freely maneuver. As you know, Almanzor razed many of the towns, abbeys and villages that had once existed there during his *aceifas*."

Again, salutes and exuberant cheers rang out among the increasingly confident leaders. Preparations for movement were to begin immediately.

# Chapter 22

## Flame of Freedom

Without waiting for all of those who were promised to join them, the huge column of Moorish warriors moved out of the environs of the city of Cordoba, proceeding generally toward the north-northwest. Most of the city people watching the spectacle hailed them, shouting their encouragement, proud and pleased to witness once again the righteous military might of the Caliphate marching out to punish their enemies and return with riches and booty. There were a few among the crowds who, while cheering with the rest, were diligently making mental notes of numbers and composition of the Moorish forces. Their reports would be hastily dispatched northward to Leon, carried by *dhimmi* riders on the strong backs of hard-riding horses.

Local Berber cavalry led the way. Trusted fighters, familiar with their chosen route, they all had experience in conducting raids into the Christian kingdoms. They were followed by the enormous force of Latumna foot soldiers marching under their own colorful banners. Behind them trailed heavily armored Arabic horsemen. Fewer in number, they were to be the shock troops of the Caliphate, committed to battle where the fighting was expected to be most intense. The next contingent consisted of the mounted warriors of the newly arrived Latumna Berbers.

The horsemen all rode at a leisurely pace. They were on friendly territory and were taking pleasure in the adulation of the watching throngs lining the roads. There was no need yet for haste. The eight hundred foot soldiers pledged by the eastern provinces were said to be making their way piecemeal in small clusters westward. This did not cause any great concern for the rest as they were supremely confident in their own prowess and the multitude of fighters at hand.

The main body of Cordoban infantry trailed behind the advanced mounted columns and Latumna foot soldiers. These were made up of local Berbers, *Saqaliba* slave warriors, common Cordobans impressed for this particular *aceifa* and, significantly, heavily armed and armored, professional Arabic infantry, most of Syrian background. All of those fighting afoot made up almost two-thirds of the Moorish host.

Comfortable on ground they considered their own, the leaders had decided not to employ flank security elements until they crossed into Leon. The dust from the slowly moving force rose into the sky and could be seen for miles. The promises of the caliph, especially those concerning the distribution of booty, had reached all of the warriors. Their mood was both light-hearted and hopeful. Few of them had ever taken part in such an expedition accompanied by so many of their own fighters. It seemed impossible to many of them that the tiny Christian so-called 'kingdoms' could mount any effective resistance to the enormous juggernaut that was now advancing upon them. The deeply resonating throbs of the drummers marching among them also seemed to proclaim invincibility. The same drums not only provided a steady marching cadence but imbued within them a sense of their own unchallenged dominance.

Caliph Sulayman rode alongside the commander of the Arabic heavy cavalry. They had fought together during various campaigns in the past and knew each other well.

"Our men appear content and confident, my Caliph, happy warriors bound for victory or paradise, both noble goals," attested the impressive captain.

The two riders presented a splendid vision of martial majesty. Both were mounted on grand white stallions, their saddles and bridles adorned with colorful, polished insets. Each man was protected by finely meshed chain mail from shoulders to knees, over which were draped finely woven linen tunics – the caliph's white, the captain's green.

"We may not have as many fighters as did the great Almanzor but our cause is equally noble and our men are, as you say, highly motivated. As you know, the various Portuguese Christian counts turned down their opportunity to join us but they were warned to remain neutral and out of our way as we march through their lands. Their only alternative was death and the destruction of all of their holdings," said Sulayman to his old comrade.

"And you are one of the few of my most trusted leaders who know that we have loosed a deadly arrow into Leon's midst in recent times. We've received just one report thus far concerning this shaft's flight. But that was most encouraging. The arrow flies true. At any time, even as we now march northward, we may learn of a fortuitous revelation that will most certainly assure that victory that will be ours."

The captain's lips turned up in a wry grin.

"And that arrow knows well four glittering quivers are awaiting its return home in Cordoba. Or perhaps seventy-two elsewhere," said the officer winsomely.

"We shall see," the caliph replied, his eyes fixed on the road forward.

***

Well before the sweating steeds and panting riders, who brought news of the advancing Cordoban army, reached Leon. much preparation was already underway. The response of the other Christian kingdoms surpassed what Felix had expected. The total of those coming from Castile, Navarre and Barcelona was just under six hundred. However, they were all mounted knights. These heavy cavalrymen were the cream of the warrior classes of their homelands as well as the flower of their nobility. Their own kings apparently trusted their light cavalry and foot soldiers to protect their homes until the knights returned from victory over the Moors.

King Alfonso had been made aware of the threat Sulayman had issued to his Christian allies in the county of Portugal. This development had ironically seemed a stroke of good fortune to the king, Sancho and their allies from the North. Even though the counts' first instinct had been to fight at their southern border, Alfonso had convinced them to abide by Sulayman's demand to allow the Moors to pass. The intent was to let them march through the least populated portions of the county and to request the country people living there make a show of fleeing at the enemy's approach. The hope was the Moors would not slow their trek to pillage the small holdings they encountered. Meanwhile, the Portuguese warriors would bide their time, anticipating an opportunity to strike the retreating Moors as they withdrew after meeting Alfonso's surprise. These forces, held back for the moment, would be in position to attack from the flank with five hundred mounted knights and twice as many infantrymen if needed.

Galicia and Asturias had both risen to support the cause of Leon as well as their own homelands. The Galicians, in particular, had turned out, as Santiago de Compostela was not only a holy city but also situated in the center of their own province. The Asturian and Galician infantry added another thousand men, half of them quite capable of being employed as archers or swordsmen as needed and a total of almost two hundred and fifty mounted knights.

Leon itself would field six hundred armored cavalry and two thousand infantry. The allies from the North, including their *Laochra* special warriors, Spartans and Magyars, would add five hundred and sixty more. Based on their own intelligence estimates, the Christians expected to be slightly outnumbered by the enemy during the main battle, which they would have to win. The Portuguese should not be initially committed but might be called upon as reserves.

In short, both sides could mobilize approximately seven thousand men for the upcoming campaign. King Alfonso, his leaders and their allies were prepared and confident. The Moors were on the move northwards and the Christians were in position waiting for them.

***

Upon crossing the border into Leonese territory, the long Moorish column deployed riders forward and to their flanks as security. These were Sulayman's long-trusted Berber cavalry, light horsemen on speedy and sure-footed mounts; all were veterans of many past raids into the Christian kingdoms. The few inhabitants they encountered in Leon's County of Portugal flew off in apparent terror at the first sight of the invaders.

As expected, no defenders appeared to confront the advancing masses of steadily advancing fighting men. The terrain consisted of ridgelines of low mountains, grassy fields and scattered patches of forest, along with small valleys cut by streams and rivers. They also passed by the ruins of abbeys and tiny villages; the remains of the deprivations of Almanzor, some twenty years earlier.

"The local people never attempted to rebuild or resettle these areas, it seems," said Sulayman. "That is good for us as it serves as a reminder to the counts of what might be in store for them if they should ever decide to resist us."

"This is a pleasant land all the same. If we could settle our people here, they would no doubt prosper," the Moorish Captain replied.

The caliph actually laughed at that.

"We have enough challenges maintaining the vast extent of our existing Empire in the Caliphate. Besides, for hundreds of years, we have left the Christians to hold their tiny 'kingdoms' in the mountainous north. That has been to our advantage as the occasional *aceifa* keeps our warriors well-honed and provides us with booty and tribute when we need it."

The officer could not take issue with that logic from his caliph. He knew, as well, the several months of winter in the mountainous North were characterized by ice and snow, an unpleasant place for him and his people. Equally sensible was the caliph's understanding that their warriors must be continually tested and blooded to assure their fighting spirit. Once again, he was impressed by Sulayman's judgement, no matter what others might say.

Over time, as the army left the territory of the counts and entered the Leonese heartland, the mountains to their east became taller and more rugged and the passes they traversed narrower. There were also low but still formidable bluffs to their west, which made them converge and move more slowly as they passed through the ravines.

At one very narrow point, covered with jagged rocks and gouges along the surface, the caliph ordered his army to a halt and rode hastily to the front of the column. When he reached the Berber chieftain waiting for him there, he asked if the forward scouts had been reporting back to him at the appointed times.

"Not for some time, my Caliph. But the ground is uneven and riding here requires care and attention so as not to injure our horses.

"What about our scouts on the flanks?" continued Sulayman.

"Same thing with them. But as you can see, on our left, the bluffs are too steep for them to clamber up and down very often. Still, at one point, I did see several of them following our course earlier this morning. And on our right, the scouts move in and out of the tree line at the base of the mountain ridge there. They are no doubt moving through the thick firs as we speak."

"I don't like this at all," complained Sulayman. "I must ride back and alert the heavy cavalry before it's too late."

At that moment, there rang out a shouted call from some distance ahead of them. Sulayman and the Berbers caught sight of one of their riders rushing madly back to them. Before they could make sense of what he was saying, his mount's fetlock became entwined in a chunk of the broken rocky debris that covered the road. Horse and rider fell hard onto the jagged stone fragments, which seemed almost embedded in the packed earth. There was a hideous piercing scream of pain from both man and beast. Then all was still.

***

Earlier, the Christian allies had decided to allow the Moorish host to advance unchallenged through the County of Portugal and into southern Galicia. With much input from his Gaelic friends, they had decided to do battle at a spot south of the river Mino, still at some distance from Compostela. First, they knew they had to prepare their battlespace and determine the most effective use of their forces to engage the enemy.

The terrain features around their chosen battlefield reminded Cormac of very similar grounds where he fought during the great Battle of Gleann Mama in Ireland on the last day of the first Millennium. A vast force of Dublin Vikings was marching to join their renegade Leinster Irish allies. The Norse were moving through a valley defile which lay below a range of small mountains when King Brian Boru and his army met them. The Irish had attacked from out of the mountains. The Vikings were scattered and chased, along with their treacherous allies, all the way back to Dublin. It was the day after that battle that Cormac liberated a young teenage orphan named *Ulf Hreda* from bondage in Dublin.

"We expected the Viking enemies to withdraw back the way they had come when we fell upon them from the mountains. Instead, they fled south, desperate to escape us. In any case, they were vanquished and we sacked Dublin the next day," explained Cormac to the allied leaders, as they all sat in their saddles atop a small mountain, looking down onto the road where they would confront the Moors.

"There are far greater numbers of combatants in our present struggle but I find many parallels to Gleann Mama. That narrow gap there, where the road is surrounded by a steep bluff on one side and equally precipitous mountain slopes on the other, forms a perfect choke point. A band of nearly one hundred Spartans, which now includes a score of brawny and well-trained Galicians among them, could form a phalanx ten wide and ten deep and repel any who dared to pass through them. They would be doubly effective if they included bands of Galician foot archers around and behind them."

The king, Sancho and Wolf were already visualizing the battle to come in their minds. Fergus had to hold himself back from immediately gathering his Spartans and moving into position. Mornak put a calming hand on the big redhead's shoulder.

"Easy, you great bull, your time is coming again, it seems," jested the affable Pict.

"We could draw up our combined forces in extended columns just inside the timberlands along the base of the mountain slopes. Their hardest-hitting force will be their heavily armored Arab cavalry. Though not as swift or nimble as the Berber riders, the shock they deliver in battle is fearful," advised Sancho. "Still, formidable as they are, our mounted knights and those of the other Christian kingdoms are more than their match. We must assure our own heavily armored knights seek them out wherever they appear on the line of battle."

The Hispanian *Campeador*, as usual, spoke from long experience in combat against the invaders and none could find fault in his judgement.

"Since Cormac has already placed our Spartans in their proper place for the upcoming battle, I request you allow us to insert our Magyars and *Laochra* where we feel they will be most helpful in supporting your hosts, King Alfonso," requested Wolf, adding, "and remember they now include some very welcome and highly motivated Galicians among them."

Wolf smiled broadly, having already trained with and been impressed by the Galician volunteers. His pleasure grew more pronounced when the king graciously nodded his assent and added his thanks.

"Let it be done as you say, Captain. And you have the gratitude of myself and all our people for joining us in this, our most desperate struggle."

The Gael bowed his head slightly and continued.

"First, I suggest that we take steps to genuinely *prepare* the ground on which we will fight. As we were coming over this mountain, I noticed a quarry with thousands of broken rocks. They were no doubt the remnants from whatever had been removed from there. They are quite close to us here. I suggest we load up as many as we can carry in our supply wagons and strew them over the surface of the narrow road. We should strive to make it appear as if, over time, the stones have merely rolled down from the mountain slopes and the bluffs on either side."

The other leaders immediately took a liking to the idea, agreeing with one another enthusiastically.

"I understand this simple step will constitute neither a barrier nor even a major impediment to their advance but it will cause the foe to move more slowly and warily. It will also complicate their ability to rapidly assemble into battle formations at the moment of our attack. We will have to collect enough debris to cover an extended distance along their route of advance. It should start from that slim gap Cormac pointed out and extend southward. Just beyond the gap, of course, is where the enemy will first encounter us."

Wolf then cast his gaze at the one man among the others who approached him in bulk and height.

"It appears, Fergus, you, your Spartans and a band of good Galician archers will be first to draw blood. Hopefully, that meets with your approval."

Grinning savagely, then bowing his head to first the king and then to his friend and Captain, Fergus replied tersely, "We very much appreciate the honor."

Smiling back, the king brought this final pre-battle assembly to its conclusion.

"Very good. Fergus, you will coordinate with our Galician friends and prepare to deploy to your assigned battle position. Now, my friends, let us swiftly perform our roles as rock collectors, then Sancho will establish the various contingents into their initial battle formations, where we will await the enemy. God be with us all."

***

The first indication that the battle was about to commence was when two hard-riding Leonese ranger scouts were seen galloping furiously back to the main army. Those familiar with them were not surprised to see two Irish scouts, Aoife and Saoirse, riding just as hard alongside them. The Leonese reported to Sancho and the king, while the women dashed off to Cormac and Wolf. The Moors were approaching along the road, with their own scouts ahead and to the flanks.

Thus warned, the waiting Hispanians were able to quickly and savagely bring down the Moorish flank scouts as they entered the tree line. Sancho observed the enemy's order of battle which was much as he expected and positioned his own forces to engage appropriately. Cormac and the *Laochra* were put in position to bolster the Hispanian infantry while the Magyars were held in reserve as a flying column.

***

As soon as the advanced scout and his mount smashed to the ground, Sulayman and the Berber chief looked beyond them to witness a sight they thought had been an exaggerated myth. A solid and compact phalanx of enormous, scarlet-robed and heavily armored giants was slowly marching toward them, wielding heavy metal shields and enormous thrusting spears.

Along narrow spaces to their sides streamed enemy archers, even now beginning to knock arrows.

"Move to the rear, my Caliph, my men will sweep them from the road," said the Berber chieftain, though the tone in his voice imparted no great confidence.

But it was too late. From the mountain slopes on their eastern flank, horns blared and drums began to thunder. They could also hear the piercing and alien shrills of strange pipes. And then, from the line of trees at the base of the mountains, thousands of Christian warriors appeared, those opposite them all mounted knights. It started with a steady canter. Lances lowered and then the knights broke into a gallop. The Moors tried to assemble in line formation to meet the attack though their movements were awkward.

The caliph was already riding back down the line trying to rejoin the heavy Arabic cavalry. All along his route, he could see other Christian forces, both cavalry and infantry, moving to intercept and attack his forces on the road. As his own warriors moved out to meet them, he knew the two armies would clash violently against each other in the fury of their initial engagement in mere moments.

The knights of Castile and the other Christian nations struck into the ranks of the hundreds of veteran Cordoban Berbers and the initial crash of horses and men was horrific. However, the heavy armor, long lances and shields of the Hispanians proved too much for the Moors in such close quarters and with so little room for the Berbers to employ their mounted agility in maneuver. Still, the knights were also suffering losses from the sharp and deadly accurate throwing spears of their enemies. In what seemed like ages but was actually a very short time, nearly five hundred Berbers were crushed under lances and swords except for the few who tried vainly to scale the bluffs.

Meanwhile, the Spartans and their Galician archer escorts continued to march slowly and inexorably southward along the road. Because of their measured pace, the shards of stone were not as much a challenge to them as they were to mounted warriors. The Spartans came upon occasional terrified enemy stragglers and made short work of them, spearing them mercilessly and then tramping over their bodies. The Galician bowmen skewered the few Moors attempting to climb the precipitous bluffs.

Trekking behind the advanced Cordoban Berber cavalry on the original line of march was the enormous column of Latumna foot soldiers. As the caliph rode warily past their lines due to the stone shards, he could see the fear and confusion on their faces as a smaller but better-armed force of Christian infantry set upon them. They had not been long in the Caliphate and whatever type of battle they may have expected did not include being hit from the flank while they were drawn in an extended line on a narrow rock-strewn road with steep bluffs to their backs.

To the caliph's astonishment, in the very center of the attacking line of Christian forces was a formation of hundreds of mail-clad warriors with heavy shields and unfamiliar flashing axes. And at the very front and center of that formation was the largest man— if it was a man—that Sulayman had ever seen. He wore a metal helmet constructed in the form of a wolf's head with large, pointed ears and mailed skirts falling to his enormous shoulders. This obvious chieftain stood well above even the largest of the big men fighting at his side. He was at the center spike position of a wedge of shields and axes. Yet he carried no shield but was armed with an impossibly massive broadsword in one hand and a chain with a spiked iron ball in the other. He cut through the massed bands of Latumna, leaving throngs of dead and wounded foemen all around him.

The Latumna had poured off the trail, rushing to meet the attackers away from the tight debris-filled road and the two opposing forces of thousands of men were now thoroughly intertwined. Yet the reason the caliph had been able to observe the alien formation of axemen was because they had already punched through their enemy's center and were now splitting into two elements to engage the still fighting Latumna warriors from their rear. Watching from his mount, Sulayman knew the inevitable result. He did not wait to witness the certain destruction of nearly two thousand Latumna, soon to take place and hastened southward, knowing his heavy Arabic cavalry would be his best protection. As he rode further south, the road became somewhat less cluttered with rocky debris and he was able to gallop more swiftly. As his course turned around a slight bend, he came upon his waiting Arabic cavalry in file along the road.

"Withdraw to the south with all haste. The Christians are pouring down from the mountains and our forward columns are lost," he commanded trying to keep his voice steady so as not to start a panic.

The battle had commenced first in the North so the Moors further south had neither seen nor heard what had already transpired. Still, they took their caliph at his word and the entire formation turned about and retreated the way they came at a brisk pace. The five hundred Latumna mounted warriors could both see and hear the spectacle of the vaunted Arabic heavy cavalry fleeing toward them. They also turned about and scattered southwards in search of refuge or sanctuary.

The enormous formations of astonished Cordoban and Lower March foot warriors were bypassed as the cavalry flowed around them. Here and there, a Cordoban rider would slow to scoop up an infantryman friend or family member to ride double with him. That did not happen very often and soon nearly three thousand warriors stood alone drawn out in an extended line along the north-south road.

The mountains to the west did not quite reach this far south along the original Moorish axis of advance and, as the northernmost Moors gazed ahead, to their right they were appalled to see thick lines of Christian heavy infantry deploying from the road and moving into deep lines in anticipation of engaging them. Even more unnerving, to their east streaming down from the line of mountains more than a thousand Hispanian knights were trotting leisurely apparently preparing to attack them from their flank.

Some of these Moorish fighters were seasoned veterans with extensive experience equipped with good armor and formidable weaponry. Many more, however, were common laborers and farm people, doing their part when summoned by the caliphate. All of them, though, were thoroughly disheartened to see their caliph, his elite heavy Arabic cavalry and even the recently imported Latumna riders flying by their ranks apparently abandoning them to deal with the northern armies on their own.

***

After the rapid destruction of the advanced Berber cavalry and huge formation of Latumna foot soldiers, the Christian allies called a halt to take stock.

“We crushed their front ranks quicker than any of us could have expected but I yet mourn the loss of our good knights to the spears of the mounted Berbers. We lost several scores of our best friends and countrymen,” lamented King Alfonso.

“That’s to be expected in even the most resoundingly victorious battle, King,” replied Wolf, “But as long as none were slain because of the ineptitude of their leaders, the pain can be easier borne. And, speaking of ineptitude, I believe I caught sight of what could only be a regally clad Caliph Sulayman fleeing south past the poor and misled Latumna foot warriors as we were slaughtering them. It was a most dishonorable spectacle."

"You weren't the only one to witness that craven coward, Wolf. He was clad in white and mounted on an equally white stallion. Many of our men recognized him," said the king. "Sancho and Cormac, what do you think is now afoot?"

Sancho responded first.

"I believe Sulayman will try to retreat as rapidly as possible with his own and the Latumna cavalry. He still has an enormous number of Moorish infantry which he believes might be an effective blocking force as we pursue him. But it's late afternoon now and he can't risk riding all night in enemy territory. He will attempt to go to ground in some place he might be able to defend and then he will see what the morning brings. I have little faith in his judgment that the remaining Moorish warriors afoot will be able to save him. No warrior becomes inspired upon seeing his supreme leader fleeing from the battlefield."

"I quite agree and we now decidedly hold the initiative. I suggest we pursue with vigor to reduce this so-called blocking force. Our infantry marching steadfastly along the road until they can deploy in line and our cavalry fanning out to attack from their flank," added Cormac.

At that point, an unlikely figure stepped out from among those assembled and moved to stand by Wolf.

"Do you think I may dare give an opinion, Captain?" asked Brother Cillian, decidedly out of place among the warriors with their dusty and blood-splattered armor and weapons and he in his clerical robes, beads and cross.

"Of course," replied Wolf and the king at the same time. The two of them looked at each other and laughed despite the seriousness of the moment.

"It is still far from over but you have already won a great victory this day, King Alfonso. This vaunted *aceifa* has proven disastrous for Sulayman. If we believe he conducted this attack to bolster his reputation and restore the unity of the Caliphate, that has failed horrendously. Our armies will, of course, destroy his isolated enemy infantry in short order. But the caliph may have given us an unexpected gift with his precipitated flight back towards his homeland."

The monk stopped for a moment to let his words sink in.

"If we pursue him and his Arabic and Latumna cavalry to a final stand and annihilate them all, Sulayman will be transformed from cowardly and failed caliph, which he is now, to a great and magnificent martyr who fell in battle against the enemies of the faithful. This could rouse the Caliphate to elect a new and more effective leader and we'd be in a worse position than before."

Despite their battle lust and confidence, none of the leaders could dispute what this wise and likeable Irish Cluniac monk had just stated.

"You are both a sage and a canny strategist for a simple and devout clergyman, dear Brother. And you are quite right. You're saying we should offer him a way to escape back to face whatever is awaiting him if I understand you," the King replied. "Agreed but first let us deal with the thousands of Moorish foot warriors who are sullying our lands even at this moment."

***

The heavy infantry element, which still strode along the road, was the strangest band on the battlefield that day. The phalanx of one hundred heavily armored red behemoths tramped inexorably toward the incredulous Moors. By now, there were hundreds more Christian infantry warriors deployed to the Spartans' left flank with Wolf, Cormac and the *Laochra* in their center. Worst of all for the Moorish enemy, mounted knights were riding in a crescent-shaped formation to strike them from their right. What the enemy could not see was a smaller and ever swifter band of mounted archers ranging far to the east to coming around and prepare to harass the Moors from their rear.

It seemed to happen all at once. The combined Christian infantry and cavalry struck the Cordobans at the exact moment. Despite the thousands of combatants involved and the savagery of the fighting, the spirit had gone out of the Moors from the moment they witnessed their abandonment. They could not expect to defeat their enemy but could only hope for some way to escape or a faithful martyr's quick death.

Before that could happen though, hundreds of men whose normal lives consisted of shepherding their herds, selling their wares, or tending fields broke off and dashed southward along the packed earth of the trail. To their horror, they came upon strangely garbed mounted archers with small, recurved bows who seemed to ride in a grand circle furiously and loose deadly arrows upon them without relent. On some occasions, with arrows spent, the Magyars rode them down and skewered them with thin light lances.

As in every engagement since the Irish had first arrived, the entire bloody affair was mercifully not a protracted one. Thousands of Moors lay dead and broken on the ground while the Hispanian casualties numbered just over one hundred.

As the Christian leaders assembled again after the short but horrifically violent battle, they once again looked up to see speeding Leonese scout rangers rushing toward them. The same two women, Aoife and Saoirse, accompanied them.

"Sulayman and about two thousand of his cavalry, including Latumnas, have managed to take refuge in one of our old abandoned and ruined fortresses atop a low mountain to our south. Despite the battered state of the old defenses there, it is a formidable position for them as the slopes are steep and there is no cover for attackers," breathlessly reported the lead scout.

"How far?" asked Sancho.

"If we leave now and ride at a moderate pace, we can be there just after dusk. The infantry will take longer," answered the excited young rider.

The Christians left some of their own to tend to the wounded and see that their dead were buried properly while the mounted warriors set off with the infantry behind them. It was late spring and the days were becoming longer, so there was still just enough light for the allies to see the ruins atop the low but still steep mountain's top. It was indeed a formidable position.

"We could starve them out easily and I know, of old, there is no source of water in that old fort," stated a grizzled veteran of many campaigns. "It is also surprisingly large enough inside for them to corral their horses but I don't think they'll resort to eating them," he concluded smiling.

"That's not the plan we discussed. Once again, to reiterate, we will offer them our terms. We will allow them to leave unmolested in the morning with their arms if they agree to leave Leon return to Cordoba and vow never to come back."

So it was, that not long after, an emissary of Christians rode slowly with torches up the summit of the mountain carrying flags of truce. Upon reaching a proper point outside the fort their leader, Sancho, called out.

"Under truce, we wish to discuss terms with the caliph and his chosen ones about resolving without bloodshed the current situation. All your other warriors have been annihilated or else you know we wouldn't be here now. We await your response."

Just as Sancho was beginning to lose his patience, the old fort's quickly improvised gate opened and four riders came out also carrying torches. The Moorish party consisted of the emir, the Captain of the Arabic cavalry, the chieftain of the Latumna warriors and a huge and fierce-looking Syrian man-at-arms clad entirely in black.

To the surprise of the Moors, the Christian leaders included the well-known *Campeador,* Sancho and three strange companions. Cormac, Wolf the Quarrelsome and Mornak the Pict, all adorned in their native panoplies of battle sat their mounts alongside the Hispanian champion. Of course, King Alfonso and Caliph Sulayman would not personally be involved in anything as vulgar as terms of truce discussions.

"The caliph is not prepared to accept your terms but offers you a chance now to leave with your lives intact. He also wants your boy king to know that the great Sulayman has many friends and warriors not only in the vast reaches of the great Caliphate but among Alfonso's own and this day is not yet over," stated the Emir, as Sancho immediately translated.

The Moors had been examining the three Clontarf veterans with suspicion and even some abhorrence at their alien participation in these talks. Wolf himself, with his lupine-formed helmet, faint silver facial scars twinkling under the torchlight and enormous broadsword slung over his shoulder, dwarfed the fearsome Syrian big man.

Yet Mornak was even more ghastly in appearance to the Moors. He had smeared his hands, face and neck with blue pigment from the woad plant, treated his hair with chalk and lime water to produce huge, stiff, distended spikes and worn his one original Pictish brat with its colorful, swirling circles that were neither Celtic, Viking, nor Saxon in origin.

"I expected this," grunted Wolf in frustration. Then, speaking in fluent Gaelic, he addressed Mornak. "You know what to do."

With a maniacal grin and Pictish cheer, Mornak slowly brought his horse closer to the Moors. He was holding a leather bag, similar to those used to carry water and offered it to the emir.

"I suspect the caliph may change his mind when you deliver this to him. Go alone, Emir, the rest of us will wait for you. Trust me, you'll return soon," declared Sancho.

The emir reluctantly accepted the satchel from the demonic apparition, which presented it to him and rode back the short distance to the fort while the others waited. Sancho had been correct as he hadn't been gone long before the emir returned with an entirely transformed demeanor.

"The caliph accepts your terms of truce. He and his loyal warriors will leave at dawn and return to the Caliphate. He also is confident King Alfonso is a man of honor and his word and that we may depart unmolested to the border," announced the emir.

"Of that you can be quite sure," replied Sancho diplomatically.

With that, the Christian party turned and walked their mounts slowly down the slope. Only Mornak among them was turned round in his saddle, casting execrations and curses upon the souls of the Moors in his own good Pictish language.

The decaying and desiccated head of Count Ramiro, which had been the satchel's only contents, had, like that of the failed assassin before him, proven successful in proving Alfonso's point.

# EPILOGUE

The next morning, the entire Christian army was assembled in formidable arrays to watch the enemy's mass of warriors move out from the ruined fortress and make their way southward along the road. The Moors kept their eyes focused straight ahead as they rode deliberately. None among the Hispanian onlookers called out or taunted them. The entire spectacle was eerily silent, the only sound the rhythmic clopping of the horses' hooves on the packed earth.

The Christians held their position until sometime later when scouts confirmed the would-be invaders had crossed back into the Caliphate. Then the entire host turned around to return to their homes.

At the head of the long columns which followed, King Alfonso rode along with Sancho, Cormac, Wolf and Brother Cillian.

"Before you arrived, I never expected I would soon be riding at the head of a massive and victorious Christian Army after destroying half a horde of invading Moors and then seeing off the rest including Caliph Sulayman himself. Even more inconceivable is that, at my side, would be two Gaelic warriors from the North and a monk from the Abbey of Cluny in France who is also an Irishman. God surely works in strange ways," said Alfonso.

Sancho looked toward the very young king he had watched grow up from infancy.

"And I would have called you mad if you had told me that you had even dreamt of such a thing, Alfonso," replied Sancho, grinning.

Brother Cillian resumed the conversation.

"I believe our great enemy has been like an aging but still defiant older man since the death of Almanzor, King. You and your valiant warriors have this day brought on the death knell of the caliphate. I suspect Sulayman will be deposed or worse before two years pass. There will be chaos and confusion afterwards and before even two decades pass, the Caliphate itself will fall into ruins. It may take one or even several hundred years after that. Still, inexorably, you and your descendants will succeed in reconquering Hispania and returning her to Christianity and its rightful people. Of that, I am sure."

Cormac and Wolf, riding on either side of the king, each put a strong hand on the young man's shoulders, nodding their assent as they all continued on their way homeward from victory on the battlefield.

When they had returned to the outskirts of the capital in Leon, it was Pyrrhus and Helena who first rode out to greet their Gaelic friends. They were grateful to find their comrades all hale and hearty and asked if the leaders might all meet in a nearby leafy grotto to discuss some new tidings.

The mood among the Clontarf veterans was jovial and boisterous, made even more so by this welcome from the dear Greek diplomats. Helena and Cormac immediately rushed to each other and embraced warmly, totally heedless of the smiles and laughs of the others who were pleased to see the two reunited. Wolf was with Aoife, Cael with Luta and even Fergus stood next to Saoirse, looking on.

"While you were away, a ship of the line arrived from Constantinople carrying Emperor Basil's most senior representative. He is a man we've known well for many years," began Pyrrhus.

"I do hope he has not come to bring you and Helena back to face justice in the Empire's capital," quipped Mornak.

This was only half in jest as both Greeks had been away from their primary imperial duties for a long time. Still, there were chuckles and smiles among their friends.

"No but it is a serious request. The emperor does indeed summon us back. But there is still more. As he has said in the past, he has been made aware of the valor and courage of the Gaelic veterans of Clontarf. He respectfully requests that we return with all haste to the capital …and that we bring as many of you as are willing with us. He feels he has great need of our service and your presence to serve as an example to others in his time of need."

"I believe we have helped set King Alfonso and all of his people on the road to ultimate victory. Now, another Christian monarch seems to require our assistance in meeting desperate challenges. What will our answer be?" queried Wolf, looking first toward Cormac.

Cheers erupted from all of those present. Cormac and Helena embraced each other even more fervently. All of them knew well they would soon be setting sail for Constantinople.

The End

# Author's Note

"Fury in Hispania" is the second in a planned medieval historical fiction trilogy featuring *Wolf the Quarrelsome*, called *Ulf Hreda* by the Vikings and *Faolán an Trodach* by the Irish. Wolf appears in the thirteenth-century Norse Icelandic Njals Saga as a nightmare to the pagan Vikings and a hero to the Celts during the historically significant Battle of Clontarf outside Dublin, Ireland, in 1014 AD. The story of his origins and the rise of the formidable band of Irish, Scots, Christian Viking men and women and one affable Pictish warrior who follow him is described in my first book in the trilogy, "Wolf of Clontarf."

In this book, I use the term "Hispania" to refer to medieval Spain which has also been historically known as "Iberia" and "Spania." No native medieval Christian Europeans ever used the term *al-Andalus*. "Hispania" is what the Romans called Spain and the name eventually evolved into medieval Latin "Spania" as the Middle Ages progressed. Iberia is a pre-Roman word and I found Hispania far more appropriate here. (Hats off to my favorite Professor of Spanish and Portuguese History, Language and Culture.)

As with much of continental Europe, Hispania was historically composed of and controlled by a variety of prehistoric indigenous peoples, migrating tribes, Romans and, temporarily, Moorish Muslims. Going back to the BC millennia, the first inhabitants of note were a people called the Iberians, hence the name Iberia. Although little is known of their exact origins, they have left archaeological evidence indicating a vibrant culture. They were also influenced by Greek, Phoenician and other Mediterranean visitors who established trading colonies. A wave of Celtic tribes began arriving around 1000 BC. Over the centuries, the Celts essentially blended with the Iberians, although each maintained some tribal areas of their own: the Iberians in the east, along the coast and the Celts in the center and north. The Romans referred to them all as simply Celtiberians. In 206 BC, the Romans invaded during the Second Punic War with the Carthaginians. Over hundreds of years of military and colonial consolidation, the Romans ruled. However, some Celtic tribes, especially in the North, maintained a strong streak of independence. As the

Roman Empire finally fell, Germanic Visigoths settled in, became Christian and Romanized and ruled until the Muslim invasion in 711 AD.

At the dawn of the second millennium, 1000 AD, the Hispanian peninsula was a seething cauldron where the former native peoples were losing their battle for survival against ruthless and all-conquering Arab and Berber invaders who had been steadily increasing their conquests for over three hundred years. Only a few small, weak Christian kingdoms were holding on in the cooler, damp mountains in the north. Indeed, all of Western civilization and the rudiments of Judeo-Christian knowledge and tradition were on the verge of being violently extinguished. Invading Viking marauders were pouring down from the north, pillaging from Russia across France and Britannia to Iceland. Magyars and other pagan steppe-riders from the east had only recently been repelled before storming through France. Seemingly unstoppable, Islamic invaders were conquering Sicily, establishing footholds in southern Italy and dominating Hispania.

"Fury in Hispania" is my fictional account of at least one of many series of events which may have initially sparked the long and arduous crusade of the Reconquista through the centuries until the native Christian peoples eventually secured their freedom from the occupying Islamic Moors. Of course, there is no historical evidence that a small band of Celtic warrior veterans of the momentous battle at Clontarf sparked the earliest struggles for the eventual Reconquista. Yet some of the characters in this novel are indeed historical people, most prominent among them, young King Alfonso of Leon. And there was (and still is) a thriving population of Celts in Spain, especially in Galicia, which I have portrayed in a prominent role in this book. So, it is at least historically plausible that they would enthusiastically join their Celtic Irish cousins in supporting their good King Alfonso in their joint battle for freedom. To conclude, let me evoke the title of my favorite song from my favorite Irish band – "Don't let the truth get in the way of a good story."

# Praise for "Wolf of Clontarf"

## SELECTED REVIEW EXCERPTS

Celtic Life International – Canadian-based Digital and Print Magazine

"Despite only recently being released, there has been a lot of love for this sweeping Irish/Viking saga since its publication last month, with a mega mélange of media coverage, including feature articles, author interviews and glowing reviews. In most cases and although understandable in an already oversaturated marketplace, that kind of hype speaks more to the muscle of a marketing team and, perhaps, less to the merit of the actual work. Thankfully, that isn't the case here, as Howley twists and turns tradition into an epic tale of power, fortune, family and love."

Gript.ie - Independent news and culture website in Ireland

"In his newly released Irish historical novel, "Wolf of Clontarf – The Irish, the Vikings and the foreigners of the World," historical fiction author, Thomas J. Howley, uses the Norse sagas and Irish annals as inspiration to bring this obscure Irishman, 'Faolán an Trodach', to vibrant and swashbuckling life."

"In this epic fantasy, Howley focuses on the international dimensions of Clontarf to tell an expansive imagined tale of global reach. His Battle of Clontarf, which was at the time a significant world event, encompasses exotic cultural visitors in Tolkienesque fashion. The shock troop infantry of the Gael and the Norse are complemented by dashing horse archers from the far steppes of Asia. It's an appealing counterfactual but why not if it adds to the epic dimensions of the story? The Wolf of Clontarf is an epic tale of tragedy, resilience, subtle romance and triumph against all odds. Another step in the seemingly insurmountable path towards Ireland's ultimate national liberation and freedom."

Irish Central – NYC/DUBLIN
News/Culture/Entertainment/Website

"An exciting new novel shines a spotlight on the mysterious hero from Irish history known as Wolf the Quarrelsome...... "Wolf of Clontarf," a new novel by Thomas J. Howley, offers an exciting look into the tumultuous chapter in Irish history when the Irish fought back the Vikings and helped to preserve the learning and culture of continental Europe and Christianity."

# CAST OF CHARACTERS
## IN ORDER OF APPEARANCE
**Historical Persons ***
**From the Norse Sagas and/or Irish Annals ****

Brian Mac Cennetigh (Brian Boru) * – High King of Ireland
Cormac Mac Mahon – Nephew of King Brian
*Faolán an Trodach* (Wolf the Quarrelsome)** – Irish War Chieftain
Basil the Porphyrogenitus* - Christian Greek Roman Emperor
Keli – Icelandic Christian Viking
Ospak of the Isle of Man* – Manx Viking who allied with King Brian
Fergus O'Roghan – Irish Captain of Spartans
Aoife of Cashel – Irish Chief of Spies
Helena Lakepeno – Imperial Greek Ambassador
Pyrrhus Lakepeno – Imperial Greek Ambassador, Helena's cousin
Luta Einarsdottir – Norse Princess, Irish Magyars weapon sister
Shlomo Ben Adret – Jewish physician/scientist, native of Hispania
Felix Santos Serra – Leonese senior diplomat
Alfonso of Leon* – Leonese King
Cael O'Cadhla – Irish Captain of Magyars
Mornak Cennelath – Pictish warrior of the Irish *Laochra an Rí*
Partha Cennelath – Mornak's adopted younger brother
King Bermudo "the Gouty"* – King Alfonso's deceased father
Elvira Garcia of Castile* – Alfonso's Queen Mother of Leon
Sancho – Alfonso's standard bearer and senior military advisor
Albin – Orphaned small boy of Francia
Bogumir Dalibor/Qatil Al Sulafia – Greek Muslim Special Warrior
Jalel – Syrian Muslim, good-natured friend of Bogumir
The Emir – Senior Syrian Muslim Leader, Bogumir's commander
Rodrigo – Hispanian former *Campeador,* Warrior Champion
Muhammed ibn'Amir Bi-llah/*Almanzor**, Cordoban Military leader
Sulayman al-Musta'in*, Ruler of the Cordoban Caliphate 1014
"Sanchuelo"*, *Almanzor's* ineffective son
Hisham*, Cloistered Caliph of Cordoba 1014
Pope Benedict*, Roman Catholic Pontiff 1014
King Heinrich*, *Romanarum Imperator,* Holy Roman Emperor 1014

Diego – Former Hispanian Sailor and warrior scout
Lorcan – Second in command of the Irish Spartans
Eoin – Aoife's younger brother
Saoirse – Member of Aoife's squadron of women Spies/Scouts
Brother Cillian – Irish Benedictine monk from the Cluny Abbey
Zaynab bint Hasan – Young victimized and liberated Moorish girl
Duke Vladislaus of Moravia – Diplomatic visitor to Leonese Court
Count Ramiro of Asturias – Alfonso's cousin, captured by Moors
"Aunt" Isabella – African former Moorish slave, Alfonso's caregiver

# About the Author

Thomas Joseph Howley, born in Boston to an Irish immigrant family, is a retired U.S. Army officer. He began his career in tanks in the Armor branch. He later transferred to Military Intelligence, spending the bulk of his career abroad, where he frequently supported or led counterespionage and counterterrorism operations. Key tours of duty included U.S. Special Operations Command and as the only U.S. officer on the primary staff of the United Nations Protection Forces (UNPROFOR) in the former Yugoslavia during the height of the civil wars there.

Earning a Master's Degree in Management, after military retirement, he was employed as a civilian operational intelligence specialist supporting U.S. Defense, Federal Law Enforcement and the Intelligence Community. In the course of his career, he has deployed to or supported security and intelligence operations on every continent except Antarctica.

He lives in New Hampshire with his wife, where he is struggling through his seventh year of studying the Irish Gaelic language. When not working on a project or at the gym, he can be found navigating the trails in the New Hampshire woodlands. *Fury in Hispania* is the second book in his planned trilogy of "Wolf the Quarrelsome."

His website is TJHowleybooks.com.

The Author and His Muse

www.ingramcontent.com/pod-product-compliance
Lightning Source LLC
LaVergne TN
LVHW090558110826
845146LV00001B/178